THE ASCENSION OF LIGHT

RYAN KIRK

OLIVERHEBERBOOKS

The Ascension of Light Copyright 2024 © Ryan Kirk

Cover design by Covers by JV Arts

Published by Oliver-Heber Books

0 9 8 7 6 5 4 3 2 1

The heart pulsed slow and steady, as if within a clan elder's calm and ancient chest, and Samora's heart beat in unison. Its adani was hers, the boundaries between them blended and smudged like a child's paints, messy and inseparable.

It was bliss. Light and warmth wrapped her in a never-ending embrace. Shadow's icy grip faded into the past, a bitter memory that rapidly lost its sting. The heart promised an eternity of joy and respite, and there was no question of choice. She swam in the light, forever content.

Someone called her name, and in so doing, wrapped a thin string of attachment around her spirit. Whether sense or memory, she couldn't say, nor did it matter, for the effect was the same. Her name drove a tiny sliver between the ancient heart and her own. The edges of unity frayed, and memories trickled through the newfound gaps. Her spirit gasped as it plunged into the freezing waters of the recent past.

The shadow's assault on the heart. Adanists from multiple clans gathered to fight a common enemy. The heart fighting to send its strength to the surface, aided by the one who walked ancient paths of knowledge. So much adani gathered and so much adani lost, countless spirits returned to a cycle older than the dragons and their watchful and sometimes malicious oversight.

Elian called her name again, his voice distant but strong. The sliver became a wedge that pried Samora apart from the heart.

Her body kept the rhythm of the heart's pulse, but now she stood separate, Samora once again. Echoes of her name called her home, but she lingered near the heart. It revealed truths long buried, hard truths, but truths necessary if humanity was to stand against the Vada and all its accompanying Debru.

A thought sent adani from her spirit toward the heart, which gladly opened to receive it. Her adani mixed again with the heart's, but now under her control. The heart pulsed, sending her adani far afield.

The Debru who had attacked the gathering ground, led by half a dozen Belogs, were no more. The shadowy remnants of their hurried passage across the land lingered, and if humanity survived the days to come, she swore she would heal the grass-lands destroyed by the Debru's mere presence. Beyond their trail, though, no sign remained. The clans had triumphed, slaying everything down to the last kettu.

Samora rejoiced in their victory, but it left a bitter stain upon her spirit. Too many had died, and though the assault had been the largest any of the clans had fought against, it represented only a fraction of the Debru's strength. The remaining Belogs stuck close to the Vada, but the Moka led squads of Debru throughout the land, far to the north and south.

Her adani traveled farther yet, far beyond the edges of the battlefield and into the lands beyond. Eventually, curiosity drove her west and south, her spirit dancing across the web of life like a spider hungrily searching for prey. Strengthened by the heart, she had no trouble stretching herself the vast distances required. She came to a stop just beyond the Vada's domain and watched.

It, too, was sensitive to adani, and turned toward her. They'd crossed paths before, back in the deadlands, and there it had toyed with her. Not so today. It stretched its spirit to the edge of its domain but didn't take a step beyond. Its gaze was slow, considered, and wary. Nothing like the confident commander she'd first encountered.

Its hesitation made no sense. It had proven it could crush her with little more than a thought. Why hide? Why send Belogs to complete a task it could have finished in moments?

It housed its spirit in a flesh the likeness of a young child, but the weight of its gaze was that of an ancient being. The chasm between perception and reality left Samora cold and queasy. She tried and failed to reconcile the difference, but the attempt made her sick.

She sent a thread of adani toward the Vada, not as a weapon, but as an invitation. Her spirit trembled as it approached the threshold between the living and the dead, but she forced stillness into the thread, hoping it would entice the Vada. She pulled the thread taut when it was no more than a few paces from the Vada's boundary and waited for its reaction.

The commander of all Debru studied the thread. Its hand reached halfway up, then froze. The Vada cocked its head to the side, then turned its back and disappeared into the shadows that swallowed it whole.

Samora let the thread of adani return to her spirit, feeling like a fisher who'd spent all day with their line in the creek, only to come home empty-handed to a hungry family. She watched the boundary, stretching her senses for any sign of the Vada's return. Only when it became clear the Vada had no interest in her did she allow her adani to return all the way back to the heart.

The heart's steady beat comforted her after the failure of her ill-conceived plan, and for a time she simply rested in its welcoming warmth. It nibbled at the edges of her adani, weakening the boundaries that separated her spirit from eternity, but the heart's promise didn't tempt her like before.

"What are you?" she asked.

It presented her with a vision, similar to the method the dragons used to communicate with her and Elian. She saw endless grasslands, not unlike those just beyond the boundaries of the gathering ground. Days and nights passed in an endless procession, and with the passing of time came the gathering of life. The cause needn't be extraordinary. Sometimes it was as insignificant as a hearty tree providing shelter and protection for a small host of animals. Birds nested in the branches and laid their eggs. Squirrels leaped from limb to limb, and deer took shelter from the burning sun. Life gathered, and in time, the web of adani knotted.

That knot called more life to it, and adani looped over itself and knotted again. Repeat for countless years, and a gathering ground was born. A small change, given enough time, changed the shape of land and adani. Samora watched, but wonder stole her voice.

Humans arrived, though not of clan or village. Their tunics were thinner than any weave Samora had seen, and their skin too light for any who spent long days in the sun. Their mastery of adani, though, needed no explanation. They weaved fresh life into the trees, looping adani within the gathering ground, much as Samora and the other healers had.

Once the amount of adani passed a particular threshold, the heart was born, weaving itself into existence as though it had always been, uncovered rather than created.

The vision faded, leaving Samora alone with the heart. It was an answer and yet not. How had the adanists known the weave? Why had they sought to create the heart at all? She asked her questions of the heart, but it remained as silent and unhelpful as the dragons.

"Why don't you answer?" she cried.

The heart rumbled, but no vision answered her question.

If the heart were a door, or a tree, something she could touch and see, she would have pounded on it until her hands bled while demanding answers. The Vada knew the truth. The heart knew the truth. Even the dragons knew the truth. All conspired to keep it from her. To keep it from the clans.

The Vada's secrecy she understood, but why the heart and the dragons?

She asked her questions again, putting the full force of her spirit behind them. She may as well have been shouting at a stone. The heart pulsed slow and steady, ignoring her pleas while strengthening every adanist in the gathering grounds.

Samora calmed the pounding of her own heart and continued her search. Perhaps the dragons, swayed by the heart's power, would answer. Maybe other faraway lands held clues to mysteries older than the clans. She was here, attached to the heart as though it beat in her own chest. She wouldn't waste the opportunity.

She skipped across the land, knowing no tiredness, no boredom, no passage of time. No stone was left unturned, no corner of the land unexamined. And for all her efforts, nothing. She learned much, but none of the truths she sought. In the end, she returned to the heart once more, empty-handed. Her exhaustion wasn't physical, but embedded deep in her spirit. No doubt the others celebrated their victory, but what joy was there in a doomed future?

The heart remained open to her, and the temptation carried more weight than before. All futures led to ruin, but if she embraced the heart, decay would never touch her.

She wavered, torn between dark visions and warm escape.

She apologized to Elian, though she knew full well he'd never hear. Then she opened herself to the heart and let it dissolve the boundaries she'd fought for so long to keep intact. This time, no voice called to pull her back.

A familiar tug pulled on her spirit, as subtle as the gentle brush of wind through her hair as it whispered its secrets.

The heart of adani called to her, but adani insisted she stay.

No logic could unravel the paradox, but once adani tugged, there was no question of what she'd do. She tore her weary spirit away from the heart's embrace, promising that if she could, she would someday return.

It beat on. Slow, steady, and patient. If she returned in a day or in a decade, it would welcome her again as though no time at all had passed.

She followed the lines of adani back to her body, still connected to the heart like two trees whose roots had grown too close together. Spirit rejoined the flesh, and it was as if she had never left.

Samora breathed deep and opened her eyes.

2

Elian's intimate history with grief did little to ease the pain of Harald's death. He'd hoped, immediately after, that his familiarity with loss would make this time easier. It didn't take long before he was proven a fool. He wept openly in front of Tera as they discussed guard duty rotations, then later lost the ability to speak when he and Warran argued about how best to approach the next council meeting. Whenever he thought the grief had passed for good, it would rise again and strike him from an unexpected direction.

Grief wasn't like other emotions. It didn't rise, crest, and then vanish like anger. It didn't lurk underneath his thoughts like despair. Grief hid itself, waiting silent and invisible until Elian convinced himself he had left it behind. Then, at absurd moments, it would leap out and stab him deep in the heart, leaving yet another wound that would never close.

He would hear Harald's name in conversation and barely react, but then he'd see another adanist with a mug of ale and would be wracked with sorrow.

The demands of his new position didn't make the process any easier. He craved time, either alone or with loved ones, but as the new leader of the Bears, he counted himself fortunate if he could finish a meal without interruption. Warran helped him understand the need and flow of supplies, and Tera knew every warrior under his command like the old friends they were. He was beyond grateful for their guidance, but the sight of them approaching, time after time, wore down what little patience he still possessed.

Five days had passed since the end of the battle, since the death of his best friend and his ascension to the head of the Bears. Five days since Samora had lost consciousness and never returned. At least, he thought it was five days. Day and night meant little anymore.

He was walking toward the healing tent when he saw Warran darting through the tents toward him like an arrow able to follow his scent. Elian slowed to a stop and allowed Warran to reach him. As always, Warran looked him up and down, as though judging whether he was worthy of whatever news he carried, before saying, "You need rest."

Of course he needed rest. Walking was as much as he could demand from his body, and that was with the aid of the heart's adani. If he'd stood anywhere besides upon the gathering ground, he'd have collapsed a day ago. They both knew it, and they both knew there was nothing to be done about it. He'd sleep when he got the chance.

"I'm fine. What's wrong?"

Warran hesitated, then took Elian at his word. "Aldo has called for the unified council to meet within a day or two. He's demanding decisions."

Elian relaxed his hands, which had formed fists of their own accord. He let out a deep breath. Adanists from all clans wandered freely in the camp, and he'd already learned the hard way it was best to pause and forge a considered response instead of blurting out his heart's deepest thoughts. "We knew this was coming, even if it is sooner than expected. Was there anything else?"

"Not from Aldo, but we'll need to move fast. We need a plan to present to the council, and it would be best if we shared it among our allies by tonight, or tomorrow, noon at the latest."

Elian closed his eyes so he wouldn't have to endure Warran's expectant gaze. He didn't have the slightest clue what the clans should do next. Leaving the gathering ground and the heart seemed foolish. Given their current state, the Vada could send one or two Belogs to finish what it had started. Here, at least, they could fight.

But only if the Vada and its forces came to them. If it desired, it could spread its poison throughout the land, and if the clans remained committed to their own safety, no one would stop it.

They were doomed if they left and doomed if they stayed, so what remained?

Elian opened his eyes and forced himself to meet Warran's gaze. It pained him to disappoint the veteran warrior, but lying did no good, either. "I don't know what to do, Warran. What are your thoughts, knowing Aldo will push so soon?"

"I don't think we can delay any longer. The healing tents have almost finished healing the last of our warriors," Warran flinched at Elian's grimace, but charged on, "so we can't use the wounded as an excuse any longer. Our best course of action is to stay here and set up more permanent lodging. I know it leaves the land exposed, but there's no point in venturing out until we have a strategy with at least some hope of succeeding."

Warran saw Elian's distaste and continued before Elian could voice his objections. "Not only that, but it's the position Aldo is most likely to take. Common sentiment among the adanists is that you'll want to lead us to battle again. If you speak first at the council and recommend caution, it'll go a long way toward convincing the others you care about our well-being. It'll also rob Aldo of some of the authority he hopes to steal from you."

It was good advice. Solid and dependable, much like the man who offered it. Elian couldn't think of better, but accepting it tasted like bitter medicine. Humans wouldn't win the war by hiding in the gathering grounds his sister had created. They would only lose more slowly.

What would Harald have done? When decisions haunted Elian, the question served as his guide through the darkness. He conjured Harald in his imagination, but the giant remained silent.

A cry from the nearby healing tent interrupted Elian's thoughts. He whirled at the sound, in time to see Brittany rush from the tent and look around. Her eyes widened when she saw Elian, and his heart sank like a stone as he feared the very worst. But then a wide smile crossed her face, the first joy he'd seen from her in days, and she called out to him, "Your sister is awake!"

Elian looked at Warran, whose joy mirrored Brittany's. The older man hurried him away. "Go on. Speak with your sister and find me after."

Elian bowed to Warran, then found the strength to run toward the healing tent. He flew past Brittany and stopped just inside the front flaps. As Brittany had claimed, Samora was awake. She was sitting up and looking around as though seeing the place for the first time. Her eyes lit up when she saw him, though, and he ran to her, jumping over empty cots in his haste. He wrapped her in a powerful embrace and held her close. "Are you hurt?"

She looked down at her hands as though they were strangers, but she shook her head. Her gaze had a distant quality, as though she looked both at her hands and something beyond, invisible to all but her.

"What happened?" he asked.

"I was with the heart, searching for answers."

Elian leaned closer. As always, it was his sister who lit their darkest moments, who served as a guide when they were lost. "What did you learn?"

"Not enough. The Vada remains in the valley to the west, planning the next stage of its assault. The Belogs are with it, but Moka are leading assaults farther north and south. I tried to speak with the Vada, but it refused to meet with me."

Half a dozen questions and objections swirled in Elian's mind at that, but words poured out of Samora like spilled tea from a tipped-over cup. "When the Vada refused to answer my questions, I asked the heart. Then I asked the dragons, and when they maintained their silence, I used the heart to send my adani as far across the world as I could. I learned much, but I couldn't uncover the history they all keep from us." She ended her report and took a deep breath, then looked up at him, hoping he might have the answers she'd failed to find.

He couldn't bear to meet her gaze. He embraced her again, then gave her space. "Tell me, please."

She did, and the only time her story faltered was near the end, when she admitted the temptation she felt when the heart promised her peace from her worries. She said little more about it, but she didn't need to. Samora was his sister, and he would understand her even if she never spoke a word again.

"I'm glad you returned," he said.

Her cheeks reddened and she looked down. "I'm sorry I couldn't find the truth."

"You have nothing to apologize for. You did more than anyone else."

"And yet not enough to matter." She held out her hand and he took it. "What happened here?"

Elian saw in her gaze that there was little she didn't know already, and that the question was an offer to share the burdens he'd carried since the battle. He took a deep, shuddering breath as grief sideswiped him once again, pooling tears in the corners of his eyes. "Harald is dead, and I now lead the Bears."

There was no surprise in her eyes, and she offered no empty but well-meaning condolences. She squeezed his hand tight and silently promised him that whatever he endured, he wouldn't endure alone. He couldn't have asked for more. With his free hand, he wiped the tears from his eyes. "I'm just glad you're back. I don't think I can do this on my own."

She nodded, and he told her all that he could about the past several days. He skipped what she would have learned from adani, instead focusing on his impressions of the other leaders, and his doubts and fears about how they would proceed. He ended by speaking of the hopeless decisions facing them.

He leaned closer, so his whisper was barely loud enough to travel to her ear. "I don't know what we do," he admitted.

"I don't, either, but our first steps seem clear."

"If they do to you, I'd love to hear them, because to me, nothing is clear," Elian said.

"We must rebuild what strength we can while the Vada considers its next move. The Moka are a problem, but we can't afford to spread our forces too thin. Loken or Lenon must lead a group of healers toward the Wolves' gathering ground. They must do what we did here and hopefully create a second heart."

"It will happen again?"

Samora nodded. "It should. The Wolves' gathering ground is already far stronger than this, so we should be able to create another heart. If the Vada gives us enough time, we might even consider doing the same to the Bears' gathering ground."

Elian started. He'd wondered, idly, if the Bears had a gathering ground, and if so, where it was. He'd always meant to ask, but there had always been something more important to take care of.

Samora understood with no need to ask. "There's no reason you would know, yet. When we first met the Bears, they were patrolling close to the northern edge of their range, and we've only forced them further north since then. Their gathering grounds are to the west and south."

"Not that far away from the Vada, then?"

"Not very, no. But while the healers are trying to create a new heart, your duty is clear, too. You need to summon the other wandering clans to battle. If we're to have even the slimmest chance of victory, we need the strength of both the Coyotes and the Scorpions. We'll need every adanist we can find."

"We can send messengers by tomorrow."

Samora shook her head. "You need to fly to them."

"I'm needed here," Elian argued.

"This is more important. If you send a messenger, there's no telling what will happen, and when they arrive, you'll have to fight Aldo for control of the groups. But if you show up on a dragon and make it clear how important the fight is..."

"Then they'll be far more inclined to accept my thoughts in the council." Elian turned the idea over in his mind for a bit. "It would probably still be good for me to take someone like Tiafel, if he's willing. Someone with some established authority who will support my claims."

Samora smiled softly. "You're already thinking like a leader."

"I'm not sure that I'd go that far. I should have thought about visiting the others first. That was a good idea."

She squeezed his hand again, paused, then said, "You know, I didn't come back out of some sense of duty or obligation."

"No?"

She shook her head. "As dark as our future looks, this is where I'm supposed to be. I don't know how yet, but if we continue to work together, we can defeat the Debru. I'm sure of it."

Elian hoped she was right, but couldn't bring himself to match her optimism. Not until they had a plan that would wipe every single Debru from the land for good.

3

Samora stood in the borrowed tent, now more her home than the house her father had built with his own two hands. Strange, when she thought about it. Home had once been sturdy walls, simple but reliable furniture, and Mother's cooking filling the air with scents of stewed carrots, potatoes, and fresh game. Now a confused drunk could tear down her walls, and the tent itself wasn't hers. It had been a couple's, once, many years ago, and used for random needs since. Every time she stepped inside, she thought not of her childhood, but of her benefactor's children. Their youngest, who still needed to be carried when the clan wandered, had forced them to build a larger shelter. Their oldest, though, had fallen in the battle to protect this fledgling gathering ground.

The tiny pouches of sage, catchweed, and willow that rested in the corner had been prepared and given to her by Brittany weeks ago, and the healer had never asked for them back, even when the line of adanists needing healing had stretched around the healing tent.

Beside the pouches lay a small knife in a sheath, given to her by Harald before he and Elian had traveled west. It had been a strange gift. Like most adanists, Samora could simply form a bound blade whenever she needed a sharp edge. He'd given it to her as if it were a sacred object, though, wrapped in layers of meaning she had yet to unravel. Her chest ached as she looked at the knife and thought of the man who was no longer here to explain his intent.

The Bears had yet to adopt her officially into the clan, but their kindnesses bound her to them stronger than any ritual or proclamation.

And in return, she brought them suffering like they hadn't experienced in generations. She couldn't see the future, no matter how desperately she wished for it, but it didn't take a seer of legend to prophesy the devastation ahead.

Samora stood still in the tent and searched for another way. A path forward that honored the gifts of the clan instead of spit on them. Adani surrounded her, embraced her, and tugged at her. She saw it now, even with her eyes open and her spirit unfocused. Its ways were now as easy to follow as the tracks a wandering clan left as it passed through open prairie.

Because she could see it, she saw the party of adanists approaching, could see the way their adani unconsciously sought hers out. The walls of her tent no longer protected her from the world beyond, and she feared she would never again feel truly alone.

Aldrick noticed them, and he shifted his position, standing directly in front of the entrance to her tent.

Samora had expected this battle but hadn't warned Aldrick. She took a step toward the front of her tent, but the gentle pressure of adani pushed against her. It was no stronger than a soft gust of wind, but she felt it as clearly as though someone had put a hand to her chest and held her away.

She stopped and waited, curious about what adani hoped to accomplish by keeping her within.

The party of adanists, five by Samora's count, stopped before

Aldrick. She couldn't see the exchange but imagined it without a problem. Aldrick was still a Wolf, though he'd openly defied several of Aldo's orders. They'd be staring daggers at one another, daring the other to move, as though the ultimate result was somehow in question.

"You would stand in my way?" Aldo asked.

"If you mean her harm," came Aldrick's measured reply.

"She's ensnared you like a fish, and you're so blind you don't even realize it."

"You can sense what she's accomplished. Her ways may not be ours, but even you can't deny the power she's delivered into our hands."

"And at what cost?" Aldo asked.

When Aldrick made no reply, Aldo continued. "We've lost more adanists in battle in the last few weeks than we've lost in the years before. A Vada has come, tearing up our sacred gathering grounds and threatening our extinction. She is not one of us, no matter her abilities. Wasn't I the one who taught you that all the strength in the world is useless unless it's controlled? She's like an archer with the strongest bow, but she lacks the vision, wisdom, and experience to aim it well."

At the conclusion of his tirade, Aldo attempted to push his way past Aldrick. As the leader of the Wolves, it was well within his rights. Aldrick stood his ground and gathered adani.

Aldo leaped back, and within the beat of a heart, all six adanists outside her tent held bound blades.

Samora took another step forward. This madness had gone on long enough, but adani resisted more strongly than before.

Why? It wasn't capable of reasoning, but she sought the reason all the same. Aldrick was skilled and didn't lack for courage, but against five he had no chance.

Samora gritted her teeth. Adani's guidance was hardly enough to restrain her. It remained subordinate to her will, and she'd see no harm come to Aldrick, at least not like this. She ignored adani and stepped toward the tent flap, ready to pull it aside. Aldo's sharp voice froze her in place, hand extended.

"You'd draw against your leader?"

"If you mean her harm," Aldrick repeated.

Samora grabbed the tent flap, ready to pull it aside, but Aldo once again froze her with his actions. With a flick of his wrist, his bound sword unraveled. The adanists guarding him followed his lead after a moment's confusion.

Aldo's voice was more considered than before. "I've known you since the day you were born. I've watched you grow from a belligerent child into a fine adanist. You've never given me any reason to doubt either your loyalty or your discernment. So, tell me, what is it you see that I don't? I refuse to believe it's simple infatuation. We raised you better than that."

Samora took a step back from the tent flap and let her outstretched hand drop to her side. Aldo's naked curiosity, while surprising, asked many of the same questions she did. She didn't question Aldrick's dedication. He'd proven it time and again over the last few weeks. He claimed it was because she was important to the future of the clans, but that explanation had never fully satisfied her. She leaned forward and listened, almost pressing her ear against the tent flaps.

Aldrick was slow in responding, but when he answered, his voice was as strong as his sword arm. "I'll not deny how much she means to me. I have never crossed paths with a woman so curious, and though she is a villager by birth, the blood of the Spiders runs through her veins. She is part of the clans every bit as much as you or I."

He paused, and Samora tried to stop the pounding of her heart in her chest. It was too loud and made listening difficult.

When he spoke again, his voice had fallen, as though he and Aldo spoke alone. "But I don't defend her just because of my feelings. I fight for her because ever since you first ordered me to watch her, I've witnessed sights that defy everything I thought I knew. I've seen gathering grounds bloom where death once reigned, seen villages made of buildings taller than trees, and watched adanists fight and win against not just one, but several Belogs.

"All of that alone would be enough to convince me she is special and should be treasured. But I've also been close enough to witness her honor. She understood the true intent behind my original orders earlier than I did, but not only did she hide nothing from me, she never pushed me away or forbade me from fulfilling my orders. There is no duplicity in her, which stands in stark contrast to the one who now stands before me."

Samora tensed, waiting for the moment half a dozen bound swords flashed into existence, but none did. A gust of wind rippled across the tent, then Aldo asked, "Is that truly how you see it?"

A moment later, Aldo said, "You've given me much to think about, and I promise you I will. But my purpose here remains unchanged. I need to speak with her, but I assure you I mean her no harm."

There was a long moment of stillness, but enough was enough. Samora opened the flap to her tent and stepped through, and finally, adani didn't resist her. Aldrick still stood in Aldo's way, torn between his old loyalties to the Wolves and his newfound dedication. She offered Aldo a quick bow, acknowledging his authority while reminding him he hadn't yet earned her respect. Aldo's answering bow almost matched her depth, which surprised her. "All who come in peace are welcome. Please, I would be honored to have you join me for a cup of tea."

At her invitation, Aldrick stepped aside and looked grateful that she had cut through his knot of conflicting loyalties.

Aldo motioned for his guards to stay where they were, and they and Aldrick relaxed as one. Samora welcomed Aldo into her tent, then closed the flap behind them. She gathered her small, cracked teapot, filled it with water from her skin, and wove adani into a flickering flame to warm the water while she collected some of her last tea leaves.

Aldo watched with undisguised interest, and as she poured the prepared tea into his cup, he said, "You prepare tea with the care of an elder."

"It's kind of you to say. I learned from my mother, who rarely accepted anything less than our best efforts."

Aldo sipped at his tea and nodded in satisfaction. "Your mother, she was a Spider, correct?"

"She was, and Father, too."

"Did she ever tell you why they left?"

"Father had some skill as an adanist, but Mother had little. As I understand it, at some point in their wandering, Father took part in a battle that left a wound upon his spirit. He lost the heart to fight, and Mother was pregnant. They sought permission to join the villages and it was granted. Mother has always told me Father was happier with a hoe in his hand than a sword, and from what little I remember of him, I believe she spoke truly."

Aldo considered this with a frown on his face. "But when the Moka reached your village, your father stood against it, did he not?"

Samora's throat tightened, and she nodded so that he wouldn't hear her voice crack.

She thanked Aldrick, for she could see no other reason for Aldo's newfound curiosity and slow reflection. She was used to every statement of hers being challenged by him, seemingly for the sole reason that she was the one who made the statement. This Aldo promised at least a chance of compromise.

"Those like your parents are not as uncommon as they used to be. My grandfather once told me he'd fought with three genera-tions of wandering adanists, and he'd never heard of one wanting to live among the villagers. Today I spend half my time leading the Wolves and half my time convincing the children to continue their training."

The admission allowed Samora a glance into a heart that had been veiled too long from her understanding.

"Mother used to tell me and Elian that most everyone desires the life they don't have, but the desire persists no matter their life. Adanists want to be farmers until the first day they spend picking and hauling stones from a field. Farmers want to be adanists until the day a Debru attacks."

Aldo's eyes shot up, and he nodded. "Your mother is wise."

"She is. She always claimed she and Father were unusual, in that their desires were true, and not just a lust for a life they didn't have."

Aldo continued to nod, but then his eyes hardened. "And what of you? Are your desires true, or do you simply long for something you cannot have?"

Samora's fingertips danced around the edge of her cup as her thoughts danced around the question. "That's a good question, and one I don't have an honest answer to."

Aldo had been bringing his tea to his lips, but the cup froze so suddenly he almost spilled on his tunic. "Then what do you want? Your voice and Elian's carry a weight I believe is undeserved, but perhaps there is common ground we can meet upon. We are entering a fraught time, when one wrong decision might doom us all."

Samora took a long sip of her tea. The leaves were some of her last, and she savored the warmth and grassy flavor of the drink. "My brother is a simple man to understand. He wants revenge upon the Debru, and will stop at nothing to see it complete. He won't be satisfied until every Debru in the land is dead."

Aldo leaned back and used his arms to support his torso. "Killing the Debru and protecting the lives of the adanists of the wandering clans are not necessarily the same goal."

"They are not," Samora agreed.

"And what about you? What do you want?"

"I want to understand."

"Understand what?"

"Everything. Why the Debru are here. What the heart beneath our feet is and why it formed. Why the dragons keep our own past a secret."

"And how does this help the wandering clans?" Aldo asked.

"Knowledge helps everyone. A farmer who understands their soil and can read the patterns of the weather will grow more crops. An adanist who has mastered their adani and can predict the behavior of the Debru will be far more effective than one who lacks those qualities."

Aldo didn't look convinced.

Samora continued, "You're no fool. You hope to preserve the lives and traditions of your clan, but I think in the deepest recesses of your heart, you understand your traditions won't save you forever. They prolong the inevitable while you hold out hope for a future that will never arrive. Even if my brother successfully summons the last of the wandering clans, you know we lack the strength to fight against the Vada."

Aldo set down his tea with so much force Samora feared the cup would crack. "Which is exactly why I'm against this foolishness. Perhaps you're right. Following tradition is a slow death instead of a fast one. So what? Life is valuable, and it shouldn't be wasted."

"Agreed, but you didn't let me finish. My brother and the wandering clans both make the same mistake. You look to strength to save you, but that time has long since passed. Our strength can no longer save us, but knowledge might."

Aldo scoffed. "You think the Vada will leave if we simply learn a history lesson?"

"No. But I believe that pursuing knowledge is our last and greatest defense against the darkness that threatens to overwhelm us. It may fail, but that doesn't mean it isn't our greatest hope."

Aldo pushed himself off his hands, and he sat straight up.

"And you think defiling our sacred gathering grounds will help you understand?"

"Without doubt. We've already learned one new way to create gathering grounds. If healers can create another heart beneath the grounds of the Wolves, we'll know we can create more. Maybe yours will be different, or stronger. It will teach us an incredible amount, I think."

"Or you might destroy the gathering ground in the attempt."

"That will not happen. Even if the technique cannot create another heart, it doesn't harm the trees. If anything, it strengthens them. It is little different from healing, except instead of closing a wound, we are reinforcing something that is already whole."

Aldo wasn't so easily convinced. "And what if you're successful, and you draw the Debru like we did here?"

Samora didn't scoff, even though she wanted to. "Your gathering ground isn't safe, no matter what actions I take. We'd done nothing to the Crow's old gathering ground, and the Debru still destroyed it without a thought. The mistake you make, repeatedly, is thinking that what was true in the past will remain true in the future. The Vada is here to wipe us out. It means to destroy the wandering clans, the villages, and the gathering grounds. Only once you accept that will we find a place to agree."

Aldo snarled, but the expression only lasted for a moment. As he reached for his teacup, his hand trembled. He saw she noticed, and it was as if she'd punched him hard in the stomach. His whole body shivered. He bent until he was almost doubled over, and his breath came in short, hard gasps.

Samora sat still while the attack passed through him. After a few silent convulsions, he mastered himself again and sat up straight. He couldn't bring himself to meet her gaze.

"It's a terrible truth to face, especially as the leader of so many," Samora said.

Aldo nodded mutely, but then he found his voice. "They're all my children, even those like Aldrick."

"I can't promise them protection, but I wish them no harm. You're right that life is good, and something worth protecting. I would like to save as many as I can. Will you help me?"

Aldo considered, then nodded, and Samora poured them another cup of tea to celebrate their new, uneasy alliance.

❧ 4 ❧

Loken whooped as the dragon that carried him and Elian north dropped through the clouds. The drop reminded Elian of running through the dense banks of fog that sometimes formed around the river valley east of their house, except faster than any pair of feet could run. Drops of water stung Elian's face, but his body provided shelter for Loken, allowing the healer all the enjoyment of the flight with less of the discomfort.

Loken shouted again as they broke through the bank of clouds and saw the land stretched out below them like a verdant green rug. Far to the east, on Elian's right, mountains rose from the rolling hills, their snowcapped peaks blending into the clouds. He grinned at the sight, and he grinned at Loken's laughter. He'd never seen the healer so carefree.

Although the only other time Loken had been on a dragon, it had been to flee a Vada as it destroyed his ancestral gathering grounds. Perhaps not the best point of comparison.

Blood pumped in his veins and adani ran like a flooded stream through his expanded channels. Untamed land passed below them as they traveled far faster than a horse could gallop. Wind blew his hair back and ripped the tears from his eyes. Despite the Debru's efforts, he was alive, and in this moment, life was good.

He was still grinning when Loken shook his shoulder and pointed to the northwest. Elian's eyes followed the line of his finger and spotted several thin plumes of smoke rising in the distance. The smoke gathered and merged into one slightly larger cloud, which drifted west on the light evening breeze. He nodded to let Loken know he'd spotted the camp, then directed the dragon toward it.

The healer had already earned his ride and more, and they hadn't even landed yet. Tracking down and summoning the other two clans was fine as far as ideas went, and Elian agreed with Samora that it was important he be the one to deliver the summons, but he hadn't had the slightest clue how to go about accomplishing the task. He was aware the other clans were to the north, but "go north" was a suggestion that encompassed an incredible amount of territory, even with the advantage of having a dragon to speed the process.

Elian had originally intended to ask Tiafel to accompany him, but Tiafel felt he was needed more in the camps, and suggested Loken as an alternative. In this, as in many decisions, Tiafel had been wise.

Loken possessed a decent familiarity with both the clans and the lands to the north. He'd wandered as a lone healer for a time before returning to the Hawks, so his knowledge was more extensive than most in the clans. It was he who had pointed Elian and the dragon in the right direction, he who had guessed where the Coyotes would be with an impressive accuracy.

Elian had the dragon circle the camp once while he studied it. The Coyotes, according to Loken, counted about as many adanists in their ranks as the Wolves, and the estimate appeared correct from the size of their camp.

Their arrival stirred up no small amount of attention. Scouts shouted and pointed, but thankfully, no bound spears flew toward them. Children stopped their games, laughed, and waved. Elian waved back, even as parents rushed to protect their children with bound shields. A handful of warriors formed spears, but no one threw them. Elian waved again, then banked the dragon away from the camp and landed what he hoped was a non-threatening distance away.

Loken leaped off first, opting to drop all the way from the dragon's back instead of climbing down like a sensible warrior. He landed well, slapping the ground with his hand and springing up like he was a child. Elian followed, though he cycled enough adani through his legs that he barely had to bend his knees. When he met Loken's gaze, the healer's smile stretched from ear to ear, a far cry from the considered, cautious man Elian knew.

Loken bowed to Elian, then turned to the Coyote camp, where a line of adanists had formed to protect the tents. "Let's hope we made a favorable impression."

They advanced together, leaving the dragon to nestle deeper into the dirt. Elian let his gaze wander across the line, waiting for any sign of an impending attack. He didn't spot any bound weapons, but he'd be surprised if the adanists weren't the blink of an eye away from forming some. Loken also ran his eyes up and down the line, but he was looking for familiar faces. After checking twice, he said, "I don't think Nimia is the leader of the Coyotes any longer. I don't see her anywhere."

Elian nodded, then almost tripped over his feet when a giant of a man appeared from near the center of the camp. He stood a full head taller than Elian, and his arms were thick and rippling with muscle. His hands looked large enough to grab Elian by the skull and crush him.

Elian swore he stared at Harald, resurrected and made whole. He almost cried out, but reason stilled his tongue.

He blinked, and the differences were there, blurred by memories of grief. This man's jawline wasn't as square as Harald's, and though his arms were all muscle, a small amount of fat had collected about his waist. His eyes were bright, but they lacked the fire that had defined Harald's intensity.

Elian quickly recovered and hurried until he was once again by Loken's side. Loken raised his hand in greeting, and Elian did the same. A moment later, the giant raised his hand, too, and some of the tension left Loken's shoulders.

"Quite an entrance, friends," the giant man called.

"The fastest way to travel, and our news requires it," Elian responded. He stopped and bowed when the giant's gaze focused on him. "My name is Elian, and I am the leader of the Bears."

"And I am Loken, second of the Hawks," Loken added.

The giant squinted hard at Loken, as though attempting to unravel a mystery. "Loken? The same one who visited years ago and healed Nimia from the disease that rotted her from the inside?"

"The same, and I'll confess I'm disappointed not to see her today. Once, I was sure she would outlive us all."

The giant laughed, and again Elian swore he looked at Harald in the flesh. It was almost the same deep, booming laugh that had kept him company for so many nights with the Bears. "She would have been the first to agree that was her plan, but a Moka spear cut short her life. Her sacrifice saved many lives, though."

Loken bowed. "Accept my deepest sympathies. She was an incredible warrior and filled with lifetimes' worth of wisdom." Several of the warriors up and down the line nodded, and the adanists finally relaxed their defenses. Many turned back to the camp to resume whatever tasks Elian and Loken had interrupted, while others came closer to greet the strangers.

Before long, Elian felt as though he'd bowed to everyone in the camp, and he found himself standing directly before the giant. He bowed one last time, and as he straightened, he found himself in a tight embrace. The giant pounded him so hard on the back, Elian worried for the health of his spine. Then two enormous hands landed on his shoulders and separated them.

"There's no need for such formality between us. You're a scrawny thing, but if Harald chose you as his second, he must have had good reasons. My name is Tassan, and you must have stories to tell, riding here on a dragon. You'll also have to tell me how Harald fell. I can only imagine it is a story we'll tell our great-grandchildren someday."

Before Elian could answer, he and Loken were half-invited, half-pulled toward the fire that was the heart of the Coyotes' camp. He ended up sitting on a log with a mug of something warm and sweet in his hands. Tassin encouraged him to share his story, so Elian did. Several of the warriors around the fire wept openly when he spoke of Harald's death.

Their tears encouraged his own, and whatever was in the drink didn't help. It made him light-headed and relaxed, and he opened himself up to memories of Harald, which only brought the tears on faster. He wiped them off his face and prepared to broach the reason they'd arrived in the first place.

Tassan stood up first. He lifted his drink high in the air and toasted Harald. Then he faced Elian. "Duel me, friend."

Surprise and drink made him slow to respond, and when he stood, his balance wavered.

Loken spoke for both of them. "Allow me the honor, Tassan. He is inexperienced in our ways."

Tassan's grin never left his face, but he shook his head slowly. "I already know your quality, Loken. But if this one wants us to ride out and fight with him, I need to know that he's worth fighting for."

"Accepted," Elian said. Tassan had already guessed his purpose, which saved Elian the discomfort of asking. The least he could do in return was honor a request for a duel.

Tassan's grin spread wider, and he led Elian, stumbling, a short way outside the camp. Many of his adanists followed, wagering with one another on the victor. There were few willing to take the risk on him.

He looked back, even though it almost cost him his balance. "Wager on me, Loken. No reason we can't both profit from tonight's adventure."

Loken bowed, then offered a considerable sum of fresh venison as his wager. Dozens of Coyote adanists eagerly accepted.

When Tassan stopped, Elian cycled a trickle of adani through his head. It cleared the drink from his thoughts, but he kept a goofy smile on his face and his limbs loose. He cycled adani through them, too, ready in case Tassan attacked quickly.

Against an adanist who knew his tricks, Elian stood little chance. The ability to bind adani was simply too great an advantage for him to overcome. He'd dueled Harald a dozen times, and the only time he'd even come close to matching his mentor was when Harald limited himself. He had one chance to defeat Tassan, and he hoped to use the opportunity to its fullest.

Tassan formed a bound sword and twirled it in his hands with effortless ease. The golden light burned the air between them, leaving an afterimage that made it look as though a wall of light blocked Elian from approaching. In response, Elian drew his knife, the one he'd inherited from his father the night a Moka visited their village. Several of the gathered adanists laughed, and more than one called to Loken, offering to increase the size of their already considerable wagers.

Tassan looked relaxed, ready, and confident. He bounced up and down on his feet, moving lightly for one so large. Elian judged his speed and decided the Coyotes' leader was just as quick as Harald, if not a little faster. He didn't appear to share his clan's low estimate of Elian's abilities, though, as he kept himself ready for any attack.

"Whenever you're ready," Tassan said.

Elian bowed again, but Tassan didn't take the opportunity to strike. He waited for Elian to make the first move.

Elian straightened and pretended to stumble, but he focused all the adani in his legs and leaped forward. He covered the space between him and Tassan in less than the blink of an eye, his knife ready.

Tassan reacted quickly, but Elian's ambush was complete. By the time Tassan's bound sword was coming down, Elian was already inside Tassan's guard. He flipped his grip on the knife and leaped, jamming the bottom of the grip up and under Tassan's chin.

Elian hadn't struck hard, but the force of the jump, combined with Tassan's surprise, toppled the giant backward. Elian followed him down, landing on top of the leader and knocking the wind from his lungs. He held the bottom of his knife against the underside of Tassan's chin for a moment longer, then disentangled himself and offered Tassan a hand.

There was silence around the circle until Tassan reached up and grabbed Elian's hand. Adani still crashed like a raging river through his limbs, so Elian had no trouble hauling Tassan up. As he did, shouts and cries of disbelief surrounded them.

Elian glanced over at Loken and saw the healer standing tall, beaming like never before. They'd be carrying enough fresh game on their way home to feed the dragons for a week.

Tassan's laughter drowned out the sounds of his clan's disbelief and complaints. "I've seen nothing like it in all my years. I can see now why Harald chose you as his successor. Were you able to beat him?"

"Never once. Once a skilled adanist knows my techniques, there's little I can do to reach them. But when I have strong adanists at my back, my sword brings down Belogs."

Tassan roared and clapped Elian on the back, threatening once again to snap his spine.

Elian coughed, then smiled to mask the pain of Tassan's friendliness.

Tassan led him back toward the fire and said, "You and I have much to discuss. I only saw him rarely, but Harald was like a brother to me. I sense some of his spirit in you, and my heart beats easier, knowing he lives so vigorously in our memories."

Tears sprang to Elian's eyes, grief surprising him yet again. He made to wipe them away, but Tassan caught his hand. "Take the time to weep, friend. No doubt your days have been filled with duties and responsibilities, leaving no time to grieve properly. Let tonight be yours, a celebration of Harald's life and a chance to mourn his premature departure from our company. Then tomorrow, you and I will mount your dragon and seek the Scorpions. I do not know how willing they will be to join our cause, but together, I feel you and I will accomplish great things."

5

K arla waited outside Samora's tent when she emerged. She raised an eyebrow at Samora's attire. "Did you run out of useful clothing?"

Instead of her typical tunic and pants, Samora had thrown on one of her dresses, long stuffed near the bottom of the pack that had traveled countless miles with her. It was a simple affair, faded over the years despite her efforts to keep it looking like her mother had just finished sewing it. Back in the village, it was the dress she'd worn to most eigthday feasts. A wide woven belt tightened the dress around her waist and secured Harald's gifted knife at her side.

Samora expected her glare was answer enough, but Karla, unfortunately, wasn't so easily intimidated.

"What are you playing at? Aldo and the others will be as likely to ignore you completely as they are to debate with you while you're wearing that. At the very least, strap on more knives and maybe a sword or two."

"There's no need to impress them with some illusion of my martial prowess, Karla. I can't and shouldn't advise them on how to fight. I go to the council to help strengthen and heal, and I don't need steel at my side for that."

Objections danced on Karla's lips, but she saw Samora's expression and decided against it. She took her customary position at Samora's side, and they walked shoulder to shoulder. Their brief journey reminded Samora of their earlier attempts to sway the council. That time, they'd retreated from the meeting with their tails between their legs. Hopefully today proved different.

She almost told Karla that there was no need to accompany her any longer, but she couldn't bring herself to say the words. True as they might be, she appreciated the older woman's companionship. Nothing could hurt her, so long as she had Karla by her side. She didn't fully understand the woman's dedication to her, but she didn't question it, either.

The walk to the council meeting barely took any time at all. The gathering ground had never been large, and the Belogs' attack had ruined a solid third of it. Grass was already regrowing, aided by the incredible amounts of adani underfoot, but the assembled clans, by unspoken agreement, hadn't rebuilt any tents in the damaged area.

The council was much reduced from its earlier days. Samora remembered a large circle filled with strong arms and fiery gazes. She'd once been afraid to even approach the assembly, but it held none of the mystique it had before. For one, there weren't nearly as many councilors present. Loken and Elian weren't here, and Harald's loss left a hole larger than his enormous frame. The Hounds, Hawks, and Bears had all lost leadership in the battle for the gathering ground, and nowhere was that more apparent than when Samora looked around the much smaller circle.

Only the Wolves' leadership remained untouched by the tragedy, and Samora feared the interactions between Kati and the Hawks and Aldo and his Wolves. Kati claimed, and Samora believed, that Aldo had deliberately withdrawn his forces early during the battle, leaving the Hawks to fight a fierce battle without support. When accused, Aldo claimed he had ordered everyone to retreat, and Kati had ignored the order.

It was a wonder the two hadn't yet come to blows, but Kati was no longer the fiery commander Samora had first met. Harald's death had made her a recluse who only emerged from her tent when duty absolutely required it. Her red-rimmed eyes stared holes into the ground, and her long blonde hair was a matted mess that hadn't seen a brush in days. Samora counted Kati as one of her closest allies in the argument to come, but she wondered just how much support the woman could offer.

Everything hinged, unfortunately, on Aldo, and despite the promises she'd secured the day before, she couldn't bring herself to trust him without reservation. For better or for worse, his actions had made the Wolves the strongest clan, and it wasn't even that close. When the dust from the battle had settled, the Hounds still numbered almost as many, but too many Hounds were injured and Tiafel had always been a cautious leader.

Normally, it would have fallen to Tiafel to start the council meeting. As the oldest of the leaders, he'd been given the honor without contest.

Today, though, Aldo stepped forward and spoke first. "Thank you all for coming. I know the last few days have been difficult, but I know I'm not alone in being increasingly worried about our future. I would like more time to mourn our losses, but I must look to my people and their needs."

Aldo paused but didn't step from the center of the circle to open the discussion up to others. "After considerable thought, I've decided it would be best if we remain within this gathering ground. It is the only place where we stand a chance against the Debru."

The proposal was the same as Samora's, and it had been previously agreed, but Samora still shifted uncomfortably as Aldo effectively took control of the clans without a fight.

Tiafel was the first to raise an objection. "What if the Vada attacks the villages? Do we ride out to meet it?"

All eyes turned to Aldo, who didn't flinch at the question. "No."

Tiafel, undeterred, continued his line of questioning. "And what of the Moka and the Debru currently wandering the land? Samora claims they march both to the north and south, and it won't be long before other villages are in danger. If we don't move to protect them soon, we may very well not have enough food come next summer."

Aldo didn't even blink. "We stay. The Coyotes and the Scorpions will have to be sufficient defense to the north. I don't think there's anything we can do for the villages to the south."

Councilors glanced at one another, as though daring another to object, but none spoke against Aldo's terrible pronouncement.

Aldo licked his lips but didn't defend his decisions further.

Samora's fist clenched, but she didn't speak out, either. Their decision was a terrible one, and she'd tossed and turned over it all night, but it was the right one. After generations of defending the villages from the Debru and their creatures, the clans had reached a point where they could no longer keep their ancient promises.

After he'd given enough time for any objections to be raised, Aldo continued. "While we continue to strengthen ourselves here, I believe we should also send a group of healers to the Wolves' gathering ground to perform the same rituals they performed here. I've spoken at length with Samora about this, and she believes that the healers' efforts will result in the creation of another heart, possibly even stronger than the one that beats beneath our feet. Given that our healers have done almost all they can here, I think it is time for them to move on, and I believe Samora should lead them."

She lifted her eyes and saw him staring at her, judging her reaction. She'd made it clear yesterday she wouldn't be the one to lead the healers to the gathering ground. With Loken gone, Lenon was the next obvious choice. Why did he now insist she leave?

A glance around the circle made the answer clear. Without either her or Elian present, Aldo would have little difficulty assuming command of the unified clans. The Wolves were already the strongest clan present, and Tiafel had no interest in leading anyone who wasn't a Hound. Under other circumstances, Kati might have delayed or confounded Aldo's grab for power, but she could barely focus enough to stand.

Most of the heads around the circle were nodding, though a few looked to her first to confirm what Aldo had said.

Thoughts raced, fast as a deer in flight. She hadn't intended to lead the healers, but she hadn't intended to stay in the camp, either. They needed answers, and they wouldn't be found here. That, too, left Aldo in firm control of the clans.

But did she even care? As far as she knew, she and Aldo agreed on the general direction the clans needed to take.

Try as she might to excuse herself, she couldn't accept her weak logic. Time and time again, Aldo had proven himself untrustworthy. He tried to acquire by guile instead of persuasion, and it cast all his promises into doubt. In his mind, had he sacrificed his gathering grounds in exchange for the leadership of the unified clans?

But what could she do? She would need to leave if she wanted to defeat the Vada. She'd hoped to leave either this day or the next.

Adani pulled her away from the gathering ground she had created, but duty wrapped its unbreakable chains tightly around her, and she stood still, caught between the two forces with no clue which path was correct. The eyes of the elders and the leaders bore into her, but even their piercing stares couldn't draw out her answer.

The Vada saved her from her dilemma. Her stomach twisted

and dropped, and her gaze was pulled to the south and west. A dark wave of shadow flooded the webs of adani that connected Samora to distant lands. Blood drained from her face as she sensed the overwhelming amount of strength the Vada casually flung about.

Moments later, others felt the same wave of shadow approaching. It left no trace in the physical world, but it felt to Samora like a wall rushing toward her.

Samora's mind, already racing from Aldo's surprise, cracked under this new threat. She stood, rooted and frozen as the shadow raced along the lines of adani. She tilted her head, fixated on the one detail that made no sense. Shadow traveled along the lines of adani, but it didn't destroy anything it passed through. It swept through, but the web of adani glowed brightly after it passed.

Panicked shouts rose from the rest of the camps. Too late to do anything, though. Several of the adanists closest to her formed shields, but their efforts would do nothing against the shadow that ripped through the land. This was like no attack they'd fought off before.

A moment before it struck, Samora's reason returned. She focused her adani in her core, cradled it tight and sheltered it as best she could with her body.

The shadow struck the gathering ground with all the force of a bolt of lightning. The heart resisted the shadow, but the Vada's attack proved to be a slippery opponent. It ducked past the heart's defenses and filled the adani channels that nourished the gathering ground.

Shadow washed over Samora, but only briefly. It felt like being submerged in mud, but when she stepped out of the muck, it slid from her without a trace. Shadow found no hold on her adani, and then it was past and the heart beat firmly under her feet and all was right with the world.

She turned, as though she could somehow see the wave of

shadow, but of course she could not. All she could see was the camp, quietly coming to realize the attack had done nothing.

She frowned and shook her head.

That couldn't be. The Vada was many things, but it was not a fool, nor were its efforts ever wasted.

Samora cast out her adani, using the heart to send it farther than she could alone.

She didn't even need its assistance. This morning, when she'd sent out her adani, she'd been surrounded by light. No more. Light still overwhelmed the darkness, but now some of the stars that she called her friends and allies had gone dark. The shadow had passed, but in passing had built nests within many of the adanists.

The council members milled about, looking at one another and asking silent questions with their gazes. Samora brought her focus in tighter, and her stomach dropped like a stone at what she sensed.

The warning on her lips never reached anyone's ears, though.

Across the circle from where Samora stood, Kati formed a bound dagger. Its customary golden light was tainted with black flecks that swirled across the blade like ash falling from the sky. Kati snarled and pointed her dagger at Aldo. "You killed my family, and your cowardice is the reason Harald no longer walks among us. Duel me now, or will you confess your cowardice among the assembly?"

Aldo took a step back as his guards rushed to protect him. He stammered, his face pale, but he didn't answer Kati's challenge.

She took a step forward and formed another dagger in her left hand, identical to the first. Tears streamed down her face, but her eyes glinted with the pent-up desire for revenge. "Then die!"

Kati leaped forward into battle, and as she did, the entire camp erupted into chaos.

6

E lian, Loken, and Tassan left the next morning on the back of the dragon, flying north and east into the rising sun. When Elian had first woken, his head had pounded as hard as it had the morning after he first met Harald. The remainder of the evening had proven that not only did Tassan fight like Harald, he drank like him, too. The Coyotes had cracked open a small cask to celebrate his arrival, and Elian swore Tassan finished half the cask on his own with little effect.

Elian had felt fine after clearing out his hangover with adani right after he woke, but now that they were in the air and the wind constantly whipped across his face, he once again felt the lingering effects of last night's celebration, some of the liquor still in his body making its presence known. He trickled the smallest extra portion of adani into his head.

The drumming in his head receded, and he silently thanked Tera once again for teaching him the trick. She'd wouldn't like that he used it as often as he did, but last night's celebrations had endeared Elian to Tassan. If the cost of gaining the Coyotes' allegiance was a hangover, he'd pay it gladly.

He rode at the front of the three, so he twisted so that his voice would carry back to Tassan. "Is there anything I should know about the Scorpions before I meet with them?"

He'd asked Loken the same question as they'd first flown north, but it had been several years since Loken had been in the area. Loken's report hadn't filled Elian with much optimism, and he hoped Tassan might share some secrets that would make his task easier.

Tassan grunted. "They're some of the toughest adanists you're likely to meet. They're a small clan, with maybe only a third the number of adanists that the Coyotes have, but if they ever picked a fight, I'd probably start searching for places to hide."

Loken had said much the same on their flight north.

"What makes them so fierce?" Elian asked.

"The mountains they call home. What you or I would call brutal and unforgiving terrain is warm and welcoming to them."

"Sounds like the warriors I want to have at my side," Elian said.

"They are, but I'm not sure even the threat of a Vada and your pet dragon here will get them to stir from their mountain."

"Why not?"

"Though they are named among the wandering clans, they don't wander like the rest of us. Their territory is much smaller, and they will be loath to abandon their villages. They hold more strictly to their oaths than the rest of us, and rightfully so."

"Because of the steel?" Elian guessed.

Tassan nodded. "The steel and the knowledge passed down within the villages they protect. If the Bears or the Hounds lose a village, there's some farmland lost and the clans need to hunt more to fill their bellies. If the Scorpions lose their villages, we lose not just the steel but the knowledge of how to mine it, create it, and forge it."

Elian considered this for a while, then asked. "Should I even be asking for their aid, then?"

"I think so. Important as the Scorpions' task is, the Vada

represents a threat to everyone, and if nothing is done, the Scorpions will fall the same as the rest of us. One of your greatest challenges will be to convince them they are at risk, too. They fight a fair number of otsoa, and the occasional kettu that wanders too far, but it's rare they fight Debru anymore. Their enemies are the land and the elements. They may well believe they're safe in their mountain strongholds."

Loken, again, had said the same. Elian's hopes for a new alliance dimmed, but all he could do was try. If Harald could find the Hawks in the middle of the deadlands, Elian could convince the Scorpions to join their fight.

Elian looked toward the mountains that grew ever larger and wondered at that. Harald had been a gifted adanist, but was still just a man. How had he so easily won the trust and loyalty of so many? Several of his strongest warriors had leaped, almost without question, at the chance to follow Harald on a suicidal mission.

The memories made him feel small. If Harald was here instead of him, perhaps humanity's future would be brighter. The Scorpions would have followed Harald without an argument.

Elian gripped the scales of the dragon tight enough that his knuckles turned white. He wasn't Harald, but Harald had trusted him. It was time to earn that trust.

Tassan shouted they needed to head a little further north and Elian obeyed. The dragon gently banked and rose so that the spires of jagged granite no longer threatened it. The terrain captured Elian's attention, and for several miles, all he could do was stare.

Snow that glittered like crystals in the early morning sunlight blanketed some of the tallest peaks, but the ones they passed over were still bare. Pine trees wedged themselves into every crevice, ledge, and crack they could find, and eagles circled overhead, watching the dragon and its passengers with wary eyes.

Loken tapped his shoulder and pointed down at a small stream running brown.

"Mud?" Elian asked.

"Iron."

Elian caught quick glimpses of narrow trails that hugged the sides of cliffs. Here and there he saw small fields, cleared now from a harvest that had likely finished weeks ago, but he saw no habitation nearby, and he wondered about the daily life of those who fought to survive upon these steep slopes.

They flew another mile, then Tassan directed them up a valley. Elian spotted the trail first, wider than any he'd seen all day. It clung to the side of the cliffs as though afraid it would fall off. Small stone bridges stood over streams that ran like tears down the side of the granite. The valley at the bottom was so densely packed with trees Elian couldn't see the ground below. Watchtowers, set in seemingly impossible locations along the ridges on either side of the valley, kept watch for danger.

"In springtime, many of those streams become rushing rivers as the snow on the peaks above melts," Tassan told Elian.

Elian held tightly to the dragon's neck and sent gratitude along their connection. He'd never considered himself particularly afraid of heights, but he'd never walked on a trail where a single misstep meant a long fall, followed by a very sudden and very fatal stop. If not for the dragon delivering them to their destination, the Scorpions' first sight of him might have been him clinging desperately to the cliff face as he shuffled up the trail.

Loken tapped him on the shoulder and pointed ahead, and Elian's eyes went wide. He'd listened to Samora's story of the enormous village to the west, and from her description, he was certain it was more impressive, but he'd never imagined a village like the one that rested at the top of the valley.

The wall drew his attention first. Made of rough-hewn stone, the stones fit together in such a way that it almost looked as if the wall had grown there naturally. It stood three times the height of a man and covered the width of the valley. Two buildings stood on top of the wall, dotted with small slits. Elian frowned, then understood. The trail bent and meandered until it reached the main gate in the wall, which was currently open. The buildings allowed archers protected places to send arrows at any invaders. Flat roofs on top of the buildings allowed adanists a clear and relatively protected view, too.

After the Moka and the otsoa had attacked his village, they'd debated building walls, but decided against it. A Moka could have destroyed any wall they built with ease, and they didn't encounter enough otsoa to justify the months of labor the wall would have taken. But if they'd known about walls like this....

Elian didn't finish the thought. The dragon flew fearlessly toward the walls and Elian could see adanists taking position on top of the buildings. He waved, then suggested that the dragon fly a little higher, just in case any adanist was a little too eager to defend their village.

He waved again as they approached, but no one raised their hand in greeting. As when he'd approached the Coyotes, he had the dragon bank above the village. He waved to all as he studied the scene below.

The village was made almost entirely of stone; the buildings squished together as though caught in an eternal embrace. The trails between the buildings had been busy, but as they flew overhead, people ran for shelter. A few children tried to wave back, but responsible adults soon pulled them into safer spaces. The adanists on the walls had spears formed and ready, and no one returned his repeated waves.

They completed their loop, and Elian looked for a place to land. The village was too tightly packed for them to land, so he searched beyond the walls. The valley they'd flown up was too steep and too narrow, but there was empty farmland behind the village. Elian directed them in that direction, and the dragon landed.

They climbed eagerly off the dragon and looked around. The air was chilly this high, but smelled fresh, unpolluted by the smoke of fires or the scent of cows and pigs. They'd landed a good quarter mile above the village's walls, and Elian made to walk toward them. Tassan's hand on his shoulder stopped him.

"Best if they come to us. They are a bit more territorial than your typical clan," the giant said.

Elian nodded, though he wanted little more than to run down to the village and explore.

It didn't take long for a party to come and meet them. The adanists came with bound spears and swords in hand, ready to throw at the slightest provocation. Elian waved again, though he started to fear he'd never receive a kind response. His eyes traveled up and down the line, seeking the warrior in command.

Tassan spoke quietly, anticipating Elian's need. "Royzen is their commander. He's the warrior with the dual swords just to the right of the center."

Elian spotted him, and a moment of careful study made him certain of Tassan's information. Physically, little distinguished him from the others. He stood as tall as Elian, though had nearly as much muscle on his frame as Alec did. The same could be said for most of the other Scorpions, though, too.

His stare gave him away, though. The others approached with barely hidden fear, their gazes darting constantly to the dragon currently nestling into their field. Royzen stared only at the adanists who'd come to visit. His eyes narrowed when he looked over Elian's shoulder. "Tassan, what are you doing here?"

He didn't raise his voice, but it carried across the field to their ears without a problem. In return, Tassan bellowed, "Came to visit!"

Royzen's gaze moved over Elian's other shoulder. The Scorpion commander recognized Elian's other companion, too, and Elian was glad he'd chosen as he had. "Loken, it has been several years since your presence has graced our halls."

Loken bowed. "An oversight I hope to correct before the sun drops below the peaks, old friend."

Finally, Royzen's weighty stare fell on Elian. "And who is this pup who travels with you?"

Elian took a step forward and bowed. "Elian, leader of the Bears."

He didn't miss the looks that passed between Royzen's entourage. Harald's legend, it seemed, had reached the high places, too. As it should.

"What happened to Harald?" Royzen asked.

"He fell in battle against six Belogs, but not before ensuring none of them would live to hurt us again."

"Six Belogs?" Royzen stared at Elian in disbelief, then laughed. "That sounds about right, though a part of me wishes he'd taken even more with him. It's grim tidings, then, is it?"

"I'm afraid so," Elian said.

"Well, be welcome. Do I need to worry about the dragon?"

"It should be fine. I wouldn't be surprised if it flew off to hunt, but your people have nothing to fear."

"My grandad once said that he'd seen a dragon, but I didn't believe him. I thought he'd gotten too deep into his cups one night."

"I can hardly blame you. I'd only known them as legends until we found them captured by Belogs."

Royzen cast a skeptical eye in Elian's direction. "You seem to have quite a collection of tales for one so young."

"I have a long history of being in the wrong place at the right time," Elian said.

"So it would seem."

They passed through the walls of the village and Elian finally saw the home of the Scorpions up close. Unlike Samora's experience of the village far to the west, here there was no gradual change in the style of buildings. There wasn't the space. As soon as they passed under the wall, they were in the shade of the tall structures, and a shiver passed through Elian's arms. Most of the homes were two or three levels high, made of stone and thick beams of lumber.

"Is there only one family per building?"

Royzen shared a questioning look with Loken and Tassan, then answered. "Not usually. Most families might have one level of a building, or sometimes two, if they've grown quite large."

Elian looked back at the wall they'd come through. The buildings filled up every available space. "What do you do if there are more people than places to put them?"

"It doesn't happen often, but when it does, we ask for volunteers to leave. There are a few villages closer to the foothills that aren't as well protected but can expand more easily."

"Can you extend the walls?"

"We could, but it would come at the cost of farmland, which is a trade we aren't willing to make. As it is, we could withstand a siege almost indefinitely, so long as the walls hold."

Royzen called him young, and he was, especially to lead a clan, but it had been a long time since he'd felt like such a child. Every time he thought he'd seen all there was to see of the world, he discovered something new that made him realize how premature he'd been made a leader.

He and Loken fell behind Tassan and Royzen, who spoke and laughed together like old friends reunited after too many years apart.

"You look like a man with a lot on his mind," Loken said.

"When I was young, I thought getting old meant learning all there was to know. Now, I'm thinking that the true sign of age is realizing how much you don't know."

"I'd agree. I traveled for years after I lost my arm and saw most of the clan territories, but sometimes I still feel as though I am just leaving my parent's tent for the first time."

Royzen led them through the maze of narrow paths that made up his village. They'd turn a corner, descend some stairs, only to turn another corner and then go up even more stairs. Between the high altitude and the constant climbing and descending, it wasn't long before Elian felt a gentle burn in his legs. He understood why the Scorpions commanded such respect. Everything about fighting here would be harder than in the plains.

He followed Royzen down a flight of stairs, and as they walked down the narrow passage between buildings, Elian realized the surroundings had subtly changed. Closer to the wall, the stonework possessed sharp edges and clean lines, no doubt achieved through the use of adani. Here, though, the stones were much more roughly shaped, and had been chiseled with physical tools.

The stone was older, too. Some were blackened and some were covered in moss. "How much earlier was this section of the city built?" he asked.

Royzen looked surprised he'd noticed, but was happy to answer the question. "Many generations. We're not sure what brought our earliest ancestors here, but they settled the land without the use of adani. Our oldest families live in homes that have stood for more than ten generations."

"Impressive," Elian said, and he meant it. His ancestors had struggled to build a life on the plains, but the mountains seemed much harder.

The clang of steel on steel drew his attention, and at first he feared a fight had broken out in the streets.

Royzen grinned at his confusion. "Just one of our smiths at work. Come with me, and I'll show you our pride and joy. One of our best smiths is near, and he's currently examining my personal weapon."

A moment later, they found themselves in the smithy. Warmth drove away the chill that had settled deep in Elian's bones, and before long, he was sweating, but he paid no mind. Three smiths worked on a long, glowing piece of steel. All wore thick leather gloves, and the woman in the middle held a long pair of tongs which gripped the burning piece of metal. She shifted it back and forth, flipped it over, then shifted it again as two men with hammers pounded on it with the rhythm of a heartbeat.

Sparks flew, settled on arms, and were ignored. Steel had always been the hardest thing Elian knew. Firm and unbreakable. Here, it was bent and molded by heat, strong arms and careful blows.

The steady rhythm of the hammers wasn't the only song within these cramped walls, though. He heard another, softer but more insistent, underneath the hammering. He looked left, where he saw a sword hanging on the wall. The sword sang, but then he stepped closer, and it wasn't the length of the blade singing, but a small gem embedded in the pommel.

The sword was one of the most beautiful pieces of metalwork he'd ever seen. Somehow, Elian knew it had seen plenty of battle and blood, but the edge looked sharp enough to shave with, and it was polished to a shine.

He reached out to touch it.

His finger brushed lightly against the gem, and adani poured into him. His channels couldn't take the pressure and he tried to pull away, but it all happened too fast, and he was too slow.

There was a flash of light, but he saw only darkness as he collapsed to the ground.

7

Surprise froze Samora in place, but only for a moment. Then she sprinted toward the battle she didn't yet understand.

That moment of surprise was all Kati needed. By the time Samora was in motion, Kati's bound daggers were already cutting down at Aldo, aimed straight at his neck. His guards threw up shields of adani, but against Kati's incredible strength, they crumbled as her blades dug into them.

Karla arrived before Samora could throw up another shield. The older adanist rarely fought with bound weapons, but the speed with which she twirled the staff in her hands reminded Samora she was no stranger to them. She blocked Kati's next strike before the point of the dagger sank into Aldo's skull, then whipped the other end of the staff into Kati's side.

The blow threw off Kati's next strike and focused Kati's full attention on Karla. She turned her daggers on the veteran adanist, cutting and slashing with wild abandon. The leader Samora knew and respected was nowhere to be found.

Karla gave up ground willingly, angling her retreat so she remained between Kati and Aldo. Despite Karla's quick retreat, her staff fell behind the speed of Kati's mad assault.

Kati landed a cut across Karla's arm, then her next attack knocked the bound staff from Karla's hand.

Then Samora reached the fight, shield prepared. Kati's next cut bounced off and she snarled, twirling one bound dagger in her hand, then raising it high and stabbing down upon Samora's defenses.

Shields had never been among her greatest strengths, and she couldn't match Kati's raw strength. The heart aided them both without regard to purpose. Her shield shattered a moment after Kati's blades stabbed into it.

Thankfully, she'd given Karla enough time to bind another staff, and Karla jabbed out at Kati.

Kati contemptuously knocked the staff aside as she raised a dagger to stab Samora. Samora searched her ally's gaze for any sign of friendship or reason but found none. Kati stabbed and Karla somehow got her staff in front of the strike, but its weaving unraveled as the sharp point of Kati's dagger stabbed into it.

Samora bound a sphere of light and whipped it at Kati's head. Kati deflected the adani with her dagger, but even as one sphere sped away, Samora had another four bound. She sent another at Kati's face, one at her chest, and two at her legs. Kati couldn't defend against them all, and Samora kept the weave of the binding tight as they struck. They must have hit like heavy stones, but Kati didn't fall.

Samora struck again, stomach twisting in dismay. Kati's daggers unraveled as she formed a dome to protect herself from the attacks that came from all directions. She blocked Samora's spheres without difficulty, but Samora wove a handful more within Kati's shield and struck her with those. Her protection became a cage, filled with bouncing adani that buffeted her.

When Kati released the shield, Samora stepped aside to avoid being struck by her own spheres. Karla rejoined the fight and whipped a newly bound staff around, catching Kati in the side of the head and sending her crumpling to the ground.

Kati's defeat gave Samora and Karla an opportunity to look around the camp for the first time since the shadow had passed through. Tents restricted much of their vision, but cries for help mingled with shouts of rage. The camp resounded with turmoil.

Samora knelt and pressed her hand against Kati's forehead. She sent a quick, subtle pulse of adani through her body, then blinked and shook her head. She'd felt this before, though not nearly so strongly. Her heart pounded in her chest.

She and Karla weren't the only two who had gathered around Kati. Aldo and his guards had stopped retreating and had come closer. Aldo's face was as red as a stormy sunset, and he looked ready to demand retribution.

Samora stood up. "The Vada's shadow has infected her. I've come across this before, but never quite like this. I'll set to healing her, but we need to spread the word."

A range of emotions passed over Aldo's face, starting with disbelief and ending with anger. "You expect me to believe that? She's been wanting revenge ever since the battle."

"I don't care whether you believe me. Kati needs help, and so do many others. Give orders to your adanists. They're to fight against anyone attacking another adanist. Aim not to kill, but you can't afford to leave your opponents conscious. There's no telling what they might do. I'll see if I can heal Kati. If I can, we should be able to heal the others as well."

Aldo stared at her in stunned disbelief. "I don't take orders from you."

Samora took two quick steps toward him, so they were face to face. The guards hadn't been expecting any sudden moves from her, and so she closed the distance without interference.

He took a step back and looked ready to run again, but then realized he wasn't up against a warrior and stiffened his spine. Samora leaned in close. "I have the dragons and I have the heart. I've tried to cooperate with you, but every moment we waste is another moment this camp tears itself apart and hands our ultimate loss to the Vada. Move your tail, or I will move it for you."

Aldo swallowed hard; his eyes as wide as the rim of Samora's favorite teacup. He prepared to argue, then took one more look into her face and thought better of it. He nodded and backed away.

Samora noted the disappointment in his guards' eyes and knew that someday there would be a price to pay, but she couldn't afford to worry about it now. Aldo turned to his guards and issued orders, which were then passed along to the various Wolves waiting nearby. The Wolves leaped into action, leaving Karla and Samora alone with Kati's unconscious form.

"He won't forget that," Karla said.

"I hope he doesn't. Perhaps someday he'll consider what serves everyone before he settles on what best serves him and his clan alone. But he's not the only one that needs to help. I'll be safe here and don't need your protection. Please, stop as many of the fights as you can."

Karla bowed. "With pleasure."

She left Samora alone with Kati. Samora bent down hastily and prepared for the healing process. Injuries mended quickly in the gathering ground, and she needed to be done before Kati woke.

She placed both hands on Kati, one near her shoulder and one near her stomach, then sent another small pulse of adani through the warrior's body. It ran smoothly through the woman's powerful adani channels until it encountered the Vada's shadow, growing, gestating within Kati's core. The shadow squirmed under adani's attention, shifting away from adani's touch like a frightened animal. Its darkness tunneled deeper into Kati's spirit than the shadow that had infected Elian.

Her hands trembled, and her breath caught. If this was the work of the Vada, a result of the shadowy wave that had passed through the gathering ground, what hope did they have? Elian's infection had grown for days and was still less than this.

She pressed her hands firmly against Kati's body. Time enough for despair later, if she gave herself the chance. Kati couldn't afford her distraction, nor her weakness and doubt.

Samora gathered adani and trickled it into Kati. First no more than the slimmest thread, then more, then more again. Light surrounded the shadow and cut off its escape. Shadow danced, shivered, and fled into whatever corners of Kati's spirit remained farthest from the light. Like the dark center of the portals, this shadow seemed to possess some rudimentary instinct, some self-preservation that made it seem as though it were alive, prey hiding from Samora's predatory advance. Her adani pressed in, burning away the shadow whenever the forces met.

Samora took comfort in that. These days, darkness was everywhere, choking the life out of all it touched. But light triumphed still.

The shadow clung, snarled, and fought. It dug hooks into Kati's spirit like burdock seeds, eager to bloom once again. Bit by bit, adani's cleansing fire burned up every remnant.

The cost was greater than Samora could have paid alone. Healing Elian had required her and Brittany both, and both had been exhausted after. Here, the heart flooded Kati with adani, guided by Samora's steady control.

Shadow tried once more to break the walls of the adani cage Samora had built, but on this battlefield, with the heart to guide her, Samora knew no equal. She allowed the shadow to rage, took a bitter satisfaction in its death throes. Then, when she'd enjoyed her petty revenge, she pressed the walls of adani together, reveling in the shadow's absolute destruction.

She let the tightly knit adani disperse naturally through Kati's body to aid in the healing, then sent another thread through the leader of the Hawks, starting at the crown of her head and traveling down to her feet. She searched every corner of Kati's body and spirit for shadow, then repeated the process once again. Only then did she decide she was satisfied, and she allowed her adani to retreat.

Samora remained kneeling and waited for Kati to wake. It didn't take long. Her eyes fluttered open, flashed with confusion as she stared up at the sky and saw Samora leaning over her. Then regret, blinking rapidly to keep tears from forming. "I'm sorry," she croaked.

"It wasn't you," Samora said.

Kati nodded, then shook her head. "It was, though. All the worst parts of me, rubbed raw, brought to the surface, and there was nothing else but the hate I've tried so hard to bury."

Samora stood and offered her a hand. Kati stared at it, hesitated, then took it. Samora pulled her to her feet. The camp still rang with the sounds of battle and chaos.

"We need you," Samora said.

Kati nodded, and together, the two adanists searched the camp for friends to save.

THE FIRE BURNED bright at the next council fire, as though mere flame might somehow keep the shadow at bay if another wave of the Vada's attack passed through. Samora welcomed the flame and embraced the warmth it offered, but she took no greater comfort from it. Everything they did, including the creation of the heart, meant nothing against the strength the Vada wielded.

She knew she had to hold on to hope, because if she didn't, what else was there, but at some point, hope felt like nothing more than another lie.

She needed Elian, missed him like she hadn't since he'd left with Harald to find the Hawks. Maybe even worse this time. The future felt dark and cold, and the fire did nothing to brighten the days ahead.

Elian did. Call it stupidity. Call it courage. Or just call it stubbornness. Whatever Samora named it, the clans needed that blind optimism, that deep-seated certainty that somehow, despite everything, tomorrow would be better than today, and the day after even better than that.

They needed it, but he wasn't here, and she was no substitute, even as she caught all the glances sent her way, seeking answers.

She had some, though not enough. She and Kati had found the pattern, the thread linking the victims of the attack together.

Aldo sat across the fire from her, as far away as he could sit and still be considered a part of the circle. She couldn't see his face, and his adani was subdued and quiet. Remorse, maybe? Or something darker?

He cleared his throat, made to speak, but Samora stood at the sound and stepped closer to the fire. Never again would he assume control of a council. Not if she could stop him. Her movement silenced him, and she met the questioning gazes of the assembled leaders.

"The Vada's attack was unlike anything we've seen the Debru use before, but the Bears and the Hounds have encountered something similar," she began.

Eyes rose from the ground to study her. The hope in their gazes stabbed at her like knives, because she had no hope to offer. Only answers, and still not enough, never enough. Still, she continued, "The attack did no damage directly, but with it, the Vada planted seeds of influence in many of our adanists."

"Why only some?" Aldo asked.

The Wolves, led by a coward, hadn't had any of their adanists turn. No doubt, Aldo likely believed it meant he and his were stronger, somehow. Chosen, or better, maybe. He witnessed tragedy and saw only another way to grab desperately at the power he sought. Best of all, perhaps an opportunity to belittle Kati and weaken the Hawks further.

"Those infected were those who suffered wounds from either Moka or Belogs in the last battle."

Samora paused, letting the fact sink through the thick layers of Aldo's skull. Then, to ensure the point was driven home, she said, "Those who were on the front lines of the fighting."

Aldo looked like he might stand and fight, argue his decisions like he had before, but no, not this time. The stares of the other leaders around the fire weighed him down and he shrank, curled into himself like a dried piece of fruit.

Samora faced the others. "The cost of the Vada's attack was greater than we can afford, but our losses were not as terrible as they could have been. Aldo and the others spread the word quickly, saving many lives."

A small favor, because they were all still fighting together, even if Aldo sometimes forgot.

"As we speak, our healers are saving the last of those who were infected by the shadow. It's not a complicated healing, but it requires more adani than most have," she said.

Tiafel saw the trickiest part of the matter. "Are we still vulnerable? Can the Vada attack us again, in the same way?"

"I don't know. I'm sure the Vada could repeat the attack, but I don't know if the shadow will take root again. All healers have searched our patients for any hint of shadow, and I've not been able to detect any in those I've healed. Based on that, I'm tempted to say we should be immune, but I can't tell you that with the certainty I wish I had."

Tiafel nodded. "And you claim you couldn't perform the healings if you weren't in the gathering ground?"

"Not as many, no. I could only have healed one, at most, over the course of a night. Lenon, who is the strongest among us, might have completed two or three healings."

"So, we're effectively trapped here?" Tiafel asked.

"No more so than before, but now we understand more clearly what venturing out may cost."

She clenched her fists, imagining a battle yet to come. One in which the Vada rested, far behind the lines of battle, while Mokas and Belogs tore through their lines. Then another wave of shadow, turning those injured into enemies.

It had been a hopeless battle already, but now it very likely meant friends turning their swords on friends.

The fire danced and leaped, as bright as ever, but the gazes of the adanists were darker than night.

꧁ 8 ꧂

E lian awoke feeling as though he was being roasted over a spit and prepared for a feast. He groaned, squinted, and struggled to pull one of his arms out of the covers wrapped tightly around him. Eventually, his hand emerged, and he wiped sweat from his brow.

Vision restored, he pushed and pulled at the covers until his torso could breathe again, though it was less a blessing than he'd hoped. The room was almost as warm as the blankets. He blinked and studied his surroundings.

The room was stone, chiseled by hand, shaped, and fitted into walls with meticulous care. Plain, heavy curtains hung over the walls, keeping the heat from the fire locked within. Massive pelts covered the stone floor, and a plate of cheese and a metal cup of clear water sat next to the bed. The cup perspired as he did, and he reached eagerly for the drink.

Elian wasn't alone. Tassan sprawled across a chair in the corner, where he'd pulled two of the hangings together to form an impromptu pillow. His soft snores filled the room, and if not for the sweat still dripping down Elian's face, he would have been tempted to dive back under his covers and follow the Coyotes' leader into the realm of dreams.

Elian sipped at the water and nibbled at the cheese as memories returned. The smiths had hammered the steel, and he'd been called toward the sword on the wall. He reached out to touch the sword, light shone, then darkness, and now, here in this room.

He closed his eyes and traced the flow of adani through his body. It ran, smooth as ever, but different. Greater. He grunted. His channels were wider than before. Not so much that he could have challenged Harald, but still much stronger. He made a fist and focused adani.

The difference was noticeable. Enough that he might even surprise Tassan if they dueled again. He grinned at the thought.

Someone knocked on the door, and Tassan was awake in an instant, looking around the room for danger. His eyes settled on Elian and his face broke out in a grin. "You had us worried there, for a bit. Come in!" he shouted to the door.

The door opened and Loken stepped through. The healer didn't seem surprised to see Elian awake. He came to the bed and, without asking permission, placed his hand on Elian's shoulder. His adani rushed through Elian, then returned to the healer. Loken stepped back, looked Elian up and down, then said, "He's healed. Stronger than before, too."

Well, there went his chance to surprise Tassan.

"What happened?" Elian asked.

"We were hoping to ask you the same," Tassan said.

"I remember little. When we were at the smithy, it felt as though the sword was calling to me. I went to touch it, and for a moment, it felt as if adani had surged through me. But then I lost consciousness, and I woke up here. How long was I out?"

"A day," Loken said.

Elian's eyes widened. He'd thought perhaps only for the afternoon. He turned his next question upon Loken. "What happened to me, then?"

Loken's shoulders rose a hair. "I wish I knew. I sensed a wave of adani pass over and through you, but it remained contained within your body. It was strong, though. More adani than a dragon possesses."

"Why was I hit with so much adani?"

Elian didn't miss the glance Loken and Tassan shared. Tassan said, "We don't know, but Royzen knows more than he's telling us. He's requested to meet as soon as you woke."

"Do you suspect him of treachery?" Elian asked.

Tassan held up his hands in denial. "Nothing like that. Royzen has been a generous host. You're in his home, and he's given freely of his scarce resources. But he started behaving strangely after the incident, and no one has said a word to us about it."

"Do you feel well enough to meet him?" Loken asked.

Elian rolled his shoulders around, twisted, and hopped a few times to loosen up his muscles. "Better than ever, actually."

Loken nodded to Tassan, who led them out of the stifling room and into the much colder halls. Elian spread his arms out, delighting in the cool air against his skin.

The hallway was longer than any Elian had seen before. It was, perhaps, only fifty paces, but that was far longer than the length of the home he'd grown up in. The stonework revealed the same meticulous attention to detail as in his room, and curtains hung everywhere. Wide windows let in natural light and provided dramatic views of the valley that stretched to the west of the village. Elian felt as though he'd descended into a richly decorated cave.

The feeling lasted until Tassan turned a corner and they stepped into the largest room Elian had ever seen. The ceiling was more than twice his height, and the room would have swallowed the home his father built as an appetizer.

A fire burned here, too, but nowhere near as hot. Fireplaces stood at each end of the long room, but only one was lit.

An enormous table, made from enough wood and stone to

build a small house, dominated the center of the room. A long bench, surface polished from years of use, ran along each side. At each end stood a tall-backed chair built largely of wood, though with a thin slab of what looked like granite as the seat. One was empty, but Royzen sat in the other, speaking with a pair of adanists who sat on the bench opposite the entrance to the room. All three looked up when Elian and his entourage entered.

Royzen didn't smile or bow. He looked at Elian as though looking at him might reveal the answer to a question he'd long asked.

Elian bowed to the leader of the Scorpions. As peers, it wasn't strictly necessary, but it was habit and polite, and manners had always served him well. "Tassan and Loken tell me of your kindness, and I wanted to thank you for your generosity. I apologize for any inconvenience I might have caused."

Royzen turned to the two he'd been speaking with. "Make sure no one overhears," he commanded.

The two men stood and bowed, and Elian and the others stepped aside as they left through the door, then split apart, each traveling in one direction down the hallway.

Royzen gestured to them to join him. Tassan sat on one bench while Loken and Elian took the other. The flame behind Royzen briefly flared to life, then resumed its slow and steady burn.

Royzen's gaze barely left Elian. "What happened to you?"

Elian told the story again, sparing no detail. The telling didn't take long, and when it ended, Royzen leaned back in his chair and brought his hand to his chin, gently stroking his beard. "I apologize for my rudeness, but I must ask. Who are you, and how is it you became leader of the Bears?"

Elian told him the story, now oft repeated, and he answered Royzen's questions as they came. He studied Royzen's reactions, wondering what it was the leader of the Scorpions was so curious about.

When he ended his story, silence descended upon the table.

Royzen studied him a moment longer, but then shook his head, stood, and paced next to the fire.

"I'm sorry to ask so much of you with so little explanation, but there is a legend among my people, and you've unexpectedly fallen into it."

"What legend?" Elian asked.

Royzen sat again at the end of the table. "The true origins of our clan are lost to history. As far as the stories tell us, our ancestors have always lived here, always called these mountains home. I am not so sure. How is it that all the other clans live happily in the fields, forests, and plains, while up above, only the Scorpions defend the mountains? I've never known the answer, but I don't believe it's because we've always been here. Everyone comes from someplace, and the Scorpions are no different. I think we simply traveled farther than the rest."

The Scorpion's leader ran his fingers across his face as though attempting to smooth the wrinkles forming near his eyes. "Regardless of our origins, our history with these mountains goes back generations. These days, our families have spilled so much blood upon the stone I don't think we'd leave, even if the Vada appeared in our midst."

Elian frowned but kept his peace.

Royzen said, "The stone you touched has a long history. My clan, like all clans, has our share of legendary heroes, but perhaps none are so famous as the man named Paelin. He was the greatest among our first adanists. He was a miner, a warrior, a lover, an artist, and one of our most brilliant thinkers."

Across the table, Tassan laughed. "Was he also twice as tall as me and able to shoot lightning from his eyes?"

Royzen's stony gaze settled on the giant and killed Tassan's mirth. "Yes. There are stories of how even the elements obeyed his commands."

Tassan nodded somberly and cleared his throat, as though a fishbone had gotten stuck within. "Of course."

Royzen resumed his story. "We have many legends about Paelin, but the one you must know is that one day, when he was mining deep in a shaft that he alone had dug, he came across an unusual stone. At first glance, it looked like some sort of clear gem, a diamond, perhaps, but when Paelin stepped close, it shone pure white."

Tassan looked as though he was more interested in learning the directions to the nearest casket of ale, but Elian leaned closer to catch every word.

"Paelin worked for three days to clear the granite away from the stone. It is said his pickaxe never ceased, that he never asked for or needed water, food, or rest. When the mountain released its prize, Paelin saw it was about the size of his fist. He claimed it was light as a feather, but no other warrior in the village could lift it. Paelin carried the mysterious gem to the surface, where the entire village stared at it in awe."

Royzen took a sip of water, then said, "The stone granted Paelin abilities beyond any normal adanist. Control over the elements, increased lifespan and strength, and more. He was a generous man by nature, and he worked with Alin, the greatest smith of that time, to forge swords with a tiny flake of the stone embedded within. It is the greatest of those swords that you touched, the one I carry as leader of the Scorpions."

Elian scratched at the back of his neck. "It's an incredible story, but I'll confess that I'm still confused. What have I done to become part of this legend?"

Royzen was eager to explain. "Ever since the days of Paelin, not a single adanist has coaxed any sort of reaction out of the stone. For generations, it has been nothing more than a chunk of diamond in a sword. Before yesterday, had you asked me, I would have told you the story was a myth, a story created to teach and inspire, but not to pass on our true history. I've held that sword since I was a young man and marveled at its craftsmanship, but not once has my presence caused the stone to react. Now here you are. Several witnesses watched the stone ignite, and you yourself report being flooded with new strength."

Royzen's gaze met Elian's. "I couldn't stop the rumors fast enough, and now many Scorpions believe you are Paelin reborn, here to save us from our last trials."

9

A pall had fallen over the camp, spread from the council's meeting to every corner of the gathering grounds. It didn't matter that life bloomed underneath their feet, or that every adanist was capable of greater weavings than ever before. Strength only mattered if it could be used to change the world, and theirs sat within them, useless. The clans were in a cage of their own creation, the latch locked tight. Samora looked north and east, for she knew her brother wandered those distant lands, and they needed him to return soon.

She wished she was as strong as him, that she could convince the clans to follow her lead with the same effortlessness he did, but such were not her gifts. She paced the tent again, looked to the north, then returned to pacing, the speed of her steps echoing the speed of her thoughts.

A surprise visitor interrupted her. She sensed her a moment before Aldrick announced her and let her in. Samora bowed as Kati entered. The woman's gaze ran around her new, gifted home. "For some reason, I thought your tent would be bigger," she said.

It was a statement uttered without malice, and Samora welcomed it. The mundane concern eased a small part of the weight that rested on Samora's heart. "It was a tent another family had outgrown when Elian and I joined the Bears. It's served me well, and my needs aren't many."

Kati opened her mouth, then shut it and grunted. "I didn't come here to talk to you about your tent. It just surprised me, is all. Sorry if it came across as rude."

"You have nothing to apologize for. I suspected your visit had a greater purpose."

Kati nodded, then bowed deeply. Samora backed up half a step and held out her hands, but Kati held the bow long past the point of simple gratitude. Eventually, slowly, she rose. "I owe you and your brother both an incredible debt. You, especially, after all you did to save me from the shadow and prevent me from killing Aldo."

"There are times when I think I should have let you. It would be one less problem to solve."

Kati snorted softly. "I understand the feeling. We can blame the shadow all we want, and it might be best to do so, but I wouldn't have tried to harm him if the thought hadn't already been lurking in my spirit. He's a coward at his core, and hungry to be recognized as a greater leader than he is, but even so, I don't think he's evil."

"Then you're a kinder person than I."

Kati shook her head. "No. He's weak and pathetic, and there's little about him I respect. Detestable as he is, though, he serves important purposes."

"A target for training archers?" Samora asked.

Kati chuckled at that, and Samora thought it was probably the first time she'd laughed since Harald had died. "That, too. No, he serves as an example. Whenever he argues against an attack, I remind myself that he's not the only adanist in the clans beholden to his fears. He's simply the one who holds enough power to speak about his fears before the council. If we are to win the hearts of every adanist in the clans, we must convince Aldo first. He is a useful balance to leaders like Harald, who, at least when they were younger, were more likely to risk too much than too little."

"I think I'd still prefer a council full of Haralds than one that has Aldo on it."

Kati answered with a sorrowful smile. "I didn't come here to talk about Aldo and the council, either. I came to give thanks, but also to help you, if I could."

"What do you mean?"

"Harald told me about the incredible control you have over adani, but he also told me you never had a talent for shields. When I attacked Aldo, you could slow me down, but not much else. Is it true?"

"Unfortunately, yes. It was my mother's greatest skill with adani, but her weaves never worked well for me."

"Then allow me to show you another one. It's not like other shielding weaves, and it rarely gets taught, because it's too complex for most and not useful in battle. You, though, might find it worthwhile." Kati held out her hand and Samora took it. They closed their eyes, and Kati began her weave.

Samora tracked the gentle threads of Kati's technique. She didn't know the other adanist well and found the woman's technique a unique blend of sheer power and subtle skill. She didn't have either the strength or subtlety of someone like Karla, but with enough years of practice, Samora could easily imagine her becoming an adanist of similar skill.

The weave began simply. Kati gathered dozens of strands of adani, weaving them across one another like a quilt. She tightened them until they formed a weak shield, then tied them off. She repeated the process, but as this quilt formed, she shifted the angle of the weave and arranged it carefully above the first layer. The process repeated, time and again, until Kati held a single weave, a stronger shield than Samora had ever sensed.

"Got it?" Kati asked.

"I do. Thank you." To be certain, Samora duplicated the process. The idea was simple enough, but she quickly confirmed Kati's claims about its weaknesses. It took too long to form, and she suspected most adanists couldn't hold so many threads at once. Completed, the weave was easy enough to hold tight, but it made little sense from a warrior's perspective. They'd be dead by the time they finished the first layer. She'd have to practice to see how quick she could become at weaving it.

"I'd hoped to try it out against the Vada when it attacked the Hawks' gathering grounds, but I couldn't control the threads over such a wide distance. At best, I can protect a person or two with it. I'm not sure how it'll stand against a Vada, but it's the strongest shield technique I know. Hopefully, you'll find it useful."

Samora reached out and took Kati's hands. "It's fantastic, thank you. I'm sorry there's nothing more I can do for you."

The corner of Kati's lips turned up, but it was only pain behind the smile. "Kill the Vada. It's what Harald would have wanted."

Samora nodded, and Kati took her leave.

She waited a time, practicing the weave a few times so Kati could depart without interruption. Then she stepped outside the tent. Despite the chill in the air, Aldrick was laying in the grass pretending to sleep in the sun. He lifted a hand to shield his face and cracked one eye open. "Where are we going?"

Kati's visit had been all the encouragement Samora had needed. Or maybe it was her earlier thoughts of Elian. Regardless, she couldn't stand the idea of pacing in her tent any longer. Any action, no matter how small, was better than mere thinking. She had one plan, that she didn't think would work, but was worth trying anyway. "To argue with some dragons. Want to come?"

He grinned. "Figured that if I stuck around long enough, something interesting would happen."

Too late, Samora realized Aldrick had likely heard every word of the conversation between her and Kati. "I'm sorry I spoke harshly against Aldo."

Aldrick grunted. "He wasn't always so quick to retreat. When he was younger, he was more like Harald than he'll probably ever admit now. But you can only lose so much before you're not willing to lose what you have left. I understand him and have some pity on him. He helped raise me into the adanist I am today. Doesn't mean I think he's our best choice for leader, though."

"What would you do, if you were in his place?"

Aldrick squirmed at the question. "It's not my place to say, really. I'm no leader, nor do I ever want to be one. In my mind, life is easier when you can find someone to believe in and follow their lead."

On the surface, it was a very Aldrick answer. He was brave and loyal, but he rarely spoke his opinions, and Samora sometimes thought of him as the perfect soldier, obedient and unquestioning.

But that was an unfair and simplistic view of the man, for he'd stood up to Aldo on her behalf, so he wasn't that obedient. There was more to him, hidden deep, and she wanted to understand his true character, so she wouldn't let him evade so easily. "You give yourself too little credit. I heard the way you stood up to Aldo, back when he visited. You may enjoy following someone's lead, but you're no slave to another's will."

"I wish I had a better reason to give you, but you'd run circles around me in any argument. My parents and my clan, even Aldo himself, raised me to trust my instincts. That advice has served me well in battle, and I'd like to think I can sense right or wrong the way you sense adani. Aldo has treated you poorly, and you've treated him with as much respect as you've been able to muster. My thoughts don't go much deeper than that."

"But what if I forced you to answer. You're the leader of the Wolves. What would you do, now?"

Aldrick gave her a pained look. "I'd help, however I could. I'd offer the services of my healers and warriors and look for some way to protect the villages and keep our oaths. You might ask me how, and I don't know how, but that would be my guiding principle: to help however I could."

They left the Bears' section of camp, and Samora said, "I'm glad Aldo chose you to spy on me."

Aldrick grinned, clearly grateful the questioning was at an end. "And I'm glad I got to spy on you, too."

They made their way through the camp, which was so quiet and still it was almost as if it was unoccupied. Most of the adanists were in their tents with their families. Those who were out moved quickly, as though afraid of the sun. She received several deep bows of appreciation and thanks, but no one spoke with her for long.

It was the first time Samora could remember feeling grateful for leaving the gathering ground. Normally she missed the vast powers at her command, but today it felt like shrugging off a heavy pack and walking freely away from the burdens that weighed her down.

The dragons, as they had been since before the Belog's attack, made their home in the abandoned fields of Samora's village. They'd nestled deeply in, and once settled, moved little. Their lack of activity still surprised her. She'd imagined they would hunt and roam far more often than they did.

"Do you think a day is short for them?" Aldrick asked.

She scrunched up her face, but Aldrick explained before she could criticize him.

"It's something I think about. You were the one who said they've been alive for a very long time. If you were that old, wouldn't you think days were really short?"

The question made her pause. "I've never really thought about it, but I suppose you're right. A day probably feels like the blink of an eye to a creature that has lived hundreds of years."

The question launched her into a thoughtful mood as they made their way to the other dragon Elian had ridden into battle when they'd been out west. They still hadn't learned the hierarchy of dragons, if there even was one, but Samora knew Elian had successfully communicated with this one, so it was her logical choice.

What else had they not understood about dragons?

She shook her head. Answering that was likely the study of a lifetime.

The dragon watched them approach, and Samora bowed once she was a few steps away. "I have questions I would like to ask you. May I?"

The dragon rumbled the affirmative, so Samora took a step forward and reached out her hand. She rested it against the dragon's scales, but she held on to her adani. The dragons had massacred most of humanity and wiped their memories like they were some sort of cattle. Elian insisted the dragons' behavior had reasonable explanations, and the dragons seemed to claim it had been to save humanity, but Samora suspected there was more they hadn't yet learned. The dragons' explanation wasn't close to providing justification for the horrors they'd inflicted on Samora's ancestors.

Yet the dragons were the closest thing humanity had to allies in this fight against the Debru, so she had little choice but to cooperate.

She gritted her teeth and sent her adani into the dragon. The technique didn't come as easily to her as to Elian, but it seeped in through the scales and mixed with the incredible reserve of adani the dragon possessed. Their spirits mixed and mingled, and Samora let them settle before forming the question in her mind.

She imagined a conversation with the Vada, the dragon beside her should she need to flee. She imagined the shield she would weave to protect them. The scene was vivid in her mind, and she pushed it to the dragon.

The dragon's rumbling laughter almost brought her to her knees. In exchange for her vision, it showed her the Vada wiping the two of them away with a flick of its hand.

Samora tried again, but the dragon was no longer interested. He collected her adani and gently pushed it away. She grimaced and thrust another vision into his spirit. She walked alone toward the Vada. They spoke at length, the Vada answering Samora's questions. She backed the vision with all the will she could muster, trying to express her determination.

The dragon's laughter subsided, and his spirit stilled, allowing her adani to once again seep through it. She knew this dragon to be brave, and more willing to "speak" with the humans than others. Samora waited, and the question that eventually formed in her own spirit was the one she expected.

Why?

Samora gathered her thoughts and tried to make them as clear as possible. *Because the Vada, at least, will show me what is true. You and it know our history, and you both demand we be dolls you play with. At least the Vada tells us we are dolls. Perhaps it will tell us more, and we will defeat it.*

The dragon's answer was succinct.

You will fail.

Once again, Samora imagined herself walking up to the Vada alone. Fail or not, they couldn't continue to fight without knowing why.

The dragon doubted, and once again, she reinforced the vision with all the will she possessed. She would have her answers, no matter what stood in her way, dragon or Vada.

The dragon's consideration was slow, and while Samora couldn't follow the details of his thoughts, she sensed him hesitate.

One guess, at least, was proven true. The dragons wanted her safe. But why? Loken could likely do everything she'd achieved, and the clans probably didn't need her to create the hearts. They only needed enough healers working together in a gathering ground.

The dragon released an unfamiliar pulse of adani, and Samora almost cried as her spirit was filled with adani from all the dragons in the field. They mixed and clashed. Sometimes they ran in parallel, other times they sparked like swords. She hadn't been prepared for the force, and for the first few moments, it was nothing but a cacophony of adani, a chaotic storm battering the flimsy house that protected her spirit.

Slowly, all too slowly, her body adjusted to the vast power of the dragons. This, then, was how the dragons conversed. Not with words but with spirit, stripped of all the pretenses, nuances, and lies that language encouraged. She couldn't focus on any one part long enough to understand, but the tenor of the discussion vibrated deep in her bones. A wiser adanist would fear walking in the spiritual halls where dragons argued, but this argument was about her, and no one had ever called her particularly wise.

Colors, sounds, and fragments of memories washed over her spirit, just beyond the edge of understanding. Her spirit, small when held against that of a dragon, bounced between different voices like a tumbleweed caught in a windstorm. Their expressions, filled with meanings deeper and more nuanced than the tongue shared by the clans, rushed over and through her, carrying a physical weight. One dragon, whose song spoke of despair and caution, weakened the muscles in her legs and almost brought her to her knees. Another, whose spirit burned with revenge, gave her the endurance to run for miles.

The arguments battered her from all sides. Her adani was stretched and kneaded like bread dough under Mother's hands. When it ended, she still stood, though her body felt as insubstantial as her spirit.

The dragon spoke to her then, not in his own language, but in simple visions she could understand. Elian had told her once that when he spoke to the dragons, he always felt like a child, and now Samora knew why. To a dragon, every human must appear as a child. Even Tiafel, old enough to have seen three generations of warriors bloom, was an infant in the scales dragons measured time with. Samora could live a dozen lifetimes and barely scratch the surface of the dragons' language.

The dragon showed her a vision of her, riding on his back across the lands, far to the west. Not to the enormous village, but some place in the mountains farther to the south. To a set of caves. To a heart, which beat beneath the mountain, and to the elder dragon, who watched over all, and whom all the younger dragons served. The vision shifted, and Samora stood before the elder.

Samora's vision ended there, the dragon careful not to imply the elder would answer her questions. The dragons would allow her to ask but promised nothing more.

She asked if Karla and Aldrick could come along, and the dragon rumbled that they could, and there was never a question of how Samora would answer. She said that they would, and that they would leave as soon as her affairs in the camp were settled.

The dragon nestled back into the field, sending one last suggestion her way. She should hurry, for time was short, and the Vada wouldn't wait for much longer.

Samora wanted to ask why they thought that, but she could sense the dragon would refuse to answer, and so she added it to the long list of questions to ask the elder.

She didn't doubt the veracity of the dragon's warning, though, and so as soon as she had disentangled her adani from the dragon's, she ran back to the camp to prepare for her visit to the elder dragon.

10

E lian stared at Royzen as though the Scorpion leader had told him the world would end at sundown. "Paelin reborn?"

Royzen shrugged and arched an eyebrow, asking silently if Elian wasn't secretly pleased.

Elian scowled, and Royzen grinned, satisfied. "Myths and legends provide light when shadow surrounds us. I do not share my people's beliefs, but I'd be a fool if I didn't recognize your gifts. Harald saw them, too. You wouldn't be standing before me otherwise."

"Is there something you would have of me?" Elian asked.

"Perhaps. You seek our aid in the fight against the Vada, do you not?"

"I do."

"You believe the Vada intend to wipe humanity from the land?"

"I do."

"Based on what? We've long endured skirmishes against the Debru, but never have I felt they've threatened us all."

Elian warmed to Royzen. The man cut straight to the heart of his questions. "The shadow of the Belogs has infected me. When consumed by that shadow, I thought as they do, and I sensed their intent as clearly as I see you standing before me. They hate us. I know not why, but that hate runs deep in their blood, and they will not be satisfied until every human life is extinguished."

Royzen's eyes narrowed. "So, you have no greater evidence than your word?"

"None, unless you count their increased attacks the past few months. We've fought more Belogs in the past few weeks than the clans have in years."

Royzen grunted at Elian's expression. "No need to turn your passions against me, leader of the Bears. Both Loken and Tassan have testified to your character, and Paelin's stone demands I take your words seriously. But there are those who rightfully believe that our place is here, and that the problems of the other wandering clans are not ours. They'll need to be persuaded, and they'll ask the same questions I'm asking now, only with less understanding."

"How can we best persuade them?" Elian asked.

"That's the same question I've wondered since you arrived," Royzen answered. He thought a moment longer, then said, "May I have one of my own healers examine you? I would trust my life to Loken and his word, but my people will trust a Scorpion over a clanless wanderer."

"Of course," Elian said.

Royzen summoned a healer, who appeared shortly thereafter, and Elian suspected she'd been waiting not far away. She was an older woman, short, and with gray hair turning white. She was all leathery skin and wiry muscle, her face darkened by the sun. He sat cross-legged on the rug while she placed her fingertips against the side of his face.

She trickled adani into him, where the deep currents of his reserve swept it up. Her adani cooled his, soothing away the sharp edges of his worry and relaxing tense muscles. He let her adani flow to every corner of his body, and she searched him from head to toe for any hint of shadow. After she'd completed one sweep, she began another.

When that ended, she allowed her adani to return. "He's free of shadow."

"Thank you," Royzen said.

The healer nodded and left the room without another word. Royzen studied Elian for a moment longer, then said, "Would you like to see Paelin's stone?"

"What do you mean?"

"At the smithy, you came in contact with a small shard, but that is all. Would you like to see the whole stone?"

Contact with a shard had knocked him unconscious for a day, but Elian couldn't deny his curiosity, especially now that he knew not to touch it. "Of course."

"Then let us go." Royzen gestured for them to follow him. As they left the receiving room, the Scorpions standing guard at the ends of the halls joined them. They descended a set of stairs, then Royzen stopped in the middle of a hall. He pulled aside a hanging, revealing a stone wall that looked the same as any other. Royzen's fingers danced across the stone, then pulled on a latch disguised to look like a jutting piece of granite. There was a click, and Royzen pushed the wall aside. It opened like a door on silent hinges.

Loken ran his hand gently across the edge of the door. "I've never seen its like."

"Made by Paelin himself, if you believe the stories. And for this, I do, and you'll soon see why," Royzen said. He led them in, and the others followed. Once they were through, Royzen closed the door behind them, and for a moment, darkness surrounded them.

Then a line of light burst into being above them. It wasn't more than the width of a finger, but it glowed pure white. The light raced down the hallway, illuminating a long, gentle staircase.

Royzen had placed his hand against the wall, and now he took it off. "Light, powered by adani. I can't explain how it works, but if there was any evidence of Paelin's skill, this is it. The light should last us long enough, so let's be off."

He started down the stairs, but Loken, Tassan, and Elian were slow to follow, their gazes locked on the impossible light.

"There's no smoke, no fire at all," Tassan said. He reached up and touched the line of light. "I can feel the adani, but it's barely a trickle."

Elian and Loken did the same. They looked at one another, but none had an explanation that satisfied them. They stared a bit longer, then followed Royzen deeper into the tunnels.

At the bottom of the staircase, the hallway took a sharp right, where another wonder greeted them. Royzen gave them time to stare.

Beautiful carvings ran along the wall, from floor to ceiling, as far as the light carried. Elian ran his hand along one, and it was smoother than an eggshell. Adani, most likely, had created these visions, but the amount of control required staggered Elian. Samora might be capable of such a feat, but he wasn't sure.

"Paelin's work?" he guessed.

Royzen nodded. "They're beautiful and haunting, but I'll confess sometimes I wish he would have simply carved words into the stone. Our philosophers have studied this hall for generations, but all they do is argue with one another over what the carvings mean. Are they visions he had, or experiences? There's a lifetime's worth of knowledge here, but we lack the key to unlock it."

Elian walked slowly down the hallway, giving himself time to absorb every scene. Though the carvings were hundreds of years old, their edges were still sharply defined. Some scenes were clearly those of battle, while others were peaceful. Elian saw farming and mining depicted, as well as marching formations of warriors.

He stopped when he came across a scene of a village burning, dragons visible in the skies above.

Royzen stopped beside him. "This one has given our philosophers plenty to argue over, and I have little doubt your arrival will fuel the flames of the arguments. Notice how tall the buildings are compared to the people? Nothing that tall has ever been built. Even our best masons couldn't raise something that size, but it's one of the few carvings in which the scale seems so out of proportion. Is it a vision, a dream, or a warning? Our philosophers have never decided."

"It's our past." Elian's voice barely rose above a whisper.

"What?"

"Long ago, dragons attacked humanity. They burned our villages to the ground and wiped our memory of the event."

Elian saw Royzen's disbelief in the set of his shoulders and the way his eyes darted between Elian and the carving. The man lived among wonder, but his belief was not so easily earned. "How do you know this?"

"My sister visited a village like the one Paelin carved. She saw the buildings and told me they stood many times as tall as your tallest tower here. I scarcely believe her, but she wouldn't lie. But how could Paelin have known? He lived well after the event, after our memories had been swept away like dust."

Royzen had no answer, but Elian didn't expect one. The pattern of his life repeated. He learned more, but with his learning came new questions, and the answers he so desperately needed never revealed themselves.

Eventually, he left the carving behind. There was more yet to learn, and hopefully, someday soon, the answers they sought.

They reached the end of the hall, which turned left and led them deeper into the mountain. Elian's stomach started to churn, and when he focused on his adani, he found it had become a storm raging in his core. Deep breaths calmed the chaos but couldn't restrain it.

Royzen touched the walls again, and the last section of hallway lit up, revealing a glimpse of an enormous chamber ahead. The other three advanced without hesitation, but Elian's steps were cautious. The storm of adani within him raged with more intensity after every step, and soon it was as though he'd run into a wall that restrained only him.

The other three stopped when they noticed.

"Are you hurt?" Loken asked.

Elian shook his head, then leaned his weight against a stone wall. It was cool against his skin, and he sighed. "I can feel it in my core. Can't you?"

They shared glances and shook their heads. Royzen studied him with particular intensity, the look of a parent trying to decide if their child was pulling a trick or telling the truth. Any other time, Elian might have detested that look, but his swirling adani consumed most of his attention. Then, decision made, Royzen reached out his hand to help Elian move forward.

Elian wasn't so convinced of the wisdom of the choice, but he didn't dare refuse Royzen's generosity. He took Royzen's hand, and Loken came to stand on his other side. Loken's adani raced quickly through him, pausing as it sensed the storm in his gut.

"Would you like me to ease your pain?" Loken asked.

Elian was sweating now but shook his head. "If it has to do with the stone, then I don't think I should mask it."

"Try to circulate more adani through your body, as though you were preparing for battle," Loken suggested.

Elian did so and breathed out a long sigh of relief. The adani hadn't enjoyed being cooped up in his core, and now it flooded his body. A few days ago, the sheer amount might have left him close to bursting, but now that his adani channels were wider than before, he could let it flow with little difficulty. "Thank you," he said.

His next few steps were easy, and he felt foolish for having a powerful adanist on either side of him, holding him up, but then they stepped over the threshold of the chamber, and Elian's legs almost collapsed underneath him. He groaned as a fresh wave of adani filled him to bursting and beyond. Fire danced across his skin as needles pierced his bones. His legs went limp as too much adani flooded through his limbs.

"Oh," Royzen said. He looked as though touching Elian was burning him, and it might very well be true. No adanist would miss the vast amount of adani flooding Elian.

Elian's reserves matched that of a dragon. Then it grew deeper. Not still, like a dragon's, but wild and turbulent, rushing through his channels like a stream forced through a narrow gorge with steep drops.

The shouts of his friends came from far away. He couldn't make out what they said, but he heard the concern in their voices.

The stone sat in the center of the chamber, resting on a pillow on top of a small stone pillar. The stone glowed brighter and brighter, until its light filled every corner of the room and banished every hint of shadow. Elian stared into it without pain, and the light entered his body through his eyes and cleansed him of any darkness and doubt.

Still, his body burned under the weight of too much adani. He couldn't think, could barely stand. If not for Loken and Royzen, he would have fallen, filled with power but unable to move.

More shouts came, from farther away this time, as he drew away from his friends. Adani surrounded him, embraced him, filled him, and became his entire world, tearing him apart as his body lost all control.

Then a blast of cold air.

No, adani, mixing with his own and that of the stone, shaping the flow. Bending it and twisting it until it ran through his channels and didn't overfill them. His channels stretched, expanded, pushed to the edge of their limits but holding, reinforced by a web of Loken's healing adani.

A fortunate choice, then, to have him with. Elian marveled at the control with which Loken turned adani to his will. Any other healer, likely, would have failed.

With Loken's aid, thoughts and memories returned.

Elian knew this strength. Had felt it before, though it had been filtered and distant.

Paelin's stone was a heart, stronger by far than the one Loken and Samora had created. A weapon, possibly, that might stand against the Vada.

But it was too strong, too powerful for human hands to wield.

Elian gripped Loken's arm. "Release your weaves, slowly. If I fade too far again, please save me."

Loken's face suggested he'd been ordered to let one of his patients die.

"It's not enough to endure. I need to control it, if I can."

Loken hesitated, then nodded. His healing weaves unraveled, and adani once again rushed through Elian's abused channels. Arms, legs, and chest burned. Elian endured the pain, then shifted adani, a little here and a little there, shoving it back into the channels where it belonged.

For a time, the fight between stone and spirit was evenly matched, but eventually, the power of the heart became too much for Elian to control. The fire in his limbs burned until he wanted to scream, and thought was once again washed away in the flood of adani.

Loken rescued him, healing weaves cooling a spirit roasted in the purifying flames of the heart. When reason returned, Elian asked Loken and Royzen to drag him back into the hallway. Remaining close to the heart was like standing too close to a bonfire, and his body could take no more.

Once they crossed over the threshold, the heart's adani vanished, a dream or a nightmare that rapidly faded from his memories. Loken and Royzen sat him against a wall, and he pressed himself against the cool stone.

"What just happened?" Royzen asked. "That stone has sat for generations without flickering once, and it was as bright as any star in the sky. And your adani—I've never felt anything like that, and I'm not sure that I ever want to again."

Elian's throat was dry. From screaming? He didn't know, his memories too indistinct. He breathed slowly and deeply, swallowed some spit down his throat so he could speak.

"It's a heart, like the one beneath the gathering ground my sister created. Stronger, though, and obviously older."

"Can you use it?" Royzen asked.

Elian shook his head. "Not as I am today. Just standing that close to it was all I could do. But someday, maybe. You said Paelin could handle it, so perhaps someday I might, too. May I return here after I've recovered?"

Royzen looked at the stone. "So long as I accompany you, then yes."

A fair deal. Elian nodded, but before he could rise, Loken was at his side, hand resting lightly against his forehead. Elian let the healer's adani trickle through him, grateful for the chill it sent down his spine.

Loken made a sound in the back of his throat. Elian's gaze darted towards him.

"Nothing bad, at least I don't think. Your adani channels have expanded again. They're wider than Harald's now."

He'd been so distracted by everything else happening, he had paid little attention to his own body. He felt his channels and agreed. They were wider than they'd been just that morning when he'd woken. The heart strengthened him. It would again, he was sure of it. But could his body endure?

He glanced down the dark hallway to the chamber, where the stone lay hidden in shadow. After the connection with the heart, he had some guess as to what it wanted. What it needed him to achieve. But how long would it be until he was strong enough to wield it?

Hopefully, they had enough time before the Vada arrived.

Heavy footsteps echoed down the hallway, and all three adanists turned to see one of the guards they'd left near the secret entrance. The man's face looked pale, but Elian wasn't sure if it was the unnatural lighting or the message he carried.

The answer came soon enough.

The guard bowed to Royzen. "Sir. Debru have been spotted approaching the bottom of the valley. They're accompanied by more otsoa than we've ever seen. Our scouts believe we'll soon be under attack."

～ 11 ～

S amora watched the mountains grow as they neared, and she let out a tight-lipped grin at the memories of their first flight west. As before, Karla and Aldrick accompanied her. Only the dragon had changed, and this one flew faster than the first. The journey had already taken two full days as they'd circled far away from the Vada's encampment and hurried toward the mountains, but Samora suspected they'd covered much more distance than that first flight.

Worry distracted Samora from the pleasures the vista offered. Aldo's influence had been severely curtailed by recent events, but the Wolves' commander was persistent in his own way, and she didn't doubt that with her gone, he'd be bargaining with the other leaders to regain the control he had lost. In her darkest moments, she feared that even if she returned with answers from the elder dragon, she'd return to a fractured alliance of clans.

Unfortunately, she couldn't be in all places at once. She hoped and expected that Tiafel would now fight harder to stay in control of council meetings, and as more of his warriors finished healing, he'd could stand more directly against Aldo's threats, but she couldn't afford to stay with the clans while more important work waited for her. She also expected Kati would rediscover her spine after the attack and work with Tiafel to keep order.

When she wasn't worrying about the clans, she worried about Elian. He should have returned by now, but there was no sign of him in the sky, and when she'd last searched for him with adani, he'd been far to the north, and of course there were Debru approaching. She couldn't guess what had happened to him or why he was so delayed, but she hoped he enjoyed more success in his endeavors than she had in hers.

Although, as they reached the mountains and flew over snow-covered peaks that threatened to blind her as they reflected the midday sun, Samora wondered if she hadn't accomplished more than she thought. The chance to meet with the elder dragon was an opportunity to learn the truth about their history and maybe, just maybe, find the key to defeating the Debru for good. She kept her hopes modest, wrapped up tight deep in her core, but it was hard not to let them out.

When she looked at the mountains, she saw hope, too. A year ago, mountains were nothing more than a story her parents had told her about, terrain she hadn't dared believe she'd ever witness. Today, not only had she seen mountains twice, but she had also flown over them on the back of a dragon. The mountains reminded her that what was once impossible was now her reality.

Today's flight was silent except for the sound of the wind rushing past their ears. The three travelers had already discussed every belief and assumption they possessed about the elder dragon, and none of it was better than a random guess. The dragon, too, seemed content, happy to return home after too long away.

The sun was high in the sky when Samora spotted the first cave, a giant shadow painted into the side of a mountain. Another appeared soon after, and before long the mountains were dotted with them. Some might have been natural, but Samora thought most were too uniform, the edges too even. It was hard to say for sure from up high, but she suspected the dragons had carved their homes in the mountains with adani.

The dragon descended and revealed more of the hidden homes. Dragon heads emerged from caves, and to the east, Samora glimpsed a group of smaller dragons twisting, diving, and chasing one another through the air. Based on their size, she assumed they were younglings. They possessed the same playful energy the children in her village once had, running and chasing each other even after a long day in the fields.

The dragon landed near the base of the tallest mountain. An enormous cave loomed before them, large enough to swallow most of the buildings from the ancient village by the sea whole. The dragon bent down so they could dismount, then gestured with his head toward the cave. Then, with a flap of his wings, he lifted back into the air and disappeared over a ridge to the west.

Aldrick scratched at the back of his neck. "He knows he's supposed to give us a ride back, too, right?"

"I suspect that when the time comes, he'll be here waiting for us," Samora said, injecting her answer with a sense of confidence she didn't feel. The dragon had promised an audience with the elder, but no more. He had said nothing about a trip back home. If she was as valuable to the dragons as she thought she might be, she worried they might attempt to keep her here, keep her safe from the rampaging Vada. She'd said as much earlier, though, when she first invited the two, so she didn't repeat her worries now. The risk was worth it.

Karla looked around, harrumphed, and marched toward the dragon cave. The shadows within didn't stir, and Samora wondered if the elder was home.

They climbed a gentle slope to the edge of the cave, but then Samora held out a hand to stop Karla as the hairs on the back of her neck stood on end. She peered deeply into the gloom of the cave and saw nothing to fear, but she wasn't so easily convinced.

"Doesn't it seem too easy?" she said.

Karla arched an eyebrow. "We had to ride three days on the back of a dragon to reach this spot, and we're surrounded by more dragons than I could count."

Samora shook her head, then extended adani toward the cave.

She gasped at the weaves draped over the entrance, hanging like invisible curtains. Karla did the same and stepped back when her adani contacted the net. "What's this?" she asked.

Samora traced the weave with her adani and tried to guess what effect the unfamiliar weaves had. They were as complex as anything she'd ever attempted, if not more so. "I thought dragons weren't capable of such complex weaves," she said.

Although that was foolish. The working of adani that had wiped humanity's memory had to have been equally complex. She'd simply seen nothing similar from the dragons since meeting them in person.

Karla didn't answer her question, lost in her own study. Even Aldrick stared.

The dragons didn't want to harm her, but did that mean they wouldn't play with her memories if given the chance? She didn't think so. Memories guided her, allowed her to shape adani in the ways dragons desired. It was possible they accepted the risk or were confident they could steal only the memories they chose, but the stakes seemed too high.

Trusting the dragons too much seemed an obvious mistake, but they wouldn't act against their own interests.

She searched the net from top to bottom, looking for weaves she understood. In time, she found one concealed within a larger knot of adani. If something came in contact with it, it would release its energy, not as fire or light, but as force.

"This is a test," she proclaimed. She shared her findings with Karla. Once the other adanist knew where to look, she found the knots everywhere. She nodded her admiration for the weave.

"So, how do we get in?" Karla asked.

Aldrick shrugged, and before anyone could stop him, he had a bound sword in his hand, and he hacked at the weaving. Samora was still connected, which gave her a glimpse into its reaction. The outer level of the knot flared as the bound sword connected. Aldrick's sword violently unraveled with an explosion of force that knocked him several paces back. He landed on his feet, then shook out his hands as if they stung.

He looked up at her and grinned. "Had to try," he said.

She would have lectured him, but the same idea had occurred to her. Sometimes the best solutions were the simplest. "Thanks."

She tried forcing the adani apart, but the elder dragon had anchored the net on all sides of the cave, and she lacked the strength to bend the weaves to her will. Next, she tried unknotting them, but they resisted her efforts there, too. She tied her hair back so it would stop falling in front of her eyes, then studied the weave again.

Then she snorted. Could it be so simple? The net of adani, complex as it was when considered as a whole, wasn't so complex when she studied its parts. It was hundreds of the oversized knots connected by strands of adani which were basic weaves. The complexity came from the way the various strands were laid on top of one another.

It reminded her of the shield Kati had taught her earlier. The pieces were simple but weaving them together made them complex and durable.

She formed the tiniest weaving of adani she'd practiced, then slid it carefully toward the net. She carefully avoided the knotting and drove it into a strand which connected two knots. The strand broke, leaving a gap just wide enough for the very tip of Aldrick's sword.

Karla shook her head. "I can barely sense the weaves you're using."

"Aldrick had the right idea. The only mistake he made was using a sword that was far too large," Samora said.

One strand at a time, she carefully guided her adani through the weak points in the net. It was slow work, but she eventually opened a gap they could walk through. "Can you sense that?" she asked her companions.

They both nodded, and Aldrick was the first to step through. He stood on the other side with a grin on his face, and Karla and Samora followed right after. As soon as they had all entered, the weaving unraveled, as though it had never existed.

They were cautious now, and Samora sent her adani ahead of them. Barely a dozen paces ahead, a solid wall of adani stood between them and the dragon's chambers. In front of the shield, another weave of incredible complexity. The three advanced together and explored the second challenge.

"The shield wall is as solid as stone to my senses," Karla reported.

"And to mine," Samora confirmed. The weave was a simple one, not that much different from the shields an adanist would cast in battle. The only difference was the strength behind it, so much adani not even Karla's strongest attack, supported by the strength of a gathering ground, would crack it open. Samora saw no trick or test in the wall. It was simply a barrier, and the test was the weaving floating before it.

"Should I cut at it?" Aldrick asked.

Samora leaned closer. "No. Whatever it is, I don't think cutting at it is the solution the dragon is looking for."

Aldrick, not to be deterred from helping, reached out and touched the knot of adani with his hand. Karla swore under her breath, but Aldrick suffered no ill effects.

"It's warm, if the cave is making you cold at all," he said.

He was a fool, but a useful one, and Samora was glad to have him. She tentatively reached out her hand and came in contact with the knot. It had a physical presence she could feel, subtly dancing under her fingertips, but as with Aldrick, it did her no harm.

She appreciated his discovery, for it was easier to examine the weaving while in contact with it. She treated it as she would a patient, sending a trickle of adani into the web and tracing its path as it ran through the weave.

This one proved more mysterious than the last. She couldn't identify any of the weaves, although there was something familiar about them she couldn't quite put her finger on. Her mind wandered, as did her adani. The pattern was hidden somewhere within. She just had to find it.

The others had lost interest by the time the answer struck Samora. The weaving felt like the knot of tiny adani channels that ran through a human's head. Once the similarity occurred to her, she saw it in every bend and twist of the weaving.

But what did it mean, and what was she supposed to accomplish?

She frowned as the flow of her adani trickled through the weaving. She let her adani return and she stepped away. Her body felt light and her stomach rumbled, but she put aside her needs for the moment. "Aldrick, could you come here, please?"

Aldrick had found a place in the cave sheltered from the breeze, but still warmed by the late-afternoon sun. He'd been resting with his eyes closed, but at her request, he leaped up and approached. "How can I help?"

"I need to check something. Do you mind?"

He shook his head, and she reached up and placed her fingertips against the side of his skull. She closed her eyes and trickled adani into him. She kept it limited to his head, tracking every bend and weave of his adani channels. It was as she'd thought. She grunted, and Karla cracked open one eye from where she'd been pretending to nap.

"Found something?" Karla asked.

"Maybe."

Samora returned to the dragon's knot and placed her hand upon it. As she trickled her adani through it, she noticed where the knot and Aldrick's mind differed, a bending in the weave hidden near the center of the knot. The answer was a healing, and nothing more. She nudged the adani channel, shifting it into the correct position and evening adani's flow. In the blink of an eye, the knot was gone, as was the barrier separating them from the elder dragon.

Samora sent her adani before her to ensure there were no more traps or tests, then nodded at the others to go ahead.

She glanced back at where the first barrier had stood and felt like she'd just completed a set of trials. The choice of challenges hardly seemed random. One to test sensitivity and control. The second to check her understanding of the human mind and healing. Her conversation with the elder dragon had already begun, but she didn't know what was being said.

Samora followed the other two as they pushed deeper into the cave. It bent slightly while maintaining its enormous dimensions. They followed the curve of the cave and came to a chamber twice as large as the entrance. It was lit from within, and Samora's attention was torn in two directions at once.

Resting in front of her was a dragon, the largest she'd ever seen. He was immense, both in size and strength. Samora's eyes ran from side to side, seeking some understandable detail she could latch onto to ground herself. His shape differed from the others, the body far longer and more sinuous than the dragons Samora knew best. The dragon shifted, segments moving and scraping against one another, reminding Samora more of an oversized snake than the allies they'd made so far. His head appeared, the most recognizably draconian part of the creature. The snout was elongated, and the horns on his head branched out like pale oak trees, and his golden eyes held her in frightening contempt.

Samora's bowels loosened, and she was glad she'd been too nervous to eat or drink much that morning. One snap of those enormous jaws would consume all three of them in a blink, and the dragon would likely consider his meal barely started.

In the back of her mind, her father's voice echoed down from many, many years ago. They'd been out in a field, and they'd come across a kettu, hunting alone. Samora had cried and tried to run, but Father had caught her. "There're many things in life you can't outrun, little one. Stand straight. Meet its gaze. Even if you want to scream and run, don't let it see your fear."

She'd listened, and the kettu had run to find its companions. Father had let it go, and Samora had always wondered why. Years later, she'd understood that he'd probably hunted the pack that night, quietly ensuring his family had a peaceful place to live.

Samora faced the dragon, stood up straight, and met its gaze. Her heart slowed and her adani explored the cavern. The dragon attracted most of her attention, but he wasn't the only interesting part of the room. She risked breaking eye contact with the dragon and looked up. The ceiling of the cavern glittered like the night sky, except the lights above were brighter. Most hung down from the tips of stalactites, their light whiter than the daisies that sometimes grew near the fields.

She recognized them immediately, the sense of them familiar. After all, she'd created one herself.

The elder dragon rested beneath dozens of hearts, each point of light stronger than the new heart beneath her gathering ground.

Like when she looked up at the night sky, the sight of so many powerful hearts made her feel small. They reminded her that for everything she'd accomplished, for everything she'd learned, it was still the barest sliver of what the elder dragon had lived through and known.

She held on tightly to that understanding, then stepped forward to meet the elder dragon at long last.

12

Elian again found himself in Royzen's receiving room, which appeared to serve many of the same functions as a central cookfire among the other wandering clans. If he wasn't at the wall, Royzen kept a constant council within. Elian, Tassan, and Loken stood quietly along the far wall as commanders rushed in and out of the room.

Elian's gaze wandered aimlessly around the room. His impressions from earlier had been of sturdiness and permanence. The Scorpion village was like his own, only bigger and stronger. The stone walls and stout defenses had impressed him, appealed to his inner child, which still lived in his small bedroom back in the village, waiting for Father to return.

Now his skin itched and the walls grew closer with every new report. He needed sun and wind, a clear view and room to move. Impressive as these walls were, they wouldn't withstand any meaningful amount of shadow, which made them little more than an illusion of safety. They were a lie, but one that was all too easy to believe.

The thin walls of his tent might not protect him like stone, but he missed them. He'd never felt trapped within them, nor did they anchor him. Now his home traveled in the sleds, providing shelter no matter where he ended a day's journey.

Royzen's walls were tight, squeezing him like the blankets he'd woken up in that morning.

He shook his head, then, at a thought, a smile crept across his face. Loken noticed. "Something funny?"

"I was just thinking that after all this time, I might finally be becoming more wandering clan than villager. I take no comfort in these walls."

"There's hope for you yet," Loken said.

More adanists came to Royzen, and thanks to his privileged listening position, Elian understood the host of problems facing the Scorpion leader. Scouts reported numerous Debru approaching the base of the valley but hadn't dared approach close enough to determine how many and of which type. A wave of otsoa ran ahead of the Debru, too many for any sane scout to try their luck against.

Almost as disturbing as the force climbing toward them was the lack of warning. If Elian understood what he heard correctly, Royzen's village maintained a series of small watchtowers along both ridges that formed the valley. He'd seen a few on the way in, but there were more than he'd spotted. They'd developed a method of communicating information back and forth, and they were one of the village's primary means of keeping safe. The towers were only accessible via narrow, treacherous trails that started in the village. The cliffs below the towers were unclimbable, or so the Scorpions believed.

None of the towers had given warning, though the scouts' report put the invading force more than close enough to be spotted by the watchtowers. Their silence hung like an ominous cloud over Royzen's every decision, their sudden and unexpected darkness adding layers of doubt and uncertainty to an already unprecedented situation.

If Debru had taken the towers, it represented the loss of no small percentage of Royzen's adanists. A critical blow before the Scorpions even realized they were under attack.

Elian had wanted another chance with the heart, but the longer he watched the procession of commanders, the clearer it became he would have to wait. The receiving room's walls continued to close in on him, and he stepped forward in between reports from Royzen's commanders.

"What?" Royzen asked.

"Let me help."

Royzen stared blankly at Elian. He'd been inundated with requests, advice, and pleas long enough that Elian could have roasted a hare over a spit, so Elian didn't blame him for being slow to understand.

"I have a dragon, and I'm not needed anywhere else. I can scout the valley for you."

Royzen stared a moment longer, then his eyes went wide. "Could you check the watchtowers, too?"

"Of course. And if we find adanists still alive, we'll provide what aid we can and return them here."

Royzen bowed deeply. "Thank you. If there's anything you need, ask any commander. I'll spread the word that you're to be granted every consideration."

Elian returned the bow. "Tassan, Loken, would you join me? If there is danger along the ridges, I'll need both spears and healing."

Loken nodded, and Tassan grunted. "I was wondering when we could get out of here."

Tassan, knowing the village best, led the way out of the hall, and they climbed several sets of stairs, emerging on a rooftop that looked over the walls and the valley below. Tassan leaped from one roof to the next, and Loken and Elian shared a questioning look before following him. They jumped across one more small gap, and then Tassan took them down a stairwell that connected with one of the narrow streets.

"A unique method of exit," Loken observed.

"My father brought me here several times when I was a child. We visited the Scorpions more often back then. Their young adanists scamper up and down the walls of the village, and if someone yells at them, they claim they're training for the days they'll have to fight in the mountains. I played frequently with them, and it provided me with a different perspective on the village. It may be unusual, but I promise this route is quickest."

Elian didn't doubt it. They were already more than halfway toward the upper wall. Even now, the walls of the buildings seemed to lean over him, and the upper gate couldn't come quickly enough. Thankfully, Tassan didn't take them across any more shortcuts, and soon they were through the upper gate and running to the dragon. He was already up and looking down the valley, as though sensing the danger that approached.

Elian put his hand against the dragon's chest, sent his adani into the creature, and made his request. The dragon was amenable to the task, but Elian caught a hint of reticence in the dragon's answer. He asked if there was a problem, but the dragon wouldn't answer. A growl escaped from the back of his throat, but the dragon was unmoved.

They mounted, and Elian urged the dragon into the sky. A stiff wind blew from the west, and once they left the shelter of Royzen's village, it cut across their exposed skin like knives. Elian pulled more adani from the dragon and warmed his body.

He guided the dragon down the heart of the valley while he leaned over and looked for signs of danger. About a mile away from the village, they came across a small pack of otsoa walking up the path.

"Should I?" Tassan asked.

"Please," Elian answered.

Harald would have formed one giant spear and laughed as he hurled it at his opponents below, but Tassan formed four small spears, more like thick needles. He tossed them with a flick of his wrist, then guided the adani with the same attention a master smith would have brought to the practice of honing a blade.

Elian squinted and looked away, prepared for a blinding light and bone-rattling blast. Tassan's raw strength almost equaled Harald's, and the adanist had never fought from a dragon before.

The otsoa glanced up in time to see their death approach, but not soon enough to flee. The bound spears struck the darkened fur of the creatures, and they looked as surprised at their deaths as Elian was by the manner in which they died.

Tassan's spears didn't even explode upon contact. They behaved more like physical arrows than bound adani, and the otsoa slumped over and collapsed, dead before they could cry for help from their masters. Tassan unraveled the weaves. The death of the otsoa hadn't created so much as a whisper of sound.

Elian glanced back. "Impressive."

Tassan bowed his head as though a humble adanist, but the wide grin on his face revealed his pride.

They encountered one other pack as they flew west, and once again, Tassan demonstrated his impressive control of adani. The monsters died just like their cousins higher up the path.

Besides the two packs, they saw no other sign of a Debru invasion. Elian made out a few of the watchtowers, dark and quiet sentinels on an otherwise bright day.

"I expected the mountains would be crawling with otsoa by now," Loken said.

Elian agreed. In the time that had passed since the initial report, the otsoa and their masters should have climbed at least halfway up the mountain pass. Possibly higher, given the Debru's speed.

Except the Debru never did as expected. Their tactics, strategies, and goals remained as mysterious as the invaders themselves. Elian searched the trees near the bottom of the valley, and he sensed Loken extend his adani to search for hidden Debru, but their searches revealed nothing. Where were the Debru?

They found part of their answer at the bottom of the trail, where it met another wide valley running north to south. Countless otsoa roamed the area, and behind them stood a tightly packed cluster of Debru. Elian thought he saw one or two Moka in the mix, but they were squeezed shoulder to shoulder, and he couldn't be sure.

He pointed the group out to Tassan. "Can you kill them?"

"With pleasure."

Tassan bound a spear, this time pulling enormous amounts of adani from the dragon. For a moment, he looked exactly like Harald in his prime, before he'd been weakened by his first battle with the Vada. He shouted, his voice almost as strong as a dragon's, then threw the spear.

The attack came as no surprise to the Debru gathered below. Shadows gathered and overlapped, like a child pulling blanket after blanket over their head to protect them from the winter's cold. Tassan's spear struck true, digging deep into the heart of the shadow before exploding. Light blasted the top levels of shadow away, but it hadn't penetrated as deep as Elian had hoped.

Tassan bound another spear, but Elian gestured for him to stop. "They're prepared, and there's no point burning your spirit for a fight you can't win."

The Debru let the shadows evaporate but took no other action against Tassan or the dragon. They sat at the intersection of the trails, patiently waiting.

But for what?

Elian ran his eyes across the mountains, down in the valleys, and even across the sky to search for the answer. Nothing moved besides the otsoa below, but for all their numbers, even they roamed in a limited range. Of course, they could have hidden an army in the thick trees of the valley and Elian would never have seen them.

Perhaps the watchtowers would hold a missing clue. Sneering at the gathered Debru, Elian banked the dragon away and flew for the south ridge, opposite the valley of the trail that ran to the village. The farthest watchtower stood on a lonely mountain; the top so vertical Elian had no choice but to agree with the Scorpions. Nothing could climb to the summit.

The watchtower itself was a small stone tower two levels tall. A pile of dried wood was stacked on the top level, a pot of oil beside it, ready to light. A hatch led to the protected room below, and it was closed. Elian flew around the tower, but there was no room for the dragon to land, and he saw no movement within. He flew on to the second one along the ridge, his stomach already sinking.

The second watchtower stood at a lower elevation than the second, and there was just enough space on the ridge for the dragon to land. The adanists hopped off the dragon and approached the silent tower, built near the edge of a deadly cliff.

"Hello?" Elian called.

Only the wind answered, strengthening and whipping across their faces. Elian drew his sword and pounded on the door to the tower. He called again, but the tower remained silent. He shared a glance with Tassan and Loken, who both signaled their readiness, then he flung open the door.

Elian jumped back and thrust his sword in front of him. Tassan threw up a shield. The door rocked back and forth on well-oiled hinges, caught in the swirling gusts of wind. Nothing launched itself from the shadows within.

Elian looped adani in his limbs and advanced. Tassan dropped the shield, though he held adani ready. Loken remained behind. The point of Elian's sword led the way into the room, and before his eyes adjusted, he called out again. Another step brought him fully into the room and the smell of decaying flesh assaulted his nose.

His eyes adjusted to the darkness, and he wished they hadn't. Four adanists, three young men and one young woman, were scattered around the room. The table which had sat in the center of the space was tipped over, the chairs broken in the fight. Blood had seeped into the cracks between the stone, turning brown as it dried.

Elian forced himself to study the bodies, even as his eyes wanted to jump away. The adanists had died quickly. Three of the four had simply been cut in half, and the other stabbed through the chest. After death, though, their bodies had served as food for the otsoa. Huge chunks of flesh were missing, and the otsoa weren't discriminate eaters.

Tassan entered behind Elian and grunted. "Doesn't look like it was much of a fight."

Elian wished he could argue, but Tassan had the right of it. The Debru had somehow caught the watchtower unawares. Each of the adanists had been killed with a single cut, and there wasn't a defensive wound among them. There was no battle here, just a slaughter. Elian stepped outside and welcomed the cold air rushing past his face. He looked east, toward the next tower. It looked as quiet as this one.

"Come on. Perhaps some may yet be saved," he said.

Tassan and Loken followed him onto the back of the dragon, and they flew to the next watchtower. Elian didn't bother dismounting. The dragon circled the tower, but no faces came to the window. They flew to the next, only to find the same. One last remained on the southern side of the valley, about two miles distant from the village wall. The dragon covered the distance in moments, and Elian let out a cry when he saw movement within the watchtower.

They landed in a clearing between tall pine trees and the watchtower just in time to see the door open as a lone Debru warrior stepped out. Its arms were painted in blood up past the elbow, and when it saw them, it made to run.

"Kill it," Elian commanded Tassan.

The giant used the dragon's adani and had a spear flying before Elian finished the command. The spear took the Debru in the back, punching clean through and unraveling before cutting into the trees behind.

Tassan grunted. "That's probably the easiest kill I've had in my life. I could get used to fighting with dragons."

Elian leaped off the dragon and strode toward the watchtower. His hopes were thin, but they still flickered.

He entered the watchtower with his sword before him, and three otsoa looked up from their feasts, green eyes glowing in the dim light of the tower. They leaped at Elian as one, but his sword sliced through them like grass, and their meal was cut short well before they finished.

He stepped outside before Loken could reach him. Tassan had dismounted on the other side of the dragon, and only his feet were visible. Elian said, "It's too late, but let's hurry to the other side. Perhaps we can rescue some."

When Elian reached the dragon, Tassan hadn't yet moved. He crouched near the ground. "What do you see?" Elian asked.

Tassan gestured at the narrow path that led from the watchtower toward the village. "Debru tracks. Maybe half a dozen, and twice that many otsoa."

"Why so few?" Elian asked.

Tassan raised an eyebrow. "For most of us, that's a considerable force."

Elian bit his tongue. His last battles had been with dragons, gathering grounds, and hearts. He'd forgotten how much stronger the average Debru was than the average adanist, but the lone Debru stepping out of the watchtower should have been reminder enough.

Besides, if there were that many Debru on this side, there might be that many on the other, too.

Tassan looked at Elian. "What do you want to do?"

Elian looked north to the other ridge, where the watchtowers stood quiet. They'd almost saved some adanists here, and there was a possibility he could save some on the other side.

He glanced down at the tracks.

The decision was no decision at all, as much as he hated the inevitability of it.

"We need to get back to the village. They should know what happened, and we can prepare them for what is coming. Climb on. We better hurry."

13

Samora stood before the dragon, still as a corpse. She'd advanced only a few paces, and though nothing stood between her and the sinuous creature, she didn't dare step closer. His golden eyes, flecked with red dark as blood, held her in place as firmly as though she'd been bound there by thick ropes.

She stared at him with no less intensity. She had no problem remembering the dragon's memories from the village by the sea, and the elder before her was the same one she'd seen then, the one that had so casually ordered the village burned and the humans' memories wiped.

Warmth spread from her core as her spirit roared, banishing the chill of the cave. She raised her head and stood tall. If the elder thought he had the right to judge her, he would regret his error.

A thin weave of adani extended from the dragon toward her, similar to the technique Karla had once used to search Samora's memories in the gathering ground. The adani paused before it reached her, silently requesting permission to continue.

Samora almost denied the elder out of spite but reconsidered. She had nothing to hide, and when Karla had attempted the same, it had opened her up to cross-examination. Perhaps the same would be true today. She nodded, and the adani reached out to caress her forehead.

Samora gasped as her past unfolded before her like a flower blooming under the bright spring sun. All her memories surfaced, and the elder considered each in turn. In less time than it took for her to draw a deep, recovering breath, the memories returned, folding in on themselves and sinking to the depths of her mind.

The elder broke off contact before Samora could examine his more ancient memories. He remained motionless, considering her as he had before.

The fire in her spirit burned brighter. She took a step forward. "I came to speak with you, not to endure your judgment and testing."

The golden eyes didn't so much as blink in response.

She took another step, though it was harder than the last. The elder wove no wall of adani, but his strength was such that it felt like a wall stood between them, anyway. "You have no right to judge me."

A rumble escaped from the back of the dragon's throat, so deep it vibrated Samora's bones and caused the cave to tremble. At first, Samora thought it was a precursor to a roar, but soon realized it was only laughter. The rumbling crescendoed, then faded, but still the dragon gave no answer. Samora's adani burned so brightly she halfway expected flames to burst from her arms, but as she prepared to step forward yet again, the world before her eyes melted away.

She blinked to clear her vision, but it remained blurry.

She blinked again, and she was back at her home, sitting at the table her father had built. A fire burned the elm trees from the nearby grove, happily devouring the fresh-cut wood with quiet crackles and the occasional surprising pops. She ran her fingertips along the surface of the table, its bumps and imperfections as familiar as the floor beneath her feet. Each and every one was present, the illusion as solid and as perfectly formed as the actual table hundreds and hundreds of miles away.

She was alone, and then she wasn't. The one who sat across from her was built like a warrior, with a broad chest and shoulders. His hair was sometimes gray and sometimes silver, depending on how the firelight played across it, but his eyes were golden, flecked with red the color of blood.

"Easier than the crude methods you and your brother use to communicate with my children," the man said, answering the question she hadn't asked.

His voice was deep and resonant, and it sounded more like he surrounded her than sat before her. It made her want to sit and listen, like a child listening to stories around the fireplace. She shook the spell of his voice off and leaned forward.

"Why the tests? I came here to speak to you."

"I wished to see for myself how your control over what you call adani has grown."

"And what have you decided?"

"Nothing, yet."

Samora's hands formed into fists on the table, and she fought to control her spirit. No small part of her wanted to weave adani into an attack and wipe the condescending look off the man's face. If she'd thought there was the smallest chance of success, she might have, but she suspected the look would only deepen if she tried.

She'd come here for more important reasons, anyway. "I've seen glimpses of your children's memories. You destroyed the village by the sea and killed countless humans. You wiped our memories and thrust us into the wild, like children without a guide. And I'm sure you know far more about the Debru than us, but you let us suffer and fight alone for generations. Why?"

The man's golden eyes turned away and stared out the window, studying a setting sun more vivid than any Samora had seen. He didn't answer, but Samora waited with all the patience she could muster.

The man sighed. "It was a gamble. One we hoped would end the war and save humanity."

"But you were winning the war. You'd driven the Debru to the brink of extinction and closed the portals."

The man waved his hand dismissively, though to Samora's eye, his hand looked more like a snake's tail swishing back and forth than a human hand. "It's ironic, isn't it? That you should barge into my home and deem me guilty of being judgmental?"

Samora failed to find the irony in the situation.

"What's worse is that you're sharply aware of how little you know. Your whole purpose in coming here was because you think the knowledge you haven't uncovered yet will somehow save you. And yet, despite this, you still think yourself righteous for passing judgment on *me*?" The man shook his head.

"You killed thousands. Perhaps tens of thousands. So, yes, I judge you, and no, I don't find it ironic."

"Ahh, but you only saw the memory of the day the decision was made. You didn't witness the years of debate that preceded it, nor did you experience our anguish as we realized we had no other choice."

Samora stood. "What does any of that matter? How many are dead because of what you decided?"

"So many more than you can guess," the man said.

It was all Samora could do not to swing her fist at the man's face. She believed the regret she heard in his voice, but what did it matter? Regret was the least he should experience. Were his punishment up to her, he'd suffer agony for the rest of his count-less days. But that wasn't why she'd come all this way. This conversation was pointless.

"How do we beat the Vada?" she asked.

"You can't."

"Let me be the one to decide what I can and can't do. What are its weaknesses? What does it want?"

"It has no weaknesses, and you already know what it wants. It seeks to destroy humanity, as you are the only creatures on this world that might one day threaten it."

Samora tossed her hands into the air. "With one breath, you tell me we can't defeat it, and with the next, you tell me humanity is the only opponent the Vada fears."

"Both facts can be true."

"How? How do we beat it and make its worst fears come true?"

"You can't."

Samora slammed her fists on the table. Her father's craftsmanship cracked under the power of her blow, and her vision trembled as the dragon withstood the assault. "You don't have the right to tell me what I can't do!"

"STOP!" roared the dragon.

Its command ripped into Samora with a physical force, and Samora staggered under the assault. Breathing became a struggle, and darkness crowded the edges of her vision. The roar echoed against the walls until it died, and slowly, Samora's breath came easier.

"You are a child who knows nothing, yet demands the rights of an elder. Have you no respect?"

"How can I? Whatever knowledge you wish it is I had, I lack because you took it away from my people."

Those golden eyes glared at her, but the dragon didn't argue. He laced his fingers together and closed his eyes, looking like Elian trying to control his temper. He sat like that for a long time, and Samora would have given almost anything to pry his head open and peer at the thoughts within. When the eyes opened and fixed on her again, Samora saw only pity.

"It's too late. Strong as you've become, it's not strong enough.

We will save as many as we can and hide you from the Vada. Perhaps your children will be strong enough to carry the burden."

"Wait…what?"

Samora's eyes grew heavy, and she yawned. Her bed was close, and the room was warm. She took a step toward her bedroom before remembering where she was and why she'd come. She summoned adani to her head to clear her thoughts, but her channels, as familiar to her as the surface of Father's table, had become twisted and strange. With a thought, she forced them back into shape, and the exhaustion lifted from her shoulders in an instant.

The dragon seemed almost as surprised as she was. For a moment, they both stared at each other, and then Samora laid into him.

"How dare you?" she accused.

"Your fight is over. It is time to rest," the dragon said. It twisted her adani channels again, harder than before, and once again, Samora's eyes grew heavy.

Samora fought the dragon's influence. She tried to force her adani channels into their healthy shapes, but the dragon's grip on her channels was absolute. Behind her, she heard both Karla and Aldrick lay down, and within a moment, the sound of their soft snores reached her ears.

Samora's focus slipped, and she thought about how she, too, would love to rest. How long had they been fighting without reprieve? She couldn't remember the last time she'd slept through the night and woken up the next morning feeling refreshed and ready for the challenges ahead.

She grimaced as another one of her channels was subtly twisted, further constricting the flow of adani within her core. The sensation brought her back to the battle she was losing.

"There's no point in fighting. This is for the best," the elder said.

He spoke like a parent to a child, unbearably condescending.

Samora's spirit flared, burning brightly enough she regained some of the ground she'd lost. She yanked one of her adani channels back into position, gritting her teeth as adani resumed some part of its smooth flow. She looked around at the illusion she was still trapped in, knowing it was a mask the elder dragon had pulled over reality.

Despite her temporary victory, the battle was as good as lost. Unless she found something to aid her, the elder would eventually overpower her. She couldn't fight against a dragon's power anymore than she could a Vada.

When she pushed out her adani, she gasped.

A sea of hearts surrounded her, each one brighter against her senses than the heart beneath the gathering ground that she'd created. All were open to her. She only had to reach out to them. She extended her adani, stretching for the ceiling of the cave.

Too late, the dragon realized her intent and tried to stop her. She hesitated, remembering how close the strength of the hearts had come to killing her earlier. But if she didn't reach, she'd soon be asleep under the dragon's weaving.

She connected with the heart before the dragon could stop her.

Adani flooded her body, then tangled up in her core as it encountered the channels the dragon had twisted. Samora doubled over, but before it could destroy her channels, it forced them into their natural paths through no effort of her own. She stood straight as the power flowed through her, and she took a step out of the vision and toward the elder.

"You don't have the right to control me," Samora said.

The dragon finally raised its head and gathered adani. Samora gathered her own, aided by the hearts, matching the dragon's strength as it increased.

She made no move to attack but didn't allow the adani under her control to be less than the dragon's. They stood, and she stared into the golden eyes, challenging the elder to attack.

The elder gathered even more power, but Samora matched it. She kept her wonder to herself. She'd never dealt with this much adani before, but her body handled it as though it was long experienced in such forces.

The dragon seemed as surprised as she was. "You shouldn't even be alive."

"And yet here I stand. We're capable of more than you believe."

The dragon released most of its adani and settled back into his resting position. He studied her for a long time, and she didn't interrupt the order of his thoughts.

Finally, he said, "Perhaps there is no harm in letting you know the truth. Join me, and I will show you why the dragons are as worried as they are about the future of this world."

Samora reappeared in her home and blinked away the disorientation she felt from jumping between the physical world and the dragon's vision. The dragon, again wearing the form of a man, held out his hand to her, an invitation to allow their adani to join.

After all she'd endured to reach this point, Samora didn't hesitate. She reached out and took the hand, and with their adani connected, the elder unveiled a significant fraction of his memories.

First came a sight Samora already knew. The meeting of the dragons, in which they decided to eliminate most of the humans. The scenes flashed quickly before her, almost too fast to track, but then settled on a new scene. One dragon landed near the summit of a mountain. The elder rested on the neighboring peak, his long body wrapped around a granite spire like a snake wrapped around a tree limb. They did not speak, but used adani to communicate. In the vision, Samora could understand them as though they spoke the human tongue.

How certain are you, truly, that this is necessary?

The elder's response came quickly. *As sure as I need to be.*

Is there no other way?

You know there isn't.

The elder waited, knowing another question lurked behind his companion's objections. They'd been in all the same discussions, and the elder's companion knew they'd once again been backed into a corner. The humans believed they neared the end of the Debru's assault, but they'd only pushed back the first wave. The second, far more dangerous, approached from the east.

The elder cast out his adani, aided by the dozens of hearts embedded in the mountains. It stretched nearly halfway across the continent, where it encountered a new portal, far wider than the small tears in space the Debru had favored in the past. This one was a new design, capable of bringing a Vada through with its army. It was targeted, as the larger portals always were, at the human settlements, the human hearts.

They couldn't destroy the portal. They'd even sent a handful of humanity's best adanists to unravel the puzzle, but they weren't making progress. The elder planned on leaving them in place until the end. Perhaps, just maybe, they'd find the answer before it was too late.

But he didn't hold out hope.

Before the elder brought his adani back, Samora sensed the portal he feared. It was a Debru circle, no different from the ones she'd learned to unravel.

Why were the dragons so afraid of the circles?

As the elder reeled his adani in, his companion spoke. *My heart is heavy with the way we treat the humans.* She *expects more from us.*

Samora, so closely linked to the dragon's emotions, expected resentment or perhaps frustration with the other dragon. Instead, she found only agreement. The elder dipped its head, and Samora brushed against the vast well of sorrow he didn't let himself feel. He didn't dare, not with what was required of him.

I know, old friend, and if there were another way, you know I'd take it. I hate what must be done as much as anyone.

How long must it continue?

Until they can protect themselves.

And what if they never can? What if we continue this cycle, repeatedly, until our spirits are as hard as the mountains we call our home?

If we must, we must, and guard our souls as well as we can.

She pulled herself away from the elder, tearing herself apart from the memories. She found herself again in the vision of her home, but she ripped it away, shredding it as she fell to her knees in the dragon's cave.

Her lungs didn't want to expand, forcing her breaths to come in short, shallow gasps. Her heart raced as though she'd just escaped a Vada on foot. Sweat beaded down her forehead.

Behind her, Aldrick and Karla slept peacefully, still under the elder's influence.

Adani flooded Samora. The hearts heeded her call, and even the elder seemed to shrink back against the strength she wielded. She stood and clenched her fists. She gritted her teeth and growled.

One betrayal had turned her against the dragons forever. It had been unforgiveable.

This? This willingness to destroy humanity, no matter how many lives were lost? She couldn't permit it. Humanity wouldn't live under the dragons' rule, not if it meant their lives were never more than pieces to be moved around the dragons' game boards. Yes, she felt the elder's regret, but regret did nothing to atone for his decision. He had still slaughtered humans, just like the Debru.

Points of light surrounded her. A dozen at first, then more, until they outnumbered even the hearts in the ceiling.

Now, now she understood why one might find refuge in violence.

The lights danced to her command, each filled with enough adani to destroy the village she'd grown up in.

Samora took a step forward, ready to end the menace of the elder.

❧ 14 ❧

The wind whipped past Elian's face as he, Loken, and Tassan raced toward the Scorpion village. With the dragon flying at full speed, it didn't take long. Elian let out a relieved breath when he saw the walls standing tall and the lookouts alert at their posts. He and his companions waved as they flew over, and the dragon landed on the far side of the village.

The guards at the upper gate informed Tassan that Royzen could be found on the western wall. Tassan led the way, but Elian's stomach tightened as they walked through the main gate into the village. The stone walls were too close. The citizens and adanists were too close. A single well-placed spear of shadow could kill dozens.

Elian tapped on Tassan's shoulder, then asked, "Would it be wise to encourage them to leave, at least until the threat has passed?"

"Wise, perhaps, but they'd never agree. We'll have to defend these walls."

Elian grimaced but followed Tassan. They found the leader of the Scorpions with little trouble, standing at the top of one of the watchtowers built along the wall. The valley stretched out before them. All was still, but Elian's eyes darted every time he thought he saw a shadow move. The Debru had to be close, but no alarm had yet been raised.

They shared their news from the watchtowers, and Royzen's face darkened as he learned of his lost adanists. The Scorpion's leader mastered himself with visible effort, then asked, "We've seen no sign of Debru. Is it possible they don't mean to attack the village?"

Tassan, thankfully, answered the question. His word carried more weight than Elian's here. "There's no telling what those shadow-cursed spawn are thinking, but the Debru we killed wasn't the only one in the area. There are more, accompanied by otsoa. The fact your watch hasn't spotted them yet only makes me think they're up to something more devious than usual."

Royzen pressed his lips tightly together and nodded.

Elian inserted himself into the discussion. "I can't speak for us all, but I'm happy to help in whatever ways I can."

Tassan grunted. "I haven't had a good fight in a bit, so you can count on my strength, as well."

Loken bowed and said, "I'm happy to help your healers as well."

Royzen bowed in return. "I'm grateful. I'll add more eyes to the walls tonight. Hopefully, that's sufficient for whatever the Debru plan."

Elian bit down hard on his lower lip. There had to be some-thing more Royzen could do, like send out parties to fight the Debru before they launched their attacks upon the walls. He started to speak, but Tassan cut him off. "I hope so, too. Would you like us to wander out and see if we can learn more about the Debru?"

"No. Night will be here before long, and they'll strike then. You can help keep watch this afternoon but rest easy for now. The battle comes later tonight."

Elian could take no more. "You'd be wiser to fight outside the walls than within. Those walls will mean nothing to the Debru."

"Perhaps not, but they mean the world to us. You haven't seen the full extent of our preparations, but I assure you, we'll easily match any force they send against us."

Royzen's attitude made it clear there would be no further debate, so Elian forced himself to nod and bow. As they left, he muttered, "Fool."

"Maybe," Tassan said, "but their chances aren't better in the field. Royzen says we defend the walls, and we promised to help him. Let the matter be as simple as that."

Elian grumbled all the way to their post, but his bitterness didn't last long against the view before them. At their post, he let his eyes drink in the valley's beauty.

It was late in the season, and verdant greens covered the valley, with pine trees and shrubs sipping contentedly from the stream that had carved the valley ages ago. From the wall he listened to the rush of water as it dropped through the narrows, and when the breeze blew up from the bottom of the valley, bending the trees as though they were dancing, he felt something resembling peace stir in his spirit for the first time in what felt like a year and more. He breathed in deep, filling his nose with the sweet scent of pine while his eyes gazed far into the distance. He tried to force the scene deep into his memories, something he could return to when needed.

Fortunately, the Debru didn't choose that moment to attack, and once Elian was sure he'd stored the memory safely away, he turned to his towering companion.

"What do you think they'll do?"

"I'm not sure. I'm not used to seeing such guile from them, but I suppose I've never seen them attack a place so fortified, either. This battlefield is as foreign to me as it is for you, I'm afraid."

Elian turned his eyes once again to the pine forest in the

valley below. The peace he'd felt watching it just moments before vanished, and he swallowed the lump in his throat as he imagined the terrors hiding within, waiting to be unleashed once the sun dipped below the horizon.

THEY KEPT watch through the afternoon, but the shadows under the pines never grew into Debru. They were relieved before nightfall, and after a quick discussion, rounded up Loken and found food. The nearest mess hall welcomed them warmly, and they were deep into their bowls when a bell clanged in the distance. They, and the other adanists in the hall, all looked up as one. The bell rang three times, then stopped.

Elian looked at their neighbor, who had gone back to finishing her stew.

She shrugged. "Three bells is the call for the watch. If we were under attack, they'd keep ringing."

Elian's skin crawled. All day he'd watched the valley, waiting for an assault that never came. The Debru were close, but none of the adanists on the wall had yet sensed any shadow approaching the village. Samora would have found them, but she wasn't here, leaving them blind to the Debru's plans. But surely, bells this night couldn't be a coincidence.

Those in the hall finished their meals silently, each man and woman with one ear cocked toward the nearest bell.

Elian barely finished his stew. He tapped his feet against the stone floor and glanced toward the door, expecting it to burst open. He reached down with his hand and brushed the hilt of his sword.

He spoke in a low voice, so only Tassan and Loken could hear him. "I'm not sure I can stand being surrounded by these stone walls for much longer. I want to know what's happening."

Loken closed his eyes, then said. "It's hard to tell with so many adanists nearby, but there's a minor commotion at the wall. Adanists are gathered near the northwestern corner."

"Do you sense any Debru?" Elian asked.

Loken shook his head. "Though it's hard to send my adani far here. The webs are less strong in the mountains. If I was on the walls, maybe, but even then, I would make no promises."

"Should we go to the walls, then?" Elian stood from the table, but neither of his companions followed his lead.

"Royzen and his commanders know where we are. We've already helped with the watch all day today. If he needs us, he'll reach out to us. Remember, we're only guests here," Tassan said.

The words had barely left Tassan's lips when an adanist rushed into the room. She looked across the assembled faces, then stopped when she saw the three visitors. She gestured for them to follow. "Royzen requests your presence," she said.

Elian smirked at Tassan, but the giant paid him no mind. They followed the slim adanist through the narrow halls and up the stone stairs to the top of the walls. Royzen stood there with his commanders, staring into the darkness as though it would surrender its secrets if he simply put enough effort into the attempt. He swore softly, then turned to the new arrivals. "The Debru are up to something, but I couldn't tell you what."

"Loken?" Elian asked.

The healer closed his eyes and sent out his adani. "There are shadows both to the north and south, along the ridges, but I can tell little else."

"Any guess as to their strength?" Royzen asked. He didn't seem surprised by the news.

"Considerable, but I can't be more specific than that. It could be one Belog, a couple of Moka, or dozens of Debru. I'm sorry I can't be more help."

"What did the bells sound for?" Elian asked.

"A guard on the wall was shot by an arrow," Royzen answered.

"I've not heard of a Debru using a bow and arrow before," Tassan muttered.

Royzen agreed. "We could bind shields, but I don't want to waste adani against arrows. I suspect we'll have more need of it soon enough."

"Adanists could take shelter in the towers. The view is sufficient, and it'll protect them from arrows," Tassan suggested.

"But if there is a Belog out there, or even a handful of Moka, they could destroy a tower with a strong enough shadow spear. I can't risk placing too many of my adanists in one place."

Elian clenched his fists. This was why they needed to abandon the walls. Against low-level Debru, they might have served as protection, but the force coming their way was too strong. He bit back his retorts and asked, "How can we help?"

"I need your strength. I don't know how they took the watchtowers without warning, but because they did, they now have control of two trails that lead straight to our walls. If you and Tassan would support the north wall, I can reassign several adanists to the south wall. We can strengthen both sides to prepare for the attack. I'm sure it'll come tonight," Royzen said.

Tassan grinned. "I thought you'd never ask. If you want, take all your adanists and stick them on the south wall. I'm sure Elian and I can protect the north on our own."

The giant ignored Elian's glare, but thankfully, Royzen wasn't so foolish as to accept the offer. "I'll leave you a little support, but I'll tell the commander to use his discretion. If the need is greater to the south, they might leave the north to you two."

Tassan waved away the Scorpion's leader. "Fine, fine. But I'm warning you, your adanists on the north wall will soon suffer from severe boredom."

Royzen shook his head and walked off, Loken close behind him. Elian stopped the healer before he escaped. "Could you do me a favor?"

"What kind of favor?"

"Go tell the dragon everything that's happening. Tell it that it should take off and leave if a Belog gets too close. We can't afford for it to get captured."

"I can't speak to the dragons," Loken said.

"Don't tell me that. I've felt the way your adani has been questing around the dragon while we've been flying. Samora tells me it's not that much different a process than healing. Offer it a little of your adani, and once it accepts it, you'll be able to imagine scenes the dragon will share. I'm sure you'll succeed. I don't dare leave the wall with Tassan wanting to take on the Debru by himself."

Loken nodded, unable to contain the gleam in his eye. "Very well, I'll do my best. Good luck. I'll be with the healers if you need me."

With that, he was off, and Elian and Tassan took cover behind the stone wall, looking north for any sign of their enemy.

THE NIGHT PASSED AT A CRAWL. The Debru strategy, such as it was, appeared to be to harass and worry the defenders without launching an actual strike. Scorpions had cleared the ground around the village wall for a hundred paces, but thick pine forest obscured Elian's view beyond that. He caught sight of shadows darting between the trees, and every so often, a lone arrow would arc into the sky and strike either the top or side of the wall.

Elian and the others remained covered behind the higher points of the wall. A quick glance was enough to tell the shadows still moved in the trees, although what they waited for was anyone's guess. The night was already dark, but the Debru seemed content to snipe at whatever brief glances they saw of their enemy.

The moon had crossed halfway across the sky when Tassan

growled. "If they make me wait much longer, I'm going to go out there for them."

"It's about time someone agreed with me. We're at their mercy, here."

Tassan nodded. "I've not seen anything like this before, and I don't like it. I'm all for supporting our host, but if they've got enough strength out there to match a Belog, we're in a heap of trouble."

Elian glanced north, but there was still nothing to see. Tassan shifted his position so he could look over the wall. An arrow skittered off the wall close to his face, and he swore at the Debru cowering behind the trees.

"I'm tempted to throw a few spears that way, and put a bit of fear in them," Tassan said as he hid back behind the wall.

"Can you sense them?"

"Not well."

Elian resisted the urge to glance back at the trees again. He'd find nothing there that he'd not seen before. "It's foolish of us to keep waiting. It plays right into the Debru's plans."

"Unless their plan is to lure us out away from the walls."

"If they have Moka or Belogs with them, they'll destroy these walls in a moment. They're waiting on something else, and we're giving them all the time in the world."

"What are you thinking?" Tassan asked.

"You throw some spears and cause a distraction. I'll jump down from another part of the wall and go hunting."

Tassan's gaze was hard. "Royzen is expecting us to guard this wall, and we told him we would. As much as I agree with you, you're usurping his command. He's relying on us."

"And this is how we can best serve him. You know that."

"I don't like it. I mean, I like it, but not like this."

Elian couldn't wait behind these walls any longer. He patted Tassan on the shoulder. "Then let me. If I draw their attention, you'll have an excuse to attack. I'll go poke them, but I'll need your protection if they poke back."

He scooted away from Tassan before the giant could object. He'd drop off a separate part of the wall to keep the attention away from Tassan, but he'd be cursed before he let the Debru attack unopposed.

Elian felt the adani running through his limbs. He was stronger than ever, but was it enough to fight against what was out there? He didn't know, but he didn't care, either. The Scorpions needed him, and he'd long ago promised himself he'd never again watch a battle while stuck behind a wall.

He took a deep breath, then leaped off the wall and charged the Debru position.

❧ 15 ❧

Adani intoxicated Samora. Lights danced around her like fireflies on a summer's night, each strong enough to level a village or destroy a Debru. She stood on the precipice of action, afraid that if she took a single step forward, she would lose her best chance at learning how to defeat the Vada.

But the memories were too vivid, the wounds too raw. Tens of thousands of voices cried out for revenge.

She took the step, and with the flick of a finger, unleashed the full might of her fury upon the elder. The swirling lights all shot forward, each aimed straight for the dragon's heart.

They froze in between the elder and Samora.

The dragon's rumbling laughter shook the floor of the cave, and Samora held out her hands for balance. Her weavings consumed her attention, but no matter how she fought to push them forward, they refused to obey.

While her attention remained on the weavings, the elder twisted her adani channels again and weakened her connections to the hearts. The lights in the cave winked out, and she tore her attention between healing her channels and pushing the attack at the dragon.

She failed at both, and the last of the lights blinked out, her greatest attack neutralized as though she'd imagined it.

The dragon took control of their shared connection and slammed her back into the vision of her home. Both she and the broad-shouldered mask of a man stood across from one another. His golden eyes glowed like small suns.

Samora fought the illusion. She pulled away, then tried tearing it apart, all to no avail. Her adani channels were still twisted and weak, and the dragon's control over her perceptions was complete. She braced herself for whatever attack the dragon would launch next.

The man shook his head, then a grin broke across his face, and he threw back his head and laughed. The laughter echoed in the cave, and Samora knew she didn't imagine the vibration in the soles of her feet.

When the laughter ended, the man wiped a tear from the corner of his eye and looked at Samora like a proud father. Samora clenched her fists and prepared to punch the smile off his face, but he sensed her intent and held up a hand.

"We are not enemies," he said.

"Right now, I'm not sure who's killed more humans, you or the Debru. That makes us enemies."

"May I show you the truth?"

Samora huffed but saw few other options. The dragon's request was more a show of politeness than a genuine question. She nodded once.

"Thank you."

The house dissolved around Samora, and she flew through the sky. Not on the back of a dragon, as she'd slowly become used to, but as the dragon itself. Her stomach flipped at the sudden change of perspective and rapid movement, and she was again glad she had eaten little before approaching the cave.

Smoke and flame rose in the distance. Samora, in the memories of the elder, flew with all the speed she was capable of. Patchwork quilts of fields passed in a blur, and as she approached the village, she spread her wings and rose higher in the sky.

The extent of the destruction stole her breath, and through the elder's memories, she sensed the depths of his despair. So much had been sacrificed to prevent this, but the Debru had returned, stronger than ever.

The burning village was larger than anything Samora had seen, far larger that even the village by the sea. It stretched across the plains, laid out in neat squares that repeated all the way toward the horizon. The homes near the edge reminded Samora of those she'd seen in the village by the sea, but they were more numerous than weeds in an unattended field.

And they were burning.

Samora expected an army, but found only a single Debru fanning the flames. A Vada. This one didn't look like a child, but appeared to be a typical adult human, except its eyes were black orbs.

The Vada watched the elder's approach and raised a hand, forming a small ball of shadow that floated before its palm. It released the orb, then turned its attention back to the destruction of the village.

The elder veered away from the orb, but it tracked the dragon's movements without a problem. When escape proved impossible, the elder summoned his immense reserve of adani and formed a small shield.

Samora understood, perhaps for the first time, why the dragons viewed her and the other adanists as children. The difference in strength between her and a dragon was immense, but the difference between her and the elder was a gulf no human could cross. She could have battered on the shield with every shred of her strength for the rest of her life and never come close to breaking through.

The Vada's attack shattered it like it was made of weak clay, exploding with such fury the evening sky was brightened by the birth of a second sun. Samora's stomach flipped again as the elder was spun through the air like a child's doll thrown in anger. Spots swam in her vision and her ears rang. Adani, long used to the deep and well-worn channels within the elder's body, twisted and crashed against itself.

Halfway to the ground, the elder regained control of his body, spread his wings, and slowed his deadly descent. His long, sinuous belly dropped so low, Samora expected it to brush across the tops of the endless rows of wheat, but she never felt the slightest touch.

The Vada didn't strike again, or at least, not against the elder. It resumed its casual destruction of the enormous village, releasing weave after weave of devastating shadow. The elder's visit had barely qualified as a distraction.

The elder leaped them forward into another time. Men and women of exceptional strength fought upon and beside a host of dragons. She tried to guess the dragons' numbers, but she couldn't accurately estimate their strength. Hundreds, at least, if not thousands. Combined with the adanists, they made the unified strength of the wandering clans look like a child's first weaving in comparison.

She fought as the elder had fought then, not as a paternalistic overseer, but as a warrior among peers. Human and dragon alike bound powerful weapons and flung them at the advancing shadows. Weaves she'd never seen before were executed with a speed and certainty even Karla would have been envious of. Had Harald fought here, he would have been like a child fighting among veterans.

For all the attention she wanted to spend on the adanists, it was the Vada, once again, that controlled the battlefield. In this memory, the Vada struggled against the onslaught of adani. One even fell, killed by a warrior's golden sword. But the rest advanced, their pace steady even after the gathered warriors thrust a mountain's worth of adani at them.

The elder leaped them away before the battle was lost, but there could be no other outcome.

They returned to Samora's childhood home, and she welcomed the familiar sights as if she had returned from a long day in the fields. She took a seat, and the elder sat across from her, once more wearing the guise of a human.

Samora swallowed her pride and offered the elder the briefest of bows. The notion raised bile in her throat, but she swallowed it down. Elian had been so certain there was more to the dragons' story, but she wondered how he'd react if he learned just how much they hadn't known.

Hopefully, she'd someday soon be able to tell him.

Her fists still clenched whenever she glanced at the dragon. No justification could cleanse the ocean's worth of blood on his claws. She'd felt his regret, but no amount of feeling sorry would earn her forgiveness. She forced her breaths through her nose and relaxed her hands. Like it or not, humans and dragons stood together against the Debru. They always had.

"Is that the true strength of the Vada? Including the one here?" she asked quietly.

"It is. If anything, this one is likely stronger. Every time they return, they've learned more. It is safe to assume the one sitting outside your lands is the strongest we've yet faced."

They'd been lucky when Elian had killed the Vada before. Beyond lucky, if what the dragon showed her was real. That had been the one moment, when the Vada stepped into their world, that it had been vulnerable, and they'd been in the perfect place to take advantage of that weakness.

Unfortunately, it had given her the wrong sense of the Vada. She'd felt its strength and been in awe, but that had only been a fraction of its true power. Ever since their first encounters, she'd imagined they were close, that if they trained a little harder or coordinated with the dragons a little better, they'd overcome the Vada.

That was nothing more than a hopeful delusion. Even if Elian was successful in recruiting the rest of the adanists from the wandering clans, all he'd accomplish would be gathering the adanists into one large group, saving the Vada the time of hunting them all down. Once again, the only possible way forward was to learn more, no matter where that knowledge originated.

"Would you tell me everything?"

"I could, but would you rather I show you, instead?"

"Please."

The walls faded, and her senses were once again trapped in a dragon's body, but this felt different from the memories she'd shared a few moments ago. The body itself felt different.

"A memory of my ancestor, the elder three generations previous," the elder said.

Given the vast number of years the elder had seen, she tried to guess how ancient this memory was, but the numbers were beyond her reckoning. The dragon flew across the land, but Samora caught no sign of human habitation. There were no fields, no homes, not even the wide tracks of the wandering clans as they patrolled the frontier.

"We witness the first meeting between human and dragon," the dragon explained.

The dragon's flight ended near the base of a cliff, where a group of humans had gathered around a fire. They were dressed in hides and were nearly as short as children. Samora watched as the dragon landed some distance away and bowed. The humans fled.

"According to our lore, the force you call adani was the first intelligence upon this world, arising from the vast interconnected web of simpler life. It first formed us dragons to protect it, guard it, and nurture it, and we did so willingly. Our bodies could hold vast amounts of adani, and with it, we became the undisputed rulers of this world."

Samora listened, but she focused mostly on the sight of the humans fleeing. They ran more like wild, startled animals than humans she knew, and she understood why the elder chose this memory specifically. "Your species is much older than ours, isn't it?"

"Much. But you are adani's crowning achievement. Adani recognized your blossoming intelligence early. It gave itself to you and tasked us as your protectors. Back then, you were a dangerous species, but not nearly so dangerous as you are today."

The memory faded, soon replaced by several others. In each, the dragons took it upon themselves to aid humanity. Here, a dragon brought a freshly killed deer to a family that appeared famished and weak. Then another dragon tore into a pack of long-fanged wolves tracking a different, helpless clan.

"You often complain that we treat you as children, even though that is rarely our intent. But you are our children. We're the ones who protected you and offered guidance, often acting without your knowledge. It was our pleasure to do so."

The quick sequence of memories ended and a longer one unfolded in front of her. This human was taller and dressed better, looking much more like a human of the wandering clans than the ones before. Dragon and human sat on opposite sides of a fire, and the human practiced different weaves of adani. After each attempt, the dragon mimicked what she'd just witnessed. Samora frowned, not quite understanding the meaning of the scene.

"As you can see, for many years, our relationship was mutually beneficial."

"How so?"

The memory faded, and they were once again in Samora's childhood home. "Dragons and adani have a history that goes back longer than you can imagine, and while humans have rarely been able to match our strength, we still need you."

"Why?"

"We lack a quality that you possess in abundance. Can you guess?"

Samora couldn't, nor was she in the mood to try.

"Dragons are long-lived and powerful. In both these domains, we outclass you by no small margin. In contrast, you humans live lives that are barely longer than the blink of an eye for us, and are made of weak flesh even a kettu can bite through. But those weaknesses have made you strong in other ways. You've had to fight and adapt to survive and because of that, you've all grown incredibly strong."

"And yet you still treat us like children."

The dragon ignored her comment and turned her toward the memory. "You may feel that way, and we may be guilty, but again, it's not our intent. Your lives are brief and short, but in that short number of years, you burn far brighter than we do. Your creativity and imagination far surpass ours, and it is your species that is always finding new ways to use adani. For all your weaknesses, it is you that teach us how to best use adani."

Samora dismissed the dragon's words as an empty platitude, but then the import of them hit her. She thought of the weaves she'd had to solve to enter the cave, and they took on a new meaning.

"You're saying that you don't come up with your own weaves?"

"Rarely, and when we do, it usually takes us many, many years. Generations, by your count. It is not for lack of effort, but there is something in our minds we cannot overcome. Our discoveries are rare, and usually an incremental improvement over what has come before. All true advances come from our younger siblings, the humans."

Samora's fists clenched again, and she tried to keep some semblance of ease in her posture. Connected as they were, though, the elder couldn't help but notice her distress. In response, it revealed another flurry of memories. In each, humanity taught dragons some new weave. First, it was the weave for fire, a bitter memory for Samora, who knew that one day, far in this memory's future, it would be that weave that would wipe out vast swaths of humanity. In another vision, a woman showed a dragon how to form weaves that altered the flow of adani, in humans, dragons, and all other species. The very attack she was currently weakened by.

Samora clenched her fists so hard tears came to her eyes. "Everything you've done to us, you first stole from us."

The elder didn't deny the accusation but continued to throw more memories at her. Different dragons, different eras, and different humans. There had to be a thread between them, but it took Samora an age to discover it.

The memories mattered. They gave Samora glimpses into a past she hadn't even come close to imagining.

But the dragon wasn't just sharing the sights and sounds of the past. The memories came loaded with so much more. Emotions and thoughts, all gifted to her without the medium of language interfering with their delivery.

She experienced the memories from the dragons' perspectives.

And yes, they looked at humanity the way that Samora imagined parents looked at their children. They were too protective, too heavy-handed, and kept humanity on too tight of a leash.

But there was no malice in their actions. There was no mistaking the warmth in the dragons' chests when the humans under their protection discovered a new weave, no mistaking the excitement when the dragons shared humanity's advances with other dragons. They reminded Samora of nothing more than proud parents.

The memories faded, and once again she was grateful to be returned to her childhood home. Though she knew it was an illusion, it was home, someplace safe that she understood. A place where she could puzzle out all the dragon had shown her.

How could the dragons show so much affection and care to

humanity, then turn around and destroy them so ruthlessly? How could they be proud parents and still be capable of visiting such destruction upon their children?

She didn't doubt what she'd seen, but she couldn't make sense of it.

"If you cared for us so much, why did you destroy us?"

"As I've said before, it was the only way we could think of to save you."

"Help me understand. For all you've shown me, I'm more lost than ever. We've fought the Debru together, so why betray us?"

"Because we thought it was the only way to protect you from the Debru. The only way we could think of to save you from yourselves."

"What?"

The walls of Samora's home faded as the dragon took her toward another memory. This one carried a different weight than the others, a darkness in the elder's heart that left her blood cold. It only grew colder when the elder spoke again.

"For you to understand anything, you must first understand this: the Debru are your ancestors."

16

Elian's feet barely touched the ground as he flew toward the Debru. A pair of growls came from within the trees, followed a moment later by the two otsoa they belonged to. Elian's sword flashed twice, slicing through the creatures as though they were paper.

In the back of his mind, he noted the difference in his speed and strength. His last few battles had pushed him to the limit of his abilities, but his contact with the hearts had expanded his adani channels. The result was a body that was stronger than he'd previously believed possible. He didn't fight upon a gathering ground, but the otsoa barely qualified as a threat.

Another dozen steps carried him into the trees, where he found two more otsoa waiting for him. One cut sliced the first in half, but the second was fast enough to avoid his first move. It bounded off a pine and tried to attack him from the side, but his sword opened it up from shoulder to hip.

The Debru were on him before the otsoa parts tumbled to a stop. They were fast, and they coordinated with one another well. The first attacked him head-on while the second approached from the side. The first clawed at him, but he was already moving and the Debru's claws tore through the side of a tree, leaving deep parallel gouges.

The second formed a blade of shadow to block Elian's cut, but it vanished like smoke when Elian's sword struck it. Elian's blade carried through the Debru without slowing. It collapsed without a sound.

He chased after the second Debru as it danced away. It formed a spear and flung it, but Elian batted the spear aside before it could stab deep into his chest. The Debru threw up a wall of shadow, but Elian cut through it and chased the Debru down. Its last defense was to form a sword of shadow, but like its companion, it lacked the strength to defend against Elian's steel.

As the second Debru collapsed, Elian spun around and searched for other enemies. Any moment now he expected one of Tassan's giant spears to come ripping through the trees, but the woods surrounding him were quiet. In the distance, a squirrel leapt from one branch to another, and the breeze from the valley below caused the pines to whisper, but the only shadows that moved were those of the trees.

Elian spun again, this time slower than before. He stepped carefully through the trees, eyes and ears straining for any shadows or movement that didn't belong.

He was alone. The otsoa and the Debru had driven out most of the wildlife, but there was no enemy force waiting in the trees.

This afternoon, Loken had sensed something. The watchtowers had fallen. An attack was imminent, but it wasn't coming from here.

Elian shifted his course so that he intercepted the narrow path that ran through the trees and out onto the northern ridge. Clouds had moved in overhead, hiding the moon and its light, but Elian could still make out tracks. It was hard to say how many, but he suspected the numbers weren't much different from what he'd seen on the southern ridge. A handful of Debru and at least a dozen otsoa. The tracks milled around the edges of the grove and traveled both east and west.

Elian let his gaze travel along the ridge, but he saw nothing that alarmed him. He watched for a moment, then followed the path to the village.

He was halfway back when he sensed the gathering of shadow in the valley below. Considering his lack of sensitivity, the fact he could feel it at all told him how great the danger was. He sprinted through the trees, coming to the edge of the cliff in time to see the true Debru assault begin.

Thick clouds cast the valley into darkness. Even so, Elian spotted the giant spear that hovered above the pine trees below. It was twice as long as he was tall, the size of weapon a Belog might prefer. No sooner had Elian laid eyes on it than it was launched, speeding toward the western wall of the village.

Elian could do nothing but watch and try to understand. The western wall was the thickest of the village, built right to the edge of a vertical drop of almost a hundred feet. Even if the spear took down the wall, what would it accomplish? The cliff face was still impossible to climb.

The few adanists on the western wall threw up a shield, but they were no match for the strength of the shadow spear. It stabbed through the shields without slowing and speared into the wall, right at the base where it was thickest.

The stone wall, ancient before Elian's father had been born, cracked under the pressure of the Debru spear. The impact echoed like thunder across the valley, and Elian held his breath as he waited for the stone wall to collapse.

It didn't, a testament to the skill and perseverance of those who had built it in ages long past.

Unfortunately, the first shadow spear wasn't the last. Several more followed, all as long and as powerful as the first. They took aim at the same place, striking near the bottom of the wall. None were so much as slowed by adani.

Royzen's stone wall never had a chance. The second spear cratered the wall, and the third dug deeper yet, blasting a small hole near the bottom. The fourth struck the hole and exploded an entire section of the wall. Stone flew into the air, accompanied by at least one unfortunate adanist who'd been standing in the wrong place at the worst time.

Elian squinted and frowned. The Debru now had a clear shot into the village, but what good did it do them?

The answer came a moment later, as the shadows in the valley below shifted and raced forward. They poured from the trees and broke against the cliff face. Then they climbed.

Elian's eyes went wide. The Debru didn't seek hand and foot holds the way a human would. They simply stabbed their claws deep into the stone and hauled themselves up as though climbing a ladder. Elian watched for a moment and suddenly understood how the watchtowers had fallen so easily.

The Scorpions had become too comfortable with their fortifications. Too comfortable being ignored by the Debru for too long. The walls that protected the village had been designed with lesser enemies in mind, not the higher-ranked Debru.

A spear of golden light flashed from the upper walls, spurring Elian into motion. The targeted Debru wove a shield of shadow above itself, and the spear skipped off.

Elian returned to the path and sprinted through the woods. The northern wall of the village came into view a moment later, and he waved to ensure no one accidentally attempted to spear him with adani. He looped adani in his legs and leaped high. He caught the lip of the wall and hauled himself over.

Tassan was nowhere to be found, but Elian wasn't surprised. It had been clear for a bit that the northern path wasn't a serious concern, and Elian expected he'd find Tassan on or near the western wall. He ran that way himself.

By the time he arrived, the battle had been joined. Tassan stood on the very northern edge of the western wall, and when

Elian first laid eyes on him, he had a spear in hand and was taking careful aim. Elian held back while he surveyed the damage.

The western wall was already a mess. Tassan and a handful of other adanists stood on the northern section of the wall. Most threw spears as fast as they could bind them, but none looked pleased by their success. On the southern side of the wall, there were far more adanists, and spears fell from the top like a deadly golden waterfall.

Tassan threw his spear, and Elian rushed forward and looked down. Vertigo twisted his stomach for a moment, but he watched Tassan's spear punch through the shield protecting the Debru and spear it off the side of the cliff. It fell to the rocks below.

Unfortunately, it was the only Debru to fall, and the rest had climbed much higher, much faster than Elian had expected. The average adanist wasn't strong enough to break through the Debru's shields, and the destruction of the wall had disorganized the defense.

Elian cursed as he saw more spears of shadow form above the trees far below. Tassan bound a shield, and others joined his cause. The Debru threw the spears. Tassan's shield barely held, but the southern side of the wall took another spear. The entire wall trembled but held.

"They have at least two Moka down there throwing those spears. If we all bound shields, we might hold them off, but those climbing Debru will be at the hole in the wall before long," Tassan said.

"I can't help with the shields or spears, but I can help defend the hole," Elian said.

"Then get to it, and good luck. If they break through, it'll be a nightmare to defend this village."

Elian clapped Tassan on the shoulder, then ran to the edge of the wall. He'd expected to jump into the gap and hold it, but a glance told him the task wouldn't be so simple. The wall hadn't been blasted clean away. Jagged granite, cut to razor-sharp edges, lay scattered haphazardly in the gap.

The closest open space was perhaps ten paces from the opening, a fragment of the path that had once run along the inside of the wall. Elian leaped for it and landed softly, then studied his new battleground.

It wouldn't go well for him. Ideally, he needed to be closer to the gap to stop the Debru from coming through but approaching risked tearing up his feet and destroying his balance.

For all the strength he'd developed, he was still as good as useless. Any other adanist could have cleared the space off in a moment, but he was stuck too far back. He might slow a Debru or three, but he couldn't block their invasion alone.

The first Debru arrived moments later. One long claw reached up and punched into the stone, then it pulled itself up and leaped forward. Its jaws opened in a terrifying smile, revealing several rows of sharpened teeth. Elian drew his sword, but the Debru sprinted north, avoiding him completely.

Before Elian could give chase, he heard a commotion on the walls. He looked up in time to see the arm of an adanist fall from the southern wall.

"Help!" someone cried from above.

Elian glanced at the fleeing figure of the one Debru that had snuck past him, then leaped back onto the walls, where he found himself in the middle of a pitched battle. He almost landed on a Debru, who turned to swipe at him. Elian brought his sword up as a shield and the edge cut through the Debru's arm. He cut again before it recovered, taking its head with his next cut.

Another Debru came over the wall and Elian cursed their foolishness. If the Debru could climb the cliffs so easily, the walls were barely the obstacle the adanists thought they were. The attack had never been focused on the gap the Moka had opened.

So much had been a distraction, keeping them guessing, while the actual assault had been remarkably straightforward.

Elian cut the Debru down, its shadow nearly powerless against his sword. The other Debru nearby noticed him, but instead of fighting, they leaped from the wall and into the village. A scream from somewhere higher up the hill told Elian other Debru were already well into the village.

"Go," Tassan shouted.

"Not yet," Elian said.

Terrible as the delay would be, he couldn't fight this battle alone. He ran for the gap, then leaped across it and landed on the northern side of the wall. He cut down the first Debru he came across before it realized he was there, but the death of their companion alerted the others. They turned, almost as one, and disengaged with the adanists they were overpowering. One after the other, they leaped into the village and disappeared down the narrow, dark alleys.

No sooner had the Debru departed than the bombardment from below resumed. The first spears that struck the northern section of the wall caused it to tremble under Elian's feet. It wouldn't last for long.

He had no command over these adanists, but they looked to him for orders all the same. He pointed his sword toward the village. "Form into teams of at least four and patrol the streets. Stay away from this wall."

"Royzen ordered us to hold this wall, no matter what." The adanist who spoke was young, younger even than Elian.

"This wall is going to fall in moments, and there's nothing any of us can do to stop it. You'll save a lot more lives this way, including, possibly, your own."

Another shadow spear from below helpfully reinforced Elian's statement. One of the commanders on the wall selected three companions, then rushed down the stairs and after the Debru. Once the first commander followed Elian's orders, the rest followed soon after.

Elian remained until the last of the adanists were off the wall.

The Debru were all up and over, so there was no point pretending to maintain the defense any longer. No more shadow spears rushed up from below, and Elian would have given up several days of food to know what the Moka planned next.

For now, though, his next steps were obvious. The Debru needed to be hunted down and killed before the Scorpion village fell.

He took one last look at the valley below, then dropped into the village to begin his hunt.

❦ 17 ❦

Samora dropped into another memory like a stone sinking into a frigid lake. The warmth of feeling that had permeated the other memories was nowhere to be found. As the vision cleared, she found herself flying above another battlefield, where human and dragon didn't fight Debru, but other humans.

Samora looked away as one woman, allied with the dragons, stabbed a spear of adani into the stomach of her enemy. The young man, barely older than a boy, grimaced and tried to weave his own weapon. A mixture of gold and shadow swirled in his hand, taking the shape of a dagger. It reminded her of Kati's attack against Aldo in the circle, though this one was different. The dagger drew her attention even as she tried to look away.

She'd never seen the two forces woven together. The Debru in her time were creatures of shadow only, just as she only knew how to weave adani. She'd believed the two couldn't mix. The sight made her sick, as though she'd eaten something rotten.

The woman in the memory must have felt the same, for she paled before the weapon. She stepped back and yanked on her spear, but the young man grabbed it with his free hand and pulled himself closer. His black eyes and bloody smile made Samora curse out loud, even though the memory wasn't hers. The woman braced her feet and pulled with all her might, but the young man's single arm was stronger. He pulled himself up the spear of adani, almost close enough to stab with the dagger.

The woman released the weaving and the spear vanished. Instead of being staggered, the young man lunged forward, almost faster than Samora's eyes could track. He buried the dagger deep into the woman's neck, then closed his eyes.

Samora saw nothing happen, but her senses flared as she perceived the woman's well of adani being pulled from the corpse by the dagger. Instead of flowing back into the world, where the adani belonged, it poured into the young man. The wound in his stomach closed, the flesh fresh and soft as a newborn child's, with no hint of a scar.

He pulled every drop of adani from the corpse, then let it collapse like a sack of dried bones. He leaped into the next fray, faster than before.

Across the battlefield, the story repeated, told in a hundred different varieties. In some battles, the adanists overcame their enemies. Though the shadow users were stronger on average than the adanists, and could heal with remarkable rapidity, a fatal blow remained fatal. The adanists were outmatched, but they outnumbered the shadow users, and they had the dragons on their side.

Samora had no choice but to watch, forced to witness what the dragon had seen this day. The feeling of her borrowed body told her this was a previous elder, and the adani under its control was awe-inspiring. It swept across the field and only the strongest of the shadow users could stand against it.

Vicious as the battle was, the outcome never seemed in doubt. The shadow users were too heavily outnumbered, and the sheer force of the dragons was too much to overcome. Too many lives were lost in the attempt, but adanists and dragons pushed the shadow users back. Samora's gaze traveled to the rear of the battlefield, where a tear in the air caught her attention.

"Many of your generations ago, there was a young man who discovered adani could make doorways to other worlds. It was considered the greatest weaving humanity had yet achieved, and even the dragons looked forward to the possibility of exploring new worlds. The first humans who traveled through the doorways came back and reported a world very similar to our own. A fair number of settlers traveled through the doorway intending to start a new civilization."

"What happened to them?" Samora asked.

"They weren't heard from for a long time. Eventually, the doorway opened again, but you can see the changes in those who returned. The settlers reported the other world didn't have adani. It was governed instead by another force, which you now call shadow. We found this more curious than threatening, and for a time, the doorways opened regularly and adanists and shadow users frequently traded."

The battle was nearly over. The dragons and adanists made one last push, driving the last of the shadow users into the black doorway. When the last shadow user stepped through, the door closed and an enormous, exhausted but triumphant cheer rose from the assembled adanists.

The elder continued. "Eventually, though, the doors closed for good, and though the adanists on this side tried to open them again, they were blocked. Later, we learned that those on the other side had found a weave that protected them from travel. We know little of what happened there, but we believe the other force, the shadow, corrupted the hearts of those who had crossed. When they eventually returned, it was much as you just saw. They still possessed the means of using adani, but it was mixed with shadow, a force that preyed upon adani with ease. They invaded in small groups at first, but more often as time passed. Villages, families, and clans fell to the invaders, and it took us far too long to realize what was happening. Once we did, though, the war began, ending with this battle. We thought this bloody day was the end, and we kept a close eye out for other doorways, but none appeared. We wouldn't see them again until I became elder, many, many years later."

"Were they Debru, then?" Samora asked.

"They were. They'd lost the ability to use adani, likely because they'd been stranded so long without it, but they'd learned shadow, and in many ways, it has proven to be the superior force."

"What do they want?"

"They've never said, but as near as we can tell, they want this world so they can control adani. Shadow becomes stronger as it absorbs adani, and we believe they want it to pursue more power."

The explanation didn't satisfy Samora, though she couldn't say why. It felt incomplete, somehow.

They returned to Samora's house, where she sat for a good while and thought through what she'd learned. Only one question hadn't been answered to her satisfaction.

"You still haven't explained why you believed it necessary to eliminate humanity."

The elder shook his head. "Not eliminate, but prune."

Samora couldn't quite control the growl that escaped the back of her throat.

"You've seen the great battles, fought between the strongest adanists humanity has ever produced and the Vada. We survived that assault, but at tremendous cost. The vast majority of the world's greatest adanists were killed in that war, and all we earned was a reprieve. Debru continued to rip new doors to our world, and our adanists weren't as strong as before. The war went back and forth for generations, and we sought an end to the continuous fighting. For many years, we'd tried to help train stronger humans, but we never had peace long enough. We, humans and dragons alike, started asking if there was some different approach."

Samora crossed her arms, still waiting for an explanation she could accept.

"The adanists at the time became obsessed with a single question: how was it the Debru could open so many doors to our world, and even our most talented adanists couldn't find theirs? The dragons still carried the knowledge of the doors, but no adanist, even once they'd been taught the weave, could find the world of shadow."

Samora leaned forward. "What did they find?"

"The Debru can sense adani. Maybe it's because of their past, or maybe it's an aspect of shadow, but they are incredibly sensitive to its use. When we sense shadow here, it is less that we sense the shadow specifically, but the hole in the web of adani. We can't track them well, but they don't have the same problem."

The last piece of understanding fell into place. "So you believed that by eliminating much of humanity, you could keep us safe?"

"We targeted those who were adanists, specifically. All humans have the ability to use adani, but only a fraction ever have. There were already very few after all the wars, but we decided to kill the rest and steal the memory of adani from you. We hoped it would lead to a lasting peace."

Samora leaned back in her chair and closed her eyes. She had her answers, finally, but they didn't bring the peace she'd hoped for. All that death, and ultimately it had resulted in nothing more than a break from the invasion. Humanity had rediscovered adani, and the Debru, in response, had returned. She had learned much, but wasn't any closer to knowing how to defeat the Vada.

"So, what now?" she asked.

The elder didn't have an immediate response. It stared out the window for a moment before speaking. "When I'd first heard you were coming, I'd hoped to measure your strength and your latent potential for growth. You've passed the tests I designed, for which you are to be commended, but I fear you don't have the strength to stand against the Vada."

Samora bit her tongue to keep herself from arguing.

"I believe it is best if we delay. Humanity's adanists are getting stronger, and perhaps the generation after yours will develop a talent strong enough to face the Vada."

"If what you say is true, the Vada will not give us the opportunity to wait. It hesitates now, but if given enough time, it will strike," Samora argued.

"Or summon more Vada, yes. It's a risk. But if we bring the remnants of humanity here, I don't think the Vada will attack. It's never destroyed our home, and this one seems more cautious than most."

Samora wasn't sure what to think. The elder spoke true. Despite the growth in her abilities over the past year, she wasn't strong enough to take on the Vada. But she couldn't imagine sitting around and hoping tomorrow would somehow be better.

An old saying of her father's came to mind, one she hadn't thought about in ages. "When something needs doing, it's best to just do it. Nothing gets easier if it sits around and waits for you."

The longer she contemplated the idea of hoping for the next generation, the more distaste she felt for it.

The dragon started, making Samora almost jump out of her seat. He narrowed his eyes at Samora.

A moment later, she felt it, too. She'd paid little attention to it as the dragon had consumed her attention, but adani whispered deep in her spirit. It didn't want to wait.

The dragon's eyes had gone wide. "What does it say?"

"That we should fight."

The elder shook his head. "It can't be." He leaned closer to Samora and searched her up and down. Then he stood and paced the small room with long strides.

"Do you really believe the Vada will leave us alone if we attempt to hide here?" Samora asked.

The elder didn't answer as he continued pacing. Finally, he slowed to a stop. "I have hopes and guesses, but I can't say for sure."

"At some point, we need to face the Vada. Perhaps there's a chance those who come after us are stronger, but it is too much of a risk. Adani believes we should roll the dice and see who wins, and I agree. Better to be free of this than sentence another generation to a life of fear."

"You might doom us all."

"So might inaction. You've seen how much my brother and I have grown in the past year. Imagine what we might yet be capable of."

The dragon made another quick back and forth through the room.

"You also have all these hearts. If you were to share them, there's no telling what humanity might accomplish."

She knew, as soon as the words left her mouth, that she'd pushed too far. The hearts, rightfully, were precious to the elder, and his golden eyes glared at her. She held up her hands in supplication. "At the least, it's something to consider."

The vision of the home vanished, and Samora stood facing the dragon directly. It snarled and sent a massive wave of adani at her.

She didn't fight against it. If she could direct the strength of the hearts, she could direct the strength of the elder dragon. She let the wave crash into her, fill her channels to bursting, and then accepted more. She began her own weaves, crowding the air of the cave with dozens of tightly bound glowing lights. For a moment, the cave was bright as day, and then she breathed out and let the adani unravel. It heated the air, driving the last of the chill from her bones.

The dragon considered, then nodded. His thought went straight to her mind.

It shall be done, then. Let us hope you haven't doomed us all.

SAMORA WOKE KARLA AND ALDRICK, who looked around as though they didn't have the slightest clue where they were. They shook their heads and cleared their thoughts, and Samora asked them if they knew what had happened.

"Elder put us to sleep," Karla grunted.

"How much do you remember?"

"It's foggy, but enough. What happened?"

"I'll tell you, but for the moment, I think it would be wise for us to leave. The dragons are about to meet, and I don't think we want to be too close."

Samora led them out of the cave and to a stone that overlooked the valley. It was big enough for all three of them to sit facing one another, and Samora welcomed the feeling of the sun on her skin as she explained everything. When she was done, her story was greeted with silence.

Karla sighed and leaned back, supporting her weight on her hands. "So, what happens next? Do the dragons fly us home?"

"I think it would be best for us to stay here for a time. Watching so many of the elder's memories has made me realize just how much we don't know. There are so many weaves I saw in just that limited time. There's a lot to learn."

Aldrick was clearly excited by the prospect, but Karla didn't seem as interested as Samora expected her to be.

"Impressive as an opportunity as that might be, I'm not sure it's what we need," Karla said.

Aldrick turned on her. "How can you say that? There are hundreds, maybe thousands, of years of history being stored within the dragon's mind. There have to be techniques there that strengthen us."

"True enough, but remember why we're here. Getting stronger isn't sufficient. The adanists that came before us might have been stronger, if what Samora tells us is true, but they fell before the Vada all the same. We need something more, so I'm not sure how much sense it makes for us to learn what we know has already failed," Karla said.

The older adanist's warning dampened their enthusiasm, but Samora wouldn't be deterred. "It's true that learning the techniques of the past won't be enough, but they may be the key that unlocks the technique we need. We'd be fools to ignore the wisdom of the past completely."

"That's fair, but all I ask is that you not get too attached to the idea that you'll find the solution in the past, because I don't think it's there. We have to find a new way."

Samora nodded, taking the advice to heart. Karla's warning was an important one. She could see, all too easily, a future in which she became so distracted by all there was to learn she forgot the reason behind the search. Karla only sought to keep her focused on what mattered most.

But Karla wasn't done. "There's something else I worry about, too."

She turned and faced Samora directly. "You've already proven you're comfortable with a wider range of techniques than most adanists, and you learn quickly. But we're also here to learn how to kill the Vada, to kill all the Debru. Will you be able to learn and teach such techniques, given your aversion to violence?"

"Of course. I understand we need to fight, and I'm happy to learn any technique to pass on to others."

Karla didn't relent. "And what if you're the only one who's proficient at the technique? Would you use it?"

Samora almost said that she would, but then she thought of the battle where the Vada had come through the doorway, the hatred and disgust she'd felt for Elian when he'd killed the Vada. "I would like to think so, but I don't know," she admitted.

Karla slid off the boulder and brushed the dust from her pants. "I know there's nothing I can say that will convince you. It's an argument you'll need to have with yourself. But you should start having it now. I fear that for all your talent and strength, the time will come when we need you to do more than you're willing and your strength will fail us. I don't want that to be our future."

❧ 18 ❧

E lian padded down the silent street while listening for the sounds of the invaders. Screams and cries came from further up the hill, but the hairs standing on the back of his neck told him danger was closer than that.

He found victims of the attack as soon as he turned the first corner. The door to their home had been busted open, the thick wooden frame as useless as paper against the strength and razor-sharp claws of the Debru. The home within was dark, but Elian stepped in to check for survivors.

There were none. All three members of the family had been in their beds when the Debru struck. The man had fallen near the door to his bedroom, and Elian imagined he'd woken when the front door of the house had shattered. The wife was a few steps behind him. Both had been torn nearly in half.

The boy in the other room hadn't stirred from his sleep. Bed and body alike had been cut in half, the work of a long shadow blade that had cut even into the stone beneath.

Elian quivered at the sight. He'd thought, after the last few months of fighting, he'd become immune to the sight of death, but he swore when he met the Debru responsible for this, he'd kill the monster slowly and painfully. No one in this house had posed the slightest threat.

This was killing for killing's sake.

Elian stepped out of the house and almost cut Tassan's head off. The giant warrior stood in the street, hands held before him in defense.

Elian sheathed his sword as a hint of shame flushed his cheeks. "Sorry, I didn't know it was you."

Tassan nodded and put his hands down. "Figured you and I would be stronger together than apart."

Elian agreed. He was strongest if he had a more traditional adanist supporting him. Tassan was an ideal partner, and together, the two of them could clear out far more of the village than Elian could alone.

"Any survivors?" Tassan asked, dipping his head toward the broken door.

"None. We need to stop the Debru before they get too deep into the village. Can you guide me?"

"I can do my best. Adani doesn't travel as well here, so the Debru aren't as easy to sense. But if we're close, I think I'll know."

"Good. What direction should we go?"

Tassan pointed his sword up the hill. "Near as I can tell, they're all working their way east."

Elian gestured Tassan forward. "Lead the way, but when you find one, be warned that I'll probably jump ahead of you."

"Only if I don't kill them first," Tassan said.

The giant warrior started up the hill, climbing a steep set of stone stairs and turning right at the next intersection. Elian followed, sword out and adani looping powerfully through his limbs. They passed homes with doors hanging off of sturdy hinges, but neither Tassan nor Elian wasted the time in checking for survivors.

Tassan turned left and took another set of stairs three at a time, Elian following easily behind. The sound of a door breaking open drew them further south, and the screams within led them to the home under assault. Elian sprinted around Tassan, lowered his shoulder, and crashed through the last bits of door still swinging back and forth on well-oiled hinges.

This family hadn't been taken unawares. The man swung an iron poker at the Debru, who batted aside the assault with a casual swipe of its arm. It raised its other arm to open the man from shoulder to stomach, but Elian arrived before the Debru could finish its deadly mission. By the time the Debru swung down, most of its arm was falling to the stone floor of the dining room.

The Debru spun and snarled in time to witness Elian cut across, taking off its head. Dark blood sprayed from the wound as the body fell, but Elian had already turned and was leaving the house. He barely heard the father cry out in relief as he strode back into the street.

"I've never seen a Debru die so easily," Tassan said.

"Lead me to the next one and I'll show you it wasn't a fluke."

"Wasn't really doubting you, but I'll happily lead you to the next. It's close."

They ran back the way they'd come, then climbed another short set of stairs to reach the next street. Tassan pointed north, but before they'd taken two steps, a pair of girls ran into the street. Their white nightgowns were stained dark with blood, but their faces were paler than the moon, still trying to shine through the clouds.

A Debru followed the girls out of the home, but a woman clutching tightly at its legs hobbled it. The Debru drug her along, and she trailed entrails and blood behind her. One of her legs ended just above the knee, but she clung to the Debru with the strength of a veteran adanist. It snarled, twisted, and stomped down on her. The crack of her spine echoed down the street.

Elian sprinted at the Debru, but it turned to the girls and the distance was too great. A spear of golden light passed just over Elian's shoulder, forcing the Debru to form a shield. The spear bounced harmlessly off the shield, causing the Debru to notice Elian and Tassan. It formed a shadow spear and flung, but Elian shifted to the side and it flew harmlessly past him.

The Debru weaved shadow into a sword. Elian cut, and though the Debru blocked easily enough, too much adani ran through Elian's body and sword. His blade passed through the Debru's and opened a deep gash in its chest. The Debru staggered back, but before it could recover, Elian stabbed deep into its heart.

His sympathy went out to the girls, but he was needed more elsewhere. "Where's the next?" he asked Tassan.

The giant pointed north, and they left the girls to grieve the remnants of their broken life alone.

They'd only gone a few houses down when a spear of adani shot through the intersection ahead of them. Elian slowed and approached cautiously. He first looked up the slope in the direction the spear had traveled, but he saw no Debru. He looked down, then saw the battle in progress.

Four adanists fought against a pair of Debru. Two moved slowly, wounded and bleeding from a dozen cuts shared between the pair. The other two stabbed their spears wildly, almost as much danger to their partners as they were to the Debru.

The Debru, in contrast, fought as though they'd spent their whole lives training together. One shielded the other from the adanists' ineffectual attacks, while the other used a shadow sword to open up fresh cuts.

Elian wasn't sure how the adanists had survived this long, but they wouldn't much longer. He shouted to draw the Debru's attention, then leaped down a flight of stairs and swung at the Debru maintaining the shield.

The second Debru let its sword drop and formed a shield, dark enough Elian couldn't see anything on the other side. His sword bit into the shield, froze for a moment, then cut through. The shield dissolved into smoke and Elian landed softly on his feet. The dissolving shield revealed a Debru in motion, kicking out at Elian with a long leg.

Elian danced back and swung up with his sword, but the Debru knew enough not to challenge the sword directly. It leaned away and formed a shadow sword of its own, half again as long as a normal sword. It stabbed at Elian and forced him to retreat up some of the stairs he'd just jumped down. When the Debru stabbed again, Elian knocked the attack away with his sword. The Debru's sword dissolved into shadow upon contact with Elian's sword, but the Debru formed another in the blink of an eye.

Tassan's spear came from the roofs above, and the Debru maintaining the shield barely protected the pair in time.

The other adanists, suddenly freed of the Debru's relentless assault, remembered their training and chose that moment to strike as well. Adani sought the Debru from all sides, and they had little choice but to both cast shields to protect themselves.

The Debru couldn't last long. The adanists wore them down, and as their shields fell, Elian's sword cut into their dark robes. In the end, one fell to Elian's blade and the other to a spear from one of the adanists.

Elian looked the small group over. He still couldn't believe that two of the adanists were standing, but the fire in their eyes told him they wouldn't accept any suggestion of rest. Instead, he offered them a slight bow, then said, "Good hunting out there."

They bowed, thanked him for his assistance, then climbed the stairs in the search for more Debru.

Elian glanced up and saw Tassan standing on the edge of a roof, looking west with a frown on his face. "What's wrong?" he asked.

"This fight is only getting started," his friend answered.

Elian clambered up the wall to see for himself. He followed the direction of Tassan's gaze, then swore under his breath.

The main path to the village was hard to see in the dark, but it crawled with shadows that raced up the road. Elian needed a moment to understand exactly what he looked at, but once he did, his stomach dropped through a hole in his gut to the ground below.

All the otsoa he'd spotted from the dragon's back earlier, the ones that had been milling around the base of the valley, now raced toward the village. No single otsoa was that much of a threat, but so many would flood the village and devour everyone who'd survived the Debru assault.

Elian pointed to the path ahead of the shadow's advance. "Why don't you make one of your most powerful spears and throw it there? I don't think otsoa can climb the way Debru did."

Tassan shook his head. "They're not alone. You probably can't sense it, but there's at least two Moka among them. I could try, but the Moka would cast a shield and block my attempt. I'd be burning adani for no reason."

Elian's mind raced. "Is there anything we can do?"

"I'm trying to think of something, but I'm not having much luck."

"We need to let Royzen know what's coming."

Tassan nodded. "Hopefully they have another way out of here, because I don't think anyone's going to want to wander out the front door anytime soon."

"Let's hurry, then. Given how fast that group is moving, it's not going to be long before they've overwhelmed us."

Elian turned toward Royzen's home near the center of the village, but Tassan didn't follow. He glanced back to ask why, but Tassan's face had lost some of its color. "What?"

Tassan pointed to the wall where they'd been standing not that long ago. "Two Moka just climbed the cliff and entered the village."

Elian cursed again. He looked up at Royzen's home, then

down at the broken wall. From where he stood, he couldn't see the Moka, but he didn't doubt Tassan's judgment.

They needed to warn Royzen, but they also needed to fight the Moka. Elian hadn't come across any Scorpions capable of handling a Moka in his time in the village. He exhaled sharply and squared his shoulders. "You go warn Royzen. I'll fight against the Moka."

"You can't take two on at once."

"Probably not, but I don't see how we have much choice."

Tassan grabbed Elian's arm and pulled him toward Royzen's home. "Stop being such a noble fool. Warning Royzen will only take a moment, then we can fight the Moka together. There's no point risking yourself like that."

Elian allowed himself to be pulled along.

The leader of the Scorpions was on the roof with several of his commanders. When Tassan and Elian reached the roof, their heads were together as they discussed the paths of the Debru.

Tassan interrupted. "I'm sorry, sir, but you've got much bigger problems to worry about."

Royzen looked up. "How so?"

"Two Moka have entered the village through the hole in the wall, and there are at least two more accompanying an enormous pack of otsoa coming up the path. They'll be here shortly."

Royzen broke apart from his commanders and went to the northwest corner of his roof, where he stared into the darkness. His fists clenched when he saw the otsoa rushing up the path, then he whirled back on Tassan. "Four Moka? You're sure?"

"At least that many, yes, sir."

Royzen chewed on his lower lip while his eyes looked to the western horizon. The discussion among the commanders had stopped and everyone waited for their leader's orders. He spoke to no one in particular. "There's no way to protect the village from four Moka, is there?"

Elian wanted to shout that there was. That he and the others had defeated not just Moka, but Belogs, in far greater numbers. But that had been with Harald, Karla, Kati, and the strength of a gathering ground and a heart. Here they had Tassan and Elian, and that wasn't nearly enough. The Scorpions fought well, but the difference in strength was too great.

Their silence answered Royzen's question, and he sighed, as though all the life had gone out of him. "Sound the orders to retreat. Gather the people outside the western gate. Have them bring nothing but the clothes on their backs."

"There's another way out?" Tassan asked.

Royzen nodded. "A narrow trail, too treacherous by far, but a safer option than sitting here and waiting to die. It'll be two days and two nights before we can reach another Scorpion village, but my people are strong. We'll survive this and come back someday with vengeance."

"How can we help?" Elian asked.

Royzen considered, then said, "Get the heart, as you call it, from below. The Debru can have the walls, but they'll never have that. Once you have it, help with the evacuation as you can."

Elian was about to object when the bells changed their cadence. They no longer rang constantly, but were struck once, then paused, then were struck once again. He assumed it was the signal to retreat.

His instinct was to run back to the battlefield, but Royzen's point was a good one. The heart underneath his home might very well be the most powerful item in the village, and he didn't want to find out what the Debru might do with it. At the very least, its loss would take a vital tool away from the adanists.

He and Tassan took the stairs, and Elian was grateful, again, for Tassan's company. He hadn't paid enough attention to the layout of Royzen's house when he'd been here earlier, but Tassan knew the way, as though he had a map in his head.

The giant found the wall hanging without problem and pulled it aside, and his finger found the hidden latch without trouble. The door swung open, but as Elian took his first step, the entire house shook as though it were a child's toy being roughly played with. Dust fell from the ceiling, and Elian wondered if the structure would hold.

"Looks like the Moka found us," Tassan noted. It sounded more like he was making an observation about the weather than declaring their doom.

"Do we have time to get it?" Elian asked.

"I'm not sure we have a choice. Hurry, now." Tassan placed his hand against the stone and the ceiling lit up as before.

Elian and Tassan ran, though the ground shook constantly under their feet. Elian kept glancing back, certain the secret entrance would soon be covered in rubble. But for all the shaking, the building didn't fall.

They turned the corner and soon came upon the chamber. Elian was prepared this time. He kept a tight rein on his adani, letting no more into his body than he already possessed. Despite his preparation, the force of the heart was still almost enough to knock him senseless. It glowed like the sun, and its adani wanted so desperately to find a new home in his body. It battered his sealed channels, looking for a gap to flood through.

Tassan grabbed the stone and put it in his pocket, suffering no ill-effects from the proximity of the stone. He glanced at Elian. "Are you all right?"

"I'll be better once I'm further from the stone. You honestly don't feel anything?"

Tassan opened and closed his fist, studying it. "I mean, I feel it, but it's not much different from riding on the dragon."

The ground rumbled again, and Tassan started for the door. "Come on, let's get out of here. We don't have that long before this whole place comes down around us."

"Lead the way. I'll be just a little behind."

Tassan did, and Elian waited a few moments to give the giant some distance. When the stone's weight was easier to bear, he followed.

When they reached the hallway of Royzen's house, there was a giant hole down the stairs. Elian stared at it a bit, then followed Tassan up the stairs, away from the gaping hole and toward Royzen. When they reached the roof, though, they came out in the middle of a terrible battlefield.

Several of the Debru had joined forces under the leadership of the Moka and were assaulting Royzen's home. The commanders, strong adanists all, fought in defense.

Royzen was holding a shield being battered by shadow, but he asked through gritted teeth, "Did you get it?"

"We did," Tassan said.

Elian wished, not for the first time, that Samora was here. In the gathering ground, she had figured out how to share the strength of the heart with all the adanists. Here, it could mean the difference between life and death for the majority of the Scorpion clan, but he had no idea what she'd done. They had the heart and all the power it provided, but it was as good as useless for them.

"Let's retreat," Royzen ordered. He dropped his shield and he and the others ran for the western edge of the roof.

The eastern edge exploded a heartbeat later, torn apart by a spear of shadow. A Debru leaped to the top of the roof and was greeted by a flurry of spears that knocked it off. It hadn't been enough to kill the monster, but it allowed the adanists to retreat to a safer street.

They were only a few houses away when Elian felt the strength of the combined Moka attack. He turned to see Royzen's house, the center of the Scorpions' power, crumble under one last, tremendous assault.

Royzen shouted at them to hurry. "Stone we can rebuild, but our lives are all we have!"

Elian tore his gaze away from the destruction and fled the Debru advance.

❧ 19 ❧

Samora and Karla emerged from the memory together. Aldrick had joined them earlier, but the experience of living through the dragon's memories unsettled him, and he begged off after a few attempts, claiming that he would rather learn from a human.

The elder had been as patient a teacher as she had ever known, often showing them the same memory time and time again while she and Karla unraveled the weavings performed. Between the two of them, though, it rarely took more than two or three showings.

Assuming they returned to the wandering clans, they'd advance the use of adani dozens of years forward. Humans in the past had used adani in dramatically different ways, from strengthening physical objects to helping to predict the weather. Samora was particularly interested in the fact many adanists followed paths similar to Elian's, strengthening the use of adani within the body instead of outside it.

Samora agreed with Karla. They wouldn't defeat the Vada with a specific weave found only in the past. She learned the weaves, not for the techniques themselves, but to understand better the ways past adanists had used adani. Before meeting the dragon, she'd only known the limited techniques of her contemporaries. Expanding her range of techniques forced her to look at adani with fresh eyes. That, she hoped, would trigger the needed breakthrough.

The two women stepped into the sunlight. Samora welcomed the warmth on her skin after the entire morning in the cave.

"We're not making any meaningful progress," Karla said.

She was wrong, but Samora understood the worry behind her claim. Predicting the weather taught her to sense adani differently, but it did nothing to drive the invasion from their lands.

"What else can we do?" she asked.

"Ask the dragon for the hearts. They've got so many we could take half and beat the Vada with our eyes closed."

Samora shivered as she remembered the dragon's reaction when she'd suggested it last. "They won't give up the hearts."

"Then we're wasting our time here. What we need is pure strength, not some esoteric technique that likely doesn't even exist."

Samora stared at the distant mountain peaks, summits glittering with a coat of fresh snow that had fallen that morning. "I don't know what else I can do. If I don't find a way to defeat the Debru, no one will. I've even convinced the dragons that I'm their best opportunity, but I fear I've lied to them."

Karla snorted. "We were all going to die anyway, so it's not like you doomed us."

Samora glared. "That's not helpful."

"It should be. You push yourself too hard and barely sleep. Unless you ease up, you're going to crack before you save us."

"There's no time to relax!"

Karla turned back to the cave. "You don't see the answer that's right in front of you. Let's get some hearts, and that will be that. Once each of our strongest adanists has a heart in their hand, we'll take on the Vada, no problem."

"The elder will kill you."

"And what if it does? We're all going to die, and if either the Debru or the dragons have their way, that'll come sooner rather than later for most. Might as well piss off a dragon while I can."

Samora let Karla go while she stewed in her frustration. The dragon had already made it clear the hearts weren't open for negotiation. Let Karla learn it for herself.

But as Karla's confident footsteps faded away, Samora's attitude shifted. The older adanist had stuck with her through more than anyone except Elian. Even loyal Aldrick hadn't supported her as long. She would be a poor friend indeed if she didn't extend Karla the same courtesy. She hurried after.

Karla shot her a grin when she heard her footsteps. "Miss me already?"

"Just figured that if anyone can save you from yourself, it's me."

"Girl, I've seen so much more than you could even imagine. You think some mere elder dragon is going to be the end of me?"

"Possibly, yes."

Karla laughed and walked with a renewed step. They roamed through the tunnel and into the dragon's home.

Back so soon?

Samora tried to speak first and explain on Karla's behalf, but the other adanist spoke too quickly. "We want your hearts."

The elder raised its head so it towered over the two adanists and roared. Samora clapped her hands over her ears as the sound shook her from head to toe. Her stomach, pleasantly full after a mid-morning snack, rumbled, and she felt the sudden urge to run outside and throw up.

Karla stood tall against the dragon's thunder. She didn't cover her ears or even wince. As the roar echoed and faded, she said, "If we're going to be allies, there will be no need for that. Argue if you wish, explain why you can't or won't share the hearts, but forget intimidating us."

The dragon rumbled, a sound that came deep from the back of its throat. Samora thought it was his form of laughter or amusement.

The elder extended his adani, inviting Samora and Karla into the shared illusion. The cave faded away, replaced by endless plains. All three stood near each other, and the golden eyes of the dragon traveled between the women. Samora waited for the inevitable tongue-lashing that was soon to follow.

Instead, the dragon dipped its head toward them. "You're right, of course, and I apologize for my rudeness. The issue of the hearts is sensitive, and I am prone to forgetting my manners."

Samora blinked and shook her head, certain she'd been training too hard and was now imagining things. She became even more certain of her madness when Karla bowed politely in return. "I understand and accept your apology. What do the hearts represent to you and the other dragons?"

The elder's stare carried him far into the past, one he didn't share with his human companions. "Only a few of the hearts grew here. Most were harvested from places all across the world over countless human generations. We started taking them because we didn't dare allow the Debru access to their strength, but most of them we took on the day we wiped humanity out, both to protect them and to serve as a reminder. We never want to forget the treachery we committed that day."

Samora ground her teeth together. The dragons didn't have the right to memorialize their betrayal. She remembered all too well the gaping hole at the center of the enormous village by the sea, and she knew now the dragons had taken that heart. The elder basked in its power daily. He was more thief than savior.

She took a step forward, but Karla gently restrained her with an arm. "I respect your desire to protect and treasure the hearts, but we've seen more success using them than any technique we may find in your memories. I suspect many of those hearts came from human settlements, so why not return them to their rightful owners?"

"Both because they aren't safe in your hands and because your generation of adanists isn't capable of handling their power. Those that came before you developed their adani channels tirelessly, but your focus on the external manipulation of adani has taken you in a different direction. Even if I were to offer them to you, they'd kill as many of your surviving adanists as the Debru would. Perhaps more."

Karla, the woman who wouldn't let anything as small as a sharp glance go unremarked, bowed again. "With all due respect, are you certain? It seems to me you're falling into the error, once again, of underestimating what we're capable of. I can understand why you view us as children, but we've achieved much in our limited lives."

The dragon looked between the two adanists again, then shrugged his massive shoulders. "We could sit and argue endlessly, but it would be a waste of time." He pointed to Karla. "I shall give you one first, as you are less valuable to us than Samora. If you live and still believe it is possible, I shall allow Samora to come in contact with one."

"I agree," Karla said.

The vision faded and they were back in the cave. The elder kept their connection, though, and extended his adani toward the ceiling, twisting a weave into an intricate pattern that stretched and touched one of the hearts. It detached from the ceiling and floated down.

This one you have a connection to. It is from the city you visited with one of my children. It is among the strongest of the hearts here, a worthy test for the ability you claim.

If Karla was afraid of taking her life in her hands, she gave no sign of it. The stone floated before her, the adani within now much easier to sense.

It was too much. When Samora had used the strength of the

heart in the gathering ground, the gathering ground had acted as a mediator of sorts. Now there was nothing between the heart and the flesh, and it felt as though Karla was about to embrace a roaring bonfire.

Samora almost warned her friend away, but there was no point. Karla was an extraordinary adanist and knew perfectly well the danger she assumed by accepting the dragon's challenge. She no doubt felt the same overwhelming strength, but she didn't flinch from her duty.

Karla took several deep breaths, then grabbed the stone. The moment she did, her entire body turned as stiff as granite. Samora tentatively extended adani toward her and recoiled from the sensation. Adani flooded through Karla, overflowing her channels like a river overflowing its banks during the spring floods. The force unraveled Karla, tearing her apart from the inside.

Karla screamed, and light poured from her open mouth. The dragon, as always, looked down on them as though exasperated by the antics of children.

But then Karla slammed her jaw shut and cut off her scream. Her nostrils flared as she forced breaths through her nose. The amount of adani tearing through her body didn't lessen one bit, but her channels grew wider and deeper until they could just barely contain the strength pouring through her limbs. Sweat beaded down her forehead, but a grin spread across her face as she gripped the stone tighter.

"See?" she said through gritted teeth. "Barely a problem at all."

That same laughing rumble escaped again from the back of the dragon's throat.

You impress me, young one. But now that you've felt the power for yourself, do you believe Samora should handle it?

"Anything I can do, Samora can learn to do, so yes." Karla let go of the stone and it floated up and away from her. She fell to her knees, gasping for air.

"That being said, the dragon might have a point. That stone damn near killed me. There aren't many among us who could handle it. Maybe only three that I can think of, off the top of my head," Karla added.

The stone floated from in front of Karla and over to Samora.

Do you wish to join in your friend's folly?

Samora stared at the heart. If she closed herself off to her senses, it seemed such a trivial task. The stone glowed with a soft light that promised warmth even in the darkest nights.

Adani told a much different story. The stone was as alive as Karla, Samora, or the dragon, and held more adani than all of them combined. To touch it was to invite death, even for the elder. Yet Karla still breathed, even though her breaths were labored and weary.

Samora was no stranger to the strength of a heart, which was why she hesitated. The heart underneath her gathering ground possessed only a fraction of the strength of this one, but her contact with it had brought her to the brink of oblivion. She cursed her fear but couldn't deny it had good reason.

If Elian were here, he'd grab it. That fool would probably try to wrap it in an embrace or stuff it in his underclothes, so it would always grant him more strength.

Before she could reason herself out of the foolishness, she reached out.

Like Karla, her body immediately went stiff, not because her muscles flexed or became rigid, but because so much adani flowed through her, she couldn't move against it. Adani over-flowed the banks of her channels, and she swore she saw light seeping out the pores of her skin.

"Don't fight it. Let it flow through you, and your body will adapt," Karla suggested.

Easy advice to give, but hard to accept. To stop fighting adani meant it would flood every corner of her body, ripping her to shreds from the inside out. It was only her extraordinary effort that kept adani under any semblance of control. But that effort couldn't last for long, and Samora surrendered before the choice was taken away from her.

Time slowed, and across the space of a heartbeat, she swore that this was the end for her. Massive, uncontrolled amounts of adani ran rampant through her body. Bone, organ, and muscle loosened as adani found every crack and space in her body and filled it beyond bursting.

Then adani, through no effort of her own, fell back into the banks of her channels, which had somehow grown wider and deeper without her noticing. The pain in her joints and muscles faded, and she felt reborn, as though she'd woken from a nap that had lasted days. Every sense grew sharper, from her vision to her awareness of adani. She could trace the flow of the elder's adani without being in contact with him.

She opened her eyes and breathed easily. Karla had returned to her feet and was watching her with the expression of someone who'd just been proven right.

The stone pulsed brightly in her hand. She wanted to run, to skip, to jump, to take Aldrick somewhere private and make love to him all night. She wanted to take the stone and wrap it tight around her skin so that she was never again without this strength.

"Try a weaving," Karla suggested. "Perhaps see how many of those orbs you can create now."

It sounded like an excellent idea, and Samora began at once. She formed a dozen, each tied with more adani than she'd ever attempted before. The dozen barely required any effort, any thought or concentration from her at all, and so she made another dozen, and then another.

Samora followed the dozens of orbs, lost in the intricate beauty of so many weavings.

Karla's voice brought her back to herself. "I think you should let go," she said.

Samora obeyed, though she wanted nothing more than to hold them and dance with adani for as long as she could.

There was so much more she could do. She only needed the time to figure out how.

Finally, she released her weaves, which unraveled into bright threads of light that quickly dissipated into the air.

"And you should let go of the stone," Karla said.

Samora clutched to it tighter.

"You've proven, beyond a doubt, what you're capable of, but we need you back," Karla said.

What was she talking about? Samora was right here. If she let go, the dragon might never let her touch the stone again.

Karla stepped over to her and gently pried her fingers away from the stone. Samora resisted for a moment, but she trusted Karla, and a moment later her hands opened, and the stone floated out of reach.

The adani in her body didn't suddenly crash, though. It continued to circulate through her channels, an amount even a dragon would have been jealous of. It faded, but slowly.

It was only then she noticed the elder, which had retreated from both her and Karla. The menacing elder looked more like a scared snake than a majestic dragon.

"What?" Samora asked.

"Do you have any idea what that felt like?" Karla asked.

Samora remembered the strength well enough, but it hadn't seemed like all that much to her. A bit more than a dragon's, perhaps.

Karla turned to the dragon, a self-satisfied look on her face. "What do you think now? How did that compare to a Vada?"

The dragon twisted and writhed, shifting one direction and then another, before finally settling down. *It's not equivalent, but it's the closest I've ever sensed.*

The elder resumed his frantic movements. *If there was another, perhaps, just perhaps.*

Samora looked at Karla. "You could hold on to the stone, too. Was my effort so much greater than yours?"

Karla's face was pale from her recent battle with the heart, but she nodded. "It was. But I'll do everything I can to match your skill."

"After a break," Samora said. She looked over at the dragon, still twisting around as though it had been wounded. "I think all of us could use one."

"Agreed," Karla said.

Both women bowed deeply to the elder, then made their way out of the cave. Samora paid little attention to the brief journey. Adani still filled her channels, making her feel as though she could climb the highest mountain peak with strength left to spare.

They met with Aldrick, who had taken shelter from the sun in the shade of a large boulder. "What happened in there?" he asked.

Samora let Karla tell the story, as she was still too distracted by the power coursing through her limbs to stitch sentences into coherent thoughts.

Karla was just finishing her retelling when they felt the elder stirring within the cave. Karla trailed off as the elder suddenly approached. In all the time they'd been present, he had never moved from the deepest recesses of the cave. A moment later, his head emerged and rose high above them.

Seeing the elder's head, outside and in the sunlight, made Samora realize just how large the elder was.

He extended his adani, and Samora and Karla linked with it.

Their environment didn't change, but the man with the golden eyes appeared before them. "We have trouble," he said.

"What?" Karla asked.

"I cannot be sure why, though I suspect it's because of what Samora just accomplished. The Vada is on the move after weeks of waiting, and it's coming this way, fast."

🦋 20 🦋

E lian and the others hadn't made it more than a few houses
further when a building ahead of them crashed down in a
storm of timber and stone. Otsoa leaped over the fresh rubble
and turned toward the cluster of adanists. For their trouble, they
were welcomed with more than a dozen golden spears. The
adanists aimed true, and only two of the monsters survived the
first wave. The survivors barely made it halfway to the adanists
before a second wave brought them down.

Royzen ordered the group south to avoid the rubble and the
Moka that had created it.

Elian's worst fears about fighting in the village were coming
true. He had no line of sight, and given that he couldn't sense the
Debru, they could attack him with very little warning. If he were
stranded, he didn't know how long he'd last.

The group dodged over one street south and Royzen looked
west. He shook his head at the sight, then continued south. A
moment later, Elian passed the street and saw what had disappointed Royzen. The street leading west was already blocked by
the rubble of destroyed buildings.

Tassan leaned over. "They're blocking us in, guiding us to where they want us to go."

Elian nodded.

"Can't say I like it. Their attacks aren't usually so clever, even when they're guided by Moka. They'd usually rather hit us with everything at once than make us dance around like this."

Elian agreed, and though he couldn't be sure, he suspected the Vada's influence behind the sudden shift in strategy. At the moment, though, it didn't matter why. They were trapped. The Scorpions had built their walls, thinking that somehow a wall would save them, protect them from the horror of the world outside. Those walls had bought them peace for a time, but now the bill for that peace was coming due.

Elian couldn't sense the Debru closing in, but he could understand the expressions on the others' faces easily enough. The enemy was squeezing them tighter even than the stone walls.

Humans didn't belong in villages, not like this. The wandering clans, the true wandering clans, knew better. Abandon the illusion of safety. Stay away from crowds. Live free, so the question of where you lay your head at night was an open one.

This, this wasn't living.

Finally, Royzen found an intersection that led west. They headed up the hill, almost at a run. Eventually they'd have to turn north again, as they'd gone too far south and traveled past the western gate, but for now they rushed for every bit of elevation they could attain.

They hadn't made it more than two streets when Royzen stopped. Elian couldn't see anything, but one adanist after the other formed spears and shields.

Tassan told him what he'd already guessed for himself. "They've got us surrounded. Up ahead is a square, where they were probably hoping to funnel us into. Royzen isn't fool enough to go there, but there's nowhere else to go."

A stiff wind blew up the valley, and the village was as quiet as the empty plains of Elian's youth. Were they the only survivors? Elian asked Tassan.

"No. Many have escaped past the western gate and are waiting for us. The Moka have singled us out, though. All their forces are here."

Tassan had barely finished when Royzen drew the sword that had waited so patiently at his hip. The stone in the pommel caught a ray of light from the moon and flashed over them.

The stone walls of the nearby buildings leaned over Elian, threatening to crush him beneath their massive, unyielding weight. He imagined the rooftops sagged under the weight of the Debru that remained just out of sight.

"There has to be a better place for us to fight," he said.

Tassan grunted. "I can't sense what's that far ahead, but Royzen is no fool. If he believes this is our best battlefield, he's likely right."

Elian's palms were wet, and he wiped them off against his pants. "Tell me what you're sensing."

"Two Moka north and two south. Both command small contingents of Debru, but it's hard to say how many. There are too many otsoa around to sense them clearly."

"What are they waiting for? Why haven't they attacked?"

"The last Debru are taking their places behind us."

Elian growled. "We can't let them attack on their own terms. What do you say to taking the fight to them?"

Tassan's eyes searched the roofs for signs of shadow, then nodded. "Sounds better than staying here."

"Go high or stay low?"

"Stay low. The buildings hide the Debru from us, but they'll protect our advance, too."

Shouts echoed down the narrow passage from near the head of the column. Elian snapped his head around and saw a wave of snarling, snapping shadows crashing down the alley. Bound spears killed the leading otsoa, and a golden shield built between two buildings stopped the rest.

Tassan's eyes went to the sky, and he was one of a dozen adanists who wove shields above Royzen's war party. The shields flashed as soon as they were finished, struck by falling spears of shadow that blended in perfectly with the cloudy night sky. Despite the strength of the assault, the shields held, which immediately struck Elian as odd. If the Moka had launched the attack, they should have penetrated.

Just as he completed the thought, the building directly ahead of him and to his right exploded into the alley. Heavy chunks of granite crushed adanists beneath their weight while dust billowed up and down the passage, choking off the survivors' air.

The dust swirled with shadows. Otsoa and Debru alike poured through the space where the building had once stood, heedless of the rubble shifting underneath their feet. One otsoa caught the throat of an adanist as she returned to her feet, yanking her back to the ground.

Elian drew his sword in time to cut down another otsoa that had similar plans for him. A Debru stumbled after the otsoa, one of its ankles dragging along at an awkward angle. It met the edge of Elian's blade and dropped without a sound.

Elian was so distracted by the destruction and death ahead of him, he almost missed the real danger.

"Above us!" Tassan shouted.

Elian took a step back and looked up in time to see a Moka standing on the edge of a roof, its arm raised high above its head and a shadow spear in hand.

Tassan and one of Royzen's adanists weaved a shield above them as the Moka hurled its deadly spear. The shadow punched through the other adanist's shield without slowing, but it found Tassan's strength more challenging.

The two forces battled above Elian's head, giving those below enough time to scatter away from the spear's path. Tassan's strength held a moment longer, then the spear cracked through his shield and struck the path below. The impact threw up dust and stone, but no one suffered more than scratches and bruises.

Elian leaped to the rooftop to meet the Moka. It threw another spear, which he batted away. Its red eyes glowed brighter.

For the briefest of moments, Elian was a child again, standing within his mother's protective shield as Father battled the Moka that attacked their home. Ice formed in his limbs, but it couldn't last against the adani roaring through his channels. He struck at the Moka, but his sword met its shadowy compatriot, and was finally stopped. Elian pushed, hoping to break the Moka's guard through force alone, but the physical strength of the monster overwhelmed him.

They passed once, then twice, and when they disengaged, Elian sported two fresh cuts across his arms. Neither was deep, but the Moka was so far unharmed.

Elian forced his adani into tighter loops, pushing it harder than he had in any battle since the fight for Samora's gathering ground. He launched himself at the Moka again, which seemed content to duel him with swords alone.

It wasn't prepared for his additional strength. Elian's first cut broke the Moka's guard, and the second took its life.

The Debru below, under the Moka's command, went mad when their commander died. Only Tassan's shields kept the adanists alive long enough for Elian to arrive and kill the three deranged Debru.

The pair's efforts bought the adanists at the rear of the column a small amount of time to gather themselves and catch their breath. Dust from the collapsed building still hung in the air ahead of them, though, and Elian didn't like what he heard. Stone cracked as shadow and adani burst against it. Men and women screamed and shouted as they fought, and far too often those sounds were cut off too soon.

"How bad is it?" Elian asked Tassan.

"The three remaining Moka are all on the other side of the collapse. They're making quick work of the surviving adanists."

Elian started forward, but Tassan grabbed his arm. "Call me a coward if you will, but those adanists are as good as dead. The Moka are ignoring us for now, and there is an open path to the gate. Consider saving yourself."

"Not while Royzen and the others are still in danger." Elian tried to pull away, but Tassan's grip on his wrist was tight.

"Respectfully, you're not thinking. We came here to recruit the Scorpions, but they're as good as gone. Even if you somehow save Royzen from three Moka, he can't contribute anything to your cause. I've never seen anyone slay Debru with such ease, and I'd be a fool to let you charge in there."

Tassan stared deep into his eyes, then, convinced his words had been heard, let go of Elian's wrist.

Elian stood, rooted in place, and weighed Tassan's words. Logically, the giant was right.

But he couldn't turn his back.

He snapped the Debru blood off his blade. "Lead the others to safety. I'll join you if I can."

Before Tassan could object, Elian strode into the dust. He picked his way carefully over the rubble, but it didn't take long to reach the other side.

He was almost too late.

The tight width of the alley made the numbers seem greater than they were, but a horde of otsoa and Debru snarled and clawed at a small circle of adanists who fought back-to-back. Royzen stood tall in the center of the circle, weaving a shield around the warriors that kept them safe from the brunt of the attacks.

Otsoa and Debru battered at the shield, and at times, it flickered and fell, but when it did, Royzen would roar and weave another. The Scorpion leader's strength didn't rival Tassan's, but he was an impressive warrior all the same. Blood fell freely from his nose and dripped down his tunic as he dug to the depths of his spirit for more adani.

The sight gave Elian pause. He'd seen too many final stands in the past year, but there was something about this one that cut deeper than the rest. Shadow surrounded the Scorpion leader, and he had no expectation of escape, but Royzen's spirit illuminated the length of the alley.

Dark shadows with red eyes moved above, and Elian saw the Moka watching the destruction of the Scorpions with smug satisfaction.

Even if he could take on all three Moka, the Debru and the otsoa were the more immediate threat. He gripped his sword and charged the horde. He sliced through several of the otsoa before they realized the danger behind them, and then he was overwhelmed.

Debru and otsoa turned as one and he faced a wall of teeth and claw. He gave up the little ground he'd won, but an otsoa still got past his defense. Just before it locked its jaws around his sword arm, a spear of adani took it in the side.

Tassan shouted and unleashed a barrage of small spears. Otsoa fell one after the other, and several Debru flinched as the spears broke through their hastily constructed shields.

Elian charged into the opening, successfully breaking through to the remaining Scorpions. Royzen and the others redoubled their efforts, and the ring of Debru cracked open.

The Moka stepped in. As they formed their spears of shadow, Royzen ordered his adanists to run. Elian led the charge west, his sword clearing a path for the others to follow. Adani flashed to both sides of him as Tassan and the other adanists aided their escape.

They almost made it to the intersection when the Moka released their spears. Buildings collapsed as their foundations were destroyed. Adanists threw up shields to protect themselves and guide the debris, but when the dust cleared, they were trapped within a ring of rubble.

More Moka spears followed the first wave, and the combined defense of the adanists did little to slow them down. Elian narrowly dodged one meant for his heart, but the force of the blast behind him knocked him down on his face. By the time he reached his feet, the battle was as good as over. Tassan and two other adanists still stood, but the spears had decimated the rest of the party.

Elian searched for Royzen and found him lying nearby. He was on his back, staring up at the cloudy sky as though he could see the stars beyond. A Moka spear had taken one of his legs clean off, and judging from the amount of blood he'd already lost, he wasn't long for this world. Elian rushed to his side.

Down the alley, the Moka formed another set of spears and Tassan and the others formed a desperate shield. It would do no good, and Elian cursed his own foolishness. He'd escaped death so many times he'd started to take it for granted.

"I'm sorry I couldn't do more," he told Royzen.

"You still can," Royzen said.

With a strong motion, which should have been impossible given his injuries, he pulled his sword and sheath from his belt and held it toward Elian. The stone embedded in the hilt glowed as it neared Elian, and Elian flinched away.

Royzen thrust the sword at him. "Take it. I'm starting to think that I was only its steward until you arrived."

Elian gulped, but the Moka were about to throw their spears and kill them all anyway, so what did it matter if he died a moment earlier? He took the sword in his hands and his world went white.

He'd felt the immense reserves of adani hidden deep within dragon's bodies, and he'd basked in the life-giving strength of the gathering grounds. Neither prepared him for the sword's adani. It traveled through the hilt into his hand and looped through his channels like a raging river. He surrendered his body to the stone, and when he opened his eyes, the world was new.

He saw with both adani and sight, a tremendous blur of color and shadow his mind needed a moment to decipher. Once it did, though, he could see the Moka as clear as day and see the Debru coming from further east.

The Moka flung their spears, but Elian leaped in front of Tassan and the others and batted aside the two meant for them. He leaped to the top of the nearest roof with the ease of taking a single step up a stairwell, then cut through the Moka guarding it before it could react to his presence.

The other two Moka fled, seeking the relative safety of the other Debru and the otsoa. Elian watched them go, then returned to Tassan and the others.

Tassan was shaking his head. "Just when I thought I'd seen everything."

"You haven't seen anything yet," Elian said.

He passed Tassan and knelt beside Royzen. Even with the strength flowing through his body, he lacked the skill and knowledge to heal the Scorpion leader. "Is there anything I can do for you?"

"For me? No. I've lived to see the fulfilment of a prophecy I never believed in, and that's more than enough. Save what's left of my clan. Have them join you in this fight so that someday, we can return and rebuild. The sword and the stone are both yours. Use them well."

Elian bowed until his forehead touched the stone, and when he rose, Royzen's gaze stared at nothing in particular. Through his dual vision, Elian saw that adani no longer flowed in him.

❧ 21 ❧

"How long do we have?" Karla asked the elder.

The dragon looked to the sky, where the sun stood near its highest point. "It will be here before the end of the day."

Samora remembered how long it had taken her and the others to get here. The Vada was starting from almost the same place but would arrive three times faster. How?

"Can we fight it? You and I, working together?" Samora asked.

For a long time, the dragon was silent, and then he said, "I do not think so, no."

"Then we have to flee."

Again, the dragon was silent, this time longer than before.

Samora turned to Karla. "We have to flee, don't we?"

Karla's face was hard, matching the expression on the elder's mask.

"What am I not understanding?" Samora asked.

Karla answered for them both. "Unless the dragons can fly much faster than we've seen, there's no point. The Vada will catch us, regardless."

Samora cursed her own foolishness. No wonder both Karla

and the elder looked as though someone had sentenced them both to death.

Her thoughts raced. If they couldn't fight and couldn't run, what remained?

Her answer would have made Elian proud. When there was no hope, there was nothing left but to fight. Better a death on her feet with some slight chance of success than a certain failure.

"We'll fight," she declared. "Until it arrives, we can continue training. If I can have Karla ready by then, perhaps we have a chance."

"No," the dragon said.

"Why not?" Samora asked.

"As much as I admire your misguided courage, it would squander the one opportunity we have to defeat the Vada. You need to escape, and you need to find someone else with the power to use the hearts."

"I will not leave you to die," Samora said.

"Then you'll be rendered unconscious and taken away. This is the way it will be, and I will hear no other option."

Karla interjected before the two could continue arguing. "What's your plan?"

"I will send as many of my children away as I dare. If my suspicion is correct, the Vada comes for me and for Samora. The children will flee to all the corners of the world, so there will be no point in the Vada chasing them all. Both of you will be on one dragon, and you will both promise not to touch a drop of adani."

"Why?" Samora asked.

"Have you listened to anything? The Debru, and the Vada particularly, are masters of sensing adani. If you use it, and especially if you use it with the heart, you'll attract the Vada again."

"So, you can't use your strength again until you're ready to battle the Vada," Karla clarified.

Samora shot her an angry glare. It was about as effective as angry glares always were against Karla, which was to say not at all. Karla's attention was solely on the elder. "May we have the hearts?"

"When you leave, you'll have them all. There is no point in them staying here, where the Vada will acquire them."

"Isn't there another way? We can't lose you now, not with everything we still have to learn," Samora said.

"Before you leave, I'll pass my memories on to my children. Several have been prepared to receive them, and in this case, it seems best to spread the knowledge wide. There is nothing more for you to do here. Gather your things and prepare to leave. There is much for me to do."

The elder broke the connection, causing his human double to instantly vanish, then hurried its sinuous body back into the cave, leaving Samora and Karla behind.

Samora stared at the mouth of the cave. Her spirit felt as hollowed out as the elder's home, cold and empty.

Karla noticed her distress and stepped closer.

Samora dug her nails into her palms. "Every time we learn something new, the Debru knock us down again. We found the wandering clans, only for them to be assaulted like never before. We used the gathering grounds, only to have them destroyed by the Debru. And now we've finally spoken with the elder dragon, and the Vada comes for him, too. When will they stop taking everything away?"

Samora had hoped for sympathy and understanding, but Karla's answer was cold. "When we kill them all. The sooner you understand that the safer we'll be."

The words landed like a slap across the face, and Karla did nothing to soften the blow. "I'll return to the camp and pack. If you want to train with the hearts, your only time is now, because once we leave, we'll have to hide."

Karla grabbed Aldrick by the shoulder and pulled him after her. "Come on. Samora's got her own work to do. We need to leave her alone."

SPHERES OF BOUND adani danced above Samora's head. In number and in strength, they were greater than she'd ever bound before, but the accomplishment did nothing to fill the emptiness that lingered in her chest.

She released the weaves, and the spheres deteriorated, unravelling into glowing strings of adani that floated upward and faded to nothing.

You've grown comfortable manipulating the hearts' adani, the elder said, and Samora bowed in acknowledgment.

When Samora had returned to the cave, he had offered to join his adani to hers, and Samora hadn't dared refuse. Though linked, the elder had left her alone as he prepared for battle. The link was like having another presence in the back of her mind, an occasional voice that wasn't hers. The elder didn't bother with creating illusions, but now addressed her thoughts.

She couldn't sense much from the connection, but the presence within her was active. He spoke with the other dragons nearby, and while she trained with the heart of the village by the sea, he unraveled the bindings securing the other hearts to the ceiling. His actions were calm and methodical, unhurried even as the Vada raced to kill them.

Samora allowed herself little distraction. She would have rather sat and observed the elder, but if this was her only opportunity to train with the hearts, there was no time. Fortunately, as the elder had observed, the training had gone well. It was less that she had to teach herself a new technique and more that she had to let go of the idea of control.

She couldn't control a heart of adani anymore than she could control the feelings of a human heart. All she could do was open herself to its strength and guide it on its way.

Once she understood that, the hearts were hers.

You still don't bind any weapons. Not the spears your generation prefers, nor any of the multitude you've learned from my own memories.

Samora raised her hand in the air and guided the adani into the shape of a spear. A shiver ran down her arm and to the base of her spine when it settled into her hand. Even Harald would never have imagined a spear like this was possible.

"It's not that I can't. The weaves are simple enough. I choose not to."

Because you detest violence?

Samora felt the weight of the spear, far lighter than one made of wood, but far more deadly. She allowed it to unravel. "No. I am not so naïve. Life and violence are inextricable. I am against suffering and needless death. Were it somehow possible, I'd much rather live alongside my enemy in peace than spill each other's blood. I've only become more convinced of that since learning what the Debru are."

The elder stopped his work on one of the remaining hearts and turned his full attention to her. *That surprises me. There isn't a single Debru that shares your mercy or your sentiments. They will kill you, every time and with every opportunity afforded to them.*

"I know. Do you know that my brother, Elian, was once infected by shadow?"

If the elder had been attentive before, now he was focused. *I did not. What happened?*

Samora told the story, ending with Elian fighting against the shadow's influence and dropping the knife. "I don't think he's truly forgiven himself for that day. We caught it early and purged it from his body, but I've seen firsthand how shadow finds all the slight flaws that make us human and magnifies them until we're turned into monsters. I don't disagree that there's no bargaining with the Debru, but I can't help but think that underneath it all, there are still humans who regret the monstrosities they've become."

Your kindness is a dangerous weakness.

"So Karla keeps telling me, but I'd be much more afraid of me without it."

I fear that if you are to be of any help against the Debru, you'll need to resolve this conflict that divides you.

The elder left her be at that, and Samora was grateful. She practiced a few more techniques, and then it was time.

My children are gathered outside for the sharing of memories. Would you care to join us?

Samora didn't have to be told how unique of a position she was in. If she knew one fact for certain about the dragons, it was their natural secrecy. She bowed low. "I'd be honored."

She and the elder exited the cave together, and Samora wondered if it was the first time human and elder had left the elder's home beside one another. Outside, the sun promised a glorious end to the day. The snow-capped mountain tops shone with reflected glory, and only a handful of small, puffy clouds braved the sun's displeasure. Five dragons waited in the clearing outside the elder's cave. They'd arranged themselves in a small circle, and waited silently for the elder to arrive.

Samora stepped off to the side. Her link with the elder hadn't been cut off, allowing her incredible access to the very heart of the ceremony. The elder joined the circle, taking the empty place left open for him. Even the breeze fell silent, as though the entire world waited with breath held tightly to see what would happen next.

The elder spoke to his children using adani and the links between them as the medium. Though Samora possessed a window into the conversation, she couldn't understand all that was being said. It was as though she was listening to a new language in which she only knew a few basic words.

The gist, though, was that the elder was honored to have the others assuming his memories. When the elder finished speaking, the dragons all bowed their heads to the ground.

She couldn't draw a comparison to anything else she'd seen in her life. Though the end of the day, and the Vada's arrival, rapidly approached, there was no haste in the dragons' actions. Some small part of her wanted to yell at them that this was no time for ceremony, but as she watched them, she wondered if she wasn't wrong, if perhaps the best time for ceremony was in the most dire of circumstances. She couldn't tear her eyes away.

The elder dipped his head toward the dragon on his immediate left, the movement mirrored by the other dragon. It looked to Samora's human gaze like something between a bow and a kiss, though it was clearly something much more than either. He repeated the process with each other dragon, each approach both intimate and noble. When the elder completed the circle, he leaned his head toward the center. The other five followed, extending their heads until all six were nearly touching.

The physical aspect of the ceremony paled compared to the flow of adani between the participants. Amid all the bowing and touching, the elder weaved a complex net of adani, linking him tightly to his children. When all the dragon heads stilled, the net lit up, blinding Samora's senses.

She couldn't understand anything through her own adani, but her link with the elder gave her a glimpse of the process. Memories weren't just shown, they were shared. They became, in some very real sense, the memories of the recipient, as real as the ones they'd lived through in their biological lives.

The extent of the memories left Samora speechless. Of course, the dragons were long-lived, and the elders the longest lived of them all, but there was more history within the elder than in Samora's wildest imaginings. She watched and tried to catch every glimpse she could, oblivious to the sun's hurried race toward the horizon.

The last memories shared were those of Samora and the last few days in the cave, and then the net was lifted, and the six incredible minds separated. The elder spoke again, his speech too draconic for Samora to understand at all. Then the six broke apart, and one of the newly minted elders joined the original elder in speaking to Samora.

This is no longer my child, but an elder. She will take you away from here now.

"I'll collect my friends, and then we can be off," Samora said. She had seen no sign of either Karla or Aldrick since she'd emerged from the cave.

They have already been summoned and will be here momentarily. I would share a few last words with you.

"Of course," Samora said.

You have often confessed you do not understand the Debru, their reasonings or their motivations. I trust you've found your answers?

"Some of them. Thanks to you, I understand the Debru's purpose, but I'll confess their tactics still confuse me."

The elder looked to the northeast, where the Vada would soon be seen. *You are not alone in this. Of all the times the Debru have invaded, this one has left us with the most questions. Despite the Vada's overwhelming power, the total number of Debru that have come through the circle is far less than we expected. Perhaps part of the solution to the Debru problem is understanding why.*

Samora bowed. "Thank you. I will strive to learn what I can."

More important than that, though, is you must understand there is no other way to save humanity than to kill the Debru.

Samora swallowed the lump that formed in her throat. "Please don't take this answer lightly, for I don't give it lightly, but of this, I still haven't convinced my heart. I still wish there was another way."

And so long as you continue to believe that, both humanity and dragons are doomed. It isn't a matter of whether anything human still lurks under that twisted, dark flesh. It's about what they are. Wherever they go, they devour adani, the very force that keeps this planet alive. You speak about wanting to live peacefully next to your enemy, but there is no way to live peacefully next to one whose very presence kills everything it touches.

Samora stared at her feet. She didn't disagree. Every word the elder spoke was true, but it didn't change her desire for a more peaceful resolution.

Your sentiment is noble, and one of the qualities that makes humanity great, the elder said.

Samora looked up. The elder rarely said anything complementary about humanity.

I've lived a long time, and fought the Debru for more years than I care to count, and there's a pattern I've noticed. Can you guess what it is?

Samora couldn't.

It's that humans always build. You've seen the cities of your ancestors, but it's true of you as well. Generations ago, even after we'd taken so much from you, you split into groups, into those who would develop the soil and build homes that lasted, and those who would protect the builders. Given enough time, you'll also build cities. There's something within you that pushes you forward, that forces you to create. It's why adani favors you, and why our hope lies in you. The Debru don't build. Even we dragons don't. These caves were carved for us by your distant ancestors. Only humans create. All the Debru know how to do is to destroy, and they'll continue destroying until they're stopped.

Samora took a deep breath to respond, but the elder cut her off. Karla and Aldrick appeared, carrying three packs between the two of them.

Time grows short, and you must be off before the Vada arrives. Hurry and collect the hearts, then be off.

It was too soon, but when Samora looked as the sun neared the horizon, she realized it might almost be too late. The Vada would be here soon. She borrowed a small sack from Karla, then ran into the cave, where dozens of hearts had been left in a glowing pile. Seeing them on the floor stole some of the majesty from them, but Samora scooped them into the sack as quickly as she could. The one she'd been training with, though, she put in her pocket.

She ran back out. Karla and Aldrick were already on the newly created elder's back.

You must hurry, the elder said.

"I don't know how to thank you for all you've done, and for what you're about to do."

Yes, you do. Kill the Debru. Rid this world of them once and for all and build something incredible after.

A sudden stone in her throat choked off her words. She nodded, then bowed deeply. The bow was returned.

Go now.

The words gave Samora the final boost she needed, and she climbed on the new elder's back. As soon as she was positioned, the dragon rose into the air, and they left the home of the dragons behind for good.

22

Tassan led the survivors through the empty streets of the Scorpion village. Everyone else was dead or had escaped, and Elian hoped there were far more of the latter than the former. The bloodstained streets and shattered doors didn't inspire much confidence, though.

The remainder of their retreat was undisturbed. Tassan looked west often, but it was more a curious gaze than one of alarm. Elian assumed Tassan would tell him if the Moka approached again.

His thoughts were elsewhere, focused on the sword that now swung at his hip. He'd placed Royzen's sword on his left, then moved his old sword from Harald to his right. Harald's sword carried more personal value, but Royzen's promised him victory against opponents he had little chance against otherwise.

So long as he didn't touch the hilt, there was no connection between him and the sword, and so long as he kept adani tightly focused in his core, the stone didn't glow. It was an extra annoyance, but he hoped that in time he'd grow used to keeping his adani on a tighter leash.

Or perhaps he'd simply walk around, lighting his surroundings everywhere he went.

What else could he do with the sword? The Moka had proved no challenge for its strength. Could he fight a Belog, or even the Vada? He licked his lips at the thought, then shook his head. No matter how strong the sword made him, the Vada would never let him close. With its power, it could tear Elian to shreds from half a mile away.

They passed through the eastern gate of the village and into the fields beyond. The dragon waited in the field, looking for all the world like it had just woken up from a long nap. Apparently, the danger had never spread this far east.

Fortunately, the dragon wasn't alone. Well over a hundred Scorpions waited in the fields, their combined breath rising as a cloud over the assembly. Many were mothers and children, but there were a fair number of adanists as well. Elian's appearance raised a cry of alarm, and one of the adanists standing guard rushed to them and asked for news.

Thankfully, one of Royzen's personal guards told the story on Elian's behalf. Word of Royzen's death shook the other adanist, but he maintained enough composure to bow toward Elian. "What now?"

Elian had been too focused on the sword and cursed his lack of foresight. He hadn't thought enough about their plans. "I understand there's a back way off this mountain," he said.

The adanist who'd been guarding the assembly paled. "There is, but if there's any other way, I'd advise against it. The trail has eroded to almost nothing in places, and on a dark night like this, it'll be far too easy to slip and fall, even for those of us used to patrolling the mountains."

Elian glanced back at the village he'd just escaped from, the village that had claimed so many. "The only other way is back through there and down the main pass."

He turned to Tassan. "Can you sense the Moka?"

The giant shook his head. "Not clearly. They're west, and they're waiting, but I couldn't tell you any more."

"Going down that pass makes us awfully tempting targets," Elian said.

The guard from the assembly spoke up. "With all due respect, the same is even more true of the other trail. If the Moka catch us there, we'll have even less room to fight than on the main trail."

Either option sounded terrible. Elian looked between the dragon and Tassan.

"What?" Tassan asked.

"If we were riding on the dragon, do you think you'd have the strength to deflect a Moka spear?"

Tassan considered the question for a moment. "I think so. At least a few."

"Then we'll send everyone down the main path. You and I will fly with the dragon and keep ahead of the rest of the group. We'll clear the way, and if the Moka are foolish enough to stop us, we'll make them suffer."

Elian didn't miss the uncertain looks that passed between the guards and Tassan, but Elian didn't blame them. They'd fought for years, and in that time, had come to accept that certain facts were inevitably true. A single warrior could rarely take on a mere Debru. The Moka and the Belogs might as well be untouchable.

Elian's arrival changed all that, but it would take time for them to understand.

Once again, it was Royzen's guard who spoke up in favor of Elian. "Normally I'd call him mad, but he is the one that rode here on a dragon, and after Royzen was killed, he used the sword to strike down a Moka in a single blow. If anyone can do it, he can."

Tassan hesitated. "It's a risk."

"No more of one than any other option," Elian answered.

Tassan deliberated a moment more, then agreed. "Very well. Let's teach the Debru what a mistake they made today."

Royzen might have passed, but the training and discipline he'd taught to his adanists lived on. The Scorpion guards untangled their chain of command with impressive haste, and it wasn't long after that they were organizing the survivors into something resembling a disciplined column. Elian and Tassan walked together toward the dragon.

"It isn't just the Moka we need to worry about. There are still hundreds of otsoa and who knows how many Debru," Tassan said.

"True, but the other threats we can deal with. The battle will be won or lost over whether we can defeat the Moka."

"Are you actually as confident as you seem? I'll not deny I'm impressed by how you killed the Moka back in the village, but do you believe the others will fall so easily?"

Elian wrapped his hand around the hilt of Royzen's sword. Adani poured through him again, and no Moka could stand in his way. He nodded once. "I am."

"Good." Tassan walked a little taller, a slight spring in his step.

Elian noticed the changes, but made no comment. He'd seen similar reactions before.

Around Harald.

No matter how dire the situation, when Harald stepped onto the battlefield, attitudes shifted. Adanists on the verge of breaking found a deeper reserve they hadn't yet tapped. Debru, who had advanced without fear, paused and sometimes retreated.

When Harald stepped into a battle, it was as though he made a promise other adanists knew he'd keep. The same sort of unspoken promise Tassan believed Elian had just made.

Elian swore to himself that he would rather die than disappoint his friend and ally.

Elian connected with the dragon and explained what he wanted to do, and the dragon rumbled its approval. When the guards signaled they were ready to begin, Elian and Tassan climbed atop the dragon and took to the air.

They circled over the village first, where Tassan found and killed a handful of otsoa roaming the streets alone and in pairs. Once they were certain they'd cleared most of the threats, they waved to the guards that the village was safe to enter. The column began its journey west by entering through the gates they'd just fled from.

Elian watched the refugees with a heavy heart.

It was all too easy to imagine the Scorpion village as the village he grew up in, the refugees below as his mother, friends, and neighbors. This morning they'd woken up to a day like any other, protected by walls that had protected their grandparents. Now they walked through the bloody remains of their home, stripped, perhaps forever, of the safety they'd believed in every day of their lives.

Elian made a silent oath, wrapping another heavy cloak of responsibility over his shoulders. If it was in his power, he'd never let what happened here happen to another village.

They circled until the column had worked its way more than halfway through the ruined village, then worked their way further west. Tassan picked off more otsoa who wandered up and down the trail, but they spotted no real threat to the column.

"Do you think they're hiding in the bottom of the valley again?" Tassan asked once he killed the last of the otsoa on the trail.

"I'm almost certain of it."

They could have landed the dragon and let Tassan use adani to more easily spot any threats, but Elian judged the risk unnecessary. Simpler and safer to assume the Moka lay in wait, eager for the first opportunity to slay the rest of the refugees.

The column reached the main western gate, and Elian waved them forward. Near the rear of the column, at least two infants were crying while their mothers tried desperately to shush them. It was unnecessary, but Elian had no easy way of telling them. The column was no secret from the Moka.

The column pushed through the wide gate and snaked their way down the trail. The dragon followed them closely overhead, but at that moment the night was quiet. Scouts walking a little ahead of the main column kept a sharp watch for enemies. They poked the dead otsoa on the road with bound swords to ensure they were as dead as they seemed.

The Moka's attack came when the column reached a narrow and treacherous section of the trail, a place where sheer cliffs rose both above the path and below it. As with the wall they'd broken down earlier in the evening, the Moka formed two enormous shadow spears that hung in the air above the valley floor. Tassan and Elian spotted the spears at almost the same time, and the dragon banked to protect the column.

Tassan gathered his adani, boosted thanks to the strength of the dragon, and wove a shield just as the Moka threw their spears. The first spent its strength uselessly against the shield, and the second brought the shield down. But by the time it broke Tassan's weave, the adanists guarding the column had formed their own shield, and the spear had burned through enough shadow the adanists could defend against the remnant.

Elian directed the dragon to the floor of the valley, where another set of shadow spears was being weaved into existence. The ground beneath the forest canopy crawled with shadow, often punctuated by flashes of the otsoa's emerald eyes.

"I'm going down," Elian told Tassan.

"Are you mad?" Tassan asked.

"Protect me."

Elian gave Tassan no other opportunity to protest. The dragon spread its wings and bled off most of its speed, and Elian leaped off the dragon's back. As he dropped through the trees, he wrapped his left hand around the hilt of Royzen's sword and flooded his body with adani.

He hit the ground hard, but his legs bent with the impact and absorbed the incredible forces with little problem. He sprang forward toward the Moka. Two of the three were looking up to keep an eye on their weavings, but the third spotted Elian and formed a sword of shadow to defend the group.

Elian drew his sword and cut, golden light flashing in the deep darkness of the valley. Light and shadow collided. Royzen's sword bit into the shadow sword, but instead of allowing its sword to be unraveled, the Moka broke contact and retreated. Elian stepped into the opening and attacked again, but this Moka was fast and clever. It retreated before Elian's attacks but didn't allow him to turn to the two forming the spears.

A golden light from above solved Elian's problems. Tassan took aim at the gathering of Moka and sent down a spear of incredible strength. It forced the Moka defender to cast a shield, but it couldn't do that and protect itself at the same time. Elian caught it as it blocked Tassan's spear, and his sword sliced clean through. The shield of shadow dropped and Tassan's spear nearly took off an arm of one of the surviving Moka.

The combination of the sudden loss of their companion and the threat from above broke the Moka's will. Their second spears unraveled without being thrown, and they fled down a narrow trail that ran through the trees with twice the speed and grace of a deer being pursued by a hunter. Elian gave chase for a dozen steps, then stopped.

Everything in the valley floor fled west. Moka, otsoa, and Debru combined into a stampede for safer lands below, and Elian saw little point in pursuing them. Powerful as he and Tassan were, they could only do so much. He watched for a time to ensure the retreat was as genuine as it looked, then went searching for a clearing where the dragon could pick him up.

Before long, he was in the air again, and Tassan was promising to throw a celebration the likes Elian had never seen. He rambled on about Elian killing two Moka in one night, but Elian's thoughts were only for the column they protected from the sky.

Protecting them tonight was a start, but it wasn't nearly enough.

He wouldn't be satisfied until they were back in the village they called home, feeling as safe as they had before.

The only way that day would come about would be when all the Debru were dead, and with the sword at his side, Elian thought he might finally have the weapon to make his long-held dreams real.

23

Samora's connection with the elder didn't fade as they put incredible distance between the dragon's home and themselves. The elder, for she hadn't yet grown used to the idea there was now more than one, rested near the top of the mountain he had called his home for hundreds of years. He had settled in a clearing that welcomed the rays of the dying sun, and he watched the sunset with all the intensity of one who knew it would be their last.

Nearly twenty of his children remained behind with him, and none possessed his calm. They flew like arrows through the valleys, ready for battle. Together, they formed the strongest fighting force the dragons had assembled in this era of humanity. The children roared, eager and optimistic for the great battle to come.

The elder wasn't without hope, but it was a light dimmer than the setting sun. What hope remained was with the humans.

Twice, Samora's preoccupation with the events happening around the dragon's home almost caused her to slip from her dragon's back. Both times Aldrick had noticed before she fell, grabbing her in his strong arms and keeping her in place. She was grateful for his constant, silent support.

The third time, Karla expelled a lengthy combination of curses that burned Samora's ears. She had the right of it, though.

Through her connection with the dragon they rode upon, Samora asked if they were far enough away to stop flying for a time. The dragon wasn't particularly excited about fulfilling the request, but Samora insisted, and the dragon relented. She suspected it had simply been waiting for an excuse. Like Samora, she shared a connection with the elder and was concerned for those she'd left behind.

Karla also wasn't pleased by the idea they stop in the middle of their retreat, but she took one look at Samora's face and relented.

The dragon settled in the clearing of an alpine forest, coming to a gentle stop and allowing the humans to climb off her back. Samora thanked the dragon, then found a comfortable place in the grass to lay down. Karla and Aldrick stretched their legs and kept watch while she closed her eyes and focused on the connection with the elder.

The sun was halfway below the mountain peaks, and Samora felt the elder's contentment at the sight as though it was her own. Despite the doom that awaited in the near future, this moment was a good one. A perfect one.

His children roared as the Vada entered the lands the dragons called their own. Through his bond with them, he saw that it had taken on a new form, one that remained true to its human ancestry, with two legs and two arms, but now with added wings that allowed it to fly faster than any dragon. The wings were wide and leathery, a slightly smaller version of dragon wings.

His children were offended, for flight was the domain of dragons and birds, and now the Debru had polluted that as well.

The elder, fresh off his days with Samora, saw the innovation as a sign that something human still remained within the monsters. They always learned, always pushed themselves to new heights. And the Vada were so far ahead of the humans here. They hadn't been set back the way humans had.

They'd acted with the best of intentions, but he would never be certain of the decision they'd made that day. He couldn't see how it could have been any other way, but there was no doubt humanity could always surprise him. The last few days were proof enough of that.

His children didn't need his guidance. They attacked the Vada together, hurling their rudimentary spheres of adani one after the other. The heat in their blood stirred his own, and he raised himself from his resting position as the last sliver of the sun dipped below the mountains. Vivid pinks and reds were splashed across the bottom of the clouds, making the elder think of blood.

He summoned all the adani within his ancient body, circulating it through channels worn smooth by countless years of use. His heart beat faster than it had in years, and somewhere deep in his stomach, fear knotted his insides.

Curious. Even after all these years, that he should fear that which he'd come to accept so long ago.

He launched himself into the sky. Off in the distance, enormous waves of adani crashed against the Vada, which flew through them as though they were as insubstantial as clouds. The mountains shook under the force of the impact. To his north, the early season snow broke loose in a small avalanche that tore down a narrow valley.

The sound and the force stirred his blood like he hadn't felt since he was a youngling, and he roared with the anticipation for battle. His imminent arrival excited the dragons already engaged in battle, and they redoubled their efforts against the seemingly invincible Vada.

Sphere after sphere of adani crashed against the Vada,

surrounding it with destructive force. The Vada cloaked itself in swirling shadow and endured the assault like a parent enduring the tantrums of a group of children.

Still, the other dragons had locked it in place, creating a target too tempting for the elder to pass up. He chose for his weapon a binding he had learned from an adanist in humanity's previous era. The adani spear had much to recommend it, but it wasted a small amount of adani, and in this battle, that small amount might represent the difference between victory and defeat.

Sitting in a clearing far away, Samora sat up. The weaving she felt through the connection was very similar to her own, in which she bound adani into a tight sphere. Here, one side of the sphere was tightened to a point.

The closest description Samora could come up with was that of an arrowhead. The point of the weaving burned with focused adani, certainly more than she'd ever felt.

He put almost all his adani into the one attack, believing this strike would be the only one the Vada allowed. If he could have controlled more within the weave, he would have given that, too, but he was at the limit of his skill and strength.

The elder launched the arrowhead into the heart of the chaos. As adani, it passed through the other spheres, launched by the children, without pausing. It struck the swirling shadow, paused, and for a moment, the whole world held its breath.

The arrowhead punched through and struck the Vada square in the chest. The Vada staggered back, and then the shield of shadow healed and hid the Vada from sight.

Samora couldn't breathe. Had it worked? This last, final gamble by the elder?

The elder roared again, inspiring his children to yet greater heights. His blow had struck true, and if they ever had an opportunity, it was now. The Vada had to be at least wounded, and if they could finish it here, the future of the world might yet be bright.

He'd never been prouder of his children. They poured every bit of adani they possessed into the assault, and it felt as though the shield of shadow collapsed underneath the effort. The elder joined, creating lesser arrowheads with all the haste available to him, then launching them at the heart of the shadow.

The shield continued to shrink under the assault, more quickly now than before, and the dragons gave it their all. Rocks and snow fell from the mountains freely, and the elder couldn't hear anything beyond the roars of his children and the clash of incredible forces.

The shield of shadow shrank again, then transformed, turning into curved slivers of darkness, sharp enough to cut the shadow off a mosquito. The scythe-like blades exploded outward, each aimed with the care of an archer attempting to hit a fleeing deer.

His children never understood the danger they were in.

The blades of shadow moved almost faster than the eye could see, and each cut through a dragon as though they were grass. Each was aimed for the heart, and none missed.

The valley, filled with the triumphant roars of dragons just moments ago, went silent. His children fell from the sky, killed with all the concern a human might show when stepping on an ant.

The elder fell with them. No shadow had come for him, but his heart had been pierced just as surely as those of his children. He landed hard in the base of the valley, but he barely felt the impact against his armored skin. He stared at nothing in particular as his children came to rest in pieces around the valley.

The Vada floated down and landed no more than a dozen paces in front of him. On its chest, where the elder's first arrowhead had struck it, there was a small wound, no bigger than one made by the tip of a knife that broke the surface of the skin. A small trickle of blood leaked from it still.

A sphere of shadow covered the Vada, but it lasted for only a moment, and when it fell away, the Vada had changed its form.

No longer did it possess wings, and no longer did it resemble an adult human.

Samora shivered as she looked, through the connection, at what appeared to be a human child, maybe no more than eight or nine. There was no wound on its chest. Only its eyes betrayed the truth of the Vada's form. They were dark, cold, and ancient.

The elder reached out with adani, not to attack, but to speak, as it did with his children and with the humans. The Vada cocked its head to the side but made no effort to interfere with the elder's attempt. Adani stretched from elder to Vada, but when it came in contact, nothing happened. It ran across the Vada's body but found nothing to connect to.

The Vada smiled, baring its teeth in a feral grin. Another shiver ran down Samora's spine at the sight. The teeth were long and sharp, too big for the face that contained them.

Do you understand?

The question went to all the elder's children, but Samora knew it was aimed straight at her.

"I do."

There was no adani in the Vada anymore, and if there was no adani, there was no humanity. No human could live without it. She wondered if this was the reason why the elder had insisted they remain connected, so she could see firsthand what she refused to believe.

Good. Then run.

"No. I will not turn away, not after the honor you've shown me. I will witness. It is the least I can offer in return."

She felt the elder rumble his disapproval, but there was a note of pride there, too.

The elder let adani return to his body, then lashed out with everything he possessed. Samora received a moment's warning thanks to her connection, but the Vada must have had none. Dozens of arrowheads appeared in the air between the elder and the Vada and launched a moment after they appeared.

Shadow appeared between the Vada and the elder, but it was quickly lost behind the light and sound of the arrowheads exploding against the shield. The elder refused to relent, binding and throwing adani as fast as he could weave. Adani sought the heart of the Vada, and Samora swore she felt the ground rumbling underneath her feet miles and miles away.

The dragon gave everything in the attempt. He spent everything but the last drop of his adani, and when the smoke and dust cleared, when the ground stopped rumbling, the Vada stood unharmed.

But not without effort. Its shields had held and prevented any of the arrowheads from piercing its heart, but its chest was rising and falling rapidly, and it didn't stand as tall as it had moments ago.

There was no doubting its strength, but it had limits, too, and the elder had almost found them.

The elder collapsed onto the stone of the valley floor, lacking the strength to support his body any longer. His heart beat slowly and his eyelids were heavy.

The Vada recovered first and snarled, whipping his hand at the elder. A thin line of shadow tore across the valley and cut straight through the elder, slicing his heart and body into pieces.

Samora's connection snapped shut and she was in the clearing alone with the dragon. She sat there for a time, staring at nothing, feeling again like life had come and scooped out her insides. Eventually she stood, but the dragon didn't stir. Whatever she suffered, the dragon's must be many times worse.

Samora had lost an ally. The dragons had lost their father.

She knew all too well what that felt like.

She walked up to the dragon and pressed her hand against its side. They made no effort at connecting. Samora only wanted the dragon to know she was present, that the dragon wasn't alone.

"We'll have our revenge," she said.

The dragon stirred to life at the words, and Samora called for

Karla and Aldrick to return. Both knew, without having to be told, what had happened. Aldrick embraced her, and Karla offered a brief bow of sympathy that Samora returned. Then they climbed on the dragon, and she took to the air.

It was time for them to run.

24

E lian watched from the back of the dragon as the last of the column walked past him. The surviving Scorpions were a ragged bunch. Rain had fallen the morning after the attack, and the passage of so many feet had turned the path into a muddy, slippery, and at times dangerous, trek. Even now, two days later, mud coated the tops of boots and the backs of legs. Several of those who shuffled past him possessed distant stares that saw nothing except the promise of a better future.

The sympathetic part of Elian wished he could share their suffering, but his promise to Royzen meant that he spent little time walking beside them. He and Tassan spent most of their days and a substantial part of their nights atop the dragon, scouting far and wide for any sign of another Debru attack. The effort left him exhausted, but he didn't dare compare his suffering with that of the survivors. He'd lost nothing but a potential ally, and they'd lost nearly everything.

For all their scouting, Elian and Tassan hadn't found many threats. They'd killed perhaps a dozen otsoa alone and in pairs, but they hadn't stumbled across a pack yet. There were no Debru to be found, and the two Moka who had escaped Elian's blade might as well have turned into smoke and vanished. Even Loken, who walked beside the survivors, hadn't been able to sense them.

Not for the first time, Elian wished he had Samora by his side. She would have sensed the nature of the attack, and even if she hadn't, she might have been strong enough to save Royzen's life. For all the strength he'd acquired, he was so much stronger so long as they were together.

He let his thoughts drift toward his sister. He hoped that she was alive and far from danger, and he hoped that by the time he returned, she'd thought of some way to defeat the Vada. She better have experienced some success, because he'd accomplished next to nothing with his efforts.

The last of the column shuffled past and continued on their way south, to another, smaller village of Scorpions. Elian and Conor, the highest ranking surviving adanist of the village, had already flown ahead to announce the arrival of the refugees. Elian suspected the village was even now hurrying to prepare for the new arrivals.

The Scorpions' future wouldn't be easy. Hundreds remained, scattered throughout the mountains and in small villages in the valley, but the core of their strength had been wiped out in the attack on Royzen's village. Food and shelter would be problems that lingered, possibly until the next harvest almost a year from now. Elian protected them today from the Debru, but he could do next to nothing about all the challenges that their future held.

His sword was strong, but time and again, he was forced to admit the limits of what a sword could do.

Tassan had walked with the refugees during Elian's last scouting run, but he pulled away from the column now, his enormous form a head taller than anyone else, and more pronounced now because he was one of the few who walked with their head held high.

The giant stopped beside him. "You have the look of a man deep in thought."

"If only thoughts alone were worth something," Elian said.

"What's on your mind?"

"Besides everything? I was thinking that you have already done so much more than anyone could ask from you, and I should return you to your clan as soon as I can."

"There will be time enough, and I'm sure they don't mind having me gone that much. I'm glad that I joined you. I've done more good here than my entire clan has done in years. Not that I had any doubts about my decision before, but I'm even more certain now that joining you was the correct choice. The time has come to fight, eh?"

"Indeed."

"But what were you truly thinking? You are no woman, thinking constantly of how wonderful I am."

Elian cracked a grin for the first time in days. Like Harald, Tassan's attitude would likely be legendary long after the warrior was gone. He'd be jesting with a Belog's shadow spear sticking from his chest.

"Just that they are in for a rough time, and there's little I can think of to help them."

Tassan shook his head. "It's no good thinking like that."

"Because?"

"Because it does no honor to the Scorpions. They're one of the toughest clans that's ever wandered this world, and you're thinking of them like some child that needs to be protected from their night terrors."

"That seems like a bit of an exaggeration."

Tassan shook his head again, more adamantly this time. "But it's not. You've got a soft heart, and I suppose at times that serves you well, but the Scorpions are proud, even now, in their defeat. Has any one of them come to you and asked you, personally, for any help?"

Elian was certain the answer was yes, but as he searched his memories, he realized that he couldn't think of a single request.

He'd helped without being asked, but even the most emaciated survivor hadn't asked for so much as a sip from Elian's waterskin.

Tassan took his silence as answer enough. "The Debru have killed many of their strongest warriors and destroyed their home, but if you aren't careful, you might become guilty of something even worse. You might steal their last and most precious possession, their pride."

"That's foolish. I'm only trying to help, however I can."

"And that's good of you. But if you don't mind me saying, you're thinking like a villager, and you're thinking about them like they're villagers, too. They might have lived behind walls and built sturdy houses, but they're still Scorpions at heart, and I'd still take any one of them as an ally."

It still sounded foolish, but Elian had asked Tassan along in the first place because he understood the Scorpions better than almost anyone else. He'd be a fool if he simply ignored his advisor's freely given advice.

"I'll think about it. Thanks for letting me know."

"Eh, don't go thinking too much. It's not good for the digestion. But if you are thinking, what are you thinking we're going to do after we get the Scorpions to the village?"

"Return you to your clan, then return to mine. I've already been gone far longer than I planned, and I fear what might have happened in my absence."

"You won't stay for a bit longer?"

Elian sensed it was a test of some sort, but the answer was the same regardless. "No. As much as I want to, the Scorpions will need to be on their own. The fight for the future is to the south, and that's where I need to be."

Tassan grinned. "There might just be hope for you yet. That's what I'd do, too."

THEY REACHED the Scorpion village by mid-afternoon that day. Elian landed the dragon a safe distance away, then hopped off. He left his hand against the dragon's side and asked if the dragon would be able to fly them one more time today. The dragon's answer was slow in coming, but he agreed.

Elian bowed in thanks. Like Tassan, the dragon had done far more than Elian had expected from him. He had saved hundreds of lives, further confirming the inherent goodness of humanity's allies. Surely, when Samora heard what the dragon had done she'd agree.

Elian joined Tassan, who stood apart from the rest of the column. Conor and the village elders spoke rapidly to one another, and Tassan's advice from earlier in the day still echoed in Elian's ears. There was no place for him here, in the middle of the Scorpions.

The discussion ended quickly and the weary column was welcomed into the village with open arms. Adanists from the village had hunted and fished all morning, and the resulting game roasted over a handful of cook fires. Pots of stew and fresh bread emerged from a few of the houses, and all gathered in and around the village square. Too many bodies tried to squeeze in the suddenly crowded space, and more than a few villagers volun-teered to sit in the grass outside the square.

Elian, Tasan, and Loken only entered after Conor invited them to join. All three ate sparingly, though Elian's stomach rumbled at the scents of so much freshly cooked food. Many hosts shared blood bonds with the refugees, and groups quickly formed. The three adanists from outside the clan found a quiet corner and ate by themselves.

"Will you be ready to leave after the meal?" Elian asked Loken.

The healer nodded in between bites of bread. "There are no healings left that require my presence."

They finished their meal long before most, and Elian kept

glancing toward where he'd left the dragon. Tassan laughed at him. "We don't need to stay until the end of the meal, if you don't want."

"Seems rude to leave so early."

Tassan shrugged. "Somehow, I doubt they're going to worry too much about us. They have greater problems to solve."

Elian leaned back against the house which they ate beside. It had been too long since he'd truly felt at ease, and he supposed he shouldn't waste this opportunity. "We can wait. We're not in that much of a rush."

With the sun warm against his face and a soft breeze from the north keeping him from getting too hot, Elian closed his eyes and enjoyed the time. His companions rested next to him, and he didn't open his eyes again until someone stood in front of him and blocked his sun. He cracked open an eye. Conor stood before him, accompanied by a few other adanists from the village.

"Is something wrong?" Elian asked.

"Are you still planning on leaving soon?" Conor asked.

"I was going to wait until the meal was over, but then, yes, I was going to leave. It's been too long since I've been home."

"Then may we speak with you?"

Elian opened his other eye, stood up, and brushed his pants off. "Of course. How can I help?"

"You haven't asked any of us yet if we're going to join your clan in the battle against the Vada."

Elian sealed his lips before blurting out his impulsive answer, which was to say that they'd already done and suffered more than enough, and their duty was here, with the families that faced a difficult future. He weighed his words carefully, knowing that his behavior over the last few days had already revealed his true opinions, and that lying would only damage their pride worse.

"To tell you the truth, I hadn't asked because I know the challenges that face the Scorpions, and I didn't want to add more burdens than those you already carry. But I know it isn't my place to decide that for you, and I apologize that I've waited as long as I have. The Bears plan on bringing the fight to the Vada as soon as we have the necessary strength. I'd like to extend you and all the adanists of the Scorpions an invitation to join us. You'll have the farthest to travel, and I imagine Tassan here will be marching the Coyotes south as soon as he returns, so you'll have to move faster than him, but if there's a clan here that has the strength to answer such a call, I now know it's the Scorpions."

Conor's chest swelled and he stood a little straighter, though the expression on his face didn't change. "We'll be there. Likely before Tassan, unless I miss my guess."

Elian didn't let so much as a sliver of a doubt cross his expression. "I'd expect nothing less."

Conor pointed to the sword at Elian's left hip, and Elian's stomach knotted. It was the one other point of contention, and he didn't want to fight the Scorpions over it.

He needed it more than they did.

He needn't have worried. "Take care of the blade for us. We've seen it kill Moka, but we're not going to be satisfied until we see it take a Vada's life."

"I'll do all I can or die in the attempt."

Conor and the other adanists bowed deeply to Elian, but he matched their bow with one of equal depth. The adanists departed, and Elian saw no other reason to stay. He nudged Tassan, who lay in the shade with his eyes closed, with his boot. Tassan made an exaggerated yawn, followed by a stretch that would have done a traveling storyteller proud. "Did I miss anything?"

"Everything, as usual. But it's time for you to get up. Our work here is done, and there's not much reason for us to stay any longer."

Tassan maintained the act. "But we've just been laying here."

Elian ignored him. "Thank you, for what you said earlier. I was wrong, but you had the right of it."

"I usually do."

The grin on Tassan's face fell. "In all seriousness, though, you did well. As well as any leader of a clan I've ever known. Those Scorpions will follow you to the ends of the world now, and I can't say they'd be wrong in doing so. You listened, even when you disagreed with me, and that's an awfully rare trait these days. You keep doing that, and you'll make a believer out of me."

Loken said, "Tassan's right. I've heard about the fight with the Moka, but I'm even more impressed now. Nicely done."

Elian turned away from them, partly so they wouldn't catch a glimpse of the color rushing to his cheeks. "What we accomplished these last days was the easy part. Now we need to find a way to make all my promises mean something. We need to find a way to defeat the Vada."

25

The flight back north and east was a quiet one. Samora said little about what she'd witnessed through the elder's connection. Karla and Aldrick had guessed the outcome from her expression alone, and none of the details of the elder's death seemed to matter much. Their worst fears around the Vada's power were confirmed. What else did they need to know?

They flew through most of that first evening, the dragon opting to fly high above the mountains, hills, and rivers below. Dawn wasn't far off when they landed, and the dragon had only relented because Samora was coming close to falling asleep and tumbling off the dragon's back. The dragon found a clearing in the middle of a grove of tall elm trees growing beside a river and landed. Samora half-dismounted, half-fell off the dragon, stumbled maybe thirty paces, then lay down. She was asleep moments after she rested the back of her head against the ground.

She woke to Karla and Aldrick conversing in hushed tones closer to the river. She blinked her eyes a few times to clear the sleep from them, then sat up. The sun hadn't yet risen above the trees in the eastern sky, so she hadn't slept long, but she felt much more her old self than she had the night before.

She sat for a while and gave her thoughts a chance to catch up with everything that had happened since she'd woken up last.

The Vada was every bit as strong as the elder's memories had led her to believe. And as the elder had so conclusively proven with its efforts, no adani remained in the monster. Though it had once been human, it wasn't any longer.

Samora's thoughts turned to her brother. That same shadow had infected him once, thanks to the Debru circles. What would have become of him if she and Brittany hadn't been able to heal him with the massive amounts of adani they'd expended? Would he be like the Debru, or would he be one of them, heart and soul, eager to wipe away humanity's last defenses?

That line of thought chilled her to her core, so she set it aside. Instinctively, she reached down to send her adani far and wide, but she stopped herself as the tips of her fingers brushed the tips of the grass. If the elder had spoken true, the Vada would be searching for her, and even this small effort might be enough to give her position away. She pressed her hand into the ground but used it to help her stand and nothing else.

Karla and Aldrick had noticed her wake, but continued their conversation, so she went instead to the dragon resting near the edge of the clearing. The dragon stretched out adani toward her, just like the previous elder. Samora froze, transported back to the cave where she'd learned so much.

She shook the memory off and accepted the dragon's adani. The life-giving force connected them, and a moment later, a woman with golden eyes stood in the space between Samora and the dragon. She stood a head taller than Samora, with dark hair that hung loose all the way down to the small of her back. She looked down at her hands as though they were strangers.

"First time?" Samora asked.

The woman nodded, and it took her a few attempts before she spoke. "There are some techniques used only by the elder. This is one. I've never taken on the form of a human before, even as an illusion."

"Did you fashion the form?"

"No." The dragon searched for the correct words. "It–arose–I suppose is what you would say."

"Thank you for speaking with me like this. I feel much more comfortable speaking to you in this manner."

"You're welcome. What did you wish to speak about?"

"The previous elder made it clear I was not to use adani in any meaningful way after the battle, but I was hoping I might learn where both my people and the Vada are. Can you send out adani and inform me?"

"I can, but I do not know if it is wise. The Vada might find the act suspicious, and home in on us as his next target."

Samora considered the argument, then decided it was a good one. As much as she wanted to know, it wouldn't be long before she was back among her people. Once they reached the gathering ground, Karla would be able to reach a considerable distance without alerting the Vada.

"I'm sorry for your loss. If there's anything I can do to help the dragons, please ask."

"My only request is the same one my father made of you. Find a way to kill the Vada. Our hand has been forced, and now we put all our hope in you."

Samora's spirit trembled, but she refused to think about the weight the dragons rested on her shoulders. There would be time enough to deal with that once the dragon couldn't see clearly into her heart.

"Do you feel strong enough to fly us today?"

"I'll be ready whenever you are."

Samora thanked the dragon, trying to hide her disappointment at not knowing what was happening in the world at large. They separated their adani, and when Samora turned around she saw that Karla and Aldrick stood behind her. She jumped, then apologized. "I didn't know you were there."

Karla, never one for niceties under any circumstance, said, "We were wondering if it was wise for us to return to the clans."

"Why wouldn't we?"

"Because the Vada is searching for you, and by returning to the clans, you put them all in danger."

"They're already in danger. I'm not sure my presence matters much."

A look passed between the other two adanists, then Karla said, "Another concern is that with the Vada now on the move, it's possible the united clans will soon be under assault."

Karla paused, as though hoping Aldrick would continue, but he didn't. Given the looks passing between the two and Karla's obvious reluctance, it didn't take Samora long to understand what they were aiming at.

"You don't think we should help them," she said.

Karla stepped forward, hands out to placate. "Only until you can help me master the hearts. Once both you and I are capable, we can rush right there. I don't like the idea, either, but we're at the point where hard decisions need to be made. Staying away from the unified clans gives us the best opportunity to develop the skills we need. They give us the best chance at fighting the Vada."

The horrible thing was, Samora understood Karla's argument. If the argument alone was all that mattered, she might have even agreed with it. Some deep part of her even craved it. She was comfortable with Karla and Aldrick. When she thought about all the bickering and infighting she could avoid, it was almost too tempting.

But in the end, there was no choice.

"We go back."

Karla started to argue, but Samora cut her off. "I understand, truly. But we won't abandon one another. Not now. It would be better for humanity to perish than for us to turn our backs on one another."

Karla put her hands on her hips, and the two women stared at one another, neither backing down in the slightest. Finally, Karla tilted her head and acknowledged Samora's victory. "As you wish."

"Good. Then let's get packed up and leave. I expect a long day of flying today, and the dragon is ready when we are."

There was a flurry of activity around the camp, but it wasn't long before they were in the air again. Like the night before, the dragon chose to go high, soaring well above the level of the scattered clouds below. They made good time, and when they settled to camp for the night, the dragon announced they would arrive at the unified clans by the end of the next day.

Neither Karla nor Aldrick brought up the idea of staying apart from the unified clans again, and Samora was grateful for that. They ate quickly and fell asleep faster, and the next morning were up and flying again before the sun had risen over the eastern horizon. Samora watched the ground as it passed far below, her thoughts wandering even faster than the dragon could fly.

Before the sun had reached its peak, they reached the western deadlands, and the sight of the desert made Samora think of Elian and the trials he'd faced here. They were nowhere close to the Debru circle and the destroyed gathering ground, but Samora wondered if they shouldn't make a quick detour. After all, it was the circle the Vada had emerged from, and perhaps there would be some clue to its strength there.

It was a slim hope, though, and she dismissed it. She'd seen circles before, and there was nothing more to learn about them. She could close it, but that would be the equivalent of standing in front of the Vada and shouting for attention.

She sat bolt upright.

"What?" Karla asked.

"All the questions we've been asking about the Vada. Like why they haven't sent more warriors. I think I know a way we might answer them."

"And how's that?"

"I need to visit the Debru circle."

Karla looked as though she'd swallowed something sour. "You've done that before, though, haven't you? If memory serves, it almost killed you, and it poisoned your brother with shadow."

"All true, but it also acted as a gate, not for my body, but for my spirit. I've been thinking about what I saw now that the elder told us who and what the Debru are. There's no doubt in my mind I saw a vision of the other world. If I return to the circle, perhaps I'll learn something more useful about the Debru."

"But what about the shadow? You can't use your adani to fight it."

"There's no need for me to fight it. I only need to survive."

Aldrick interrupted the argument. "It sounds like you have a plan."

"I'll step into the very edge of the circle, then tempt the shadow with the barest adani. Once it attacks, I'll let it surround me, and if it acts like it has in the past, I'll have a vision of the other world. You two will remain just on the other edge of the circle, and you can pull me out before it's too late."

"Why not send me instead?" Karla asked.

"I've done it before and know what to expect. In the worst case, I also have the control over adani necessary to attack the circle directly. It's better if it's me."

Karla weighed Samora's arguments, then shook her head. "I don't think you should. It's too much risk for too little gain."

"If it were up to you, you'd hide me in some quiet corner of the world and keep me safe until there was no one left to protect," Samora snapped.

"You're the only weapon we have! We can't afford to waste you."

"But I'm not yet strong enough, and I won't get any stronger sitting around trying to think of ways to improve my abilities. We get stronger by pushing ourselves as hard as we can, over and over, until there's nothing in the world that can stand in our way."

Karla met her stare, but soon turned away, surrendering the argument. Samora turned her glare to Aldrick, but his answer was simple. "I'll go wherever you go."

Samora's features relaxed, and the warmth in her chest spread. She bowed to Aldrick, as deeply as it was possible while riding on a dragon and turned halfway around. Then she connected with the dragon and asked the elder to change her course.

THE CIRCLE in the heart of the deadlands wasn't obvious from the air. Unlike the circles in the lands of the wandering clans, here there was no sharp boundary separating life from death. The whole land was dead, which made seeing the boundary an exercise in futility. The Vada had also taken every Debru with it, leaving the circle itself unguarded.

It being unguarded made Samora nervous, but she was already committed to her course. The dragon landed a safe distance away and the three adanists neared the circle. Unable to sense it, Samora let Karla and Aldrick lead the way.

Karla and Aldrick claimed it was easy to spot with adani, but Samora held hers tightly within her body, so she was denied even that knowledge. In the end, Aldrick drew a line with his foot to denote the boundary.

"You won't be talked out of this?" Karla asked. She remained frustrated but hid it better than before.

"It'll be helpful. Besides, you've already saved my life more times than I can count. What's one more time between friends?"

Karla gave her a hard stare, then chuckled and shook her

head. "You've come a long way from the frightened girl I first met."

Samora stared at the line Aldrick had drawn in the sand. Her knees grew weak, and although she'd already relieved herself, she felt like she needed to again. "Maybe not so much as you think."

Delaying would only make it worse, though. She looked at both Aldrick and Karla, standing next to the line in the sand, ready to pull her back to safety. Satisfied, she took a deep breath and stepped across the line.

She'd halfway expected the shadow to leap at her immediately, but the circle didn't react to her presence. A stiff breeze blew dust from west to east, and Samora shielded her eyes until it passed. The circle might not be reacting violently, but it still pulled hard on her adani. It brought back memories of her and Elian discovering that first circle by their house, the discovery that had started all of this.

Now it was time to end it. She bound a single, weak spear and threw it toward the center of the circle.

That caught its attention. A dark cloud appeared near the center and raced for Samora. She opened herself to it and allowed it to surround her.

Where the shadow touched skin, it felt as though cold worms crawled across her. The strength of this circle was far beyond the ones she'd encountered before, the shadow at the heart of it darker and deeper than those closer to the wandering clans. Now surrounded by the shadow, Samora felt the depth of the wound the Vada had caused, sensed the tear in reality that led to another world. It was still open, and shadow tugged her gently toward the center.

She set her feet. It could surround her, but she wouldn't let it drag her in. She had a world to save.

Shadow choked the light from the sky, casting her into a deeper gloom. It sucked adani from her body like a leech hungry for blood. Samora possessed far more now than in her previous forays into the circles, but she still fought to slow the loss to a trickle. She intended to be here for a while.

Darkness closed in as the wet tendrils of shadow wrapped her ever more tightly in their deadly embrace. Her sight faded until it was a perfect blackness, and then she found herself on the other side again.

Samora's host wasn't so weak as before, though she wasn't as strong as she'd once been. A steel sword hung at her side, and shadow danced like flame up and down the length of the blade.

Samora's heart beat in unison with that of her host. As she sank deeper into the vision, her senses sharpened. Her host possessed no adani. Shadow had consumed her whole, yet when her host looked down at her hands, they were human and not Debru. This host was far stronger than the other humans Samora had visited.

Her host stood on top of a rise and stared at the mountains to the west. Near one of the lower peaks, a bright light shone, warmer and more welcoming than the sun that had disappeared behind the clouds that never dissipated.

Her host's hand went to her sword. She tugged at it once to ensure it wasn't stuck in the sheath, then sheathed it again and resumed her trek.

Samora couldn't see into her host's thoughts, but she could sense the emotion running through her veins.

She didn't know how it was possible, but her host had chosen a fateful path. She planned to kill all the Debru on the world, then turn the blade upon herself.

❧ 26 ❧

E lian and Loken said farewell to Tassan. The giant warrior had tried to get them to stay the night for a feast, but they'd politely declined. Elian wanted nothing more than to return to the Bears, and Loken seemed eager to be among the Hawks once again.

Once they were in the air, Elian said, "I can't decide what I'm expecting. I'm hoping that when we return, the unified clans are still together, healed, and stronger than before, but I fear that when we arrive, it'll be only the Bears waiting for me."

"Funny. I would have thought all your worries would be focused on one particular young woman."

Elian's face turned redder than the setting sun. "Truth be told, I'd thought this trip would give me some time to sort out my feelings. But we've been so busy, I'm feeling even less certain about everything than before. What if she got bored of waiting for me and chose someone else?"

"I know I'm not that much older than you, but I've traveled more than you have, so can I give you some advice on how to think properly about it?"

"Please."

"Stop thinking about it so much. Do you like her?"

"I do."

"And do you believe that she likes you?"

"I do."

"Then that's all you need to worry about. There's never any telling what tomorrow will bring, so let go of those worries. If you decide to get bonded, that's a bit different, but for what you have? Enjoy what you can when you can."

Elian glanced back, but Loken had a distant look on his face, so he didn't pry further. The healer's words made him even more eager to return.

The rolling hills and deep forests of the northern clans gave way to the prairie and grasslands more familiar to Elian. He spotted no fields yet, but suspected they weren't far off. Their dragon was unsettled, his adani as chaotic as a springtime storm, but whenever he tried to ask why, the dragon sealed himself off. Maybe they'd have an answer soon, as the dragon flew faster than Elian expected. The dragon was in as much a hurry as he was.

"We're almost there," Elian said later.

"Is that so?"

"I recognize that grove. If you look closely, you can see the land there was once a field. We're nearing the farthest north my village's farmers reached before the Debru drove us back."

"This far? Aren't we still miles away from your village?"

"My father told me that the fields weren't contiguous. The farmers searched far and wide for the best land, and apparently a few wanted to live close to the village but still be separate."

Loken grunted. "Must be a village thing."

"What's that?"

"The desire to be separated from others. I suppose there are those in the wandering clans who value their privacy, but to be separated from the clan is a fate as good as death. In fact, it is often the worst punishment we can sentence a warrior to, one few leaders ever hand out."

"You exile people from the clan?"

"Not often, but it's happened before. Most who are exiled die soon after."

"What about you and Karla? Both of you have lived full lives traveling as you see fit."

"We're the exception that proves the rule. For both of us to survive, we've had to learn a wide variety of new skills. We have to be able to hunt, cook, clean, and heal, all on our own. When traveling, there's no one else to set a watch, so we have to learn to sleep light or sleep while extending our adani to danger. It's not that it's not possible to live alone, but it's unlikely. More to my point, very few are even interested in trying. Karla's case is unique, as she's lived for so long, and I only left after losing my arm and nearly losing my sanity."

Elian shook his head. "For all I learn about the wandering clans, there are times like right now that I realize there is still so much left to learn."

"With any luck, you'll have a whole lifetime ahead of you to do so," Loken said.

Elian spotted more familiar landmarks, and it wasn't much longer before he spotted Samora's gathering ground and all the people and dragons surrounding it. They circled once to gather more information.

Their first look was satisfying. Judging by the number of tents still in the gathering ground, the unified clans hadn't broken up and gone their separate ways. Elian didn't believe for a moment it meant all the discord between them had been resolved, but it put the worst of his fears to rest. So long as humanity remained united, they had a chance.

Their loop around the dragons' temporary nests was almost as discouraging as the loop over the unified clans had been encouraging. All the dragons remained, but all seemed to share whatever problem afflicted the dragon they rode on. Elian was used to the dragons being alert and active, even when they didn't move

RYAN KIRK

much. Today most seemed to be asleep, their massive heads tucked tightly into their bodies.

Their dragon landed in the same place he had taken off from so long ago. Off in the direction of the camp, Elian saw that his arrival was already stirring up attention, but he pushed those problems aside as he hopped off the dragon. He remained near and pressed his hand against the dragon's side.

"What's wrong?"

Sorrow traveled freely through the connection, but the dragon shared no vision with Elian to show him the source of the grief.

"If there's anything you need from us, just ask," Elian said.

He turned away and faced the assembled adanists standing between the dragons' nests and the gathering ground. His left hand neared the new sword at his hip, but he didn't dare touch it. Simply passing his hand close to it provided him strength enough for whatever awaited him.

As he got closer to the group, he saw that it consisted of many of the leaders and elders of the unified clans. Aldo, of course, was there, having pushed himself to the front and center of the group. But Warran and Kati were there, too, and both looked to be in better spirits than when he'd seen them last.

Aldo was the first to greet him with a deep bow. "It's an honor to have you back, Elian."

The bow was too deep, and the words scraped across Elian's ears like sandpaper, but Elian had long ago given up on expecting sincerity from Aldo. He bowed in return and wondered what he could say that was truthful. "I'm excited to see all of you here. I'm sorry that my journey took so long."

Warran interjected before Aldo could speak again. "There's no need to worry about us. Were you successful in your recruitment?"

"I was. We'll have both Coyote and Scorpion adanists here before long, and we'll truly be able to call ourselves a unified clan."

Aldo's eyes glinted like steel at Elian's mention of a unified clan, but he buried the reaction so quickly Elian wondered if he'd imagined it. The other faces lit up, though, and they hounded Elian with additional questions.

Knowing he'd need to tell the full story; Elian encouraged them to follow him as he returned to his tent. He spoke as they walked, recounting everything that had happened since he'd left. Not for the first time, he was grateful for Loken's company, as the veteran healer confirmed and expanded on Elian's story when he was needed.

Elian grimaced when Aldo challenged him about the assault on the Scorpion village. "Surely they weren't Moka, but simply strong Debru."

Loken spoke before Elian could launch a heated defense. "I can assure you, Aldo, they were Moka, and strong ones, too. Though we'll never know, I suspect the Vada delegated the destruction of the Scorpion village to them."

The objection danced on Aldo's lips, and Elian could well imagine what he would say. *"They couldn't have been Moka if Elian could cut through them so easily."*

But the words never escaped. Aldo sealed his doubts away while the others complimented Elian on his bravery.

Someday soon, matters between him and Aldo were going to reach a head. He'd rather Aldo be more open with his doubts, because doing so gave him a chance to refute Aldo publicly. Instead, Aldo wrapped his doubts up tightly in his soul, where they grew and festered. Elian didn't look forward to the day Aldo took action on everything he'd held onto so secretly for so long.

Elian tried to minimize his role in the events, but there was no way of avoiding the fact that the sword at his side had given him the strength to kill Moka. By the time they reached his tent, almost all questions had come to focus on that, and Elian didn't have the answers they sought.

The sun had just fallen, and with the coming of the evening

came Elian's exhaustion. He stood outside his tent, answering as many questions as he could, but his limbs started to feel heavy, and his eyelids drooped.

Kati was the first to notice. "Sorry for all the questions, but you can imagine our excitement at the news you bring. Since you and your sister left, the camp has been quiet, which has been good for us. We've trained together and rested, and thankfully we haven't had as much as a single kettu wander our way."

Her description of the past weeks perked his ears up. "There's been that little Debru activity?"

Kati nodded. "The only development here since you left has been the dragons and their moods, but we don't know a thing about what caused it."

"They're mourning something, or someone, but I don't know who or what. They won't let me in to tell me."

"Regardless, it's been quiet here, and we've appreciated the peace. We're as ready as we'll ever be for whatever comes next."

"I'm glad to hear it. Has there been any word of my sister?"

Warran shook his head.

"I see." Elian hadn't expected one, but the lack of word from her left him almost as unsettled as the dragons. "For tonight, I must get some rest, but tomorrow I look forward to speaking with you all some more and discussing what we should do next."

The leaders took their cue to leave, and one by one they left Elian alone until only Warran remained.

"Has it truly been so quiet?" Elian asked.

"It has, much to all our surprise. Aldo's even been more pleasant since both you and Samora left, though his attitude returned the moment he saw a dragon in the air. I'll confess I still never have a clue what's going through that man's head."

"That makes two of us, but it's a problem I'm not going to worry about until tomorrow. Do you have any word of Capricia?"

"No. I know she's been busy among the Hawks, but I've been too busy with the Bears to pay much attention."

"And how are the Bears?"

"Wounded, but healing well. The loss of Harald cut us more deeply than I think even you can imagine, and I know you loved him well. But nothing will keep us down for long. They'll be eager to have you back, I think."

Elian bowed deeply. "Thank you for your leadership while I was away."

"You're more than welcome. So long as you don't make a habit out of leaving for long stretches of time, I'll never mind."

"Of course. Thank you again."

Warran bowed and left, and Elian opened the flap to his tent and stepped inside. As soon as the flap closed behind him, he sagged and gave a great exhale.

It was good to be back.

He let his hand drift very close to the sword and the stone embedded in the hilt began to glow. Fresh adani poured into his channels and he welcomed the surge of strength.

The light also revealed that he wasn't alone.

"What's that?" Capricia asked.

Elian jumped and almost screamed like a child, then caught ahold of himself. It took a moment for his heart to stop trying to escape out of his chest, but once it did, he laughed. Capricia joined him, and he stumbled over and collapsed next to her. "You scared the daylights out of me."

Her laughter lasted longer than his own, and he decided he liked the way the sound filled his tent. He wouldn't be opposed to hearing it more often.

"I'll have to tell the others. Most of the Hawks say I'm not a great hunter, but I'd say that ambush just about killed you with a word."

"I'm afraid you have the right of it. But I'll have to ask you to keep this a secret. If your story were to get out, my reputation would be ruined."

Capricia scoffed. "Reputation? While you've been gone, I've

done nothing but go around telling people that you jump at shadows and always need my rescuing. There's nothing left to save."

Elian chuckled and shook his head, but the smile fell too quickly off his face. "I can't tell you how much it means to me that you're here. Before you'd scared me, I'd intended to drop off my pack and come find you."

Her smile remained. "To tell you the truth, I was surprised by how much I missed you, too."

She held out her thumb and forefinger, barely separated from one another. "It was about this much. I'd expected it to be more."

"You wound me."

"Maybe you should learn to fight back."

"My mother taught me to never strike an unarmed opponent."

Capricia laughed at that, then made to leave. "I'm sure you're exhausted, but I wanted to greet you before you went to sleep. I've missed you, too."

Elian reached out and grabbed her wrist. "You don't need to leave, you know."

The smile on her face grew wider. "I was hoping you might say that."

✣ 27 ✣

Samora's host moved through the shadow world, undeterred by the vast, barren wasteland. Even as her strength waned and she shuffled and almost fell, she continued on. Samora had no control over the vision. Sometimes it seemed as though Samora was trapped, watching events unfold at the same speed they would have transpired if she had lived them herself. Then time would seem to skip and bend, and the mountains off in the distance were that much closer.

Samora tried to push the vision forward, but her efforts amounted to nothing in this space. At this rate, she would have risked the Debru circle for nothing more than the chance to watch this woman walking.

Given that she could do nothing, though, Samora resigned herself to making the most of the opportunity. Aldrick and Karla would pull her out before it was too late. All she had to do was relax and observe, so that was what she did.

This world wasn't dead in the same way the deadlands were. Dark grasses and bushes grew near sources of water, but they were widely scattered and not plentiful. Trunks of desiccated trees could sometimes be seen near the path, evidence of a world that had once known more life.

Samora looked up to the sky. If she'd seen the same clouds back home, she would have closed the shutters over the windows and prepared for an imminent storm. The clouds had the same dark bottom she associated with thunderclouds that stretched miles high into the sky, but here, there was no moisture in the air, and she doubted they carried any rain.

She rarely felt the refreshing sensation of a cool breeze against her skin, either. The air was as still as the rest of the world, lacking any sense of life. It wasn't quite hot, but it was warm, as if she was in her home and someone had sealed the doors and windows too tightly to let fresh air in.

Sometimes she would see the bones of an animal that had fallen. The bones weren't bleached by the sun, nor did they have the bite marks of scavengers. What decay they'd experienced had come from time and time alone.

The world couldn't have looked like this when the first Debru ancestors arrived. No one, no matter what reasons they had to leave their world, would have fled to a place like this.

Once, this place must have been like their own world, or perhaps even better. Now, though, it could hardly support life.

Perhaps the elder dragon hadn't been entirely correct about the Debru's motivations. Maybe it wasn't just about adani, but about survival. They'd been given a wonderful world and destroyed it by exercising the power of shadow. Now they needed someplace new to live. Someplace else to greedily devour.

Samora's host ate sparingly from her pack, but she never attempted to hunt. What food she had was likely all she possessed. By the time she reached the base of the mountain she was nearly out of food, but she found the trail of stairs carved into the side of the stone and climbed without hesitation.

Her pace increased the closer she came to the glowing light. Samora's window into her thoughts was limited, but she noticed enough to guess how the woman viewed her purpose. The food in her pack was nearly empty, but she made no effort to find more. She wasn't like the woman Samora had haunted before, who had looked to the summit as though salvation was waiting for her. This woman held out no hope for herself. She planned to fight, and if she died, she died. If she won, well, that was just a slower death sentence.

She stopped short of the light, took off her pack, and had a few small bites to eat. She rummaged around the bottom and pulled out a small carving of a human figure. Crude cuts had been worn smooth by months of worrying attention. She ran her thumb across the figure, then raised it to her lips and kissed its forehead.

The figure went into her pocket, but the rest of the pack remained behind. As far as she knew, she was the last human left.

She took one more deep breath, then drew her sword and ascended the rest of the stairs.

She came to a wide rock ledge, the stone beneath her feet too smooth to be the result of any natural process. An intricate circular symbol had been carved within the stone; its edges as sharp as any knife blade. Her eyes glanced over the symbol, following the geometric curves as they danced and intersected. It pulled her attention, and she forcibly ripped her gaze away. A person, if they weren't careful, could lose their spirit in such a pattern.

The bodies around the circle were evidence enough of that. Enthralled by the power of the Vada and their esoteric knowledge, the poor fools had traveled from points around the world to take part in the dark ritual. They'd come believing they'd be rewarded, though for what she couldn't imagine. Their only reward was to have their strength and their spirits pulled from their bodies.

More than two dozen had powered this great work, and from what she could sense, only three still lived, and just barely at that. They were the ones closest to the Vada, unlucky enough to be drained last.

She didn't care to imagine their agony. Her husband had fallen for the Vada's promises and wandered away years ago. His body wasn't here, but she knew well enough it was somewhere else, part of the gruesome remains of the same process completed elsewhere. Only this one remained.

The Vada noticed her. Its dark eyes went wide. Chained by the ritual, completely focused on keeping the doorway open, there was nothing it could do against her. Under any other circumstance, it would have killed her with barely a blink of its eyes.

They were never alone, though. How many of these doors had she closed now? A dozen? Two? It had all blended together after a time. Their defense was always the same.

Now.

A Belog emerged from the stones obscured in shadow behind the Vada, launching its enormous bulk at her. She retreated, angling herself so that the symbol was between her and the Vada's defender. It charged, too confident by far in its own strength. The symbol slowed it, expecting the Belog to step through, but the Vada controlled the passage, and it groaned as it fought to keep the Belog here.

She'd been waiting for just this moment. She ended her retreat and leaped forward, sword carving through the enormous muscles in the Belog's legs. Unable to support itself, it collapsed, swiping at her as it fell. She cut off its hand for its trouble, and then its neck was low enough for her to cut. Her sword sang in her hand, and it found its way between the Belog's vertebrae with practiced ease. The Belog's head fell from its neck, too dead to even be surprised by how fast it had perished.

The shadow within her demanded release, but she kept it locked tightly in her body. Soon, very soon, she could let it go for good. But not quite yet. The last of her prey remained. Then it would be over.

The Vada's eyes bulged in its sockets, which was about all the motion it was capable of.

She advanced slowly, allowing herself to savor the moment, the completion of so many years of training and hunting.

Then the Vada smiled. It screamed, and the shadows she'd once thought were stones stirred to life.

She cursed to herself. Of course. Here were all the elders and mothers who were waiting to cross over, the one doorway held open by a Vada. Sleeping and still, saved from the needs of food and water, waiting for the moment when the call would come, when it would be safe to cross over.

Now awake, and so fast.

It didn't matter. She leaped toward the Vada with all the speed her training and shadow had gifted her. If she could kill the Vada, nothing else mattered. They would all die here, on this world they'd destroyed.

She didn't make it halfway. Thirty spears of shadow stabbed down from the sky and fixed her in place, the symbol beneath her gladly drinking her blood and growing stronger as a result. She tried to dissolve the spears and execute one final cut, but the powers arrayed against her were far too strong. Already, most of the elders were settling down to return to sleep, but one remained, a fierce looking Belog with a scar down the side of his face. He formed a last shadow spear, and she screamed, her throat ripped apart by despair, as he flung it at her head.

She'd been so close.

SAMORA SCREAMED, too, as her eyes snapped open and she found herself under the bright light of her own sun. She shivered as the warmth soaked through her skin. She panted as the fear drained out of her body. Aldrick and Karla kneeled beside her, faces sick with worry.

RYAN KIRK

"Move," she croaked at Aldrick, who was blocking some of her sun.

He obeyed without question, joining Karla on the other side. The sun soaked deeper into her, and she imagined the light reaching down to her bones, driving the shadow from within. After a few deep breaths, she felt like herself again, the experience fading into memory.

She tracked the flow of her adani closely, watching the way it moved and seeking any difference at all.

"Would you check me for shadow? I can't feel any, but I don't trust myself yet," she said to Karla.

The older woman put her hand against Samora's chest and extended a thin line of adani. It was caught by the adani already flowing in Samora's channels, and before long, Karla's adani had been everywhere. She let the adani return. "You feel fine to me."

"Thank you, both of you. I'm sorry if I worried you, but the risk was worth it."

"Was it?" Karla asked.

"I know why there's only the one Vada, and why their forces aren't as great as the elder expected, so yes, I think it was."

"Care to share?" Karla asked.

Samora did, describing what she'd seen in detail.

When she finished, Aldrick asked, "And you think this is something current? Not a vision of the past?"

"I can't be sure, but it didn't feel that way. It also explains a fair amount of the Debru's behavior. Once the Vada here eliminates all threats, it'll call for the others to come through, and they'll make this world their home again."

Karla and Aldrick chewed on that while Samora brushed herself off and stood up. She walked away from the others to give herself a modicum of privacy. She was sure there was no shadow within her, but that didn't mean she felt fine. The darkness of that world lingered, deep in her bones, and she wished, if such a thing were possible, that she could forget all that she'd seen in that realm.

Life, even for someone who grew up in the village like her, could be short, brutal, and mean, but those forces were opposed by friendship, family, and love. She'd never call her life a paradise, and she wasn't sure she wanted it to be. Kindness meant the most when people were suffering.

But that world was something else. There was no hope or kindness to be found. Even her last host's actions, noble as they were from Samora's perspective, had been driven only by thoughts of hate and revenge. She hadn't wanted to save anyone. She'd only wanted to make sure they all died together.

Contact with that kind of darkness left a chill in her spirit she wasn't sure any amount of sunlight would banish. Her previous visions of the other world had left her nightmares for weeks, and she suspected the same would be true this time.

Samora spun on her heel. "We should close this circle."

"We already went over this," Karla said.

"But now we know more. If we close this circle, the Debru won't be able to come through. We'll be safe."

"Except we don't know that. We don't know if the Vada on the other side has the strength to open another doorway. If it does, you'll have given your position away for nothing, and we'll have lost our best chance at winning this war for good."

"The host believed she was the last human left, and there were only a few survivors in the circle. I think it's worth the risk."

Karla pressed the palms of her hands against her eyes, then tugged on her hair. "When did you start sounding so much like your brother? We can't afford to gamble, not now. You may well be right, but from what you told me, your host didn't exactly strike me as being terribly aware. She didn't even notice the elder Debru collected behind the Vada! I don't think we should stake our entire future on what she thought was true."

Samora bowed her head. Karla was right.

She'd let her own feelings about the circle and the darkness within override her reason. It could work, but the risk wasn't worth it, and the circle they knew about was probably better than one they didn't. If they couldn't find a way to defeat the Vada, they could always come here and try. The circle wasn't going anywhere.

"You're right. I'm sorry. I just want this circle and everything it represents gone from this world."

"Soon, girl. Soon."

Samora nodded, took a steadying breath, then said, "Well, if nothing else, we've learned something else valuable to help us against the Vada. I think it's time for us to finally return home."

❧ 28 ❧

Elian woke late the next day to the comforting, familiar sounds of the camp busy with the work of the day. A group of adanists were training together not too far from his tent while children ran after one another, playing whatever game was most popular this week. Muffled conversations seeped through the tent walls, and Elian smiled.

The tent was already warm thanks to the morning sun, and sometime during the night, he and Capricia had tossed off most of their covers. She lay pressed against his left side, her head using his left bicep and shoulder as a pillow, her left arm and leg draped over him. Her soft, even breathing tickled his ear, and he swore he wouldn't move until she woke.

More than once, he glanced over to assure himself this was real and not some particularly vivid dream. Of all the wonders he'd experienced over the past year, this was the one he had the hardest time believing was true. The only other girl he'd cared for had been Sara, someone he'd grown up with in the village. He'd tried to pursue a relationship for years, but in the end, she'd chosen Gabe, the closest thing to an enemy Elian had known grown up.

Capricia and Sara were nothing alike. Elian wasn't sure Sara had ever held a knife in her life, and Capricia was a seasoned warrior who'd survived the Hawk's deadly expedition to reclaim their gathering ground. Sara rarely asked questions about anything, whereas Capricia asked questions about everything. Sara had never expressed an interest in adani, even when Mother had taught all the children in the village the basics. Capricia's sensitivity to the force was impressive, among the best of adanists.

The more time he spent with Capricia, the more he wondered if his affection for Sara had only been due to Sara being the only girl about his age around.

If there'd been one true downside to living in the village, it was that he hadn't known many people. True, under normal circumstances the wandering clans rarely interacted with one another, but they usually met with other clans once or twice a year. They traveled, and that travel made their world bigger, not just in the land they covered, but the people they met along the way.

It cast Mother and Father's decision to leave the wandering clans in a new light. He never would have made the same choice, but he wondered now if the only reason they'd been able to make that choice with their whole hearts was because they'd been in the wandering clans first. They'd found one another, so it didn't matter after if their world shrank.

Capricia stirred, and the motion of her body against his stirred him, too. Her breathing shifted, and a slow smile grew across her face. "Well, good morning to you, too."

After, they dressed.

"Were you awake long?" she asked.

"A bit. Not much."

"You seemed deep in thought."

"I was thinking about my parents and their decision to leave the wandering clans."

Her deft fingers froze, just for a moment, before they resumed braiding her hair. "And what were you thinking about your parents?"

"That the only reason they could make the decision to leave was because they'd already found one another."

Her hands paused again, but she quickly resumed.

"And that I think that even though I understand them better now, I don't think I could make the same decision. Once this is all over and the Debru are defeated, I think I'm still going to want to wander with the clans. The world is too wide to stay in one place," he said.

The grin returned to her face. "For a moment, I was worried you were about to ask me to stay in the village with you. I don't think I could. There's too much I want to see."

"Would you be interested in seeing it together?"

The grin grew wider. "Maybe."

"Only maybe?"

"Maybe."

She leaned away as he playfully swiped at her, then rose smoothly to her feet. "I've distracted you for long enough. I'm sure the leaders and the elders are beside themselves waiting for you to appear, so you best get going."

He groaned. "You're much better company than the elders."

"Of course I am, but that doesn't change what you need to do. I'll find you in time for the evening meal."

She stepped out of the tent, breaking the spell that had fallen over him. He finished dressing and followed soon after, blinking in the bright light of the sun. He shaded his eyes with his hand as he looked around. Two Bears stood to the south of his tent, and another two stood to the north. At a glance, each pair appeared deep in conversation, but something about their posture bothered him. He pretended to stretch while watching them.

If they were having real conversations, he was secretly a dragon in disguise. All four Bears kept a sharp eye on their surroundings, barely looking at the person they were supposed to be talking to. All four were among Harald and Warran's most loyal, which meant they'd been assigned to watch him.

He almost let it pass, but decided it was better if everything was in the open. He spoke loud enough for all four to hear. "You can stop pretending, now."

Their expressions ranged from perfectly innocent to shame-faced, letting Elian know he'd been right. They approached.

"Why are the four of you out here guarding me?"

Alec, the adanist who had first attempted to train him when he joined the Bears, spoke for the group. "Apologies, but Warran ordered it."

"Why?"

"You'd have to ask him. I assume he thinks you're in some sort of danger, but he didn't tell us."

"Your protection is appreciated, but not needed. Go resume your normal duties."

No one moved.

"Did I miss something? Am I not the leader of the Bears anymore?" Elian asked.

"No, you are. It's just that Warran was quite explicit in his orders, and after the last few weeks, we'd all feel better knowing you have a bit of extra protection around you," Alec answered.

"But if I ordered you, you'd listen?"

"Against our wishes, but yes."

Elian sighed to himself. Their presence was unnecessary, but hardly harmful, and if they wanted to stand guard, he supposed he could allow it for a while. When he saw Warran they could straighten the problem out. "Very well. Where can I find the elders and leaders these days?"

"Tiafel and the Hounds host the unified council," Alec said.

That was another, slightly unexpected piece of good news. Elian would have bet a fair amount of his food that Aldo had somehow manipulated the council into being hosted by the Wolves, but the fact that he hadn't boded well.

Alec led the way, with Elian ending up surrounded by the two pairs of adanists. The presence of the guards deterred other adanists from speaking with Elian, which meant they made it to the council circle quickly.

Despite the presence of the heart and the strength of the gathering ground, grass struggled to grow here. There'd been so many feet on the ground recently that even now the grass was pressed down. Anyplace else and this circle would be nothing but dirt.

The other leaders and elders were already present, including Warran. Elian was used to arguments in the council, but today the different clans were all mixed together, talking and laughing as though they'd been the best of friends for years.

The sight caused Elian to pause before he'd fully entered the circle. How long had he secretly imagined exactly this scene? After the Vada destroyed the Hawks' gathering ground, he'd known the only possible chance the clans had was to join together and unify.

Every effort of his had failed. Sure, the clans had come together, but they were unified in name only. By the time he'd left to find Tassan and the Coyotes, he'd despaired of ever achieving true unity.

He stepped into the circle and was warmly welcomed. He bowed to the circle and said, "It's great to be back, and to see such harmony between the clans."

The elders and leaders shuffled around the circle until they were arranged by clan. Elian stood next to Warran, but didn't ask about the guards. The proper time for that was later.

Tiafel opened the council meeting. "We're here today to welcome Elian back and discuss our next plans. I suspect most have heard of Elian's adventures since he last joined us, but perhaps he could give a full recounting to everyone here."

Elian was glad to do so, and told the story as quickly as he could.

He couldn't have asked for a more attentive audience. No leader interrupted his telling, and when he finished, even Aldo looked impressed by his exploits. Each and every member of the unified council expressed their admiration at what he'd accomplished, but memories of the fallen Scorpion village prevented him from feeling any sense of pride in his actions. Yes, he'd helped the survivors, but it meant nothing until the Debru were destroyed.

Tiafel must have noticed the expression on his face, because he said, "You should be proud of what you've accomplished. The arrival of the Coyotes and the Scorpions will be a historic moment, the first time all the clans have gathered since we parted ways all those generations ago."

"It is cause for celebration, but let's not forget that not all the clans that parted back then will be here. Spider and Crow are gone, and though it pains me to admit it, the Hawks are on the brink of destruction as well," Kati said.

Heads nodded around the circle while Elian focused on the leader of the Hawks, who stood tall on the other side of the circle. She'd lost weight since he'd seen her last, and the hollows under her eyes made her look as though she hadn't slept since he left, but her back was straight, and she met his look with a confident one of her own.

True as the facts were, the comment seemed designed to minimize his accomplishment. Why did she bring it up now? Wasn't she an ally?

She was. Elian refused to believe otherwise. Which meant there was something else happening in this circle, a battle he hadn't realized he was fighting. But who was fighting who, and what did they battle over?

After a moment of silence for the lost, Aldo pushed the conversation forward. "It's true we are reduced from the height of our strength, but Elian has brought together the greatest collection of adanists we've seen in our lifetimes. The question we need to confront is what we do with that strength."

Elian's head spun. What had happened in his absence, that Kati would seem to be against him and Aldo supporting him?

Aldo didn't give him the chance to straighten out his thoughts. He faced Elian and asked, "Elian, it was your plan to gather all the adanists here. What would you have us do?"

Fortunately, Elian had spent considerable time thinking about that very question. "You'll have to forgive me, leaders, as I haven't yet had a chance to learn all that has happened in my absence, but I believe my strategy should be effective. If there's one thing my time with the Scorpions has reminded me of, it's that we need the strength of a gathering ground to fight the Debru. Without the power of the heart, the Debru are simply too strong. Given that, we'll have to find a way to lure the Vada to a gathering ground and hit it with everything we have. I'm sure that with our combined might, we'll be successful."

Aldo nodded along to everything Elian said. "Has anyone told you yet that the Wolves' gathering ground has been successfully strengthened by Lenon and his group of healers? We have a second heart now." Aldo gestured at Elian's sword. "Apologies. I mean we have a third heart now."

"Congratulations are in order. Is it stronger than this one?"

"According to Lenon, yes, considerably."

"Has there been any discussion of moving the clans to your gathering ground?" Elian asked.

"Discussion, yes, but no decision. We wanted to wait until you returned with news of either success or failure."

"And how do you lean, now?"

Aldo gave a small, non-committal shrug. "It is of little import to me. At some point, perhaps once all the clans are gathered, we'll should consider moving, but for now, there seems little reason to disturb the routines we've developed."

"If the heart in your gathering ground is stronger, we should make haste for it. Now that Elian is back, there's no reason to delay," Kati argued.

"What about Samora?" Warran asked.

"She can sense us wherever we go. If she's capable of finding us, I don't doubt that she will," Kati said, so quickly Elian was sure she'd expected the argument.

He shuffled back another half-step, hoping to avoid the leaders' focus. Aldo, though, wouldn't let him go. "What do you say, Elian?"

His mind raced. He knew Aldo's question was a trap, but how? Elian considered others' positions and wondered what might be at stake. But he was no closer to an answer when Warran said, "Elian and I haven't yet had time to speak, Aldo."

"What does that matter? He's already said he believes we should lure the Vada toward us." Aldo faced Elian again. "Do you believe it would be best to lure it here, or to lure it to the Wolves' gathering ground?"

Finally, Elian saw the barest outlines of the trap Aldo had laid for him. It was the same sticking point as before. The gathering grounds were sacred territory to the wandering clans, an attitude Elian had never fully been able to adopt. The gathering grounds gave the adanists the strength to fight the Debru. It was foolish to ignore their potential when survival was on the line. But tradition didn't bend easily, and Aldo had positioned himself as the bearer of the old ways.

What would Harald do?

Elian grinned. He wouldn't care about anything Aldo said. Trap or not, the course of action they needed to take was clear. "I believe we should prepare to move the clans to the Wolves' gathering ground. If the heart there is stronger, that's where we need to be."

The debate didn't end with Elian's opinion. Some leaders feared leaving their current camp, sure the Vada would strike as they traveled from one gathering ground to the next. Others argued for staying and using the Wolves' ground as a retreat.

Elian noted who said what, regaining the rhythms of the debates that defined the unified council. The afternoon's meeting ended with a decision to meet again the next morning and take a final vote. As they parted ways, Warran grabbed Elian's wrist and pulled him away.

The guards followed, ensuring the two of them maintained their privacy. Once they were back in their own camp, Warran finally slowed. "It was a foolish thing you did back there, though I suppose the fault is my own. I didn't think Aldo would press so hard so quickly."

Elian looked past the insult. "What happened in my absence?"

"Aldo happened, same as always. His tactics changed, though. Instead of lambasting you in council meetings, he's acted as the supportive but skeptical leader. In one breath he acknowledges all that you and Samora have done, but in the next, he's among friends, privately questioning whether the clans are better off than before or not."

Warran looked around, sighed, and said, "There are rumors circulating that the Vada only came and attacked *because* of you and Samora. The fact that it's been so quiet since the two of you departed only strengthens their case."

So that had been what he had missed. "That's why Kati brought up the loss of the Spiders and the Crows. She was reminding the council the Debru had been attacking long before Samora and I joined the Bears."

Warran nodded. "But the counterargument is that even the Spiders and the Crows were only set upon after you two were born."

That brought Elian up short. "They're arguing the Debru have increased their attacks because *my sister and I were born?*"

"Although I disagree with the idea, it's not as far-fetched as it may seem. You've said yourself it seems as though the Debru have a particular fascination with you and your sister. The Spiders were your parent's clan, and the Moka that broke through our lines the night your father died made a line straight for your village. If I were the enemy commander, I'd do everything in my power to destroy you two."

"But we were just children, and hardly powerful."

Warran shrugged. "The problem with the argument is that it will be made regardless. The only way to conclusively disprove it is to ask the Vada and somehow be convinced it would answer truthfully."

Elian rolled his head in a circle and shook his arms out, fighting the tension that built in his body. Whenever he thought he'd seen the worst humanity was capable of, someone found a new depth to sink to. Responding in anger did little good. "What do they want?"

"It's hard to tell, as everything is rumors and hearsay. Alec believes that those who are most persuaded want you and Samora dead, which was why he convinced me to set the guards around you. I believe Aldo is building support to have you and Samora exiled from the clans, perhaps to be sent back to your village. But he's always been nearly impossible to predict, so it's hard to say."

"Why was I fool at the council?"

"The rumors about the Debru only attacking because of you and your sister isn't the only rumor spreading through the camp. The other one is that you're a war-obsessed leader who is more than happy to sacrifice the clans and our gathering grounds for your petty desire for revenge."

"And by arguing we should move to the Wolves' gathering grounds, I'm only lending support for that belief."

Warran nodded again. "Like all the best deceptions, it's rooted in a seed of truth, and you don't need to deny it to my face. Though you've become more like one of us over the past few months, and though I'll support your leadership of the Bears until my dying breath, you're still not one of us. You don't think like us, and your values don't exactly match ours. Aldo has simply taken this truth and twisted it into something darker."

"If the heart there is stronger, it only makes sense for us to go there," Elian said.

"You'll find no argument here. I'm only telling you what you're fighting against. A fair number of adanists are starting to believe that so long as you and Samora are gone, they and their gathering grounds will be safe. For what it's worth, I think Aldo genuinely believes that, too. Or at least, he comes as close to believing it as a man like Aldo can believe anything."

"Any suggestions for how I should proceed?"

Warran bowed and prepared to part ways. "Nothing that you wouldn't think of on your own. But I would encourage you to be cautious. The Debru aren't your only enemies."

29

The sight of familiar fields loosened the tightness in Samora's chest she hadn't even been aware of. The dragon descended from its high altitude and flew no more than a hundred feet above the rolling plains. With the sun on her face and the wind in her hair, she forgot about her problems and basked in the simple beauty of flight.

Returning home couldn't banish completely the chill in her bones, but it came close.

After so many miles of travel, the last leg of the trip ended with a surprising suddenness. The dragon crossed the final miles in a flash, then slowed as it approached the field where all the other dragons waited.

Their arrival caused a stir among the assembled dragons. Usually disinterested in the comings and goings of individual dragons, now all raised their heads and watched with sharp eyes. As Samora and the others came in for a landing, they rose from their resting positions and shuffled into a circle. From above, the scene almost made Samora laugh. For all their grace and strength in the air, the dragons were often awkward on the ground.

"They've gathered to greet their elder," Karla said.

Samora silently cursed herself for not figuring that out first. In her mind, the elder was still the dragon she'd learned from in the cave, not this child they rode back home.

But the elder was dead, sacrificing himself so that she might live and fight, and now the dragons' world had been shaken just as hers had been. They landed in the center of the circle as gentle as the first snowflakes of the season falling from the sky. With so much draconic attention upon them, they descended carefully. Aldrick and Karla took steps to leave, but Samora said, "Wait."

She turned back to the dragon, the child who had so recently become an elder, and gave her a formal bow, as deep as she could comfortably bend with her pack on her back. Karla and Aldrick, both quick studies, mirrored her gesture, and the elder dipped her head in return. She stretched out adani to Samora, who accepted it.

The fiery woman appeared before her. "I do not know what happens next."

"Neither do I, but I believe that between my brother and I, we'll find a way to defeat the Vada. It isn't invincible. Until then, I'm sure there is much for you and your family to discuss. As always, our fields and our game are yours to use as you please, and if there's anything you need from us, please, don't hesitate to ask. I'm sure I'll be coming to speak with you soon."

The illusion before her offered a short bow. "Thank you for witnessing his death. It meant everything to him."

"It was the least I could do. He very possibly gave us the keys to defeating the Debru once and for all."

Dragon and human parted on peaceful terms, and the children made a gap in the circle for the travelers to pass through. As they left the circle of dragons, Samora felt the deep and interconnected waves of adani pass between the dragons, that mysterious language that carried so much more meaning than human words.

Their arrival attracted human attention, too. A handful of guards left their position near the camp's edge and came to meet the new arrivals. The three were immediately recognized and the guards gave them free passage into the camp.

Glad as she was to be home, for this was where she considered her home to be now, she was surprised by her visceral reaction to being among so many people again. She'd missed the clans while she'd been gone, but her excitement at returning barely lasted any time at all. She caught herself thinking about where she might need to go next, and she shook her head.

"Do you think you're going to need me for anything soon?" Karla asked.

"Nothing that I can think of. Where can I find you if I need you?"

"Oh, I'll be around. Tonight, I'm hoping I might be able to corner a lonely wolf."

Aldrick visibly blanched and Samora grinned. "Good hunting, then."

Karla parted ways from them, wandering toward the Wolves' encampment. Aldrick didn't follow her. "Aldo will kill her if he finds out," he said.

"I'd like to see him try. You're not heading that direction, too?"

Aldrick blushed and brought his hand up to scratch the back of his neck. "Um–"

"Because if you don't have any place else to be, I wouldn't mind your company."

His bashfulness fell away. "In that case, I'd be honored to join you. Are you going to see your brother?"

"I am." She paused, catching the slight hesitation in his voice. "Why? You have nothing to fear from him."

"I know that." Aldrick stared down at his boots. "Doesn't mean he doesn't intimidate me sometimes. He's killed a Vada, several Belogs, and who knows how many other Debru. I really, really don't want to be the one who upsets him."

She grinned at his discomfort. "I suppose you'll have to stay on my good side, then, won't you?"

His grin was shaky, as though it might fall into a frown at any moment. "I suppose I will. I'm up for the challenge."

She took his hand, her own heart pounding faster as she declared her feelings publicly. They weaved their way through the tents into the Bear's encampment. She found Elian near the center of the camp, deep in discussion with Warran and a handful of the Bears' elders.

He glanced up as she arrived, then returned his gaze to the elder who was speaking. A moment later, his head shot up and his eyes went wide. He blinked quickly. "Samora, is that you?"

"I should think so."

He was up and across the circle in a heartbeat, moving faster than any human should. She saw his eyes glance down and see her hand in Aldrick's, and he hesitated, but too briefly for anyone else to notice. Then he embraced her tightly, squeezing the air from her lungs. She let go of Aldrick's hand and reached around him, only able to pat him lightly on the back. He'd filled out even more since she'd last seen him.

When they broke apart, she saw that wasn't the only change in him. She'd left him alone for a couple of weeks and he'd gone and matured by several years. Unfortunately, it seemed to her as though no small part of that maturation had been fueled by grief. It hadn't dimmed his spirit, though. His eyes were hard and focused, burning with an inner light she wondered if he recognized.

It had been easy to mock Aldrick for his fear of her brother earlier, but after some time away, she understood. He radiated strength and determination in a way few people she'd come across did. If he continued along this path, he'd soon be a force of nature unto himself, like adani in human form.

She was so preoccupied by the changes that had come over him that she didn't immediately notice the sword at his side. It wasn't until she collected herself that she felt its incredible outpouring of adani. Even without extending her senses she felt its power. She looked down and saw the stone embedded in the pommel.

She couldn't help but laugh, which brought a confused smile to Elian's face. He followed the line of her gaze. "You find something entertaining about my sword?"

She slung the pack off her shoulders and pulled out the precious sack of hearts. She untied the cord that bound it shut and held it open so he could see inside. "Not at all. It's just that you and I went our separate ways, and we returned with the same gift. Of course, yours would come attached to a sword."

She hadn't thought it was possible for his eyes to get any wider, but at the sight of so many hearts, she feared his eyes were in danger of dropping out of their sockets. "There are so many!"

When he recovered from the sight, he remembered his manners. "Sorry, Aldrick, but I couldn't believe it was really my sister. How are you?"

"Well, sir, thank you."

Elian reached out, his arm like a snake attacking unsuspecting prey, and pulled a very surprised Aldrick toward him. He wrapped the Wolf adanist in an embrace, then let him go. Aldrick's knees seemed weak, and Samora feared he might fall, so she took his hand to support him.

"Thank you for guarding my sister on her adventures. It means the world to me," Elian said.

"Of course, sir."

"And there's no need for formality here. Elian is fine." He grimaced. "I'm sorry I can't spend more time with you, but I'm in the middle of discussing our food supplies with the elders. Can we meet tonight for supper? I'll invite Capricia, as well."

"That sounds lovely," Samora said. "That gives me the opportunity to take a bath and finally put this pack down."

"It's agreed, then. We can eat outside my tent tonight. I'll look forward to seeing you there. We have much to talk about."

HER TIME alone with Aldrick ended too soon. They'd each bathed in the nearby stream, then returned to her tent together. As the sun dipped toward the horizon they decided to enjoy one more bath, then hurried toward Elian's private fire. The day had been a warm one, but the night promised to be cold.

Samora stopped Aldrick before they reached the ring of guards surrounding Elian. Through the gap in the tents, she saw him sitting in the grass next to Capricia, and he seemed like a different man than the one she'd met this afternoon. The light in his eyes hadn't disappeared, but it had taken on a different quality, a warmth and softness it hadn't possessed earlier. He and Capricia sat shoulder to shoulder, speaking quietly. Elian's smile was easy, and hers was wide.

"It's good to see him like this," she told Aldrick.

She pulled him onward. They were already a little late, thanks to the amount of time they'd spent together earlier, and she was eager to hear her brother's stories, and to tell him her own.

Together, they had to be able to figure out how to beat the Vada. Perhaps even tonight.

Alec stopped them and fixed a glare on Aldrick. "Just so you know, we're not allowing any adani to be used near him. If we sense anything from you, we're coming in fast."

Aldrick bowed. "I understand."

Alec's glare softened, and he let himself smile. "Good. Enjoy your meal. He's been looking forward to seeing you for a long time."

They joined Elian and Capricia at the fire, and there were embraces and greetings all around. Elian treated Aldrick as though he were already family, and Samora thanked him for it.

She'd expected him to be more overprotective, but there wasn't a trace of it to be found in his actions or words. They sat around the fire, keeping warm against the cold of the encroaching night. They feasted on roast pork from the village, a rare treat these days, while Samora and Elian took turns telling the tales of their adventures.

Samora went first, and she was fascinated by watching the emotions cross his face. He did, of course, have a look of smug self-satisfaction when she revealed how much more there was to human-dragon history, but he looked more conflicted about their decisions than he had before. The elder's decision to trust her and sacrifice himself at the end, though, nearly brought him to tears.

When Elian excused himself to relieve himself outside the camp, Aldrick said, "He wears his emotions so openly."

"He always has, despite his best efforts. When he was young, he tried so hard to mask them, but I think the depth of his feelings has always been his greatest strength. I'm glad to see him freely expressing them, now," Samora said.

"Someday, I'd like to hear more about what he was like when he was younger," Capricia said.

"I'll be glad to tell you, but we'll have to be far, far away from him. Otherwise, he might find out and I'm not sure he'll ever forgive me."

Elian returned then. "Talking about me?"

"Of course," Samora said.

After he settled back down, she encouraged him to share his story. He did, painting Tassan in such a light that Samora was more than eager to meet him. Her heart fell, though, at the story of the Scorpion village. Elian's self-judgment, as always, was harsh. "If I hadn't been so useless, we might have found a way to save more of the Scorpions."

She stopped him before his tirade went too far. "Is that truly how you feel?"

He nodded.

"Can't you see how if not for you, they all would have died?"

"Maybe, but if I'd been stronger, I could have saved more."

"Do you not see your own strength?"

Elian's laugh was bitter. "How could I not? It's all anyone talks about. I'm not blind to it. I'm grateful for what I can do, but unless I improve what I'm weak at, I'll never be enough to defeat the Vada."

For all he'd changed, he hadn't changed at all. No other person would so easily claim they were going to kill a Vada, and he believed it, too. He wasn't that far off, either. She didn't extend her adani toward him, but she felt the extent of his strength all the same. He wasn't there yet, but the Vada's power was within sight.

"Perhaps not alone, but you're not alone. I have a heart as well."

Elian's eyes bore into her. "And I've no doubt your skill is impressive, but can you use them as they'll need to be used? What you've learned and what you've seen has only confirmed that the Debru must die. I ask you, honestly, can you do that? Or will you hesitate in the crucial moment?"

She couldn't match the intensity of his gaze, and her eyes drifted to the fire now burning low. "I know what must be done, but I'll not lie and claim a certainty I don't feel."

"Unfortunately, until you do, I must push forward as though I'm alone. I mean no offense, but you understand, don't you?"

Samora swallowed the stone in her throat. "I do."

Capricia broke the long moment of awkward silence that followed. "I think the most important question is what we do next. You and Samora are both here, so the council will soon demand a plan."

Elian again looked at Samora as he answered. "Unfortunately, Samora and I need more time. We're still not strong enough."

Samora nodded her agreement. "If Aldo is using your desire to use the Wolves' gathering ground against you, perhaps you should suggest to the council that we stay here for a time. There is a risk in decamping, and I wouldn't put it past the Vada to strike in our moment of weakness. By staying here, you kick a leg out from Aldo's arguments, and I can't imagine the gain from moving to a stronger heart would be that great."

Elian pondered for a time, then said, "You might be right. So, we stay here, train to get stronger, and wait for the others to arrive?"

"Yes, and now you also know how to lure the Vada here. Assuming you've mastered your new strength, once the Coyotes and the Scorpions arrive, I'll send out adani and summon the Vada for the final battle."

Elian nodded, but then the seriousness fell from his face, and he looked like the child she remembered. "It's great having you back. Let's not separate again until all this is over."

"Agreed."

"So, you and Aldrick. How did that come to be?" Elian asked.

Samora blinked, her mind frozen by the sudden change of subject. Elian laughed out loud, and Samora blushed.

Capricia, wisely, unstoppered the flask and poured a round of drinks for them all, and for the rest of the evening, the worries of the world fell away.

30

E lian woke up late the next morning and groaned. He pressed his palms hard against his forehead, trying to push the headache away. It laughed at his futile efforts and pounded all the harder.

"Feeling it?" Capricia asked.

"Who hit me over the head last night? I demand justice."

Capricia laughed, and the joyful sound banished his aches, if only for a moment. "I'm afraid you have only yourself to blame for your suffering."

"I never would have guessed Aldrick was capable of drinking so much. That wasn't a battle I was prepared for."

She laughed again, but this time it did little to drive away the pain of his poor decisions.

Though he could all too easily imagine Tara frowning at him, he ran a trickle of adani through his head and cleared the headache away. Enjoyable as last night had been, he couldn't afford to have an addled mind today.

"You're going to need to teach me that trick someday," Capricia said.

"All you need to do is send the smallest bit of adani into your head. Although I don't think you should do it too often. I think it might be a bit too easy to ruin the adani channels up there, and they're narrow enough as it is."

"You make it sound so easy, but I don't have that kind of control over my adani. I can brute force a bit into a limb, but it's rough and only lasts for a few moments. I'm afraid that if I tried, I'd spend the rest of my life unable to speak."

"When all this is over, I'd be happy to teach you more. At least as much as I'm capable of."

She rolled onto her back and stared up at the ceiling of the tent. "Do you often think about after?"

"Not that often. Why?"

"The wandering clans are all I've ever known, but there isn't much reason to wander if the Debru are gone. What do we do? Do we keep wandering, just because it's what we're used to? Or do we set aside our weapons and pick up scythes and hoes like the villagers?"

Elian joined her in the careful consideration of the top of his tent. "I really don't know. I haven't thought much past killing all the Debru. What would you do? Say we succeed, and all the Debru are gone from the world for good. How would you spend your time?"

"I think I'd want to travel more. Wandering is in my blood, and there's so much more to the world than we know. If it were safe, I'd travel farther than any human in our generation has traveled. I'd want to learn everything there is to learn."

Elian didn't have any problem imagining it. Every day, walking and exploring. Every night, gathered around a fire discussing what they'd seen. The sort of living he felt like he could get used to pretty quickly. "Would you care for some company?"

She looked at him and bit her lower lip. "Are you serious?"

He shifted so he was on his side facing her. "Very."

"I'd like that," she said.

"Then it's a plan." He held her close, kissed her, then rolled out of bed. "What are you doing today?"

"I told Kati I would help train a younger group of adanists this afternoon. There's a number of children who've been training together since the clans unified, and a handful are almost of the age and skill necessary to join as full-fledged members of the clan."

"Do they join the unified clan, or do they remain with the clan of their birth?"

"Their birth. I don't think anyone expects the unified clan to exist once the threat of the Debru is taken care of."

"I suppose that's true."

"You don't sound pleased."

"I like having all of the wandering clans together. We're stronger when we fight beside each other, capable of more."

"We're also packed into a space that's too small, and we've been still for too long. Sure, there are moments of kindness and friendship, but the elders also have their hands full with small arguments that break out into fights. We aren't meant to be together like this."

Elian finished dressing and tied his sword to his hip. It still tugged on his adani, but he'd grown more used to holding on tight to his own. The stone barely flickered as he tested the sheath to ensure it was secure. "I suppose as long as we make it through the battle with the Vada, it doesn't matter that much. I do wish the wandering clans could set aside their differences better."

"You and every elder here. What are you going to do—take part in today's council meeting?"

Elian shook his head. "There's little to accomplish there. I'm going to head outside the camp and practice with this sword. There's more strength there, I just need to figure out how to unlock it."

"Good luck. See you tonight?"

"Of course. Good luck training the young ones."

With that, he left, though no small part of him wanted to stay in the tent forever and let the troubles of the world pass him by. In that tent was his perfect world, unmarred by the Debru and the petty infighting of the clans.

As expected, Alec and the others followed him through the camp. Elian wasn't sure when they found time to rest, but he didn't bother asking. They'd only take offense.

He left the camp and headed east, putting the full might of the unified clans between him and any threats that might approach. After hearing Samora's story yesterday, he feared that his training might call the Vada, but he didn't see that he had much choice. He couldn't face the Vada as he was, and the sword promised more. He'd felt that clearly during his battle with the Moka.

Once he'd put a rise in the land between him and the camp, he began his training. Alec and the others spread out in a wide circle, giving him plenty of space to move freely. He shifted the flow of adani in his channels, looping it through limbs, lungs, and heart. He ran through the forms he'd been taught, and he caught Alec's smile of satisfaction when he practiced one Alec had taught him what felt like a lifetime ago.

Once he'd stretched his channels, he steadied himself, then took the sword in his hands. Even though he'd prepared for the crashing waves of adani, the force of it still took his breath away. He surrendered to the flow of strength and his channels stretched to encompass the wealth of adani.

His limbs twitched, eager to pounce like a hunter finally looming over its prey. Even his thoughts seemed quicker. He squeezed the hilt tightly, fighting his body's urge to jump, leap, and cut. Practicing his forms with this new strength was a worthwhile cause, but he sensed his quest for greater strength took him in a different direction.

He turned his attention inside, to the minutiae of how the new adani flowed through his body. The channels in his hands and forearms had widened the most, and when he took one of his hands off the sword and made a fist, he was certain he could punch through stone.

He shook out his hand and it blurred with the speed of his movement. Once it was loose, he placed it back on the sword.

There was more strength here, but where? Even as the heart's strength coursed through his limbs, it longed for more. But how?

Elian launched himself into some of the forms his old master had taught him, crossing the width of the circle his guards had formed with a few feather-light steps. He leaped into the air, for a brief moment a dragon without wings. He landed, absorbing the force easily with adani-filled legs, then crossed the circle again, the movement of his sword barely visible to the eye.

A deep breath stilled his body as adani surged through his channels. He ignored the looks his guards gave him, a mixture of misplaced hope and awe that did no one any good. Despite his efforts, the amount of adani in his body hadn't decreased a bit, the heart able to fuel his movement without problem.

The heart's longing was still there, as obvious to him as the desire in Capricia's eyes the night before. It wanted something more from him, but what was there to give?

Focus. Everything he needed was already inside him.

Adani looped through his limbs, faster than thought. He tracked it through the myriad channels, listened for any wisdom it was willing to impart. How did he get closer to the heart?

His focus shattered and he cleared his throat. Did it need his blood?

He drew the sword lightly across his forearm, surprised by how easily it split the layers of his skin. His blood coated the edge of the blade, but he felt no change in the heart's outpouring of adani or his. He looped extra adani around the wound and watched it close, leaving the skin unblemished.

That, at least, brought a smile to his face. Finally, here was a skill Samora would approve of.

Unfortunately, blood wasn't the answer to summoning the full extent of the heart's strength. He ran through another set of forms, unable to contain his strength any longer. He pushed harder than before, jumping higher into the sky and moving faster. Adani-filled legs screamed as they were pushed to their physical limit, but the heart still hadn't released more than a fraction of its power.

He was breathing easily even as he finished his forms. His muscles were sore and complained, but adani helped them recover quickly.

He went again, as hard as before. His legs burned and his arms and back ached from controlling the sword at such speeds, but still he ran through his forms. Somewhere ahead he was sure there was a limit. All he needed was to find it and break through.

Except there was no limit. Adani rushed to heal his legs and arms, and there was more than enough to go around. Once he became used to the feeling of being exhausted, he realized there was no end to how long he could fight.

He came to a stop, and once again felt as relaxed as though he'd just woken up from a long nap after just a moment's break. Sweat poured down his face and soaked his shirt, but he could have fought Moka without a problem.

It was a remarkable discovery, and worth the training alone, but it wasn't what he sought.

He went deep inside his body again, tracing the flow of adani through his limbs. He found no detail that he'd missed before, but before he gave up hope for the day, he turned his attention toward his core.

His core required little direct attention. Adani looped more naturally here, so there was less to gain than when he focused on looping adani tighter within his limbs. When he flooded his body with adani, the core naturally grew stronger.

As adani raced through his core, it hit a slight bump, barely noticeable except for the fact he was searching for anything odd. He focused in on that bump, thinking that one of his channels had gotten knotted up when he wasn't paying attention. A closer examination revealed no knot, but the bump remained. He probed it with all the attention he could muster, but it held tightly to its secrets.

It reminded him of the shadow the Belogs had once infected him with, but it wasn't quite the same. No matter how much adani from the heart he threw at it, the bump remained, some sort of permanent blight on his spirit. It wasn't shadow, but a void, an emptiness that needed to be filled.

But not with his adani. He pushed everything he could from the heart toward it, but adani just flowed around, as though it was a rock in a stream.

Eventually, he gave up. The day faded quickly and his ability to concentrate had been weakened by the day's exertions. He'd made progress today, even if he hadn't figured out how to get stronger.

Perhaps his body simply wasn't ready. Using the heart demanded almost everything he had, and his adani channels were still unused to the heart's strength.

As soon as he sheathed the sword, he tracked the flow of adani through his body, wondering if the prolonged use had hurt him in any way. Fortunately, all was well.

He frowned. There was no more bump in his core.

Still weary from channeling the heart's strength all day, he reached down with his left hand and grasped the hilt. Power once more flowed through him, and once more the tiny void in his soul appeared.

He let go and shook his head. A mystery for another day. Perhaps Samora would have some clue as to what was happening. Maybe the flow of adani in his body needed to shift when there was so much. He rubbed his eyes and yawned. His body felt fine, but his mind was exhausted. The guards returned with him to his tent, where he hid from the world and stretched while he considered what he'd learned.

The sun had already fallen by the time Capricia returned. She looked about as exhausted as Elian's head felt, but she smiled when she saw him, and they sat down at the fire together. Their meal wasn't nearly as extensive as it had been the night before. The Bears kept trying to give him the best of everything, but he was content with the same food most ate.

Capricia's day had been as busy as she'd expected. The youths had been eager, though not many appreciated her techniques. Like Samora, she relied more on precise control of her weaves than sheer power, and the young men, in particular, were not impressed.

"I'm not sure I would have been, either," Elian admitted. "Granted, I can't do anything you can do, but I didn't realize how much power there was in control until lately."

"Maybe you should be the one to come instruct them. I can guarantee they'd listen to you, especially after today."

"Why after today?"

"Your guards from this afternoon got excited after they returned. Started telling everyone what they'd seen you do. To hear them tell it, you can move so fast you can't even be seen."

"Do they also think I can kill a Debru with an angry stare?"

"They might. It's probably a good thing you aren't eating with the rest of the Bears tonight. I'd suspect you'd be inundated with requests to perform for them."

"No thanks."

"And speaking of celebrating, when one of my friends heard about your feats, she gave me this."

Capricia pulled out a flask and Elian's stomach did a flip. He held out his hands. "After last night, I think I'm good for a while. I won't stop you if you're interested, though."

Capricia shrugged. "Your loss. My friend says that it came

from Aldo's personal stock. Consider it preemptive revenge for all the problems he has yet to cause."

She took a long sip. "Ahh, that's good."

Elian snatched the flask from her. "You'd think you were trying to get me drunk."

"And what if I am? Are you going to hit me with one of those Debru-killing stares you're so famous for?"

Elian shook his head and took a sip. His body protested, but one didn't often get a chance to sample another leader's drink. Such treasures were carefully guarded.

It was among the best he'd ever tasted. Strong, burning down the throat, but smooth with a hint of sweetness. He took another small sip, then handed the flask back to Capricia. She took another long pull, offered it to him again, and when he refused, stoppered it back up.

"Despite everything, life isn't too bad, is it?" he asked.

Capricia collapsed to the side, falling hard against the ground.

"Capricia?" He moved toward her, but his limbs were suddenly heavy. He grasped the hilt of his sword and adani flooded his body, but even that force wasn't enough to save him. Darkness crowded the edges of his vision, and he fell forward as the void swallowed him whole.

❧ 31 ❧

Samora meandered through familiar fields, one foot in the past and one in the future. Aldrick and three other adanists followed behind her, searching horizon and sky for any sign of danger, any clue the Vada's temporary peace was about to be shattered. The gray, cloudy skies would have hidden any advance, though.

She'd argued that she could visit the village alone. It was only a few miles, a walk she'd made countless times before. None had listened.

She wasn't Samora anymore, not to the unified clans. She'd become something more, and the elders didn't want her assuming any unnecessary risks. Samora understood, but she and the elders disagreed about what exactly qualified.

She'd dreamed last night, and in that dream, she'd traveled the length and breadth of the land. Some part vision, some part imagination, she'd seen the Coyotes and the Scorpions racing closer, pursued by otsoa and persistent Debru.

It wasn't just the last strength of the clans nearing, though. All the Debru, all the monsters they brought with them through the portal, approached, too. As she flew high above, the wind passing through her as though she was a wisp of a cloud, it looked like all the world, light and shadow, swirled closer to her humble gathering ground.

When she'd woken from the dream, she'd stared at the ceiling of her tent, unsettled in a way she found difficult to describe. The feeling didn't fade as the sun crawled above the horizon, either.

Her desire to return home grew from the seeds of that unsettled feeling, a childhood desire to be safely within the walls of her home, watching Mother baking bread for the family. She didn't know how closely her dream corresponded to reality, but her sense was that they had some time yet. Like a storm gathering its strength beyond the horizon, the Vada was coming, but it wasn't ready yet.

The elders had compromised, allowing her to leave only under the protection of a group of strong adanists. She consented, although she demanded they remain behind her, allowing her at least the illusion that she was alone.

She summited the last hill between her and the village. The homes were so familiar, but the surrounding fields had been trampled when the clans had made camp outside the village boundary. It was home, but changed, and no matter how she wished it, she couldn't return it to the way it had been.

What was true of the houses was true of the people, too. Once, she would have been ignored as she walked between the homes. Her desire for silence and solitude had been well known, and she'd wandered like a ghost among her own neighbors. Now, though, word of her accomplishments had spread, and the villagers bowed deep in her direction. She bid them to rise, and some did, but others didn't, waiting until she passed to rise and continue upon their days.

She would have given them anything in her power to return to how it had been, to let her drift like a ghost.

Mother was pulling late season weeds out of the garden when Samora arrived. The guards tried to stay close, but Samora kept them back with a wave of her hand. They froze, torn between their orders from their elders and her wishes, but then Aldrick bowed and took a few steps back. The others followed his lead.

Mother glanced up. "Guards now? And strong ones, given the amount of adani I'm sensing from them. The rumors about you must have some truth to them."

"Depends on what you've heard."

Mother stood from her garden and brushed her hands off on her pants. She was into her forties now, but she'd never lost the grace of movement that had come from her days as a Spider adanist. She glanced between the guards and her daughter, and with a mother's intuition, asked if Samora wanted to come in.

"Please."

Samora followed her mother inside, feeling like a guest in the home she'd grown up in. Inside the door she paused and looked around. The elder dragon had gotten every detail of the home correct, but it had still always felt like a copy. A home wasn't a home unless it had family within.

"Tea?" Mother asked.

"Yes, thank you."

Mother carefully hung their well-used pot over the fire and prepared a small handful of tea leaves. There weren't many left in the container, but Mother wasn't stingy with what little remained. Samora sat quietly at the table, using the preparation time to organize the thoughts that had become a jumbled mess in her head, like the chaos of discarded clothes and toys that had once filled the room she and Elian had shared when they were both younger.

Mother poured the tea and Samora warmed her hand on the cup. She inhaled deeply, then took a tentative sip. "Wonderful," she said.

Mother took a sip, too. "It tastes better when you or Elian are home."

Mother didn't pry but waited in silence for Samora to unload her burdens.

"Did Father ever regret leaving the Spiders?" Samora asked.

"Sometimes. It was hardest for him in the year leading up to his death. It was clear, even to us here in the villages, that the Debru were making dramatic moves against the clans, and Jace sometimes felt as though he'd abandoned his duty."

"Did he consider returning?"

Mother shook her head. "Never. Whatever regrets he had, they were nothing compared to how he felt about being close to the three of us. But why do you ask?"

"In the past few months, I've discovered techniques and abilities that give humanity a fighting chance against the Debru. Unfortunately, at the moment, I'm the only one who can use them. Soon I hope to have others trained, and Elian's been getting stronger with every passing day, but for now, it's just me."

Mother quietly refilled their cups with tea, silently encouraging Samora to take all the time she needed.

It was unfair, as though Samora was pushing a bale of hay off her chest and forcing it on her mother, but she couldn't carry the weight alone. "If nothing changes, I'll have to face the Vada directly. I worry I might not be strong enough to win, but I fear I will be strong enough, but lack the conviction to kill it. Humanity's fate can't rest on my shoulders."

Having freed her fears, she curled into a ball, bringing her knees to her chest, and resting her heels on the front edge of the chair. She wrapped her arms around her legs and stared at the table.

Mother watched her, then finished her cup of tea and stood up. She disappeared into her bedroom, and for a terrifying moment, Samora knew Mother was going to close the door behind her and shut her coward of a daughter out of her life for good.

The door remained open, and mother shuffled around. She

reappeared with her old comb in her hand, and she took the seat directly beside Samora. Without a word, she began combing her daughter's hair, running it slowly from her scalp as far as it would go. She didn't worry at the tangles she found, but removed the comb and brought it back up to the scalp.

Samora almost objected that she wasn't a child any longer, but at the first touch of the comb, she relented. Pleasant shivers ran down her spine as the comb straightened and gently pulled at her hair. Thoughts and worries fell away, like climbers losing grip of their holds. Her eyes grew heavy, and though she never fell asleep, she closed them and let the feeling of the combing become her entire world.

She had no idea how long she sat there, but she would have for the rest of her life, if she'd been given the chance. Mother finished combing her hair, then braided it. When that was done, she returned the comb to her room, then took the chair she'd first sat in, across from Samora.

"I don't have the answers you seek, as much as I wish I did. You surpassed me in matters of adani long ago, and now it sounds as though you've gone much further. But I can still make you tea, listen to your problems, and comb your hair."

"Those are the same things you did for me when I was a child."

"The role of mother doesn't change all that much over the years. It's how I showed my love to you when you were younger, and it's how I can show my love to you today."

Samora swallowed the lump that formed in her throat. She'd been right to come here. She hadn't received what she'd hoped for, but she'd been given exactly what she needed. "Thank you."

"You're welcome, but you know there's no need to thank me. You are always more than welcome here, always more than welcome to share your burdens."

Samora stood and wrapped her mother in an embrace. The motion must have caught Mother by surprise, because she was slow to respond, but after a moment, she stood and wrapped her arms around her daughter.

Whan Samora broke away, Mother said, "Do you remember the last words your father said?"

"Of course." How many times had she gone back to that moment, both in memory and nightmare? "My steps are light."

"Do you know what he meant?"

"That he died content."

"In a way. When he was younger, Jace had a master who developed a unique style of fighting with adani, fighting with a greater number of smaller bindings instead of putting as much strength into a single spear as possible. In a way, some of your techniques remind me of his. The ultimate goal of the style was to move quickly, without conscious thought, to be able to strike in any direction in an instant. To accomplish this, an adanist needed to fight with both their body and their will in perfect alignment. One who could do so was considered to possess 'a light step,' in his master's words."

Samora leaned forward. In all their discussions about Father, none of this had ever come up.

"Jace became one of his master's more advanced students, but he could never break through that final barrier. He could never act without thought. He confessed to me, later, that he believed it was because he'd never given his heart to the mission of the clans. True happiness, for him, was here, working the land and watching you two grow up."

The lump in Samora's throat reappeared. She'd hardly known him, their future together stolen by the Debru.

"When he said that, what he meant is that in that last battle with the Moka, he'd broken through the barrier. He'd finally found something worth fighting for."

Samora nodded, but Mother wasn't finished. She tapped the side of her head.

"When Jace died, you took refuge here, and that's fine. Your curiosity and reason have taken you further than I ever dreamed possible. But for this, it's not enough to know it here," she tapped the side of Samora's head, "you need to know it here." She tapped Samora's chest.

Samora nodded again, and they embraced, and Samora took her leave.

Aldrick was the first to greet her, his eyes filled with unspoken questions she wasn't ready to answer. He accepted her silence without question, and in the privacy of her thoughts, she thanked him for that acceptance. At times, he seemed so simple and obedient, but anyone who thought as much was a blind fool.

He believed in her. Whether she explained herself or not, he stood by her side, defending her against anyone.

She hoped she was someone worthy of such belief.

Night fell as they began their way back to camp, but despite her guards' worried looks to the sky, she walked slowly.

It was too easy to get lost in thoughts. Given the opportunity, she'd do almost nothing else. Tonight, she pushed them away. She focused on the clouds gathering overhead, the rising humidity in the air as the storm approached from the west, on the solid, dependable presence of Aldrick ahead of her.

The Debru wanted to take all of this from her. From everyone.

The first flickering of lightning had started to light the horizon far to the west when the messenger from the camps found them, breathless from running as fast as her feet could carry her.

"It's your brother. He and Capricia have been poisoned, and no one can heal him. Loken and Lenon are afraid he's about to die."

32

Samora saw the tents nearing, but she could barely say how she'd gotten there. Hurried footsteps in the night, illuminated by distant lightning, thunder chasing them across the prairie. Talk of betrayal, of an exodus of the clans, the words known but their meaning lost in the haze of panic that dulled her senses. Then, among the tents, guided by Aldrick's steady hand.

His grip on her hand became everything. So long as she followed that hand, all would be well. It had to be well.

Adani churned, as violent inside her core as the approaching storm.

Voices, shouts, and questions surrounded her like an angry swarm of mosquitos, but none could reach her. The camp was lit as though it were day, yet it lacked the warmth it usually possessed. Something indefinable had been stolen, cut out like flesh that had rotted away.

Aldrick pulled her through a circle of adanists, their power held tightly, ready for battle, grating against her senses. Then through a tent, more brightly lit than the night outside. He let her go, and she grasped for his hand before looking up and seeing Brittany, Loken, and Lenon looking back at her.

Their lips moved and sound poured into her ears, but she held up a hand for them to stop. She searched the tent and saw them, Elian paler than the sheet covering him and Capricia on her side, a thin stream of vomit running from the corner of her mouth to a pail carefully positioned beneath the cot she lay on.

The sight snapped her back, and the world was sharp again.

"What happened to them?"

Loken answered. "Sweetroot. Quite a bit, I'd think."

Samora frowned. "I'm not familiar."

"It's a plant not found anywhere near here. When boiled into a tea, it creates a clear, tasteless liquid. Very poisonous, and particularly dangerous to adanists, as it seems to effect adani channels as well as the blood."

"Is there a cure?"

Lenon spoke for the healers. "There is, and it's been given to both of them. Capricia's response is more similar to what I've seen before. She'll need to vomit out everything in her stomach, and if she survives, she'll need to drink nothing but water and some broth for the next few days to clear out her body."

His words wrapped themselves like a stone around her heart. "If she survives?"

Lenon shrugged. "Survival depends on how much she had, how long it was since she drank it, and her own constitution. Thankfully, she and Elian were under watch, so it couldn't have been long before they were noticed and rushed here. A nearly empty flask was found next to them, no doubt the method of delivery, but we don't know how much they drank. She's strong, but there's really no telling. We'll keep a close eye on her, but it's anyone's guess whether or not she pulls out of it."

"And my brother?"

Loken stepped forward to answer that question. "A more diffi-cult question. Like Capricia, he's been given the cure for sweet-root, and he's vomited a little, though much less than her. If not for his channels, I'd say he had a great chance of surviving."

"What's wrong with his channels?"

"Sweetroot causes them to wither and twist. For most adanists, this is an unfortunate problem, but rarely a dangerous one. Healing can restore the adani channels with little difficulty. There's only one problem: his adani channels have grown too deep. None of us have strength enough to heal them."

Samora's frown deepened. "All three of you, here, with the assistance of the heart?"

Disappointment lined their faces, their silence answer enough.

What had Elian done to himself? She'd sensed the latent strength within him well enough the night before, but how had he put himself beyond the healing of these three, especially in a gathering ground?

She reached the cot he rested on and placed the tips of her fingers against his shoulder. A brief pulse of adani raced from her fingertips through his body, like a pebble thrown into a massive cave. It didn't travel far, but she understood.

Her own channels had expanded to allow her to manipulate the strength of a heart, but Elian's were deeper, wider, and stronger. If she put a heart in his hand, he'd manipulate its strength as though he'd been born to it.

No matter how far she advanced, he was always one step ahead of her, stronger than she could imagine.

She lifted her fingertips off his shoulder as her adani returned. It was no wonder the others hadn't been able to manipulate his channels.

"If you were to join us," Loken suggested, "we might be strong enough to heal his channels."

"I won't be enough."

"But you manipulate the hearts better than anyone," Loken said.

"When the three of you worked together, you all pulled from the same heart. One heart, working through three spirits. If I were to join you, it would still be one heart, only channeled through four spirits. The amount of adani would barely change, and being as I bring so little of my own, I'm actually among the worst of your choices."

Brittany, the youngest and the weakest of the healers present, finally spoke. "I refuse to believe there isn't something we can do."

"There is," Samora admitted.

She'd known the moment she'd felt her adani return. An answer that carried its own poison.

"What?" Brittany asked.

"I use the power of the heart I carry. Stronger than the one beneath our feet, and directly upon him, not mediated by the gathering ground. If there's anything that can save him, it's that."

"Then do that, if that's all that will save him."

Samora bit her lower lip. "I need time to think. Is his life in immediate danger?"

Loken said, "No, though if something isn't done by dawn, I worry he might not recover."

"That's enough time, thanks." She strode from the tent, hurrying as though otsoa were chasing her.

———

KARLA RUBBED the sleep from her eyes as Samora finished telling her what had happened.

"I see your dilemma. If you use the heart, the Vada will have no doubt where you are. But if you don't, Elian may die, and he's our single best candidate for helping you kill the Vada," Karla said.

"And he's my brother," Samora added.

Karla didn't deliberate nearly so long as Samora had expected she might. "It's not much of a decision. If we assume the Vada is intelligent, it must already guess that you're here. The risk is worth it."

Samora surprised the other adanist when she flung her hands around Karla's neck and pulled her close. "Thank you!"

Aldrick waited for her outside the tent, the lines of concern etched on his face visible even at night. "What did she say?"

"That I should attempt the healing."

It had been the same advice he'd given her earlier. "Good. Then let's get it done."

She took his hand and squeezed it. "Thank you."

"For what?"

"Everything."

They raced through the camp together, and when they reached the healing tent, they found Loken, Lenon, and Brittany waiting for them. Samora explained what she was about to do.

"What do you need from us?" Loken asked.

"To keep a close watch. I've never attempted anything like this, so I'm not sure it's within my ability. I'm counting on you to make sure I don't go too far, and to clean up whatever mess I might make in the process."

They agreed without hesitation, each hurrying to prepare the tent for the healing. Brittany collected the herbs she thought might be most useful while Lenon heated a fresh pot of water. Loken sat in quiet meditation beside Elian. If Samora's efforts turned against either her or Elian, he was the one most likely able to save them from disaster.

Despite their haste, time crawled for Samora. Now that the decision to use the heart had been made, every moment they waited was a moment wasted. She tried to follow Loken's example and meditate, but in the end, she preferred pacing. The repetitive movement allowed her to focus on the task ahead of her.

As soon as Brittany and Lenon announced they were ready, Samora knelt beside Elian. She took the heart from her pocket and unwrapped it from the layers of cloth she'd kept it in. Loken's eyes went wide, but Samora took it in her left hand and held it tight.

Adani crashed over her like water falling from a great height. Her body stiffened at the rush of power flooding through her limbs, but the experience was familiar to her now, and she kept her body relaxed. Her channels were already adapted to the strength of the heart, so they flexed and extended quickly, absorbing the adani and letting it flow freely through her body.

She reached down and placed her hand on Elian's chest, sending enough adani into his body to kill a lesser adanist. His body accepted the flood of power eagerly, and the heart from the destroyed village by the sea possessed more than enough strength to fill his channels. The twists and blockages of his channels were as obvious as a child trying to hide by standing tall in the middle of an empty village square, and thanks to the power of the heart, Samora began the long and slow process of healing her brother.

The technique wasn't any different than the healings she'd done before, but the scale of the powers was new and unexplored territory. She found that the scale mattered little. Her body was adapted to the new levels of power, so as long as she maintained her focus, the incredible amounts of adani behaved exactly as she expected it to.

She sensed the results almost immediately. Under the gentle but unrelenting pressure of her healing, his channels began to recover. Those that had withered and shrunk expanded and came back to life. Like a clan of adanists fighting their way through a group of Debru, she pushed forward, working her way more deeply into his damaged core, healing the wounds she found as she went.

She only stopped when she couldn't sense anything left to heal. She'd gone through his channels time and time again, ensuring that not the slightest imperfection remained. By the time she finished, his body allowed the heart's adani to flow through it with the ease of a warrior who'd known such strength for years.

He was a remarkable man. She'd always hoped that he would reach incredible heights, but she'd never imagined his determination would carry him so far.

Despite her healing, he didn't wake. When she asked why, Loken said, "Remember it wasn't just about adani. His body still needs to reject the sweetroot."

The four of them sat a silent vigil. The morning sun turned the eastern horizon various hues of pink, but the camp didn't stir its way to life the way it usually did. All waited in silence to see how the events of the night would transpire.

Elian vomited just after the sun broke over the horizon. Then he opened his eyes, and a moment later he was sitting up, though the effort cost him. He swayed back and forth, and the four healers were right beside him. He looked around, confused by the sudden attention.

His body couldn't handle the activity of his spirit, though, and he fell back. Loken and Lenon guided him back down to the comfort of the cot. He closed his eyes, though Samora could tell from the pattern of his breathing that he wasn't asleep.

When he'd gathered his strength, he rolled over onto his side and looked around the tent. His eyes found Capricia and Samora could see the tension drop from his shoulders. "How is she?"

"She's well enough for now, and we have high hopes that she'll pull through. We've done all we can, though. The rest is up to her," Samora said.

Elian clenched his fist and the heart, which Samora had placed back within the layers of cloth in her hand, began to glow in response to his adani. She swore the air around Elian bent, like air that shimmered near the horizon under a midday sun. He wasn't even connected to the heart, but it responded to his strength anyway. But then she blinked, and his incredible strength had returned to normal, at least for him.

She reached out and grabbed his arm, offering her silent support. The muscles in his arm quivered with tension, and she noticed, though he tried to hide them, the tears that trickled down his cheek.

She didn't know much about the future, but she was certain of one thing.

She didn't want to be Aldo this day.

❧ 33 ❧

The sun had risen, and the unified clans were awake, but the camp remained quiet outside the walls of the healing tent. Elian sat beside Capricia, waiting to see if Aldo's treachery had stolen her from his life or not. Brittany occasionally joined them to check on Capricia, but otherwise the two of them were alone.

Samora and the other healers had told him what had happened. He'd heard every word, but it was as though the news had barely penetrated past his ears.

Capricia needed to survive.

A part of him knew the clans waited to hear what he'd decided. Warran and the other remaining elders had politely asked to meet, but he'd so far denied them. He imagined marching after Aldo and the other traitors, the unified clans at his back. But every time he did, he had to push the thought away. It brought his blood to a boil, and he didn't trust what would happen if he allowed himself to fulfill his darkest desires.

So he sat and waited. At times, his mind was empty. Those were the times he appreciated. He could sit and stare at Capricia, memorizing every curve of her face, every faint scar that represented the lifetime of battle she'd survived.

Poison couldn't kill her. Not after everything she'd fought.

The longer he waited, the farther his thoughts drifted. Every moment he wasted here was a moment Aldo and his conspirators raced away from the justice they so richly deserved. Aldo's treachery had divided the clans, and many, not just Wolves, had fled the gathering ground last night as Elian and Capricia fought to hold onto their lives. He should be chasing Aldo, but he couldn't leave Capricia's side.

When his thoughts started to run away from him, started to focus too much on the events outside the healing tent, he spoke to her. Lenon had told him that people could hear even though they seemed unconscious. Elian wasn't sure he believed, but once he started speaking, he found it difficult to stop. He spoke of anything that wasn't about the present moment, anything to keep the rage churning his stomach at bay.

"Growing up in the village, there was this girl I liked. Or, at least, I thought I had liked her. Maybe I was only interested in her because she was one of the only girls around my age in the village. Her name was Sara, and we played together when we were children. Anyway, I'd carried this secret desire for her in my heart for a long time, and I was certain that someday I'd bond with her, and we'd have a farm somewhere close to my father's land. Or, if it was a day I believed I'd become an adanist, that she'd leave the village with me, and we'd join the wandering clans."

The recollection brought an empty smile to his face as he shook his head. "I was a fool, but worse than that, I was a blind fool. I was so certain of my future that I didn't even notice that my feelings for her weren't returned. One day, I found her and Gabe, another boy in our village, kissing in the grove. They didn't know I saw them, but I must have run for miles before I stopped."

Elian held up his hand, made a fist, then released it. "I swore I was going to kill Gabe. He'd taken something I thought was mine."

He swallowed hard. "Of course, I know now that Sara wasn't mine, that the dream I'd constructed in my head was nothing more than a dream. But that was how I felt at the time, and it wasn't until Mother calmed me down that I felt like it was safe for me to return home."

He hung his head. "It's the same now. I've always liked you, and then one day I realized I loved you. If you come out of this, I'm going to ask for your hand. We can have Kati or Warran bond us. But right now, all I can think about is killing Aldo. I can think of a dozen reasons why it's a terrible idea for humanity, but I don't care. I want to take my sword and make him suffer."

Capricia didn't answer, and Elian was grateful she didn't. He would have treasured her advice, but he didn't want her to see him like this, so consumed by emotions he couldn't control. He fought to bring them back under his command, at least until he remembered Kati and Harald arguing about him long ago, when they'd met in the Hawks' gathering ground. Kati had argued that Elian didn't need to control his emotions, and Harald had reluctantly agreed.

Elian stopped trying to tie his emotions into a knot or force them into a box. He stood and swore, cursing Aldo's cowardice and promising vengeance. He clenched his fists and imagined beating Aldo until his face was bloody and raw.

The moment passed, and his anger, no longer contained, dissipated like a Debru weaving cut apart by his sword. His outburst left him a little emptier inside, but when he saw Capricia laying there, beyond his help, tears came unbidden. He let them come, allowing himself the space to cry, heedless of anyone who might wander into the tent.

But like anger, the sorrow, too, passed through him, leaving him lighter as it passed. He sat down next to her and held her hand in his own, running his thumb along the back of her hand. He stared at nothing in particular, content to be by her side.

Samora found him in the same position when she came into the tent later. "How is she?" she asked.

"Same, near as I can tell."

"May I?"

Elian placed Capricia's hand by her side, then stood to give his sister room. Samora placed her hand gently across Capricia's forehead and closed her eyes. A slow smile spread across her face. "She'll make a full recovery," she said.

Elian's heart leaped, but he eyed Samora as though she was one of the village elders who, at the spring planting, had promised the farmers a bountiful harvest in the autumn. "How can you know?"

"Her adani is flowing much more smoothly, particularly in the channels around her stomach. Thanks to the other healers, she vomited out most, if not all, of the sweetroot. I can't say for sure, but I expect she'll be on her feet, if a little unsteady, by the end of the day."

Elian threw an embrace around his sister. "Thank you."

Samora didn't respond immediately, taken aback by the unexpected display of affection. Then her smile grew a little wider. "I didn't do that much."

"You saved my life, again," Elian said. "I'm starting to lose count of how many times that's happened."

"No need to count. You know I'll save your life as many times as I can."

Elian let Samora go and took a step back. "No matter how strong I get, I'm always a step behind you."

She started at that. "That's how I feel about you. You shouldn't sell your own abilities short."

Knowing that Capricia would live, Elian felt as though the ropes tying him to her bedside had been cut. "Do you know when she'll wake?"

Samora, as she had since she was a young girl, saw to the heart of his question. "I don't, but I think if you want to speak to the elders, you have time."

"Any idea what I should tell them?"

"No, but I trust you. Whatever you decide to do, I believe it will be best, not just for you, but for the clans and for humanity."

She left the tent, leaving him alone with his thoughts. He sat with Capricia, weighing his choices, but when he squeezed her hand to bid her farewell, he still wasn't sure what path he'd order the clans down.

HE SUMMONED the elders to the Bears' central campfire, but the request was almost unnecessary. His departure from the healing tent was observed by adanists from each of the unified clans. Word had spread long before he'd sent it, and they gathered not long after he'd gotten settled. He'd hoped to speak with Warran first, but he'd already delayed too long.

He looked around the reduced group. Aldo, obviously, was long gone, but it looked as though all the Wolves' elders had joined him in his departure. Wolves still remained in the camp, though only a small number, and they kept themselves apart from the rest of the camp. Accusations of betrayal were tossed around whenever they were mentioned, but Elian expected the opposite was closer to the truth. Those Wolves remained loyal to his vision, and they remained, knowing the scorn that would be heaped on them.

Elian turned to one of the Bears standing guard around the circle. "Find Aldrick. He might be with my sister, or he might be among the Wolves. Ask him to join us, please."

He didn't miss the fire in the guard's eyes as she bowed.

"Kindly, please. He's a friend."

The guard bit back her retort, nodded again, then left to find him.

The rest of the circle had gone silent, and the weight of their judgment made it difficult for Elian to breathe. Those here had stayed, but he'd be a fool to assume their utter and complete loyalty. The unification of the clans balanced on the edge of a blade, and a single mistake could cut them apart for good.

Kati and Loken, representing the Hawks, looked ready to march to war for him. After the blood they'd spilled together, their loyalty came as no surprise, but he silently thanked them for it, nevertheless. Tiafel looked as though he'd aged a decade in the past few days, and he'd looked old before. He'd lost the most warriors of any other clan to Aldo's design, and Elian couldn't guess what thoughts ran through his mind. Then again, he'd never been able to guess the wily elder's innermost thoughts. Warran, sitting beside Elian, didn't look much better. Only a few Bears had joined Aldo, but each one felt like a deeper betrayal, coming from Elian's own clan.

Altogether, the group felt brittle, as though the ties that had once bound them tightly had frozen in the winter snows and were ready to snap.

Elian opened the gathering with the good news. "Thank you, all of you, for your support. Aldo and I rarely agreed, but I never believed he would stoop to such a measure. Thanks to the efforts of Loken, Lenon, Brittany, and my sister, I survived and feel as good as I ever have."

The mention of every healer by name was intentional, a reminder that he'd only been healed because of the combined efforts of almost every clan present.

"Not only that, but I just learned that Capricia is expected to make a full recovery. She consumed much more of the sweetroot than I, but thanks to the actions of the same healers, she was quickly treated, and she remains strong."

Kati bowed to him at the news. "Thank you for letting us know."

As she finished speaking, Aldrick arrived in the circle. He looked as though Elian had asked him to walk into a dragon's open mouth. And from the looks he received from the other elders, Elian might have. "Sir, you wanted to see me?"

Elian gave him the briefest of bows, hoping to put him at ease. "Yes, and thank you for your haste. I'm afraid I don't know the situation among the remaining Wolves, but I was hoping I could appoint you, at least temporarily, to serve as elder for those of your clan who chose to stay."

Aldrick took half a step back and held up his hands as though warding off a blow. "I'm honored, but I'm hardly the one you should ask, sir. I'm not qualified."

"You're as true a Wolf as I've ever met, and I trust you as much as I trust everyone else in this circle. How are you not qualified?"

Aldrick hung his head. "Perhaps it is best if the Wolves have no elder upon the council, sir. After the actions of our leader, I'm not sure we deserve to have our voice heard."

"Nonsense!"

His outburst caused several heads around the circle to snap up.

"I have no intention of punishing anyone simply because of their association with another. Does anyone among us question, directly, Aldrick's honor? If so, speak now, so I may know if he's worthy to sit among us."

"He's a Wolf, isn't that enough to keep him away?" Kati asked.

"Not even close. Every clan here had at least one adanist who joined Aldo in his treachery. Should we dismiss ourselves, too, because we were friends with those who left?"

Kati looked down at the ground, unwilling to meet his stare.

Tiafel looked as though he might say something, but for the moment, he kept his own counsel.

No one else spoke, though Elian gave them plenty of time to object. Then he said, "Please, join us, Aldrick. After, you may speak with the other Wolves and determine who among you is best suited to sit upon the unified council, though my own recommendation is that they nominate you. For what you've done to protect my sister, you have my eternal trust."

Color rushed to Aldrick's cheeks, and he took his place among the other elders.

Elian looked around the circle before tackling the most difficult questions. Kati didn't like his decision about Aldrick, but he hadn't lost her loyalty. Tiafel still looked thoughtful, and Warran nodded.

Elian cleared his throat and said, "Now, to the matter we're all thinking about. I'll confess my own mind is unsettled in regard to Aldo. Poisoning me and Capricia was enough to make me want to settle our differences with a sword, but I'm even more upset that he would tear us apart when we most need unity. Tiafel, I'm certain you're well informed as to the extent of the treachery. Where do we stand now? What was Aldo hoping to have happen?"

Tiafel tugged at his beard. "From what I've been able to gather, Aldo hoped that killing you would solve several of his problems. First, he truly believes the Debru have only increased their assaults on the clans thanks to the presence of you and Samora. I'm not sure what plans he put in place to kill Samora, and I apologize for my rudeness, but considerable suspicion has been cast upon Aldrick. Many whisper that he was ordered to get close to Samora only so that he could kill her when the time was right."

Aldrick was on his feet before Tiafel finished speaking. "That's not true!"

The guards around the circle turned their attention to the

argument, and even Elian felt the hairs on his arms stand on end as they gathered adani to protect their elders.

Elian reached down with his left hand and grabbed the hilt of his sword. It greeted him with the familiar flood of adani, but once he surrendered to it, his sight sharpened, revealing the paths of adani around the circle. The heart glowed like a second sun beneath their feet, and every blade of grass and weed sparkled with excess adani. Several of the elders had gathered theirs, focusing it in preparation for a weaving.

Aldrick didn't. If any of the elders or guards decided to attack, they'd kill him before he could even try to raise a shield.

Was he that devious, or innocent?

Aldrick didn't beg or plea. His face twisted in anger, but he kept it under tight control. "I'll do anything to prove my innocence. Just tell me what I need to do."

"What if I asked you to leave my sister alone and never see her again?" Elian asked.

Aldrick turned to him. The fire in his eyes hadn't died, but his face might as well have been carved from stone. He met Elian's stare without backing down.

"Anything but that," he said.

Elian bowed his head, then gestured for everyone to sit. "We shall get to the truth of the matter, but for now, I trust Aldrick."

"You're too close to him, sir," Kati said. "It prevents you from seeing the obvious treachery."

"Perhaps. But I choose to extend Aldrick my trust. Not only that, but I trust my sister and her judgment. We will find the truth, but I won't dismiss anyone based on a rumor. Now, Tiafel, please proceed."

"Of course, sir. It is also believed Aldo wanted you and Samora dead in the hope that the clans would return to their traditional ways. He believed we were safer wandering our designated lands, or at the least, he believed independence worth the additional risk. It was that appeal to tradition, I think, that won over many converts from the other clans. Numbers aren't exact, but I believe that with his departure, we have lost about one in three of our adanists."

"And what of his plans now?" Elian asked.

"Uncertain, but I believe he intends to return to the Wolves' gathering ground to wait and see what happens. If we assume his worldview, the Vada will attack this gathering ground, killing us all and destroying the land. But then it should retreat, and he and the others will return to the old ways."

"Thank you. What would you do if you were the sole decision-maker in the unified clans?"

Tiafel considered that question for a good long time. "I'd let him go. Wicked and foolish as he might be, he might still be right. We'd considered splitting our forces before, and so long as they reach the gathering ground, they might be useful."

Kati disagreed. "Such treachery can't go unpunished. We hunt him down and kill him, using the dragons if we must. Those who followed him can be given an opportunity to recant, but he must die."

"Warran?" Elian asked.

"Let him go. There's no point in risking our lives until the Vada is defeated. Then, maybe, we can bring our forces to bear against him."

"And Aldrick?" Elian asked.

The younger warrior looked up, surprised to be asked. Elian knew how deeply Aldrick respected Aldo, so he was surprised when the newly appointed leader answered quickly. "Kill him. He's a disgrace of a leader."

Elian had called the council to order uncertain of his own beliefs, but as every eye turned to him for the final judgment, the answer was obvious. It wasn't the answer his heart wanted, but it was the right answer.

"We let him go," Elian said. He held up a hand to stall any objections.

"It is not that I don't want him to suffer for his crimes. I do. But I've always said, and I believe this with every piece of my heart, that the only battle that really matters is between humanity and the Debru. Pursuing him risks our forces, both because we'd be leaving the protection of the gathering ground, and because we'd be fighting a group of battle-hardened adanists. I may hate what he did, but I won't let that hate doom humanity. Our battle is here, against the Vada. Once we've defeated it, then we can ask ourselves once again what we should do about Aldo."

The verdict, as he'd imagined, earned mixed but predictable reactions. Kati growled but accepted the judgment. Aldrick clenched his fists and stared hard at the ground, and both Warran and Tiafel looked pleased by the decision.

"Prepare the camp for battle. I want all the tents brought closer together so that we can defend them more easily when the Vada arrives. Set up new watches among those that remain so we're always prepared. Have your adanists practice with the heart's power. If anyone is particularly talented at channeling it, let me or Samora know, because we might set a heart aside just for them. Let's move. I don't think the final battle will be long, now."

❧ 34 ❧

Word of the arguments and decisions made at the unified council spread through the camp like wildfire, and even Samora was swept up in the destruction. Aldrick's name was on everyone's lips, and opinion about him seemed evenly divided. Several concerned adanists came to Samora and suggested that Aldrick be restricted to the Wolves' section of the camp, which was quickly becoming considered a place of outcasts and traitors who had yet to reveal their true nature. Some praised Elian's faith in his allies, although plenty called her brother a fool.

She had more people seek her out in the immediate aftermath of the council than she'd talked to in weeks. She tried to be polite, but soon asked the guards that still surrounded her to ensure her privacy. In better days, she would have fled the camps and wandered the wild, seeking someplace quiet, but she had no desire to tempt the Vada to visit again.

Her tent was the only place in the gathering ground she was free from wandering eyes, so she went straight there.

Alec, who currently led her guards, stopped her before she entered. "When he shows up, what do you want me to do?"

"Let him in."

He nodded, and she silently thanked him for his acceptance. She slid through the opening in her tent and closed it behind her. She didn't feel like sitting, so she paced while she waited. Alec had the right of it. Aldrick would be here soon, and she would have to answer him then.

It wasn't as though the thought of betrayal hadn't occurred to her. A guard from a hostile clan, suddenly deciding that she was the most important person in the world? It could be love, respect, or affection, or it could have been something more sinister. She'd never been the subject of such affection, so how would she know? She believed in her senses and her instincts, but she'd been wrong before.

How would she know?

She wished she had her mother to guide her through. She remained aloof from the dramas that captured the clans' attention, and she had a sharp eye for what was best for her daughter.

Samora was no closer to an answer when his adani approached. It was turbulent, which could have meant anything at all. Was he an innocent man, coming to plead his case, or a guilty man, using his one last opportunity to strike?

She was tempted to gather her own adani, but then she hated herself for thinking that way. Elian had chosen to trust him, but if rumors from the council were true, he'd only trusted Aldrick because he believed in her judgment.

Elian shouldn't put her on such a high pedestal. She didn't know what she was doing.

"Samora?" Aldrick had stopped outside her tent, but she heard his voice tremble through the hides.

She hated herself for doing it, but she extended her adani toward him, searching for any clue as to his intentions. Light flowed easily through his body. He hadn't gathered it for immediate use, but was that because he possessed no ill intentions, or because her guards watched him like eagles, ready to strike the moment they sensed focused adani?

"Come in," she said.

He did, stopping just inside the flap. She stood on the opposite side of the tent, but it felt as though the entire deadlands separated them.

He stared hard at the ground and his cheeks were flushed. He dug into the dirt with the toe of his boot, and his fists were jammed deep in his pockets.

Seeing him like this, Samora longed to leap across the tent and wrap him in her arms. How many times had she relied on his calm, quiet strength? How many times had she believed in herself because he had believed in her?

At that moment, she hated the clans and the world even more than the days after Father had died, for they had broken something beautiful, and she wasn't sure it could be put back together.

"Look me in the eye and tell me it isn't true," she demanded.

He stared at the ground a moment longer, then, as though lifting an enormous fallen log, he lifted his head and met her gaze. "It isn't true."

The deadlands between them vanished, and Samora crossed the tent and nuzzled into his chest. His arms hung loosely at his side, but her presence gave his arms strength, and he reached up and wrapped her up in a tight embrace.

"Just like that?" he asked.

"Just like that."

"How?"

She liked the way he smelled, the light scent of his sweat pleasant and comforting. "Trust is a choice. My mother taught me that the only way to judge a person was by their actions, and you've done nothing but earn my trust since we met. I'd be a fool to throw that away because of a rumor."

He kissed the top of her head. "Some would say you're a fool for trusting so easily."

She shook her head, nuzzling a bit harder against his chest. "It wasn't so easily earned. You've fought for me, defended me, and traveled untold distances with me. All of that and more is what earned my trust. Those that doubt me want me to throw that trust away at the first sign of trouble, but that isn't trust, and that's not the life I choose to live."

He trembled, but the moment passed quickly. "You know I'd do anything for you, don't you?"

"I do."

THEY SPENT time in the tent, relaxing together and speaking of nothing in particular. Political storms and Vada might lurk beyond the walls, but for a few precious moments, all else was forgotten.

"What do you want to do when all this is over?" Aldrick asked.

"I don't know."

He rolled onto his side and propped his head on his hand. "You don't know?"

"That's what I said."

"You don't have any dreams? Any hopes?"

"I hope that I'm living in peace, and I can put all this madness behind me."

Aldrick wasn't so easily satisfied. "But what will you do?"

"I haven't spent much time thinking about it."

"Now seems as good a time as any. Don't go too deep into thought. What's your first reaction, your first instinct?"

The decision came easy, almost without thought. "I think I'd want to keep studying adani. Spend more time with the elder dragons and pick through their memories. I've learned a lot since I left my home—more than I'd ever imagined, but it's barely anything when I measure it against all that's left. If the knowledge of adani was that city we discovered by the sea, I'd say that I've only explored the first room of the first house."

Aldrick whistled softly. "So little? Really?"

Samora warmed to her subject. "Really. We've learned plenty about how to manipulate adani, and we know it's intricately connected to life across the world, but what else do we know? How did it arise? Was it here before all life, or did it arise from life? It clearly possesses either consciousness or something akin to it, but how?"

Aldrick stared at the ceiling of the tent. "Those seem like difficult questions to answer. Maybe even impossible."

"Maybe," Samora agreed, "but if I could do whatever I wanted with my life, I think that would be it. Not only would it satisfy my curiosity, but it would help humanity, too. We might have other enemies out there we don't even know about."

"What do you mean?"

Samora gestured toward the west. "Since the day we've been born, we've considered the Debru the enemy. And they are, yes, but why? Because there's another force in the universe. We call it shadow, but it took the adanists and captured them. If you ask me, our real enemy isn't the Debru, it's shadow."

"That's an unsettling thought. That means that even if we defeat the Debru, our war isn't over."

"No, I think if we defeat the Debru, if we kill this Vada, the war will be over in our lifetimes. But the universe is a violent place, and I'm not sure defeating the Debru means the shadow is also vanquished. Our descendants need to be prepared, and I'd like to help them if I could."

"We'll have to make some descendants first," Aldrick said, a mischievous grin on his face.

Samora laughed, kissed him, then pushed him away.

"True, and we will, but not right now."

Aldrick hid his disappointment well, then grew curious as Samora sat up and started braiding her hair. "What are you thinking?"

"Nothing specific, but talking to you about the future

reminded me that we won't have a future unless we figure out how to defeat the Vada. I should speak with Elian."

Aldrick rose, too. "Then I'll stand guard, as before."

Samora kissed him again. "I'd like that very much."

SAMORA IGNORED the suspicious looks Aldrick endured as he walked a few paces behind her, senses alert for threats. The rumors wouldn't die, likely not until the battle with the Debru was over. She didn't allow herself to doubt him, for if she did, she feared the entire world would collapse around her.

They tried the healing tent first, but Elian wasn't there. Samora checked in on Capricia. Her adani flowed smoothly and her breathing was deep and even. She concurred with Brittany. Elian's love was safe, so long as she continued resting.

The Bears' central fire was likewise empty, leaving Samora with the choice of training grounds or tent. Knowing her brother, she made straight for the training grounds.

Elian was there, his new sword in hand. Samora stood a safe distance away and watched, still in awe of Elian's newfound abilities. He'd always been stronger and faster than most thanks to the way his body used adani but watching him now made it clear he'd reached an entirely new level of strength. He moved faster than the tip of a dragon's tail and his cuts were strong enough to slice a house in two.

The heart embedded in the hilt of the sword shone as Elian used it, leaving an intricate trail of light behind as it spun and cut through the air. Samora almost wished the sun would go down, so that she could watch the light dance through the night.

Elian sheathed the sword when he was finished, a casual move that happened so fast Samora barely noticed. One moment the sword was in hand, the next, it was in its sheath, and she wasn't entirely sure anything had happened in between.

"How are you feeling?" Samora asked.

"Good, mostly. I still feel half a step behind, but I'm not sure if that's true or if it's just me wanting to push myself harder."

"It's impressive you can push yourself any further at all. I've never seen such speed, not even in the elder dragon's memories."

Elian grunted. "Still doesn't feel like enough. I've got some small idea of the Vada's strength, and I don't match it, yet."

"You don't."

Elian accepted her assessment without complaint or objection, and she was struck by his complete trust in her.

His eyes wandered up and over her shoulder to where Aldrick stood guard. He grinned. "Good for you."

"If I can't trust him after all we've been through, I'm not sure I could ever trust anyone again."

"I know what you mean. If anyone accused Capricia, they'd have a black eye before they finished." He paused. "So, what are you thinking?"

"I wanted to talk about how we prepare for the Vada. Now that I've revealed where I am, it's possible that we'll be attacked at any moment."

Elian nodded. "Agreed, and I've already asked the clans to prepare for an immediate attack."

Samora had seen the clans bringing their tents together as she'd made the journey to find Elian and had assumed as much. "Good."

"I'm also hoping to pair adanists with hearts. Would that be acceptable?"

"Of course, although don't get your hopes up too high. The hearts are incredibly difficult to manipulate."

Elian nodded. "I was also thinking the time has come to have you send your adani out so we can understand what's happening in the world. No point hiding you anymore, is there?"

"Probably not, unless you're worried me using adani again might pull the Vada here."

Elian shook his head. "I don't think it's that irrational. When it attacks, it will be its reasoned choice, not because you were exploring with your adani."

"Do you want me to search now?"

Elian looked around and shrugged. "Why not? I'm as curious as you are."

Samora sat cross-legged in the grass and placed her palms against the ground. She closed her eyes and ran through the familiar routine, using the heart beneath the gathering ground to strengthen her efforts. Her adani shot out in all directions, and she opened her mind as the world came to her.

She found the Vada first, the darkness of the shadow unmistakable. It had returned to the camp it shared with its army a few days west of the clans' position. It sensed her, of that she had no doubt, but it turned away, as though uninterested. If anything, she'd say it delighted in ignoring her.

Why?

Her adani pushed farther, but there was little of interest. Eventually it came across a large group of adanists wandering south from far up north. Samora assumed the group was Tassan and the other adanists Elian had recruited, but they were several days away, even if they pushed themselves to the brink of their endurance.

She called her adani back, the frown deepening on her face.

"What's wrong?" Elian asked.

She told him what she had sensed, from the casual disdain of the Vada to the reinforcements soon to arrive. "I can't figure out why the Vada now seems so smug. When it came for the elder dragon, it was serious."

Elian sat down next to her. "Maybe it believes that without the old elder, we're helpless against its power."

"Then why is it waiting?"

Elian thought for a bit but came no closer to an answer than she did. Eventually, he asked, "Did Aldo and the others make it to the Wolves' gathering ground?"

"I didn't think to check. They must have, because I didn't sense them anywhere else."

Once again, Samora closed her eyes, and this time she sent her adani north, toward the Wolves' gathering ground. She sensed the heart within, and she agreed with what the others had told her. It was stronger than the one she'd created here. That was good. The more hearts they had, the better.

But no matter how long she looked, she couldn't sense the presence of adanists in the other gathering ground. It wasn't an easy task, akin to looking for the flame of a candle while staring at the sun, but she should have sensed something. As near as she could tell, the gathering ground was empty.

She kept searching, up until the moment her stomach sank down to the bottom of her gut. It couldn't be.

She brought her adani back, but searched every mile of land between here and the Wolves' gathering ground, wandering several miles east and west, too, just in case Aldo and the others had been forced to take a wide route.

Nothing.

She opened her eyes when adani returned to her, and she met Elian's stare. As he had since they were children, it seemed as though he had read the news in her posture and expression.

"It's bad, isn't it?" he asked.

She slowly nodded. "I think they're gone."

✾ 35 ✾

Warran and Tera trailed after Elian as he tried to leave
them behind.

"You can't just leave! And certainly not with Samora," Warran
said.

Elian kept walking. The discussion was already over, even if
they didn't recognize it. They'd argued with him, even after he'd
made his plans perfectly clear. Now they sought to stop him as he
put them into motion.

Tera, by far the more aggressive of the two, leaped around him
and stood in his way. He tried to walk around her, but she side-
stepped and forced a confrontation. She kept her voice low, so
that it wouldn't carry throughout the camp, but there was no
doubting the fire in her words. "Take a moment and listen, fool.
You've worked hard to prove you're more reasonable than Harald
was. Don't start throwing that away because Warran's trying to
talk some sense into your brick of a head."

Elian's glare could have frozen an entire field, but Tera wasn't
impressed. She stood her ground while Warran stepped around
Elian's back and joined them.

"There's nothing to gain," the elder said.

"We need to check for survivors, and I need to see with my own eyes," Elian said.

Warran opened his mouth to object, but Elian said, "He tried to poison me and Capricia."

Warran shut his jaw, his lips in a tight line. "At least take an escort."

"Samora will pay attention. If the Vada begins to move, we'll hurry back here."

Warran grimaced, then sighed and nodded. "Fine."

"Thank you."

Elian left the two behind. As he left the Bear camp, Alec and the other guards circled around him and escorted him to the dragon's nests. Once they were free of the tents, Alec said, "You might not like to hear this, but I understand where they're coming from. Can't say I like the idea of you wandering off alone."

"There's no point risking anyone else. Samora and I on a dragon can be there and back before most people even know we're gone."

Alec didn't argue, but he wasn't pleased to be staying behind.

They met Samora, who stood beside the new elder. "She's agreed to take us," Samora said.

Elian bowed to the dragon. "Thank you."

They climbed on top of the dragon and took off without delay. The elder's powerful wings lifted them into the sky, and they raced north, following the path Aldo and the other traitors had left. Enough feet had fled the camp that they'd blazed a trail the siblings could follow in the dark.

The speed of their flight brought tears to Elian's eyes. At least, that was what he told himself to calm the turbulent storm of emotions raging in his chest. He'd dreamed of meeting Aldo again, with the traitorous leader scrambling away from the tip of his sword. Still, if Samora's senses were to be trusted, it meant that nearly a third of humanity's remaining strength had just been wiped out.

Because of a treachery that had never needed to happen.

Even when they disagreed, they were stronger together.

Since he'd woken, Elian had tried to put himself in Aldo's position, imagining what it would be like to believe that he and Samora were the true danger. But even if he accepted that, he couldn't bring himself to poison an ally.

Thanks to the elder dragon's haste, they found the traitors before long. It wasn't hard.

It looked like the world had risen up and taken its vengeance. Wild grasses, trees, and brush had been torn up alongside flesh, bone, muscle, and dirt. It had all been tossed together and ground up like a cook chopping different vegetables for a stew.

Elian's stomach churned at the sight as the dragon circled slowly overhead. The limbs that were on the surface or sticking up from the mess showed no signs of predation. The attack had frightened the nearby scavengers so badly they hadn't returned despite the feast waiting for them.

There was no point in looking for survivors, but Elian asked the elder to land, anyway.

It did so, remaining a hundred paces away from the edge of the destruction.

"Sis?" Elian asked.

"Of course." Samora took a heart in her hand, sat down, and pressed both hands into the soil. Even Elian felt the adani pulse out from her as she searched near and far for information. His own search focused on the outskirts of the destruction.

He saw no reason to walk within the churned-up ground. Nothing there lived, except perhaps some hardy grassland seeds designed to endure the harshest of prairie conditions. He didn't think he'd even find a mostly whole body.

Instead, he looked for other tracks, any sign of what forces had ambushed the traitors. That the Vada had been behind the attack came as no surprise. He and Samora had already guessed as much. It was the only one of the Debru fast enough to strike the traitors and return to its forces by the time Samora pushed out her adani. The destruction beside him only confirmed it. The land reminded him of the first attack he'd seen, when the Vada had chewed up an entire gathering ground.

His quick search confirmed his suspicion. As near as he could tell, not even a kettu had been present for the massacre.

By the time he'd made a complete circle, Samora had opened her eyes. "No survivors nearby, although that's not surprising. The Debru are on the move, too."

Elian started. "They're coming for us?"

She shook her head. "No, they're heading for the unified clans."

He was already halfway to the dragon when he saw she hadn't moved. "Samora?"

"There's no need to rush. I don't think they're actually attacking. It's the whole camp. Debru, Belogs, the Vada, everyone. They're moving slow."

"Sounds an awful lot like an attack to me."

"I think it's a message."

"How so?"

Samora's face was pale. "We're trapped. Anyone who tries to leave will be killed. Without the power of the hearts, they won't stand a chance. And you and I are trapped, too. If we leave, it'll attack the clans."

Elian looked south and west, though the Debru were far beyond his sight. "Why not just kill us?"

His sister shrugged. "Why take the risk? If I'm right, the Debru here are about all that are left. Once, the Vada may have thought it could roll right over us, but it's being cautious now. When we fight at the gathering ground, the advantage is ours. But we can't stay there forever. It can starve us out within days by hunting those that leave the gathering grounds' protection."

"And if we try to protect those who leave, it'll attack the clans." Elian swore. "I liked it better when the Debru just attacked without a strategy."

Samora nodded. "Regardless, we should return to the gathering grounds. We can see if I'm right about this being a feint, and we can spread the news about Aldo and the others."

Elian took one last look at the torn-up fields.

"I suppose we won't have to worry about Aldo splitting apart the clans anymore," Samora said.

Elian swore again and clenched his fist. "Shortsighted coward. All this death was so damn pointless. I might have detested Aldo, but there's no honor in this. It's just a waste."

They turned from the scene and returned to the dragon, who was eager to return them to the safety of the gathering grounds.

UPON HIS RETURN, Elian informed Warran and the other elders of the fate of Aldo and the other traitors. He watched the same battle he'd just experienced play out across their faces. The satisfaction of knowing the traitors had brought their own doom upon them warred with the knowledge that so many friends and family had died for no good reason.

Once they'd accepted the news, Elian hurried straight for the healing tent. He needed Capricia's presence now, even if she hadn't yet woken. She widened his perspective just by being near.

Brittany was alone in the tent when he arrived, and she looked up from the preparation of herbs she was working on. When she saw who her intruder was, she tilted her head toward the back of the tent. "No change, though I suspect it won't be long before she wakes."

Elian bowed in thanks and padded over to the back of the tent. The folding stool he'd spent so much time on earlier was still there, and he took a seat beside her.

He was no healer, but he believed Brittany was right. All the color had returned to Capricia's cheeks, and she breathed with the same deep and even pattern she did when she was fast asleep. He reached out, took her hand, and rubbed his thumb gently across the back of her knuckles. He let his mind go empty, seeking peace in the silence.

Sometime later, her hand tightened on his, and he squeezed in return.

"Aldrick?" she asked, the corner of her lip turning up in a smile.

Elian snorted. "Unfortunately, I think his affection belongs to my sister. You'll have to settle for me."

"Poor me." She gripped his hand tighter and cracked open her eyes. "Aldo?"

He nodded. "He's dead."

"You?"

"No. He took all those who agreed with him away, but after they left the gathering ground, they were killed by the Vada."

She closed her eyes again, and a tear trickled down the side of her cheek. "I'm sorry."

Elian shook his head. "There's nothing to apologize over."

"I brought it. Made you drink it, even when you didn't want to."

"But it was Aldo's private stash, and I think we can both agree it was delicious."

She grinned at that, then used her free hand to wipe the tears from her eyes. "Too much of a hangover for me, though."

"Same. I might be done with liquor for a while."

"You and me both."

They fell into silence, and Elian felt the knots that had been tightened around his chest slowly loosen. Capricia was back, and no matter what else happened, that was all he needed.

"I heard you, you know."

Elian's eyebrows rose. "You did?"

Capricia nodded, and blood rushed to Elian's cheeks as he remembered all he'd said. He hadn't really believed the healers had spoken true about her hearing while unconscious. "Everything?"

"I think so."

Elian got off his stool and took a knee, bowing his head. It was too soon, but this decision was the easiest he'd made in weeks. "Will you bond with me?"

"Of course I will. I've been considering it ever since Kati asked you and I to scout the Debru."

Elian's head shot up. "That long?"

She nodded. "I've never met someone else who puts others so consistently before themselves. You could have left me behind that day, and I wouldn't have even blamed you. But you came back, and now that I know you better, I know you'll always come back, always fight for anyone."

Elian leaned over and kissed her, and when their lips broke apart, she said, "Now, get out of here. I'm exhausted and need to go back to sleep, and I'm certain you have more important places to be."

"There's nowhere more important to me than being by your side."

She waved his thought away. "You know what I mean. Find a way to defeat the Vada. I'm sure I'll be here for a day or two yet."

Elian kissed her again, then left, his heart light despite the tragedy that surrounded him.

SAMORA'S GUESSES about the Vada's behavior turned out to be prophetic. As soon as they returned to the gathering ground, she'd sent out her adani again, and the Vada and its assorted followers had halted in their tracks. They didn't return to the valley they'd been camped out in for weeks, but they didn't come any closer.

To Elian, it felt as though the Vada held a sword over his head, ready to cut down the moment he moved. He walked around the camp, knowing he needed to be seen, but his thoughts wandered as he sought a way out of the clever box the Vada had put him in.

They couldn't stay, but they couldn't leave. What remained?

He had no answer. Thankfully, they had several weeks of food on the sleds, taken from Elian's village before they'd left. Supplemented by wild game, it should have been enough to last them through the winter. Still, it gave him a bit of room to think.

He spent most of the rest of the day in training with the sword gifted to him by Royzen. Adani from the heart within the sword strengthened his limbs and sped his cuts, but it wasn't long before he once again felt as though he'd reached the limit of his new capabilities. They were impressive, but he doubted if they were sufficient.

The hole in his adani remained. He tried pushing adani there, he tried wrapping adani in tight loops around it, he even pulled adani away from the hole. Nothing worked.

Eventually, he gave up. His skills would serve the clans well in battle, and Samora explored her own paths to victory. Hope remained. He sheathed his sword, wiped the sweat from his brow, then returned to the camp.

Samora found him sitting with the small number of Wolves that had chosen to abandon Aldo and remain behind. They'd chosen well, but many of their friends and family were gone now, adding a fresh layer of grief to the mess of emotions that threatened to overwhelm them. Elian sat with them, talking of nothing in particular, simply content to be with them as they grieved and figured out what came next.

Samora sat down beside him. "Mind if I borrow you for a bit?"

"Of course. Did you figure out what the hole in my spirit is?"

His sister shook her head. "Still don't have the slightest, but I think you'll appreciate what I have discovered."

Samora led him out of the camps to the eastern edge of the gathering grounds. She crossed the boundary without hesitation, but Elian's stomach clenched, as though simply stepping outside the boundary for a moment would summon the Vada. She walked past the sleds and Elian caught up with her. "Where are we going?"

"Just up ahead. I only need us to be farther away from the gathering ground."

Elian held the rest of his questions. Samora would tell him in due time, and she wouldn't lead him someplace that would put the rest of the clans in danger. She stopped near the top of a rise in the land, leaving them a clear view of the gathering ground and the clans camped within it.

His spirit sank at the sight. After the attack that had killed Harald and Aldo's betrayal, the camp was a fraction of the size it had been. Only a few hundred adanists remained, and the view forced Elian to admit that even if they found a way to destroy the Vada, it might not be enough.

Samora drew his attention away from the camp when she squatted down and started digging in the dirt.

"What are you doing?"

"Digging a hole."

Elian snorted. If she wanted to keep her secrets to herself, that was fine, he supposed. He let her have the moment, certain she was building up to something he'd be impressed by.

She dug the hole quickly, and it reminded him of simpler days when she would help Mother with the garden beside the house. The longer he watched, the more it reminded him.

Then she reached into her pocket and pulled out something small. Given what he'd just been thinking about, he wondered if it was a seed.

He couldn't help himself. "Seems like a poor time to start a garden."

She rolled her eyes but made no other response.

Whatever she was carrying had been wrapped in a handkerchief, and when she unwrapped it, Elian saw that it was a small stone. He inhaled sharply. "That's one of the hearts, isn't it?"

"The final gift from the elder dragon."

Samora took the stone, laid it carefully in the finger-sized hole she'd made, then covered it up with soil. Elian frowned. She'd said she'd received several from the elder dragon, but it hardly seemed like they should be burying them.

A moment later, he felt it. The heart beat, and it felt as though a child had been born, as though the ground beneath his feet pulsed with new life. The wild grasses under his feet regained their vigor, transforming from slowly browning stalks to a spring-like green.

Samora grinned at the look on his face. "I knew you'd be impressed."

"How fast does it spread? How far is the effect? What happens when–"

Samora held up a hand to stop the barrage of questions. "To all your questions, I don't know. This was just a random thought of mine that proved to work. I'll keep studying it, though, so you'll have your answers soon."

"You can make a gathering ground wherever you want," Elian said.

Samora carried his thoughts to their logical conclusion. "Which means the clans aren't stuck here. Once we're ready, if we want, we can bring the fight to the Vada."

❧ 36 ❧

The days flew by like the migratory birds fleeing south before the encroaching winter. Samora divided her time between experimenting with planting the hearts in the ground, training her own abilities with the hearts, watching and learning from Elian's training, and seeking others to train with the hearts.

It was the last task that disappointed her most. She'd thought, back in the elder's cave, that adapting to the strength of the hearts was a skill she could teach to others. And she might still be right, but there was nothing she could teach in the time they had. Controlling the strength of even the smallest hearts required a level of control over adani few of the clans' adanists possessed.

Time and again she bumped up against the limits of the training methods that had worked so well for the clans. Almost every adanist could bind a spear in their sleep, and most could cast a shield with equal ease. There were some, like Aldrick, who'd taken naturally to other bindings, such as a sword or knife, but the training philosophy behind each of the techniques limited future growth.

The warriors of the wandering clans had learned that it was better to be a master of one or two bindings instead of becoming more widely proficient. And to this point in the clans' battles, the teaching had been correct. It was far more important to be able to form a spear or shield in the blink of an eye, exhausted and injured, than it was to play around with esoteric weaves that would rarely be used.

Unfortunately, the teaching established habits that would take months to break. The process of binding adani was for most so instinctive, they'd forgotten how to control adani in other ways. As a gifted adanist from a village, where she hadn't had to fight to survive, Samora hadn't been so limited. Karla, likewise, had spent so much time wandering on her own and exploring the different uses of adani that she was capable of harnessing the strength of one of the lesser hearts.

Few others were. Loken had intermittent success, and one young woman named Alera, who'd just come of age among the Hounds, could sometimes use the heart for brief moments as well. Others showed promise, but it would be weeks or months before that promise was realized.

When she'd complained to Elian, he'd shrugged and said, "It's unfortunate, but we have other options. To tell the truth, I think your discovery about planting the hearts is more promising than the idea of equipping individuals with them. A gathering ground strengthens everyone, not just a select few."

Those experiments were more encouraging. A single heart planted in the ground affected adanists for hundreds of paces in all directions. Unlike the gathering grounds, there was no hard and fast boundary that defined the edge of the heart's influence. Instead, those closest to the heart felt its influence most strongly, while those farther away felt it less.

She'd also tried planting multiple hearts at once. They released more adani, but the benefit to adanists was small. Most adanists could only channel so much in the first place, so planting a dozen was barely more beneficial than planting one. The adani spread a bit further, but not much.

The strategy she'd devised with the elders was straightforward, then. When the time for battle came, a handful of representatives from each of the clans would plant the hearts, creating a wide field that would assist the adanists as though they were fighting on a gathering ground. Both Samora and Elian had concerns about simply planting the hearts and leaving them where anyone, human or Debru, could scoop them up, but it was widely believed there was only one more battle to fight. The fate of the stones would be determined by the victor, not by their location.

All that remained was Samora's training, which she most often conducted with Karla. Their combined efforts, though, resulted in few gains greater than what she had already achieved in the elder's cave. She could harness the power of a heart and use it as she saw fit. The longer she exposed herself to the heart's power, the more capable she became of wielding it for longer.

And as she did, sometimes she swore she could feel the miniscule hole in her adani that Elian told her he'd felt, but it was as resistant to her inquiries as his was. No manipulation she knew could seal the hole, and to her senses, it almost felt as though it didn't want to be sealed. It wanted something more, but what, she couldn't begin to guess.

Her explorations were interrupted by Karla's arrival. The elder adanist took one look at the dozens of spheres floating above Samora's outstretched palm and shook her head. "I know you can bind a spear, girl."

Samora released the spheres and chose to ignore the comment. It would only lead to an argument they'd had too many times already. "You said you were too busy for training today, so what brings you out here?"

"Your brother asked me to find you. Says he wants to meet with you and a number of others down by the dragons."

"Did he give any reason why?"

"No, but he had that self-satisfied look he gets whenever he thinks he's doing something clever."

Samora barked a quick laugh. She was all too familiar with that look. He'd had it since he was a child, and in the past, it had usually meant a fair amount of trouble for her. "I feel like maybe I should run the other way."

"Please don't. I told Elian I'd bring you, and I don't want to chase you down."

"Like you could catch me."

Karla rubbed the side of her temple with a hand. "Youth these days. No respect for their elders."

Samora gestured for Karla to lead the way. Karla did, then asked, "What have you sensed recently?"

"Nothing that's changed. The northern clans are two or three days away, depending on how hard they push the pace. The Vada and all its minions are sitting in the same place they've been sitting since the day Elian and I left."

"Any sense of what it's up to in there?"

"The shadow is too thick. I can feel incredible powers moving within, but I don't have a clue what any of them mean."

"Everything that monster does makes me uneasy. It's too clever by far, if you ask me."

They reached the north side of the gathering ground where the dragons had made their nests. Elian and a surprising number of adanists stood around the dragon that had carried Samora, Karla, and Aldrick back to the gathering ground, the new elder.

Elian grinned and waved when he saw them, and Karla's observation was confirmed. He very much had the look he got whenever he thought he'd come up with a particularly clever idea.

"Thanks for coming," he said. "I thought it was important that you be here, too."

Samora looked around the circle and tried to understand why.

Everyone else was either a leader or an elder, and she had no place here.

Elian began. "The first news I wanted to share is known to some of us, but not to all. Aldrick, I'll turn it over to you."

Aldrick stepped forward, and Samora saw how hard he tried to look like the leader he wasn't yet prepared to be. The Wolves had nominated him their new leader and he'd accepted, though he'd privately told Samora that he hoped to soon be free of the burden. He was a warrior, happiest with a sword in hand and an enemy in front of him he could cut. Council meetings were worse than battle for him.

He cleared his throat and bowed to Elian. "The past few days have been difficult for me and the remaining Wolves. All of us have lost friends and family in Aldo's betrayal and subsequent demise, and our position among the clans has been rightfully contested. Once we were one of the strongest southern clans, but now we are one of, if not the, weakest. After much conversation with my adanists, we've made a difficult decision. Today, I come before the council and formally request that the Wolves be absorbed by the Bears. The Wolves who remain would be honored to serve under Elian's leadership."

Samora started. He'd told her nothing of this, though they'd seen little of each other in the past few days. Her time had been consumed by training and learning, and now she understood what he'd been so busy with.

Elian had obviously already known, but the others in the circle looked as surprised as Samora. Karla just grunted and scratched at an itch on the side of her leg.

"It's me who is honored by the trust and faith you show in me, Aldrick. We've already talked privately, but I'll say now in front of all that I'd be honored to have your Wolves join the Bears. We're in need of strong warriors, and the Wolves are strong."

Her brother looked around the circle. "I've spoken at length with Warran, and I understand there is no official precedent regarding such decisions. I accept the loyalty of the Wolves, but I wanted the rest of the council to speak first. From now until the end of the Debru, we're fighting together, and I'll do nothing to upset that."

Tiafel said, "I have no problem with it if you don't."

The longer Samora had to get used to the idea, the more impressive Aldrick's decision seemed. The Wolves were so greatly reduced it would be difficult for them to contribute meaningfully to future battles. Even more problematic, those that remained weren't trusted by many in the clans. Joining the Bears solved both of Aldrick's most pressing problems.

Kati looked between Aldrick and Elian. "If we're joining clans, then the Hawks would like to join the Bears, too."

The entire circle went silent, and Elian looked as surprised as everyone else. "Sorry. What?"

"We were in discussions with the Bears about joining before Harald's death, as you well know," Kati said, "but we've been fairly occupied since then."

"When we last spoke about it, you didn't think your adanists would agree."

"True, but a lot has happened since then. We've lost even more strong warriors, and you've proven yourself time and again. As you're always saying, we're stronger together."

Elian made his decision with surprising speed. "Only on the condition that you become my second."

Kati scoffed. "You're not going to ask Warran?"

Warran answered for himself. "Elian knows I don't care about the title or the role. I'll continue to serve the clan as I always have, no matter what title you give me."

"Then I accept," Kati said.

Samora blinked as she tried to keep up with the changes. Just a few moments ago there had been four unified clans in the gathering grounds, and now there were two.

Several gazes turned to Tiafel, who shook his head. "I respect you, Elian, but the Hounds will remain our own clan."

Elian looked relieved. "I wouldn't expect anything less."

Her brother turned to the elder dragon. "But now that there are fewer clans, it occurred to me that perhaps it is time for another clan to join us."

Samora couldn't keep up with her brother's ideas, but Karla barked a harsh laugh. "You want to make the dragons a clan?

Elian didn't see the humor in the situation. "I do. They've fought beside us, aided us in ways both big and small, and sacrificed almost as much as any wandering clan. You all know that I believe the only way we win against the Debru is if we fight together, and that means human and dragon, too."

He spoke to the circle of elders, but he looked only at Samora, his question directed as much at her as everyone else.

Dueling memories fought for supremacy in her thoughts. The sight of flames consuming buildings and bones wrestled against the elder's final stand against the Vada. She couldn't find the space in her spirit to forgive the dragons, but the elder's ultimate sacrifice carried a surprising weight. Perhaps it was time for her to think more about the future than dwell on the sins of the past.

"I believe the dragons have more than earned the honor of becoming one of the wandering clans," Samora said.

Elian allowed himself a little smile and bowed his head toward Samora. The other clan leaders had little to add, and Elian's suggestion was carried.

Her brother turned to the newest elder, who had been looking upon their proceedings with undisguised interest. The only time Samora had seen its like was when she had studied under the elder. "Great elder, we would be honored to have the dragons join humanity as a wandering clan. Do you accept this honor?" Elian asked.

The dragon considered the council for a brief moment, then bowed its head toward them. After it raised its head to the sky and let out a long roar loud enough to make the clouds tremble in fear throughout the nesting ground, the other dragons joined in a shout loud enough to frighten the Vada. For a moment, at least, it gave her the courage to believe they might survive the winter.

The Vada answered the challenge

Even though Samora hadn't extended her adani, she felt the gathering of shadow as clearly as if it had formed directly beside her. The weave reminded her of the spheres she preferred, though it was more complex by far.

The other leaders and councilors felt the weaving a moment after her, and every eye except Elian's turned to the west.

"What is it?" Elian asked.

"The Vada is weaving an attack. Some form of shadow sphere."

Elian's decision was made in a heartbeat. "Retreat to the gathering ground. Everyone, prepare to create shields."

He turned to the dragons. "You'll likely be safest in the gathering ground, but if you want to fly, I will understand."

The elder dragon bowed, and the dragons took to the air, heading east. The humans ran toward the gathering ground, shouting orders as they approached the camp.

Samora's stomach dropped when the Vada launched the attack. It didn't seem real. She thought she'd understood its power, but how could anyone focus a weave over such vast distances?

They reached the gathering ground in time, and all eyes turned to the sky for any sign of the sphere. Samora joined them for a time, but there was little she could add. Instead, she sent her adani down and out.

She found the sphere with little problem. Though it sped through the air, such was its strength that it killed the ground it passed above.

Samora let out a cry and she almost collapsed. Only Aldrick's quick reaction held her up.

Elian was by her side an instant later. "What's wrong?'

Samora's tongue was dry and heavy in her mouth, as helpless as she was. As helpless as she'd always been. With effort, she forced the words past suddenly parched lips. "It's not coming for us," she said.

Elian frowned.

Samora clutched his arm, one of the only solid things in the world she could still trust. "It's heading toward our village."

Elian stared at Samora, certain he was trapped in a nightmare, for even life, in all its cruelty, wouldn't dare. Did the Vada know that it struck the hearts, not of the clans' gathering ground, but of the siblings who dared oppose it?

He straightened. On a dragon, perhaps, he could reach the village in time to do some good. As he turned to leave, though, Samora's hand tightened on his arm. He looked down and she shook her head, tears in her eyes.

To the south of the camp, there was a flash of light, brighter than the sun on a summer day. Elian saw his shadow clearly cast by the false sun, which faded much more slowly than it had appeared. He forced himself to face the light, to witness and to remember. The light dimmed as a cloud of dust and debris rose high into the air, easily visible miles away.

A rumble passed through the ground, not strong enough to throw people from their feet, but enough to rattle Elian's teeth. He clenched his jaw shut as he flexed his fists.

"I need to see," he said.

Samora kept her grip on his arm, and at first, he thought she might be trying to keep him from leaving, but she was only using him to raise herself up. "I'm coming with," she said.

Elian nodded, then told Warran they would return soon.

"Of course, sir. Should we attempt a rescue effort?"

Elian glanced at the cloud of debris, still expanding. "I don't think that will be necessary but thank you."

Warran bowed. "If there's anything we can do, all you have to do is ask."

Elian escorted Samora away. They walked through a soft chorus of condolences, but for the most part, they were left alone, and he swore that if it was within his power, he'd find a way to thank the clans for their kindness. The dragons were already returning to the nest, and Elian led them to the dragon he'd saved from the Belogs in the deadlands, the dragon that had carried Samora to the enormous village by the sea.

Elian had come to think of the dragon as a friend, and he wanted to be surrounded by friends today. He connected his adani to the dragon's and asked if he would be kind enough to carry them both to the village and the dragon readily agreed. They climbed on and were in the air in a moment.

The flight was blissfully short, too short for thoughts to catch up. They tried to reach Elian, but he pushed them away. So long as he didn't think, there'd be no grief. For now, all he needed to do was to witness. To see, with his own eyes, that the Vada was every bit a monster.

The dragon landed as close as he could, and Elian thanked him as both he and Samora slid off.

The surrounding land remained familiar, but what stood before them did not. The Vada's weaving hadn't simply destroyed the village. It had caused the village to disappear completely. The ground was cratered, maybe three times Elian's height in the deepest point, where the village square had once stood. Everything that had been within the space the crater occupied was simply gone. Elian hadn't seen a single window frame, a single piece of broken furniture, not even a scrap of cloth on their flight in.

In a few years, once grass, animal, and tree had reclaimed the land, there'd be nothing to tell their descendants that a village had bloomed here. That two brave souls had left the clans and tried to build a more peaceful life here.

In a way, the complete disappearance of the village provided Elian a wonderful temptation. It gave him space to believe Mother still lived. With no corpse to wash and no bones to bury, it was as if she wasn't gone at all.

But she was.

The thought slapped him across the face, then slapped him again.

Once again, he'd been able to do nothing but watch. For all the strength he'd gained, he still couldn't protect the people he loved. He was still too weak, the same as he'd always been.

Samora took his hand and held it in her own. She pulled him forward, and together they made a slow loop of the crater. She said nothing, but she held his hand as though she was grasping at the hilt of a sword.

He wished there was something he could say that would comfort her. Something that would take some of her pain away. If it had been possible, he would have taken her pain and carried it upon his own shoulders. But that wasn't how life worked, not at all, and the best he could do was share her grief.

Their loop allowed them to witness the destruction from all angles, but there was nothing to learn. There was no debris in any direction, no sign of life within the crater. Elian's spirit wilted as they walked over the grass that had died as the sphere had approached the village, but it returned once they reached the live grass.

They stopped where they began and stared at the place of their birth.

The full weight of Mother's loss hadn't yet struck, and some part of Elian hoped it never would, though he knew that it would surround him when he least expected it.

Samora stared into the abyss with him, and when she spoke, it was just loud enough for him to hear. "It needs to die," she said.

Elian nodded and squeezed her hand. They let go of one another, and without another word turned back to the dragon.

It was time for them to launch their war on the Vada.

BY THE TIME they returned to the camp, Elian had his thoughts fixed firmly on the future. Hopefully, there'd come a day in the future when he had the time and space to mourn, but to surrender to his emotions now would leave him helpless when the clans needed him most. They couldn't delay any longer.

Most of the clan leaders and elders were waiting for them when they returned. In answer to their silent questions, Elian said, "There's nothing left. Nothing at all."

Before he could drown under a fresh wave of condolences, he said, "We have a larger problem. If the Vada can launch attacks that far, it stands to reason it can hit us here. It also means it can likely hit the northern clans as they finish their approach. We need to establish more powerful defenses. Samora, can you and Loken divide up those who have some ability with the hearts? I'll let you two best judge how to divide them, but we'll need to fly a handful over to Tassan and the others, while leaving a few here to protect the gathering grounds."

Samora nodded, but Karla objected before she could begin. "I hate to be the one saying this, but someone has to. Are you certain that sending any of the hearts away is wise? With all of them here, we might be able to block an attack from the Vada, but if we split them, I'm far less certain."

"You'd have me leave Tassan and our northern allies undefended?"

"I'd have you consider it, yes. I'd rather have half of us alive than all of us dead."

Samora interjected. "There are other options, too. The gathering ground is too small to fit the dragons, and they're capable of binding simple shields. Assuming the elder is willing, we can use most of the hearts here but send most, if not all, the dragons to protect the arriving adanists."

All agreed, and Elian gave the orders. He wanted Samora to join him traveling north, but she convinced him it was wiser for her to protect the gathering ground. She suggested Karla join instead, and the elder adanist agreed.

Once they were on the dragons and safely away, Karla asked, "What happened to Samora? She didn't say much, but I could see the change in her. Will she be able to fight when the time comes?"

"For the first time, I think the answer is 'yes.'"

"Good. I'm sorry it cost you your mother, but considering the stakes we're fighting for, I'd consider the loss worth it."

Elian turned his head slowly and fixed her with a stare he hoped would be sufficient to remind her that he, too, had just lost his mother, but she was almost as impervious as a Vada.

"I'm not worried about you having the will to fight. If anything, you need to learn caution."

Elian stared at her a moment longer, then snorted and turned away. Karla was Karla, and there was nothing in the world that would change her.

They reached the clans without incident, sooner than Elian had expected. Tassan had pushed his clan hard. Most of the dragons flew in a protective circle while the dragon carrying Elian and Karla landed in front of the clan.

Tassan stood in the very front of the line, and he was halfway to Elian before Elian had finished dismounting. He barely had time to set his feet before the giant had picked him up again in an embrace that would have killed a small bear. Elian grunted as he was forced to exhale every bit of air in his lungs, but he couldn't stop the smile that spread across his face when Tassan put him down.

"I can't tell you how good it is to see you're alive, young Bear," Tassan said. "We sensed the Vada's attack and worried you were no more."

Mention of the attack wiped the smile from Elian's face. "The gathering ground stands, for the attack wasn't aimed at us. It was, instead, aimed at the village Samora and I are from."

Tassan's face hardened, and Elian saw a side of the man he'd only glimpsed in the chaos of the Scorpion village. "I'm truly sorry, Elian. We'll make them pay though, won't we?"

Elian nodded. "With their lives."

Tassan's eyes rose to the sky. "I take it that's why there are more dragons in the sky than I thought were even alive?"

"If the Vada could reach out and destroy a village, we feared it would do the same to you. The dragons have agreed to protect the rest of your advance, and Karla has agreed to help as well."

Tassan's grin returned at the mention of Karla's name, and his eyes glinted in a way Elian hadn't yet seen. He bowed, too deeply, to the clanless adanist. "My fox, it's been a long, long time."

"And here I thought you'd forgotten me," Karla said.

"I'm more likely to defeat a Vada with a single blow than I am to forget you."

"Have you settled down and bonded yet?" Karla asked.

"I have."

"A shame. Memories don't keep me warm on these cold nights."

Tassan's laughter was loud enough to make Elian want to cover his ears. "I'll be sure to warn the young men of the danger wandering the camp tonight."

"You'll do no such thing, or I'll have words with your wife," Karla said.

"I'm afraid she already knows my past better than I do, so

your threats are empty, friend. She'd actually be pleased to meet you, I think."

The two returned to the clans, walking shoulder to shoulder, leaving Elian standing beside the dragon. He rubbed at his eyes and shook his head. He didn't want to think about it. Not at all.

They were here, and with the dragon's help, they'd keep the Coyotes and the Scorpions safe.

That was all that mattered.

His stomach twisted and flipped, just as it had earlier in the day. He turned south and swore. He couldn't see anything, the attack far too far away, but there was no doubting what it had been.

Then there was nothing. The dragons continued to fly in the same patterns they'd established when they arrived, so it didn't seem like the attack was heading toward them, but someone, somewhere, was on the receiving end of the Vada's wrath.

He couldn't lose Samora.

He didn't notice when Karla returned and stood next to him. "It wasn't aimed at the gathering ground."

"Where, then?"

"Tough for me to tell, but I think it was sent to the village south of yours."

Elian pressed his palm against the dragon, and it was only by focusing on the dragon's well of adani that he controlled his reaction. He took deep breaths, and he felt, more than saw, Tassan come up behind him.

"Can your clans march through the night?" Elian asked.

"I'm not sure we have much of a choice. We won't stop until we've reached the gathering grounds."

"Good. Once you're there, we'll take some time to rest. We'll need some time to prepare our strategy and decide our roles. But then we strike, whether we think we're ready or not. It's time to bring this war to an end."

❦ 38 ❦

Samora sat among the other Bear adanists and sharpened the knives she would carry into battle. If the battle turned in such a way she needed the weapons, humanity was as good as doomed, but it gave her something to do with her hands as the inevitable summoning approached. Her hands guided the blade across the whetstone with even, sure strokes, and when she held her hand up so it was level with her gaze, it didn't so much as tremble.

She kept waiting for the fear to arrive, to steal her breath and make her heart pound, but it kept its distance. The matter had become a simple one. She was going to kill the Vada, no matter the cost. No one else would be forced to endure the loss of so many loved ones to invaders. The worries that had churned her stomach for so long were gone, leaving nothing but a cold emptiness behind.

The Coyotes and Scorpions had arrived early that morning, and Elian had ordered them to rest. With the sun high in the sky, everyone wondered if Elian would begin the battle today or tomorrow. The Vada had destroyed a third village this morning, casting a deep silence over the assembly. It felt to Samora like the calm that settled over the land immediately before a fierce summer storm.

When this one broke and the clans attacked, the ensuing battle would be one for the ages.

Assuming anyone survived the battle to tell the story.

Someone approached from her left, and when she looked up, she expected Aldrick's steady presence. Instead, Brittany came and sat down beside her. Samora welcomed her with a quick bow of the head, then returned her focus to the edges of her knives.

Brittany squirmed against the silence, struggling to find the words to express whatever had brought her to the fire. Samora imagined that whatever it was, it must have weighed heavily on her spirit, for there was no end to the preparations she'd be making for the upcoming battle. She and the other healers would have no tent to protect them once the spears began to fall.

"I'm sorry about your village," Brittany began. "I keep trying to imagine what it would be like to lose the whole clan in one attack, and I can't. If there's ever anything I can do, just let me know and it'll be done."

"Thank you," Samora said.

Brittany nodded, tapped her heels, but didn't leave.

Samora took one last look at her knife and sheathed it. "There's nothing you need to apologize for."

Brittany started, eyes wide as though Samora had somehow stolen the thoughts from her mind. She recovered quickly, used, now, to Samora's keen insights.

"I still feel like I should. I haven't always seen the world the same way you and Elian do, and you two have taught me I wasn't as eager for change as I thought I was. Part of me has always known you're doing what you think is best, but it's hard to accept that when it's your friends and family dying in the process."

Samora almost repeated that there was no need to apologize, but now that Brittany had started, there was no stopping her.

"I was unkind and cruel, and I'm sorry. Please, accept this as an offering."

Brittany pulled out from one of the many pockets sewn into her cloak a pouch designed to carry wet herbs. Samora opened it and sniffed but couldn't place the scents within.

"A concoction of my own design," Brittany explained. With gentle but firm fingers, she pulled the drawstrings on the pouch tight again. "Best not to let it get exposed to too much air."

"What does it do?"

"It's a powerful healing salve. Hopefully, suitable for the battlefield. If you come across an injury that you don't have time to heal, just slather that across it and run a small amount of adani through the salve."

"It takes adani?"

"It'll work fine without, but with, it's something special. The mixture of herbs reacts with adani, creating a local but potent healing. It should close up large cuts, mend torn muscle, and possibly even heal broken bones, assuming they've been set properly."

"If half of what you claim is true, this is incredible."

Brittany nodded, clearly pleased with herself. "It's something I've been working on for quite some time. Loken helped me with the last bit I hadn't figured out on my own. If we survive this, I'm hoping to make more. It could help a lot of people."

"Once you get this out to all the clans, you'll probably have saved more lives than any adanist in history."

Brittany blushed, then stood. "We've got to survive this first, so let's work on that."

"Agreed. And Brittany, take care of yourself. I'm sorry I won't be around to help you today."

"You've got much bigger problems. Just kill that Vada and come back alive."

Samora nodded and pulled out her other knife to sharpen.

The word came down from Elian and the council not long after. They marched on the Vada in the morning.

THE REST of the day and that night somehow passed in a blur that lasted forever. Feasts were held around each of the campfires, and Samora was surprised, yet again, by the adanists' ability to keep tomorrow's worries locked firmly in the future. Warriors shouted toasts to one another in between arguments over who would kill the most Debru the next day. Others stayed close to their families, their preparations quieter. But though she searched, she didn't see any outward sign the adanists shared the fears that made her gut feel like a block of ice.

That night, with Aldrick, she confessed her lack of understanding. "It's all I can do not to vomit," she said.

"And if we were left alone, we might feel the same. We take our strength from one another, though. Judge us if you will, but it's harder to run when your friend is beside you. You both might be so scared that you want to piss your pants, but you won't retreat so long as the warrior next to you is stepping forward." He ran his hand through her hair, and her eyelids grew heavy. So long as he remained by her side, the worries of the world grew lighter.

"Besides, you need to remember that most of us have been looking forward to this day since we were children. We've spent most of our lives being driven back by the Debru, but I don't know a single warrior who hasn't dreamed of being part of the final battle for this world."

Samora stirred at that. "Hopefully, after tomorrow, we can give our children better dreams."

"I hope so, too."

They fell asleep, hands and bodies intertwined, and didn't wake until the sun's rise.

CAPRICIA FOUND Elian training near the edge of the gathering ground, Royzen's sword glowing in his hands as he cut through the darkness. She watched as he ran through his forms and waited for him to finish. After a particularly quick set of cuts, the gem dulled as he sheathed the sword and turned to her. "I thought you were going to get some rest," he said.

"So did I, but our bed is cold, and I was promised company tonight."

He had promised, but he hadn't expected peace to be quite so elusive. Normally a few rounds of practice would be enough to put his mind at ease, but the storm of thoughts and emotions churning through him showed no sign of letting go.

"Is there anything in particular that's bothering you?" she asked.

"Besides the stakes?"

"Yes, besides those."

"I need to be stronger. As I am, I'm not strong enough to defeat the Vada."

"Good for us, then, that all will be fighting together with the largest collection of adanists in living memory."

Elian smiled but shook his head. "That's not quite what I mean. I know there's another level of strength, something more we can do with the hearts, I just haven't found it yet. If I haven't by tomorrow, it'll be too late. Once again, I won't be strong enough to protect the people I love."

Capricia wrapped her arms around him. "It's not all up to you, you know."

"I know, but it feels like time and again, I'm unable to stop those I love from dying."

"I hate to be the bearer of bad tidings, but that'll be true for you no matter how strong you get."

"You know what I mean."

She gave him a squeeze, then took a step back. "Did I ever tell you that when I started my training, I was a slow learner?"

"No, you haven't."

"It's true. I was often so distracted by adani I didn't have the focus necessary to weave anything. I eventually learned, but I was behind the others and often got beat badly. Then I'd get in my own way, too focused on my losses to ever win a duel. My master said something after one of my losses that really stuck with me."

"What did he say?"

"He told me to stop telling myself stories. That my past was tying me up in knots and that I wouldn't be able to fight until I freed myself of them."

"Easier said than done."

"Sure, but if you can kill a Moka with a single cut, I think you're plenty capable."

Elian pulled her toward him and wrapped her in his arms. He knew about how she'd take the request, but he asked it anyway. "Would you consider staying here tomorrow? Keep watch over the others who remain?"

"Not a chance," she said.

He was about to object, but she silenced him first. "Don't you think I feel the same whenever you march into battle?"

Blood rushed to his cheeks, and she noticed. She pulled him gently in the direction of the camp. "Come on. There's nothing you can learn between now and the battle, and you're going to need your rest."

"I'm not sure I'll be able to sleep."

Her grin was mischievous. "Leave that part to me. I'm sure we can come up with something that will distract you."

ELIAN WOKE THE NEXT MORNING, perhaps not feeling refreshed, but ready for the battle to come. Capricia was already moving around the tent, getting ready. Elian watched for a moment, then joined her. He strapped Royzen's sword to his left hip, but he made sure the one Harald had given him was on his right. In answer to Capricia's unspoken question, he said, "I want a spare."

When her stare didn't subside, he confessed, "And I want to have it by my side. I realize it might be foolish, but it makes me feel like he's following me into battle."

"That's not foolish," Capricia said.

Once they were ready, Elian embraced her again. He wanted to tell her to be safe, but that was foolish. He settled instead for, "Fight well."

"You, too."

Elian emerged into the middle of the clans preparing for battle. Adanists said their farewells to their families. Those who couldn't fight would remain behind in the gathering ground. Elian acknowledged everyone who greeted him, but he made quick time to the front line, where the council was gathered.

"How are the preparations?" he asked.

Kati answered. "Nothing of note to report. The Vada has been silent since the attack yesterday, but I find it hard to believe it will let us approach without opposition. Otherwise, it's as we planned. The hearts have been scattered throughout the line, and those who can make use of them have them in hand. I can't talk to the dragons, but they're all up and moving about, so I'm guessing they're ready. We'll be ready to leave soon."

"Thank you. I suppose I'll go check on the dragons, then."

Elian made his way to the nest, where the dragons were all up and moving. He found the elder and approached. Before he got too close, he felt the dragon's adani wash over him. He'd not had the experience before, but Samora had told him of it, so he opened himself up, allowing the adani to connect.

A young woman with golden eyes appeared before him. Even

though he'd been expecting it, her sudden appearance where there'd been no one before startled him.

"Is there any change to our plans?" she asked.

"No. We're about ready to leave, and once we do, we'd still like you to provide protection. We expect the Vada will attack, and it will take all of us working together to create shields strong enough to protect ourselves."

The dragon bowed. "Of course. And once the battle begins?"

"I'll let you use your best judgment. Drop as much adani on the Debru as you can, and if you find other ways to help, I'd be much obliged. I don't think there will be any retreat today. We'll either win or die trying."

"And we'll join you."

Elian bowed deeply. "We owe you much. Thank you."

The dragon returned the bow and vanished as quickly as she'd appeared. Elian blinked, then shook his head. He turned back to the camp.

The sun had just peeked over the horizon by the time they began their march. Samora's last check with her adani had placed the Vada less than ten miles away, so the fight would begin by midday.

Elian and his recently enlarged Bears were the center of the line, with the Hounds to the south and the Coyotes and Scorpions to the north. They marched through fields Elian had worked as a child, and Elian wondered if there would ever be another harvest. Any farmers who had toiled in these fields were gone, and none in the wandering clans knew the ways of tilling, weeding, planting, and tending.

He let the thoughts slide from his mind. His attention needed to be here and here alone.

Samora ran a little ahead of the others every couple of miles to send out her adani, but as near as she could tell, the Vada and the rest of the Debru waited patiently for them to arrive.

Midway through the morning, though, that all changed.

Elian felt the twisting in his stomach, uncomfortably familiar these past two days. He wasn't alone, and the clans responded as they'd discussed. The Hounds, Scorpions, and Coyotes all pressed closer to the Bears, and every adanist capable of creating a shield helped weave one overhead. Samora, Karla, and Loken, the three adanists most capable of using the hearts, provided almost all the strength.

The dragons, likewise, circled close and added their considerable strength to the shield. The air in front of the adanists glowed with golden light, which only made the approach of the sphere more pronounced, a stain in sky that grew rapidly as it rushed toward them.

They braced their feet and raised their arms to shield their eyes, and there wasn't time for anything else.

The Vada's attack crashed into the shield, bending the air as though it were a sheet scrunched up by a child. Adanists shouted as they focused their adani into the shield and several dragons roared. The light ahead of them grew brighter, until it filled the sky with a pure white light.

The blast shook Elian's bones, but it didn't knock him off his feet. When the pure white light faded, the golden light of the shield remained, even if it had been dimmed by the Vada's attack. For a moment, they all stared at it, and then Elian raised his fist and shouted. Cheers raced across the assembled adanists, joined by the roar of dragons.

The Vada had struck, and for the first time, humanity had stood against it.

Elian motioned them forward and they marched, hearts beating with hope.

❧ 39 ❧

Samora had never been this close to the Vada, and the proximity agitated her adani like an angry child churning butter. It felt as though the Vada stood directly in front of her, its shadow was so overwhelming. She clutched at the heart in her pocket, all that remained of her ancestors who had built by the sea and took strength from their sacrifice.

The feel of the Vada was so close, Samora swore she felt the emotions that stormed within it. The Vada hated adani, hated even more the people that wielded it well.

Too late, Samora realized her adani and the Vada's shadow were intertwining, similar to the way adani mixed with the dragons. It should have been impossible, yet there was no denying what she sensed. She remembered, then, those memories of the earliest shadow users, who mixed shadow and adani with ease. Perhaps the skill hadn't been entirely lost. She almost pulled away, but the insights she gained were too valuable.

It hated what it could not have. The Vada's blood longed for adani, longed for the light and warmth which it could never again enjoy. Every human and every dragon would die, and then it would call the elders through. They would replenish their weakened bodies on the vast strength of the hearts, then spread shadow across the land, devouring every scrap of adani on this pathetic world.

And when they were done, when they had killed this world just as they had the last, they'd open a portal to a new world and do the same. In time, shadow would rule all.

The Vada ordered its armies into motion, and Samora paled at the size of the force lurking within the shadow. Only dozens of rank-and-file Debru remained, no more than had attacked the gathering ground before. Unfortunately, they were joined by dozens of Moka and nearly a dozen Belogs. By themselves, they would have been an almost impossible force, but they were joined by the Vada, whose strength still defied understanding.

Samora pulled her adani back and informed Elian of what she'd learned. He thanked her for the information, and the firm set of his jaw told her he'd hoped for fewer enemies.

The two armies were less than a mile apart when the sky ahead darkened. Samora had listened to Elian's tale of the destruction of the Hawks' gathering ground, but she had never seen the Vada's strength in person. It was as if someone had spilled a pail of ink across the sky, and it oozed and slid toward them.

Up and down the line, faces paled and steps faltered as they watched the stain expand, threatening to block the midday sun. Elian gripped his sword and let the gem shine bright, but it was a small point of hope against the gathering sea of darkness. The expression on her brother's face let her know that he was well aware, and he had that same look in his eyes he always got when he contemplated something stupid.

It was too early for that, but his instincts pointed in the right direction. The clans needed light, and she had plenty to offer. She held tight to the heart and gathered her weaves, forming sphere after sphere. They blinked into existence across the line, from Hound to Coyote. Dozens, then more, then over a hundred, easily the most complex weaving she'd ever attempted.

Nothing about the weave was easy, but it wasn't as hard as she'd expected. She held the weaves, allowing all an opportunity to see them leading the way. Then she released them, raining the assembled adani down to the adanists. It strengthened limbs and spirits. Faces regained their color and warriors marched bravely toward the shadow.

The clans came to a rise in the land and Elian called a halt. The rise ran roughly north to south, and across a shallow valley, an opposing rise mirrored it. Samora understood little of battle-field tactics, but she understood well enough that if the clans were caught in the valley the Debru would delight in dropping deadly shadow down on them. Already the leading edge of the dark cloud could be seen cresting the opposing ridge.

Elian glanced to Kati, who nodded. "Plant the hearts," he ordered.

The command was passed up and down the line, and nearly a dozen adanists took a knee and thrust their hands deep into the soil. They planted their precious seeds like farmers in a hurry, then covered the holes and packed the dirt down with their feet.

Adani surged through the land beneath their feet. Grasses stood up straighter, just like the adanists who faced the shadow. The spirits that surrounded her grew in proportion to the amount of adani available.

If they had one surprise against the Vada, it was this, that they had discovered a way to bring their gathering grounds with them. If the Vada was surprised, or concerned, it made no show of the fact. The shadow gathering on the opposing rise grew wider and darker, and though Samora knew what the shadow hid, she saw nothing through the darkness.

"Sister, would you see if you could bring us some light?" Elian asked.

Samora weaved her spheres once again, fewer this time, but

stronger. The last time she'd thrown this attack in anger had been at the elder dragon in his cave, but she hadn't really thought she'd hurt him. She closed her eyes and remembered the crater where her village had been. Today, she very much wanted to hurt the Debru.

Once the weaves were complete, she launched them across the shallow valley. The spheres raced toward the darkness, dropping into the shadow like small stones thrown into a pond. Shadow rippled where the light entered, then reformed as though nothing had happened.

Samora still sensed her weaves, fighting against the Vada's protective shadow. Instead of forcing them deeper, she drove each straight down. They struck the ground and exploded, the blast ripping the outer shreds of the shadow apart. Light and heat washed over the faces of the assembled adanists, and a cheer rose from the crowd, though Samora doubted she'd done much harm. Otsoa and kettu were likely her only victims, but they'd died by the score.

Before the echoes of her blast had finished dying in the valley, enormous weaves of bound adani dropped from the sky, the dragons joining the fight. Light crashed against shadow, and while no blast penetrated deeply, the display of raw power strengthened the hearts of the wandering clans.

They hadn't expected much from these initial attacks, but causing damage had never been the primary aim. Despite the Vada's overwhelming power, they had one advantage, even more pronounced now that they could create a gathering ground wherever they went. They could be replenished by the world and the adani surrounding them. The Debru only had the shadow within. The longer the battle lasted, the greater the parity the adanists expected.

The Vada, it seemed, thought much the same. As the last of the dragons' attacks faded against the shadow, it allowed the protective barrier to drop, revealing a vast assembly of powerful foes. The numbers were no different than Samora had felt earlier, but seeing the enormous forms of the Moka and the Belog made those numbers seem a lot larger than they had earlier.

Near the center of the enemy line, well behind the front, protected by four of the largest Belogs Samora had ever seen, stood the Vada, once again wearing the guise of a child. Not even the Debru approached too close to their leader, making the Vada an obvious target for Samora's next attack.

Before she could begin the weave, it had formed a spear of shadow and sent it casually flying toward the wandering clans. Cries went up among the adanists, and Samora joined them in weaving a hastily constructed shield.

The spear didn't have anywhere near the Vada's full strength behind it, but even so, it nearly cracked the combined shield. Samora groaned under the intense pressure, calling upon a considerable amount of strength from her heart. The heart obeyed, but she didn't like the way her adani channels struggled under the load. They hadn't yet found the limit of the hearts, but their bodies were all too fallible.

By the time they'd dealt with the spear, otsoa, kettu, and Debru were halfway across the valley, several Moka and Belogs leading the charge.

Elian drew his sword, the heart embedded in the pommel shining white with adani. He pointed the sword down into the valley and the adanists obeyed. Bound spears fell from the sky, crashing into the advance like heavy rain from a summer thunderstorm. Belogs and Moka cast shields above their weaker brethren, but the adanists continued to pour on the pressure. Dragons joined in from above, and Samora observed the results.

The average adanist, pulling from the power of the hearts, was slightly stronger than a Debru, but probably not as strong as the Moka. Fortunately, the battles rarely came down to a single adanist against one of the Vada's minions. Adanists attacked together, choosing their targets carefully. Most chose to focus on the Moka.

Spears battered the Moka shields. Sometimes they were aided by their larger cousins the Belogs, in which case, the adanists switched to a different target. At other times, the Moka was strong enough to withstand even the efforts of several adanists fighting together. But there were times, promising times, when the Moka's shield fell against the assault of several adanists working together. In those moments, the Moka and the Debru under its protection died as spears rained down.

The dragons also contributed to the effort, focusing their attention on the more powerful Belogs and keeping them from aiding too many of their smaller companions.

Samora couldn't spare them much attention, though, as she sensed the Vada prepare another attack. Like the last, this one used the barest fraction of its strength, but with so many adanists focused on the charge, Samora didn't think they had the power to shield themselves. Elian noticed the attack, too, and was about to order shields, when Samora stopped him.

"Leave it to me," she said.

He looked doubtfully at her, then nodded.

Then he paid the Vada no mind, his trust in her complete.

Samora worked through the weave she'd learned from Karla long before, layering one weave over the next, hoping it would be enough. She couldn't spread the weave out over the entire line, but all she had to do was intercept the spear and it should be enough.

The Vada threw, and Samora had just enough time to layer one more weave over the top of the others. She whipped the weave north, to where the Scorpions were pouring out all their pent-up rage upon the charging Debru.

She'd never been great at catching anything, but adani guided her, almost pulling the shield into place. The spear struck her weaves in the center, and Samora dropped to her knees as she competed directly with the Vada.

Any normal shield would have broken under the Vada's strength, but the pattern of weaves held as the spear spent most of its energy against it. Still, Samora knew it wouldn't be quite enough. She and the heart weren't enough.

Just as the spear was about to break through the last fragments of the shield, a powerful blast of adani struck it from above. The spear vanished and the dragon flew overhead, roaring in satisfaction. Samora grinned as she recognized the dragon Elian had freed from the clutches of the Debru so long ago, the one that had flown her across most of the known world and deep into the unknown corners.

She raised a fist in triumph.

Across the valley, the Vada formed another casual spear. As the dragon banked, the Vada let fly. Samora began weaving another shield, but the process was too complex and took her too long.

"No!" she cried.

She was only halfway finished when the Vada's spear caught the dragon in the chest. Its armored scales were no match for the Vada's strength, and spear punched through as though the dragon's scales were as soft as the skin of a newborn.

The dragon probably didn't even have time to feel pain. The spear exploded inside the dragon's body, raining Debru and adanist alike in hard scale and soft organ. Samora watched the neck spin, lopsided due to the weight of the head, until it crashed down not more than a hundred paces ahead of her. It crushed two otsoa beneath it, and Samora swore she saw the dragon's eyes blink once before staring off into nothing.

The Debru charge was close now, smaller than it had been when it had started, but still enough to sow chaos and death among the wandering clans.

Samora, though, saw only the Vada, forming yet another

spear. Her weave was still half finished, and she quickly tied the rest of it together.

The Vada looked straight at her, shadow spear in hand, and Samora braced her feet in preparation for the attack.

But the Vada didn't throw. Instead, he stabbed the spear into the ground, as though it were a walking stick, and he was out for a stroll among the rolling hills.

Samora stood, confused, for a moment, before her stomach twisted at the way adani died in the valley. She'd felt this sensation before, just before Harald died.

With a curse, she positioned her weave beneath her and jumped. The Vada's spear thrust up from the ground, aimed exactly where her lungs had been a moment ago. The spear struck the shield and exploded on contact. The force of the blast flung Samora through the air like a rag doll, and when she struck the ground, her world went black.

❧ 40 ❧

Being forced to watch the exchange of adani and shadow made Elian want to charge headfirst into battle. His blood boiled as he stared at the Vada standing alone on the other side of the valley. The Belogs and Moka that so frightened his allies meant nothing. They were no more than debris he needed to clear away before he met the Vada with his steel. Vengeance called to him, louder than the sounds of the battle.

But endure he did. The Vada's time was near, but it hadn't arrived yet. He forced himself to wait, to stand tall as shadows approached. Samora and the Vada exchanged their first blows, and spears of shadow rose from the ground as bits of dragon rained from the sky.

Elian endured, and then the shadow reached the boundary of their freshly planted gathering ground and he attacked, unleashing everything he'd held within since the first moment he'd seen the crater where his village had once stood.

He'd left his village with Samora to protect it. He'd failed at that. All that remained was avenging the dead, and there were so many dead.

His sword passed through the first Debru. It had tried to stop his cut with a shadow sword, but it wisped away like a cloud in the wind as his steel made contact. The edge of his blade opened the Debru from shoulder to torso, and it fell, twitching, onto the gathering ground.

Not all duels were so one-sided. Kati fended off two Debru who had joined forces to cut her down, and an entire pack of otsoa lunged at Warran. Elian was left alone, his enemies streaming either to his left or to his right.

Elian used the moment of peace to leap to Kati's aid. Her bound daggers kept her safely away from the Debru's dark spears, but their joint efforts were sufficient to keep her from dealing any damage in return. His arrival tipped the scale in Kati's favor. While one Debru tried and failed to withstand his flurry of cuts, the other fell to Kati's powerful daggers and quick strikes.

She dipped her head in thanks, but as her gaze rose, her eyes went wide. He followed her gaze to see two Moka, nearly the size of Belogs, lumbering toward them. Glowing red eyes were fixed on him, leaving little doubt as to their intentions.

He ran at them, a pair of Kati's thrown daggers leading the way. The Moka in front, standing nearly twice the size of Elian, brushed the daggers away as though they'd been mosquitos bothering him. One dagger killed an otsoa, while another injured one of the Debru. The Moka's stare never wavered.

Elian cut across, but his sword was blocked by a wall of shadow weaved by the Mokas working together. He grunted, then looped more adani through his sword. The edge took on a faint golden glow and it sliced through the binding, revealing both Mokas holding swords and waiting.

Their combined attacks forced him to retreat a step, but then a bound dagger caught the Moka on Elian's left in the face, leaving a wide gash across the Moka's cheek. Elian cut and cut again at the Moka as it regained its focus. One attack across the back of the Moka's thighs sent it to its knees, where another cut nearly severed its head. The sword bit into the ancient flesh and the head flopped to the side.

He and Kati both turned their attention onto the second Moka. His steel and her bound daggers proved too much for the giant creature, and it, too, soon fell among the dead.

The Moka's death bought them a moment to look around. Their lines held for the moment, but the fighting was fierce and the strongest of the Vada's creatures were still to come. Directly to the south, Elian spotted Aldrick leading the warriors who had once been Wolves. Aldrick and the others stood strong, and Elian watched the other warrior fight. He wasn't gifted with the same strength as Samora, but his skill with a bound blade in hand was considerable. Elian almost went to help, but Aldrick and the others hadn't faltered, and there were worse enemies approaching.

The Belogs came as though Elian's thoughts had summoned them. Karla greeted their arrival with a blast of lightning that sent otsoa and kettu running for cover, but the Belogs advanced fearlessly.

It was time to test his sword and his newfound strength against the Belogs. If he couldn't fight them, what good would he be against the Vada?

Elian breathed in deep, then ran toward the nearest Belog. A handful of kettu tried to slow him down, but his sword flashed under the midday sun and their bodies fell behind him. The Debru standing between him and the Belog shifted beyond the reach of his sword.

He noted the shifts in their strategy but spared little time to consider the implications. The Belog waited for him, and he was eager to test his strength.

He brought his sword up to meet the Belog's first cut, and the Belog's shadow sword slid off his as he angled his blade over his head. As the sword passed over his shoulder he stepped forward and snapped a cut at the Belog's leg, but it stepped backward and avoided his blade.

Elian prepared to cut again, but the Belog formed a shield and swiped at him. He cut with his sword, hoping to slice the shield in half, but the shadow overpowered him and sent him flying backward. He almost kept his feet when he landed, but surrendered his body to gravity as he rolled over his back and shoulder before returning to his feet.

Elian gripped the hilt of his sword tighter.

The other Belogs had struck the front lines, and the force of their advance bent the lines close to breaking. Karla's distinctive lightning strikes had stopped, and most concerning, Samora's attacks had also stopped.

He might have retreated, but the Belog had no interest in letting him flee. Its long strides ate up the distance between them, and it hurled half a dozen shadow spears at him to keep him occupied.

He slapped the spears away, but the distraction cost him any chance of influencing other parts of the battle. The Belog attacked him viciously, combining strikes from its sword, hastily bound spears of shadow, and shields that formed in less than the blink of an eye. It was all Elian could do to keep himself alive.

The Belog's foot caught him by surprise, flinging him once again through the air. This time, Elian hit the ground hard, tumbling end over end once before sprawling across the grass. An eager kettu lunged for his neck, and he barely got his sword up in time to defend himself. He pushed himself back to his feet, but he stood on weak legs that threatened to give out at any moment.

Dark thoughts stained his spirit.

All his efforts, all his training, everything he'd learned and done for the clans since leaving his village, all of it had been for nothing. He'd been a fool to believe that he could become anything more than what he'd been the day his father died: a coward hiding behind a shield.

If he couldn't beat a single Belog, what hope did he have against the Vada standing in the distance, twirling a shadow spear of incredible power as nonchalantly as a child playing with a new toy?

He'd gained strength, but no amount of strength could mask the truth.

And now here he was, alone against a Belog as the people he'd led into battle died behind him. Father wasn't here to save him anymore. Even Harald, who had taken Father's place for a time, was gone.

It wasn't the Belog's curse that poisoned his thoughts. It was simply...truth.

He was nothing, and all his pain and suffering stemmed from the fact he believed he was something.

Another volley of the Belog's shadow spears bracketed him, preventing him from escaping, though he saw now that any escape was pointless.

He let go of the hopes that had carried him this far. He wouldn't be the one who saved the clans, nor would he be the man that struck down the Vada. Those stories, if they existed, belonged to other warriors, other leaders. He was just a man with a sword, standing against the Debru, and wasn't that all he'd ever wanted?

The adani crashing through his limbs calmed, flowing instead like a wide and deceptively calm river, the placid surface hiding a deep and strong current. His breaths slowed and grew even, and he looped adani through his limbs the way Loken had shown him. The heart in his sword poured even more adani into his channels, which welcomed the fresh strength and mixed it easily with his own.

The advancing Belog paused, but Elian took no advantage of the hesitation, opting to neither advance nor retreat. He was right where he belonged. The Belog's hesitation only lasted long enough for a hungry pair of kettu to lunge for his ankles. He didn't bother defending. Jaws closed on his ankle and calf, but their teeth were too weak to break through his adani-enhanced skin. They let go and howled in frustration, but Elian paid them no mind. Their success provoked the Belog, though. It rushed toward him, its pounding feet causing the ground to shake. Elian watched, feeling as though the attack was aimed at someone else. The Belog's sword cut down at him, but it was slow, as if the Belog wasn't really trying. A small step to the side allowed the sword to pass harmlessly over Elian's shoulder, leaving Elian with an open cut at the Belog's leg. Royzen's sword glowed brightly as Elian carved through the massive calf.

The Belog's leg gave out and it came crashing to the ground. Elian caught his first glance at the exposed neck and all his desires for vengeance crashed through the momentary calm that had fallen over him. He shouted loud enough for all his warriors to see, then whipped his glowing sword across the back of the Belog's neck. It sliced through flesh and bone like soft bread, and the Belog's head fell from its shoulders.

His defiance was witnessed by both sides of the valley. Scattered cheers rose from the clans, and on the other side, the Vada took a step forward, its first since the battle began. Elian dared it to come across the valley, but for the moment it did not.

So be it.

He looked to his own lines and understood why. The Debru had allowed him an uninterrupted duel with the Belog, but they'd used that time to great effect. Up and down the line the clans were close to breaking, overwhelmed by the enemies the Vada cast against them. Samora and her techniques were nowhere to be found. No matter.

He'd killed one Belog by himself, and the others would soon taste his steel. He ran back into the battle, eager for Debru blood.

❧ 41 ❧

Samora woke to a rough hand shaking her shoulder. Her eyes popped open as she remembered where she was and what had happened. She patted herself down, taking a moment to ensure she was still healthy and whole. Her neck and head hurt, but she seemed otherwise unhurt.

"Sure, you're alive, and safe for now, but I'm not going to be able to hold this forever," a familiar voice said.

Samora noticed Karla then for the first time. One of her arms was caked in mud, and a trickle of blood ran from a thin cut above her right ear, but she looked well otherwise. She kneeled beside Samora, holding a dome of a shield above them as the battle raged in every direction.

Karla's efforts to protect Samora hadn't gone unnoticed. Three Debru surrounded the shield and they stabbed at it with dark spears. Karla's strength kept them at bay, but it wouldn't last forever.

"If it's all the same to you, I'd be thrilled to drop this shield and rejoin the fight. It won't be long before a Moka or a Belog finds us."

Samora scrambled to a sitting position. Her head hurt and her vision swam as she rose, but a trickle of adani to her head cured the worst of her problems. "Of course. How long was I out?"

"Not very. I think everyone lost track of your adani when you passed out, so the Vada didn't dare launch another attack. Now, weave us some weapons so we can get out of here."

Samora knew it was a test, but the memories of her village were still too fresh for her to fail this one. She didn't use the heart, though she ensured it was still at hand. She bound three spheres of light and nodded to Karla.

Her old friend only hesitated a moment before returning the nod and dropping the shield. She weaved a sword, but it would be too late. Three dark spears sought to skewer them, but Samora released her attack.

Each of her spheres struck true, punching through the skulls of the Debru like arrows. Their spears vanished before they struck, and Samora felt a grim satisfaction at the sound of their bodies slumping to the ground.

"Impressive," Karla said.

The scene she woke to wasn't encouraging. Moka and Belogs roamed among the clans, and even with the additional strength of their impromptu gathering grounds, the clans weren't having much luck against them. Nor did they appear to focus much effort on the more powerful foes, as their attention was consumed by the smaller creatures swarming all over them.

One of the Belogs fell and Elian appeared behind it, cutting through its head and sending a cheer up among several of the adanists.

Helpful as it was, though, it wouldn't be enough.

"Keep an eye on the Vada for me," Samora said.

Karla nodded, and Samora took hold of the heart once again. The strength rushing through her limbs cleared her aches and worries and she formed a single sphere, pushing all the adani she could into it.

She tightened the weave, pulling a corner of the sphere into a point and aiming it at the nearest Belog. She thanked the old elder dragon for teaching her the technique.

"Better hurry," Karla said as she began weaving a shield.

Samora couldn't spare the attention. The Belog swung its massive sword, cutting down two adanists too busy fighting through a horde of kettu to realize the danger they were in.

She launched the weave. It flew faster than any arrow and struck the Belog in the side of the head. The sharpened point of adani pierced the thick skin and sliced through the bone as though it was made of jam. The strength of the Belog's swing twisted it in a half circle as it collapsed, killing a handful of unfortunate kettu that found themselves suddenly deprived of the Belog's protection.

Samora's attack received no cheer, as the Belog's death caught even the nearby adanists by surprise.

Karla shoved Samora out of the way as an enormous spear of shadow jutted out of the ground and tried to impale her. Samora looked up and saw the Vada holding the other end of the spear across the valley. It let the spear dissipate, and then the Vada and all its attendants advanced upon the battle.

"Well, that got its attention," Karla observed.

"Might as well take out a few more Belogs while I can, then," Samora said.

"I don't think it's going to let you have the time."

Samora looked up to see the Vada form another spear in its hand and toss it lazily into the air. It floated, almost as if it was a child's kite, before starting its slow descent. Samora swore and weaved a shield to protect the clans. She stopped the spear in time, but barely.

No sooner had the first spear dissipated than the Vada sent the next flying through the air.

Samora hurried to weave another shield, stopping the spear only moments before it struck the clans.

"I hate to be the one that says this, girl, but you might just need to let one of those fall," Karla said.

"Not a chance. See what you can do to kill the Belogs. I'll protect the clans."

The Vada threw one spear and then another, pushing Samora's abilities to their limit. Just as Samora feared she had failed, the dragons roared overhead and dropped powerful spheres of adani on the Vada. They lacked the strength to hurt it, but their efforts were powerful enough the Vada was forced to defend, granting Samora a brief break.

Shouts from the south caught Samora's attention. A pair of Belogs there had finally broken through the lines, surrounded by three or four Moka. Tiafel and the Hounds were in disarray, but Kati didn't have the Bears to spare to help.

Samora swore. They hadn't even dealt with the Vada yet.

The dragons circled like hawks closing in on their prey, weaving enormous spheres of adani as they swooped and dived. The Vada flicked a dark spear at one dragon that flew too close, and the dragon was no match for the spear. Darkness punched through its chest and blasted out its back, cutting the spine in half. The unfortunate dragon roared as it plummeted from the sky. Its strong wings flapped limply, and it died when it crashed into the valley, its neck snapping as it struck the ground at an unnatural angle.

Samora tore her eyes away as the remaining dragons tried and failed to enact vengeance for their fallen sibling. She finished her weave and launched it at one of the two Belogs tormenting the Hounds. Her aim was true and the Belog fell in a heap, but then the Vada threw another spear and she was forced to weave another shield. The second Belog laid into the surviving Hounds, almost as if it could make up for its partner's absence with enthusiasm alone.

The truth was obvious for all to see. They'd mastered the

hearts and unified the clans, but none of it added up to a damn thing.

Then the Vada held up its small hand, the mischievous grin of a child upon its face. Several spheres of darkness floated above its open palm, a dark mirror of Samora's favored technique. She felt them even without extending her adani. The Vada put real strength into the spheres, so much so it made the earlier spears seem like toys in comparison.

She couldn't block those. She wasn't even sure she could stop one.

The Vada flicked them toward the clans, nothing more than a child tossing a ball. The spheres spread and flew over Samara's head, falling toward the rear of the clans' lines where there were few Debru. Samora weaved a shield to block the nearest sphere, which dropped toward the place where Brittany, Loken, Lenon and the other healers were hard at work.

Shadow struck shield. Every fiber of Samora's being lit on fire as the heart flooded massive amounts of adani through her channels. Moments stretched into eternity, and all Samora could do was let more adani pass through her into the weave she'd prepared. When the shadow faded she found herself on her knees, the ground shaking from the impact of the two other spheres.

Her efforts, though, had been successful. The healers lived. Her body was as empty as the elder dragon's cave, a vast unoccupied space. The hole she had felt in training was easier to sense, a void that begged to be filled. With what, though, she was no closer to understanding.

The front half of an otsoa tumbled to a stop beside her and she turned to see Karla fighting off a press of Debru and otsoa. She was a wonder, dual blades of adani serving as shield and weapon alike. Golden light sliced shadow to ribbon, dancing like summer lightning against the pitch darkness of towering storm clouds.

Samora rose to her feet, swaying as she fought for balance. Her world had gone strangely silent, her ears stuffed with impenetrable cloth. Though shadows surrounded her, light filled her spirit, entering her both from the ground below and the heart strapped to her wrist. She blinked and her vision changed.

She saw not just the bodies and the blood, grassland and sky, but adani and shadow, locked in a pitched battle for control of this world. Each adanist was a point of light, burning brightly against the chaotic shadow that swirled, darted, and smothered. When an adanist died, their light winked out, snuffed from the world like a candle blown out at night.

There was so much more light than darkness. Adanists were overwhelmed by shadow, but the world was still light, and the hearts glowed brightest of all.

She blinked and her vision returned to normal, but the impression remained. The entire world was with them.

True as it might be, the knowledge did her little good. The Vada's power still overwhelmed them, and if shadow secured its hold today, the rest of the world's light would eventually fade.

She bound a dozen of the small darts and threw them, clearing the surrounding area of enemies. She stood beside Karla and surveyed the battlefield, though the process only took a moment. Aldrick and his precious Wolves still fought, and the Bears' line held strong. Tassan, to the north, fought like Harald would have were he alive. But it wasn't enough.

Their defeat was inevitable. The Belogs and the Moka churned through the line of adanists.

Brave warriors did everything within their power to fight back. Not far from Samora, Alec and Tera fought together, trying to bring a Moka to its knees with their combined strength. Both of them together only slightly overpowered the Moka, but it was a slow duel of attrition.

On Samora's other side, Kati fought with the few warriors that had originally been Hawks. Her daggers kept her adanists safe, and Samora saw Capricia was still among their number, which eased Samora's heart.

Somewhere up ahead, her brother fought, but she couldn't see him over the press of bodies. Only the fact that some of the strongest Debru kept dying somewhere up ahead let her know.

They couldn't continue to fight like this, though. This battle of attrition favored the Vada, who still hadn't committed all of its forces.

"The Vada is the only enemy that matters," Samora said.

"Thinking about charging down there?" Karla asked.

Samora shook her head. "There's no need. It's plenty close enough."

She formed a dozen of her darts, sharpened as tight as she could pull the weaves. Adani poured from the heart, through her will, into the weapons, and when they were complete, she rained them down on the Vada's head.

It formed a shield of shadow overhead, and though Samora pushed each of her darts with all her strength, they barely penetrated the Vada's shield. The darts exploded as they expended their adani, sending out a wave of force that blew Samora's hair back.

"Try just one," Karla suggested. She launched a bright spear into the side of an otsoa that came too close.

Samora's thoughts had run in the same direction, and she began a new weave, focusing on tightening adani into an edge so sharp it could cut the wing off a mosquito. She threw it as soon as it was ready, but the Vada was prepared, another shield of shadow forming before it.

Adani and shadow met again, and the point of Samora's dart cut deeper into the darkness than any of her previous attempts. The heart helped her push, like a giant hand shoving the dart closer to the Vada. Shadow slid to each side of the dart, seeking desperately to hold it but failing to find purchase. The dart slowed but didn't stop, and then with a sudden burst of speed it was through.

The Vada's shield blocked her sight, but she sensed enough. That deep darkness that was the Vada shifted suddenly, so quickly it was almost as if it had vanished and reappeared in another place. Her dart passed through—something—before slicing into the ground.

No amount of shadow could block the light that erupted from behind the wall of darkness. Shadow billowed and strained to contain the force, and though it was mostly successful, the light that burst through warmed Samora's spirits.

She'd cut the bastard. She was sure of it.

Her confirmation came a moment later.as the Vada dropped the shield. Black blood leaked from its right arm, but as she watched, the wound stitched itself together.

She cursed silently to herself, but hope remained. She'd hurt it, and if she could hurt it, she could kill it.

Samora began to recreate the same weave, but she'd barely started when the Vada unveiled more of its power.

The inky darkness that had been floating haphazardly through the air grew thicker, blocking the sun from the sky and thickening the air. Every breath tasted like smoke, and the air coated her tongue and tried to strangle any expression of adani.

In the midst of the assault on her senses, the Vada raised its now-healed right arm. A black sphere, somehow darker than the void that grew around them, formed.

Samora sensed its power, and tears trickled down her cheek. No one had ever misled her into thinking life was fair, but she and Elian and so many others had worked so hard to learn and grow stronger.

How had they fallen this short?

She began weaving a shield, a masterpiece greater than anything she'd ever bound before. The threads of adani ran from the south tip of their line all the way to the north. It was hopeless and pointless, but sometimes all that was left was to fight. Elian, too far ahead of the others to shield, would understand. It meant nothing to their success, but her spirit would perish proudly, and that would have to be enough

Belog, Moka, and Debru, along with their otsoa and kettu, all of whom had been pushing deeper and deeper into the lines of adanists, suddenly turned and started running the other way, back toward the Vada.

She worked quickly, but the Vada held its attack, its confident silence the last damning insult to her weakness.

Too late, she realized that Karla was saying something. The weave was almost finished, and she spared a fraction of her attention for the older adanist who'd helped her in so many ways. "I'm sorry, what?"

"I said that I'm proud of you, and that I think Aldrick is good for you. That simple stability will be good for your wandering mind and spirit."

Samora didn't have time to answer, and she wouldn't have known what to say if she did. The Vada sensed the completion of her weave and with a flick of a finger, sent the sphere of shadow toward the clans.

The sphere split into many before it struck, and Samora dug her feet into the ground to brace against the impact. The shadows struck her weave, and it was as if someone had suddenly crushed her between two mountains.

The breath was driven from her lungs and her muscles and adani channels burned as the heart gave everything it had to stop the attack. Her scream died in her parched throat, escaping her lips more like a high-pitched whine.

She focused only on the weave. On protecting the others against the shadow, if she could. Her own life would be over soon, but if she could somehow just hold the weave, it would all be fine.

Except she couldn't hold the weave. It unraveled, as she'd known it must, against the pure force of the Vada's attack.

Until Karla joined the battle, glowing like a pair of suns, so bright Samora couldn't help but sense her. The woman was holding not just the heart Samora had given her, suitable for her ability, but another, nearly as strong as the one Samora wielded. She pulled from both hearts and from the new gathering ground, funneling more adani through her body than a single spirit could ever endure.

Karla's massive infusion of adani reinforced the weaves of Samora's shields just as they were about to unravel. Karla and Samora screamed together, and for the briefest of moments, Samora saw all of Karla's life, far more than she'd seen in the Wolves' gathering ground so long ago. Their adani was linked, and against the Vada, it mostly held.

Blasts shook the land and knocked breath from lungs, but the vast majority of the Vada's strength burned itself against the shield, and surviving adanists continued, somehow, to survive.

Samora's elation was short lived as she sensed the final remnant of the Vada's attack, aimed straight for her. It was the strongest of the spheres, the one which all others had split off from, and it raced toward her. Her adani channels still worked, but her mind was still after the battle she'd just survived. No weave came to mind.

Then Karla appeared before her, like a ghost somehow rising from its burial site. Samora didn't understand how she was still alive, much less standing. The adani she'd just channeled would have killed a family of dragons.

She took the sphere of shadow in the chest, and somehow, using the power of both the hearts, still burning bright in her hands, she stopped the last fragment of the Vada's attack.

Adani and shadow dueled, and then there was a flash of light mixed with dark, dark shadow, and Karla was gone, her body erased as though she'd never been anything more than a dream, and the blast slammed into Samora, lifted her off her feet, and tossed her far away.

❧ 42 ❧

E lian fought with Royzen's sword, handed down from Paelin's time, imagining the former leader of the Scorpions by his side as he cut through any enemy who challenged him. He hoped that if some shred of Royzen's spirit was present, it was proud of Elian's use of the weapon.

Never before had a sword felt so natural in his hands. The sword Harald had first given him, which still hung off Elian's right hip, was a fine one, well balanced and sharp even after months of heavy use, but it couldn't compare to the work of art he now used.

Royzen's blade was a bit longer than his old sword but felt as light as a knife. At times, it seemed to leap into place of its own will. He couldn't tell how much of the weapon's elegance came from adani and how much came from the physical craftsmanship, but the final result was unquestioned.

The longer he fought with it, the more convinced he became that the swordsmith hadn't just added a heart to the pommel of the weapon. He had worked adani into the steel itself. It was almost as though the sword was alive.

Together, they worked their way through the horde of enemies that sought to destroy the clans. Mere Debru tended to make themselves scarce when Elian neared, but the Moka and Belogs eagerly challenged him.

Sword met shadow as the heart in the pommel glowed, a single shining star in a dark sky. As Belogs and Moka pressed in, he lost himself in the fight. Shadows reached for him, and he cut them back, then he'd lash out and maybe deliver a fatal blow. There was time for nothing but instinct, but instinct and the sword were enough to keep him alive.

The pressure continued to mount, though, as more Moka and Belogs joined the fight. They became less interested in dueling, and more in overwhelming him with their numbers. He pushed in the Vada's direction, but the spears and swords of his enemies were as thick as a wall.

He leaped forward when a gap opened between two Belogs, then swore when a Moka stopped his advance.

It was the same as always, the lesson he seemed to never learn.

No matter how strong he became, it wasn't enough. Even with a legendary sword in hand, all he could do was watch as the Debru tore his world apart.

Just as it seemed his defense was about to break, the pressure against him eased. He'd been fighting off three or four Moka and a Belog, and then suddenly he was alone.

Samora.

She must have found a way to drive the Debru back. Elian swayed on his feet but found the strength to grin. She had always been the smarter one.

The rapidly darkening sky told him that his hope had been misplaced. The dark clouds sheltering the Vada and other Debru from the sun had always been a nuisance, but this was something different. The air itself darkened, and a sour and bitter taste coated his tongue.

Elian slowly turned to see the Vada holding a dark sphere over its head, an attack very similar to the one that had killed the dragon on Elian's ill-fated scouting expedition.

The Vada threw the sphere, which almost immediately split into dozens of smaller spheres. Most flew over Elian's head, and the strength of each was such that it killed the grass it flew over. Elian didn't know how the clans would survive the assault, but he had his own problem, as one of the spheres sped straight for his heart.

Without the ability to weave a shield, he did the only thing he could think of. He swung his sword at the sphere and hoped for the best.

His blow froze the sphere in place, and it felt as though Elian had tried to cut through stone. He grunted and flexed his wrists, drawing more power from the heart to guide the sword through the attack.

The sphere wouldn't cut, though. Dark tendrils wrapped around the steel, and Elian shouted, contributing some of his adani to the cause.

The sphere cracked and Elian put even more of his strength into the sword. Finally, the sphere gave up the fight and his sword cut through, Each half of the sphere sped off to one side, and the explosions that resulted from the contact of the spheres into the ground knocked him forward and off his feet.

He landed hard, and as he fought to return to his feet, another blast, much larger than the first, knocked him down again and squeezed the air from his lungs. He twisted his head and looked back. All he saw was the dust and dirt in the air, the lines of adanists now cloaked in the darkness that spread over everything and choked the life from the world.

Samora couldn't be dead. He had no evidence to support his belief, but she couldn't. Somehow, he would know if she had fallen. But she wouldn't last long, not under that oppressive darkness with the Vada unleashing attacks like that.

He pushed himself to his feet. Thanks to the sudden retreat of the Belogs and Moka, he had the most open shot yet toward the Vada, and before he could allow himself the time to question his decision, he charged forward.

His adani-fueled legs ate up the distance, and the Vada's soldiers were slow to react. A pair of Moka drifted into Elian's way, but they were on the weaker end of Moka, and their shadow couldn't stop his steel. He cut them down quickly and continued on, only to find himself face to leg with a Belog.

The enormous monster cut, but too slow, and Elian struck at the exposed leg. The Belog cast a shield over itself, which slowed Elian's blade long enough for it to retreat a step.

Elian cursed. He needed a way through and quick, and this Belog was content to stand as a shield, preventing him from reaching the Vada.

The Belog took a few extra steps back, then half-turned to the Vada behind it. It bowed, then stepped out of Elian's way. Now there was nothing between Elian and the Vada. The monster had once again taken the guise of a human child, the illusion ruined only by its ink-dark eyes and its confident, comfortable grip on the sword of shadow.

"After all that hiding, you're just going to let me close?" Elian asked. He sensed the Debru gathering around him, closing off his escape, but what did it matter? If he could kill the Vada, it was all over.

"Your sister has already been defeated, so all that remains is to demonstrate the errors of your thinking," the Vada replied, in a voice far too deep and scratchy to ever emerge from a child's throat.

Elian hadn't expected a response, and for a moment he stood and stared before responding. "Samora's not dead," he said.

"Not dead but defeated. She knows now she can do nothing against me, and I'm eager to teach you the same lesson."

"Foolish to take such a risk."

"You may think so, but from where I stand, there is no risk.

For too long I feared you had reached a level sufficient to threaten me, but I see now I worried over nothing. Come. Let us end this, for I have more important tasks to complete today."

Elian didn't need further encouragement. He looped adani tightly through his limbs and leaped forward, covering the remaining distance between them in three long strides. His cut was blindingly fast, and he put all the force of his spirit behind it.

The Vada batted it aside with contempt and responded.

Elian didn't so much see the strike as sense it, the darkness of the Vada's blade overwhelming and obvious even to his poor senses. Instinct alone saved him, and he raised his sword to block the blow.

Shadow and steel collided, and Elian was launched twenty paces back, tumbling end over end. Both his hands had gone numb, but he held onto the sword, for his life depended on it. When he finally came to a stop, he was on his back staring up at the sky. Two Belogs stared down at him, but they made no attempt to strike.

Elian took a long breath, then rolled to his feet. His arms ached from the force of the last blow, but he was otherwise unharmed. He shook his arms out, took a fighting stance, and advanced on the Vada, who waited on him as though bored.

Elian kept tight control of his cuts, searching for some weakness in the Vada's defense.

It didn't take him long to realize the truth, though.

He wasn't even close in speed or strength to the Vada. The heart fueled his limbs and strengthened his sword, but the Vada lazily blocked each and every cut, without apparent effort.

Then the Vada's sword blurred again, and again Elian was saved only by instinct. He ended facedown this time, Royzen's sword several paces away.

Still, the Belog and Moka that surrounded him didn't bother to attack, their indifference an insult Elian could hardly bear. He crawled toward the sword and picked it back up, thankful he could rely on the heart's strength to stand again.

Two shuddering, deep breaths cleared most of the despair from his heart.

"I'll grant you this, you don't lack for courage, and you've caused more problems than any adanists since the last war, so take some pride in that," the Vada said.

Elian looked down at his sword. The heart still glowed as bright as before, but his body was near its limit. He'd finally found a battle he couldn't escape from.

No matter.

His enemy was before him, and he had the world's most powerful sword in his hand. It was all the opportunity he'd ever dreamed of having, and if he failed, he'd join Mother and Father in death. There were far more horrible fates.

He looped adani as tightly as he ever had, frustrated yet again by the small hole in his spirit he didn't know how to fill. Once he'd filled himself with all the strength his channels could handle, he advanced on the Vada.

This time, it didn't even give him the chance to attack. It cut first, but his vision was sharp enough he almost saw the cut. He set his feet and blocked.

The Vada's blow broke Royzen's sword, but it didn't shatter like a normal sword. It exploded. Elian closed his eyes and looked away as steel shrapnel raced away from the impact. The hilt shattered and crumbled in his hands, and the force knocked him off his feet again.

The heart, freed from its prison, fell to the ground and tumbled in front of his face before stopping.

Elian stared at it, unblinking, unable to believe what had just happened.

He'd had one weapon, one chance to kill the Vada, and now it was no more.

He closed his eyes and waited for the Vada's sword to end his life.

❧ 43 ❧

Samora stared at the place Karla had stood a moment ago, simultaneously sure of what she had seen and also confident it was impossible. Two foot-sized divots in the loose soil were all that remained, dug deep from the pressure of the attack she'd defended against.

Up and down the lines, adanists were returning to their feet. Many looked at their hands or pressed their palms against their torso, as though convincing themselves they still lived.

They did, thanks to Karla's sacrifice, but the same trick wouldn't work again. Samora's left arm twitched. then spasmed as her body absorbed and distributed the excess adani from her efforts. She could, maybe, weave the same shield again, but it wouldn't matter. Without Karla, the next attack would break through no matter what she did.

The battle was over. That knowledge was written on the faces of everyone she saw.

Somewhere near the northern edge of the line, a giant spear appeared, and it was as though the ghost of Harald had returned for one more fight. Backs straightened, and those standing helped those who had already surrendered to return to their feet.

Samora watched, unable to summon the strength to move, or to care. Nothing they did mattered.

Movement beside her almost made her jump. She turned her head to see Kati standing beside her. The Bears' second looked north, eyes fixed on the giant spear. "Tassan," she said.

Samora nodded, unsure what was expected of her.

"He reminds me so much of Harald sometimes. That fool would have given almost anything to be here, to witness this last stand."

Samora nodded again.

Kati took her hand. "Will you stand with me? I swear he looked at you and Elian as his own children, and I'd be honored to have you by my side."

"You beat me to it," another voice said from behind the pair. Tera joined them, though she was walking with a pronounced limp. She wasn't alone, and Samora's eyes widened when she noticed Brittany following Tera.

The healer noticed Samora's look and shrugged. "Not much need for healing, is there? Everyone I was treating is struggling toward the line. If there's anyone left after, I'm sure I'll be busy, but until then, I might as well join you."

Samora stared at the ground. She'd been ready to give up. Ready to let the Vada strike the final blow.

Nothing about their situation had changed, but Samora couldn't let these women down. They'd helped her and Elian time and again, supporting them as they'd found their place among the clans. She nodded again, for the final time. "Of course," she said.

She straightened and turned to face the Vada, just in time for another surprise.

Elian was before it, on the ground and hurt, but still moving.

She summoned the strength of the heart, filling her weary body with adani and weaving it into a single powerful dart.

Her effort earned her no cheers from the exhausted clans, but they took it as an order to begin their assault. They started walking forward, silently marching toward their end.

———

ELIAN BLINKED AND GROANED. The expected blow from the Vada didn't fall, and when he cracked open an eye, he saw the Vada staring into the distance. Elian flopped his head over. The clans looked ragged and broken, but they marched down the side of the valley toward the Debru, who looked confused as to why the humans would be attempting such an advance.

It didn't take Elian's eyes long to find what had captured the Vada's attention. A dart, brighter than the sun, hovered above the center of the line. He couldn't sense the adani, but he knew what that dart represented.

Samora lived.

Elian flopped his head back over and rolled onto his side. He stretched out his hand and grabbed the heart which had once been embedded in the pommel of his sword.

The Vada's gaze drifted between the clans and him, then returned to the clans.

It spoke, though there was no need for it to do so. Their commands passed through shadow. No, the command was meant for him to hear. For him to despair.

"Don't let her get close. Kill them all," it said.

The Debru leaped forward, Belogs and Moka leading the way. Elian groaned, his muscles weak after the abuse he'd piled on them during the fight. He swayed on his feet, but he held the heart to his chest and allowed adani to trickle back into his body. "Now you're without defenders."

The Vada laughed, a bitter, rasping sound that set Elian's teeth on edge. "You couldn't even scratch me when you had that sword. What do you think you can do now? Watch your sister die, and once she's gone, I'll end your misery for you."

Elian put his hand on the sword Harald had given him, still whole and resting on his right hip. "I've still got a weapon."

The Vada laughed again and ignored Elian.

Worse, it was right to do so. He'd given everything in the last fight. He clutched tighter at the heart, taking what comfort he could in its strength.

The heart's adani strengthened and faded, beating in time with his own heart. Elian closed his eyes so he could sense it more clearly. The beat of the heart grew louder, slowly pushing away the sounds of the Debru advance.

It had traveled all the way from the mountains of the Scorpion stronghold to the plains west of his village, carried by generations of Scorpion leaders. It seemed a shame to leave it here, now.

Such an ignominious end for such an incredible gem.

He pressed his hand tighter around it, but it didn't hurt his palm to do so. He squeezed tighter, swearing that no matter what would happen, he would protect it until his dying breath. In response, it seemed to shift in his grasp, seemed to come alive.

It wanted something.

He stilled the thoughts that suddenly raced through his mind and forced himself to listen. He remained unconvinced by Samora's belief that adani guided her, but he'd seen too much not to be open to the idea.

So, he listened, waiting for adani to reveal its intent.

Adani flowed from the stone to his hand, pulled like water falling from the edge of a cliff. He focused on that sensation.

His body wanted more than just the stone's adani.

It wanted the stone.

Elian opened his eyes and cracked open his palm. The stone sat within, but it almost felt as though it had burrowed partway into his skin, like a leech, except that the stone gave instead of took. He stared, and as he did, his vision shifted. His hand grew lighter and he could trace the flow of adani within it, running through channels both wide and narrow, branching out until it reached every part of his body.

The stone was much the same, etched with channels that mirrored those in his body.

They looked the same. Two different manifestations of the same force. The only difference was in their brightness. Compared to the stone, Elian was almost as dark as shadow. Even if he could accept the heart into his body, it would kill him. He needed Samora. She'd always been the stronger one, but an army of Debru stood between him and her.

He looked up to see if he could find a way to her, but his gaze stopped on a luminous presence hovering over his shoulder. Another manifestation of adani, though different from any he'd seen before. It reminded him of the threads of adani that some-times floated through the gathering ground, glowing softly at night. A knot of spirit and energy, briefly unmoored from the ground that sustained it, though this one seemed larger and brighter than those, almost as bright as a candle's flickering flame.

He nearly jumped out of his skin when the light spoke. "Do it, Elian."

"Harald?" It couldn't be. It had to be nothing more than a trick of his imagination, and yet, somehow, he was sure of what he sensed.

"There's no time to delay. Everything hinges on the edge of a blade, and our fates could fall either way."

"I'm not strong enough. This will kill me."

"You've always been strong enough. You've just never realized it."

The light at his shoulder unraveled, its adani spreading through the impossibly complex web that surrounded Elian. He watched it until he couldn't track any part of it, then returned his attention to the heart.

What did he have to lose?

He allowed the heart to melt into his hand.

The rush of strength was every bit as strong as holding the gem and allowing the adani within, but not much stronger. Elian was disappointed, but to his altered sight, it looked as if the stone was crawling up his arm. He felt nothing, but it moved faster the closer it came to his torso. It crawled through his left shoulder and dropped into his core, where it settled.

A moment later, his stomach caught fire.

He wrapped his arms around his gut and doubled over as the heart filled the void he hadn't known how to fill and forged new connections with his body. Adani surged into every nook and cranny of his body, stronger than anything he'd felt before. His own channels expanded to accept the heart's offering.

The heart offered more than mere strength, though. It carried with it memories, the lives of all who had wielded it through the generations. He could trace his lineage all the way back, to the stone's first uncovering. He saw Paelin, and swore that Paelin saw him, too.

Then it was done, a flash of agony that passed nearly as fast as he could breathe.

His acceptance of the heart did not go unnoticed. The Vada formed a sword and struck down, but Elian danced back, and the sword missed. The Vada stepped forward and cut again, but Elian saw the cut and stepped aside.

He used his left hand to draw Harald's sword, then positioned himself to defend against the Vada's next blow. It came without hesitation, the Vada revealing a determination Elian hadn't seen before. Elian parried and cut, and the Vada took a step back.

He needed a moment to realize what had just happened, but when he did, he felt the first hope bloom in his chest since the battle began. He strode forward, but the Vada didn't retreat. Half a dozen dark spheres appeared in the air between them and attacked Elian from all sides. He couldn't defend, but he knew a technique that wasn't his own. He strengthened his body with adani and took the blows.

The force crashed upon him, but he stood and bore it with only minor difficulty. When the dust cleared, he remained standing, his body sore but unharmed, no worse than if he'd been punched hard a few times.

He cut at the Vada, but the Vada was prepared and blocked his cut. Their swords passed and passed again, and though the battle was much closer than it had been before, Elian was still outmatched.

The difference wasn't much, but in the end, it would be enough.

Elian tried to loop the adani in his limbs tighter, but there were no further gains to be made with the techniques he'd once relied on. His body was as strong as he could make it.

He pressed the attack, hoping that at the least, the Vada would make a mistake he could exploit, but the Vada was too careful. It was all too happy to retreat if its sword started to falter, too happy to drop spheres of shadow on him if he came too close.

Elian shouted. He was too close!

He attacked again, but to no better results. He pressed harder, only to take a dark sphere to the face that rocked him back and put him on the defensive. The only thing that kept him alive was the Vada's unwillingness to commit itself fully. It struck only when it was certain of its safety, allowing him to recover. Still, he couldn't gain the upper hand, and soon the Belogs and the rest would walk over the clan survivors.

He leaped at the Vada once more, hoping that this time, he would finally find a gap in its armor.

❧ 44 ❧

Samora had intended her dart for the Vada, but the Belogs proved the more immediate threat. They were only moments away from slamming into the clans' line when Samora split her attack in two and sent the darts for the Belogs. Both struck true, slicing into the tough flesh like a razor through a ripe berry.

The darts dug in deep before releasing the incredible energies bound within them, and the two bright flashes of light were soon followed by the welcome sight of two Belogs falling to the ground. Her darts had opened enormous cavities in their chests. Ribs had been blown outward, dark blood poured freely from the wounds, and viscera coated the Moka who had tried to serve as the Belogs' protection.

Samora noticed every detail. She witnessed the destruction her skills had wrought, and she was satisfied. Her spirit leaped at the sight of the falling monsters.

Her actions caught the attention of every Belog on the battle-field. Many turned toward her, and she welcomed their advance. Every Belog that focused on her left another adanist alone, and thanks to the heart, she could at least defend herself.

She began another set of weaves but was interrupted by a tug on her adani. Her gaze rose above the valley to the other side, where Elian and the Vada stood across from one another. He had changed somehow, though from here, she couldn't tell how.

Elian leaped at the Vada, so quickly he seemed to blur, like a mirage in the heat. The Vada did the same, and sword met shadow, too fast for Samora to catch any of the details. She only saw them clash, then break apart, then clash again, leaving her more with the impression of an incredible fight than the sight of one.

She'd watched him train, and he was so much faster than before. But how? She saw no light from the sword.

The Belogs grew close, but her curiosity overwhelmed her sense, and she extended adani toward her brother.

And staggered back as she encountered the adani within him.

It was far greater than any human. Greater than any dragon, including the elder. Greater even than one of the hearts. In all her adventures, she was certain she'd never felt adani so strong.

He'd reached a new level, but how?

She kept her adani on him, and the reason didn't take long to find. The heart was within him. The one from the sword, unless she missed her guess. It filled the gap they'd discovered within their adani channels.

Tera, Brittany, and Kati all began binding and throwing adani as fast as their bodies and skills would allow. Their efforts slowed the Debru advance, forcing the monsters to bind shields to protect themselves against the onslaught, but it wouldn't last long.

Could she do the same?

Knowing what he had done wasn't the same as knowing how he'd done it, but if he could do it, she must be able to. In adani, at least, she'd always been ahead of him. She was already connected with the heart at her wrist. She opened herself to it completely, and their strength rose and fell in unison.

"We could use your help!" Tera cried.

Samora heard only the beat of the heart. She closed her eyes and felt it, a slight pull exerted by her body on the stone. She focused in on that sensation and felt the heart begin to melt into her adani channels. It sank into her arm, crawled toward her shoulder, and fell through her torso until it reached her core, nestling in as though it had already belonged.

The rush of adani nearly brought her to her knees, and the memories of the enormous village by the sea almost completed her fall. The heart stored memories, much the same way the elders of the dragons did. It held onto events both big and small, and Samora could trace the line all the way to the heart's development, when the village was barely large enough to be called a village.

Suddenly, the dragon's decision to store and protect the hearts took on yet another dimension.

He may have nearly destroyed humanity, but he had tried to preserve it, too.

"Samora!"

Brittany's shout brought her thoughts racing from the past to the present. She opened her eyes to see the ranks of Debru crash against the adanists.

In response, she formed a dart and took aim at the nearest Belog. It sensed her attack and bound a shield of shadow, but it seemed wispy and insubstantial now. She flicked her finger forward and the dart shot toward the Belog. It shattered the shield without slowing and struck the Belog in the chest. The dart burrowed in deep and exploded, and Samora weaved an effortless shield that kept the adanists protecting her safe from the Belog's shattered ribs and shredded organs.

As bone and body slid down her shield she bound another dart, and then another, sending them after the Belogs that sought her head.

The once-fearsome creatures couldn't stand against her

attacks, their shields next to useless. Dart after dart struck deep into the clans' enemies, and one by one, they fell. When the Belogs close to her were dead, she turned her attention to the Moka, whose advance had stalled once their commanders started dying.

"Adanists! Shields!" Samora called, her voice echoing across the valley.

Her command was heeded, and every adanist who heard cast a shield between them and the Debru. Samora began picking off the Moka, and as each Moka died, the Debru under its command went mad, ripped free of whatever control the Moka kept them under.

Adanists took shelter behind their shield wall, and Samora continued her relentless campaign against the Debru. Belogs and Moka were what mattered. So long as they fought within the gathering ground created by the planted hearts, the warriors of the wandering clans should be able to fight mere Debru.

The Belogs and Moka attempted to stage a counteroffensive. Several weaved strong spears and flung them toward her, but her shields handled the attacks without problem. If she gave them time to coordinate, they might have endangered her, but her sudden ascension had caught them unprepared.

In response, she gave them a taste of the nightmare they had visited for so long upon humanity. Her darts arced down, ignoring dark shields and killing those who tried to hide. The dragons, now encouraged to return thanks to the Belogs' sudden preoccupation with survival, dropped back down on the battlefield, sending waves of destructive adani across the crazed Debru.

When the last of the Belogs fell, she turned her attention once again to Elian and the Vada. All would be for nought if the Vada still won, and she feared its power remained sufficient. She watched the battle for a few moments, and although it was difficult to be sure, she believed Elian was still losing. He occupied the Vada, which had allowed Samora to destroy its most powerful warriors, but the battle wasn't yet won.

She stretched her adani to the sky and connected with the elder, who came down to sweep up Samora in a claw. The flight across the valley took only a moment, and the dragon gently dropped Samora into the dirt, safely away from the duel but close enough Samora could reach it quickly.

Samora thanked the elder and ran toward the duel, weaving a dart as she did. As soon as she had a clear view of the Vada, she threw the dart. It burned its way through the air, but the Vada leaped back and threw up a shield to protect itself from Elian's sword and Samora's attack.

Elian chased after the Vada and Samora realized her mistake too late. The dart struck the shield and the resulting blast knocked Elian off his feet. He rolled over his back and was standing again a moment later. He glanced back, his eyes blazing with golden light.

At first, she thought he would yell at her, but as soon as he saw her, his jaw dropped. "You figured it out, too, didn't you?"

She nodded.

"Good. It's too strong for me," he said.

"Together, then?"

"Together."

The shield protecting the Vada faded and it stood before them, still in the guise of a child. Samora didn't flinch from the sight. It stared at them, then looked to the battlefield, where the remains of the Debru were being killed by the dragons and adanists working together.

Samora tensed, expecting it to release an attack in that direction. Elian's posture shifted, clearly ready to do the same. The Vada watched the destruction of its forces but made no effort to intervene. Finally, it turned back to them, and Samora involuntarily took a step back from the force of its gaze. The air around it began to shimmer.

"Now!" Elian shouted.

He leaped forward, sword trailing behind him as he raced with impossible speed toward the Vada. Samora bound a dart, wrapping it with more adani than her previous attacks. She waited for an opening.

It never arrived.

The shimmering air that surrounded the Vada expanded and darkened. Elian skidded to a stop, but the force of the expanding wave of power still picked him up and tossed him backward. He went flying past Samora, but she barely had time to shout after him before the wave crashed over her and sent her flying.

Land and sky switched places and spun wildly, and Samora tried to relax her body in preparation for the impact.

When it came, though, it was gentler than she expected.

Elian had caught her and put her gently down. His sword was sheathed, and he was staring at the place the Vada had once stood. Once Samora checked to ensure all her body was where she expected it to be, she followed his stare.

The child dissipated before their eyes, what was solid boiling away and turning into a dark mist.

"What's happening?" Elian asked.

Sight provided Samora no answers, so she extended her adani toward the shadow. Adani fought against her, but she pushed it closer regardless.

"I think we're seeing its true form, untethered from any of the disguises it normally uses," she answered.

"How bad is it?"

"It's not using any strength to assume a new form, so it has more to spare, but I'm not sure that will be our greatest challenge."

"What will be?"

Samora gestured at the shapeless form before them. "How do we kill something without form?"

Elian shrugged, then drew his sword. Samora saw it was the one Harald had given him, not the one he'd brought back from the Scorpion village.

He pointed the blade at the Vada. "Let's start with steel."

❧ 45 ❧

E lian cautiously advanced toward the shifting, malevolent form. The Vada no longer looked like a child, but the inky darkness still maintained the approximate form of a human. Despite this new development, he remained hopeful. He and Samora fought together. Nothing was beyond them. Even if this was its true form, there had to be a way to kill it, a vital part his sword could cut. He just had to find it.

A long needle of darkness shot from the Vada, aimed straight for Elian's heart. He slapped at the needle, only to realize too late that it was less a needle and more a long thorn suddenly extended from the Vada's body. It kept its connection, and his slap did nothing to protect him. His sword stopped in the middle of his deflection.

Elian slipped to the side, wincing as the needle sliced through the meaty part of his right arm. Shadow rushed in to fill the wound, but with the aid of the heart, Elian shoved the shadow out and sealed the wound tight.

Another thorn shot from the Vada, and this time Elian had the sense to use both hands. Steel met shadow, and this time, shadow lost.

Elian's victory was short-lived. Thorn after thorn shot from the Vada's body, each one retracted as it was blocked, but all strong, and all working together to keep Elian from advancing. He was just about to call for Samora's aid when the first of her darts arrived.

And passed straight through the shifting form of the Vada. A hole opened where the dart would have struck, and it made no contact. Elian swore, but Samora shifted her strategy before the words finished leaving his lips.

He couldn't help but smile as the lights appeared in the darkness that hung over their heads, like stars that had snuck close when no one was looking. He quickly lost track of how many she formed, and she formed them in all directions, cutting off any route of escape. The spheres neared the Vada, eventually coalescing into a dome of light.

The Vada thrust spears of shadow in all directions and Elian hugged the ground as the energies collided. Samora shoved adani closer, and then the world erupted.

The blast barely ruffled Elian's hair, and when he looked up, he saw a translucent wall of golden light protecting him from the worst destruction. Sweat beaded down Samora's brow, but she held the weave without much concern. She glanced at him. "It's not dead yet. I'm not strong enough on my own."

Elian pushed himself to his feet, and as a strong northern wind blew the dust from the blast away, he leaped back into the battle. This time, the Vada was slow and weak. It thrust one of its thorns out at Elian, but he was able to deflect it without problem.

Samora kept the Vada busy with more spheres, too many for it to dodge the way it had her powerful darts.

Torn between the two siblings, the Vada was as good as beaten. Elian approached, planning to hack the formless darkness until he cut something that made it hurt. He took his first swing, only to have the darkness form a hand that grabbed at his wrist and pulled him closer.

Four other hands formed and pulled him in, shadow surrounding him, trying to seep into every cut and pore of his body. He would have sworn, except that opening his mouth would have invited another invasion of shadow.

It had never been weak, but now that it had lured him in, Samora couldn't attack.

Elian struggled, but the Vada lifted him in the air and locked him in place, surrounding him like a cocoon that cut him off from the air his lungs desperately craved. He sensed the Vada's satisfaction, this elegant solution to the two siblings who refused to surrender. Tear them apart. Use one as a shield against the other.

And Elian was too weak to fight against it. Too weak to do anything but be the shield the Vada desperately needed.

Elian fought and twisted, adani burning in his limbs, but alone, the Vada was stronger. Elian could sense the core of it, a heart darker than black, but he couldn't make the slightest move to cut it, and Samora would never dare attack, not with him inside. It had been difficult enough for her to convince herself to attack the Debru in the first place.

He wouldn't give up. They couldn't lose, not now. But there was nothing else for him to do. No matter how he fought, no matter how he struggled, the Vada remained, as always, one step ahead of him. Darkness blocked his vision, and he knew that soon his lungs would give out.

SAMORA STOOD, frozen in place, as the Vada seemed to swallow Elian whole. She continued forming spheres, if for no other reason than to give herself something to do, but she couldn't use a single one. She could kill him just as easily as she could kill the Vada. Easier, most likely.

His adani was weak, either because she couldn't sense it through the shadow or because he was dying. Maybe both.

And that settled it.

If she did nothing, he was certain to die, but if she attacked, he might yet survive. It was unlikely, but possible. Either way, he was as good as dead, punished for charging into battle one time too many.

"I'm sorry," she said, as she dropped the full weight of her newfound power on the Vada.

BLACK TURNED TO GRAY, and then light cracked through the shadow. It grew lighter and lighter, and before long he had to close his eyes. The impacts rocked his body, like being hit with a hammer over and over, and as the Vada jerked under the assault, Elian's limbs cracked and broke.

He screamed through sealed lips, his lungs burned desperately for air, and then suddenly, he was loose. Not free, but the Vada's grip lost some of its incredible strength, Samora's assault too much for it to bear while holding so tightly to Elian.

He gripped the hilt of the sword and gritted his teeth, having some sense of the pain he was about to inflict on himself. He wasn't sure he'd survive, but it was their only chance.

One cut was all he had.

Samora's spheres continued to strike, turning the Vada and its prisoner into jam.

Now.

Elian looped his adani as tightly as he could. He twisted and cut one handed, aiming for the spot he had sensed before. The Vada tried to hold, but its strength was torn in too many different directions.

It moved its core instinctively, but it was forced along lines of shadow, no doubt similar to Elian's adani channels. He shifted the path of the blade, his body screaming as bones ground against bones and muscles failed to respond to his commands.

But the blade cut through the spot, and then the Vada was gone.

Several spheres of adani struck Elian directly, and even though he was surrounded by light, his world went dark, a smile on his lips.

❧ 46 ❧

Samora sensed the destruction of the Vada before she saw it. Light and shadow mixed with dust, grass, and blood, obscuring her vision, but the overwhelming pressure of the Vada vanished, as though it had dropped off the side of a mountain and disappeared.

She restrained her spheres as she quested with adani for the Vada's hiding place, because it was impossible that so much strength could disappear so quickly. And yet, no matter how far she searched, no trace of it remained. What shadow lingered on the battlefield was weak in comparison. Debru fled or went mad as the last of their commanders died at the hands of heart-strengthened adanists.

Still, realization came slowly. For so long, defeating the Vada had been the focus of all her attention, the end of the journey she'd been walking on for what felt like forever, a destination she never honestly thought she'd reach. Blind optimism was Elian's quality, not hers.

It couldn't be over.

But only thin wisps of shadow remained to press against her adani, and those wisps fled, the same way the villagers she'd grown up with had fled when otsoa had invaded and destroyed so many lives.

It couldn't be over, but there was no Vada before her, only her brother, broken and bloody, and though she couldn't quite bring herself to believe they'd won, the sight of him tore her from her confusion. Elian needed her help. Everything else in the world could wait.

She ran to him, looking left and right, still more than halfway expecting the Vada to appear again, but there was only the sun overhead and the prairie grasses, and then she was by his side, hand on his shoulder, questing through his body with adani.

He was on the verge of death, and though his adani burned as brightly as the sun, it couldn't heal him without direction. She turned all her strength to shaping adani, to repairing what had been broken, and even with the heart burning in her core, it took everything she had.

The curse of his new strength was that no one but her could heal him. Only her newfound strength was sufficient to mend his broken body.

But she was here, and once she'd healed up the most immediately fatal of his wounds, she carried him back to the gathering ground, where other adanists and hearts could help. He was light in her arms, like a child, and she marveled at this new gift of strength, adani manifesting in her body as physical force.

Her return to the gathering ground marked the beginning of one of the longest afternoons of her life, which had followed one of the longest mornings. There was so much that needed to be done, and the first was to ensure that Elian lived. She saw the look Brittany gave her as the Bear's healer sent her adani through Elian, the sorrow for a loss that hadn't happened quite yet. But Brittany didn't understand what Samora could do, and together, they brought Elian from the brink of death back to health.

As Samora worked her healings, she feared that the hearts would give out, that they would fade now that the need for their strength had passed. She worked quickly, not only because Elian's condition required it, but because she feared she might lose the strength she'd been gifted. How long would the world grant her such strength?

Elian's healing came first, but he was hardly the only adanist needing Samora's attention. At times, she wondered if every single wandering adanist would sport a scar from the battle against the Vada, like some sort of communal mark of pride. No one she saw had escaped unscathed, and if not for the power of the hearts, many more would have died. Even so, it was one of the bloodiest days in the history of the wandering clans.

Samora, Brittany, Loken, Lenon, and the other healers couldn't save every life, but they pulled many away from the edge of death. The hearts gave their strength freely, and though Samora never stopped worrying about the well of strength drying up, it never did. There was always enough for the next healing, and then the one after that.

After they completed the last healing, there was still more to do. Those who died were to be buried, and the hearts gave of their strength for that, too. She twisted a shield of adani until it served as an oversized shovel and dug a mass grave.

She'd carved the grave with a ramp, and she watched as warriors began carrying the dead down into the grave, laying them gently down, side by side. Adanists formed a line, and only one person went down at a time, often taking a moment or three with the departed before climbing back up the ramp. She looked for Karla's corpse, but it never came by, her final sacrifice having consumed her entire body.

The burial ceremony, if it even deserved the name, was short, guided more by necessity and exhaustion than by the honor the dead deserved. But the wandering clans were nothing if not pragmatic, and they were nothing if not familiar with the loss of their loved ones, and they treated the mass burial little differently than any other death. Soon, they would move on, leaving the dead behind, their eyes set on a future just as uncertain as yesterday's, even if it was safer.

Once the burial was over and the dirt had been poured back on top of the bodies, Samora shuffled away from the rest of the clans, sat down in tall grass, and let the events of the day, which had been chasing her since the Vada's death, finally catch up to her.

The enormity of what she'd helped accomplish didn't settle onto Samora's shoulders until she'd been sitting for some time, and the sun had gone down.

The moment the realization finally struck with all the force it possessed, it took her breath away. The Vada was dead, and a part of her wanted to smile and laugh and leap through the fields like she had when she was a child before Father had died. But another part of her couldn't so easily shrug off the unbearable cost of the war. The list of the dead had grown so long. For her, it started with Father and ended with Karla, but it had claimed Mother, Harald, the elder dragon, and so many more. Names and faces she could only carry in her memory, until that too would fade and there'd be nothing left of them at all.

She didn't know what she should feel, and she almost wished there was something more for her to do so she wouldn't have to think about any of it. Action was the only escape from being trapped with her feelings, but she couldn't think of anything more that needed to be done.

Aldrick's strong, familiar hands settled on her shoulders. She'd been so distracted by her thoughts she hadn't even sensed his approach. "Would you like to be alone?" he asked.

"Wouldn't mind a companion, actually."

He pressed his thumbs into the muscles between her shoulder blades and her spine. She sighed as he drove out some of the tension in her back. The simple feeling of his hands on her back gave her strength, reminded her that whatever burdens she was fated to carry, she didn't have to carry them alone. He rubbed the back of her neck, then sat down beside her.

He looked to be in terrible shape. Blood, dust, and mud covered him from head to toe, and he moved with the slowness of a man who'd just run the full day without rest. She glanced at a pair of parallel cuts on his left arm, already red and inflamed. The healers hadn't been able to pay any attention to the minor cuts and bruises earlier, and come morning, there'd need to be another round of healings to drive out infection.

Aldrick noticed the object of her gaze, started to hide it, then stopped when he realized how foolish that would be. "It's nothing."

She reached out a hand, he sighed, and gave her his arm. The healing only took a moment, and then the bloody scars were fresh skin, cleaner than the rest of his arm. She stared, first at his arm, then at her hand. Already her body adapted to this new level of ability, and it began to feel normal, even if her new strength was anything but.

What would she do now? Everything had been to this end, to acquire the strength necessary to defeat the Debru, but now that they were dead, to what end did she bend this new strength?

"Thanks," he said, pulling her back to the present.

She nodded, her thoughts still traveling in other directions.

"Kati is meeting with the surviving elders and leaders later tonight. Not so much to make any decisions, but to start thinking about what's next for the clans. We're invited."

Samora could well imagine the arguments and discussions sure to follow. Days of debate, followed by a decision, followed by more discussions. She'd be surrounded by people every day, each of them asking her questions, looking to her with expectations no adanist could fulfill. They'd make her an elder before she'd seen thirty summers.

And if she wanted, that would be her life. Leading the

wandering clans for the rest of her days, dealing with their squabbles as they made their way into this new world.

She shuddered at the thoughts, and in that moment, realized her body and spirit knew her future, even if her reason hadn't yet caught up. Karla had abandoned her leadership of a clan, but Samora had never blundered into leadership in the first place. She could follow her mentor's footsteps tonight, and it had to be tonight, because if she waited for morning there would be more to do. Duties would pull her closer to the clans, and it would be harder to leave. She turned so she could take Aldrick's hand and look him in the eye. "If I told you I wanted to leave tonight, would you join me?"

His look told her that he understood that this leaving wouldn't be just for a day or a week. He stared off into the distance, but only for a moment. She sensed he'd already made this decision, long before she'd asked, and he only needed to find a reason to justify it to himself.

"I would."

The weight of her visions of the future fell from her spirit, and she smiled for the first time since the Vada had been defeated. Her limbs filled with a sudden excited energy, which was good, as his agreement meant there were now many small tasks that demanded her attention.

There would be goodbyes to endure, thanks to give, and arrangements to be made, though as she made a list in her head, not so many as she would have expected. Despite her contributions to the wandering clans, she'd always been more adjacent to them than part of them. She had no official roles or duties that needed to be filled by other willing volunteers. Aldrick had more than her, though his decision to join the Wolves to the Bears made his leaving easier, and she wondered if he'd considered that, too, when he'd offered to merge the clans.

They kissed and went their separate ways, and Samora said her farewells and packed her bag. It was a familiar practice; one she'd gone through dozens of times in the last several months, but this time, it wasn't just routine. She went through her pack carefully, choosing what she would take with her and what she wouldn't, each decision weighted with a sense of finality.

Still, settling her affairs took less time than Samora expected, and the elder dragon she'd traveled on before agreed to join them, at least for a time. The dragons, too, had decisions to make, especially now that there were so many elders. This one, like Samora, had no desire to be part of the discussions, and was more than happy to explore lands lost to the memories of her ancestors.

Aldrick joined her late, closer to morning than she'd expected, but he was ready.

"What about your brother?" he asked.

"He'll find me." Of this, Samora was sure. She'd left enough clues for him to follow. "Are you ready?"

"For this, with you?" He paused. "Of course."

They climbed on the back of the elder, who did Samora the kindness of circling once in the sky. Samora looked down at the clans, who seemed so much smaller than when she'd first met them. But they'd grow again, bigger and stronger than before. Elian would see to that.

She said a silent farewell to the clans, and she and Aldrick flew north, the whole world ahead of them.

❧ 47 ❧

Elian woke inside of a tent, which he considered to be very good news, indeed. First, because he'd woken up, which he'd been less than certain about when he'd been losing consciousness. Second, because a tent meant he'd woken up among the clans, which was yet more proof that they had won.

He let that thought wash over him, simply basking in the knowledge that they were alive and that they'd be alive for some time to come.

He smiled.

"You're awake," a very familiar and very welcome voice said next to him.

He tilted his head to see Capricia sitting beside his cot. Her left arm was in a sling, she had a nasty cut that looked like it had just missed her right eye, and she was covered in dirt and blood, but she was smiling at him, too, and at the moment, that was all that mattered.

"And you're alive," he said.

"Thanks to you and Samora. If your legend hadn't been big enough before, it's enormous now."

Once, he'd dreamed of becoming an adanist of legend. Now

he'd give all of it away for a single lazy afternoon with Capricia. "Can't say I care much about that. What happened?"

Her gaze went distant. "We won, but the cost was enormous. Tiafel died in the fighting, and now Lenon is talking about how they'll join the Bears, too. The surviving Scorpions won't, they're eager to return to their mountains. Tassan and his Coyotes, though, might be joining you as well. Add all the survivors together, and you might just barely have enough adanists for one full-strength clan."

Elian's throat tightened. He'd known the cost would be high, but a part of him had always hoped it wouldn't be. She offered him a waterskin, and he grabbed it and brought it to his lips. It was only after he'd finished taking a few tentative sips that he realized what he'd done and how easily he'd done it. "I don't hurt anywhere."

"You have your sister to thank for that. She brought you back to camp, and the first thing she did was heal you. When I saw how you looked, I didn't think you were going to survive. I've never seen anyone recover from such injuries, and I've certainly never seen someone return to full health so quickly."

He noticed then that she had been crying, her tears streaking through the mud and blood on her face.

"How is it that I'm healthy and your arm is still in a sling?"

"Samora and the others prioritized those who were most wounded yesterday. Brittany, Lenon, Loken, and a handful of others are healing now, but they started with the most severely injured. My time won't be for a while, yet. There's something else you need to know." Capricia paused, not wanting to share whatever it was.

"What?"

"Your sister and Aldrick left on one of the elder dragons. Nobody knows where she went or when she'll be back. There are some rumors floating around that she left for good."

Elian closed his eyes, fearing the worst. "Was she hurt?"

"Physically, she looked fine, as far as anyone could tell. A few cuts and bruises, but she came through better than most. Otherwise, I'm not sure. I've always had a hard time figuring out what's going on in her head, and that was true today, too. Once she could convince herself she wasn't needed, she vanished."

Elian opened his eyes and stared at the roof of the tent, slowly coming to terms with everything Capricia told him. They'd won, but it didn't feel like it. All he could think about were the losses. "How are the clans?"

Capricia swallowed hard. "Wounded, and badly. There might be less than two hundred adanists left, and after the Vada attacked the villages, it's possible there's less than five thousand humans left in the world. At least, that's the rumor going around."

Elian sat up. Harald's sword rested next to him. The heart still beat within his core, and he didn't think he'd ever be rid of it. Not that he wanted to. With it, there was no limit to what he might someday accomplish. He wiggled his toes, moved his legs, twisted his torso, but couldn't find anything wrong with him. He felt well rested.

"How long was I out?"

"Not quite a day. It's late morning the day after the battle."

"Will you walk with me?"

"Of course."

Elian's first responsibility was within the healing tent. Before leaving, he went from warrior to warrior. The healers hadn't had time to set up many cots, so they rested most of the severely wounded on blankets. Elian squatted or kneeled next to each, speaking briefly to them before moving on. Then he thanked the healers and stepped outside the tent.

The scene that greeted him was like no clan camp he'd seen before. They hadn't brought much in the way of supplies, but they hadn't bargained on the exhaustion they'd feel after the battle was over. They had no tents, no bedrolls, and no more food than what they'd been able to carry in a single sled. The healers had brought a little extra, but even that had amounted to little more than a few tents and the supplies they'd need to deal with the wounded.

So adanists sat in circles, scattered across the plains. Taken as a whole, they were a battered and bruised bunch. Elian saw no one who had survived without injury.

Still, they were alive, and the Debru weren't. He looked toward the valley. Debru corpses littered the grass, but Elian saw no human bodies.

"What happened after we defeated the Vada?" he asked.

"There was a bit of a pitched battle, but our strongest adanists were able to clear out the clumps of Debru we were struggling with. The rest broke and took the otsoa and kettu with them. After, we collected our adanists and buried them together. We wanted them under the soil quickly. I can lead you in that direction, if you'd like."

"Thank you."

His emergence from the tent didn't go unnoticed. Those closest to the tent stood, and one by one, they bowed deeply. Elian shook his head. He didn't deserve any more respect than they had earned. To his mounting horror, others in the camp stood and did the same, until nearly the entire camp bowed in his direction.

Elian swallowed hard, then dropped to his knees. He bowed, first to those to the north, then to those to the west, then to those in the south. He pressed his forehead to the ground each time, holding each bow for a count of ten. When he finally rose, the prairie was quiet enough he could have heard a field mouse thirty paces away. He gestured that they should sit and return to their rest, and then he began the long process of visiting each of the groups.

Most of his visits were variations of a single experience. He told the story of his victory over the Vada time and again, answering their questions to the best of his ability. Many had questions about what came next, and to that, Elian wished he had better answers. Most everyone agreed all the Belog and Moka had been killed, but Debru, otsoa, and kettu still roamed the land. The worst of the danger was past, but they weren't yet completely safe. There was still more fighting ahead of the wandering clans, though few wanted to consider it.

As Elian stood after speaking to one group, he caught sight of a lone figure approaching. Her long, blond hair was matted and dirty, and her clothes were covered in mud and blood, but she stood tall as she shuffled over to them, favoring her right leg.

Kati started to bow, but Elian hurried forward and stopped her with an embrace. "Not you," he said.

In his arms, her strength gave out for a moment, and he held her up. The moment passed, and she took a step back, her brief weakness unnoticed by anyone else.

"The clans are yours, whenever you're ready," she said. "Clan, really. Only the Scorpions are for sure going to remain separate."

He let his gaze travel once more around the broken and the wounded, and he shook his head. "Soon, but not yet. For now, we rest. We tend to our wounded, and we grieve those we lost. I'll need to speak to Samora, too, before I'm ready to make any decisions."

"Of course," Kati said.

"I'm sorry to ask for more after all you already given, but will you continue leading until I've spoken with Samora? All that matters to me is rest and recovery. Anything more can wait a day or two."

"It would be my honor," Kati said, though the way her eyes sank into the back of her skull made Elian feel guilty for asking.

"I am sorry to ask you," he repeated, "but there's no one I trust more, and I hope the clans need little while I seek my sister. It shouldn't take long."

Some of the life seemed to return to her gaze as she nodded.

She was about to turn away when Elian said, "Kati, he spoke to me."

She looked confused, but then her eyes narrowed, as though she was a mother catching her son in a lie.

"It's true, although I can't explain it. His spirit formed some knot of adani, and he spoke to me when I needed him most. He gave me the courage I needed when I was lacking."

For a long time, she held his gaze, and then finally, she nodded, and she looked to the sky as if she expected to find Harald there. "That sounds like something he would do. He was proud of you. Proud like you were his own son."

Elian swallowed the lump that suddenly appeared in his throat and sniffed. He nodded, not trusting himself to speak.

Kati turned away. "Two days, and then I'll demand a decision."

Elian bowed to her, thanking her not just for her leadership today, but for all she'd done since they'd met.

AFTER VISITING the last of the small groups, Elian asked Capricia to guide him to where the dead had been buried. She led him south and east, several hundred paces from the nearest collection of adanists.

The work was obviously that of adani, and Elian thought he detected Samora's hand in it. She'd carved a long furrow in the ground, then, after the bodies were buried, had pushed the dirt back over and stamped it down. What would have taken the survivors a day took Samora barely any time at all.

Elian took a knee beside the grave and rested his hand on the freshly disturbed soil. The burial site was rich with adani, the spirits of the dead lingering together before they were inevitably pulled to all corners of the land and possibly beyond.

"Thank you," he whispered.

Adani surged through his fingertips and up his arm, and he took it as their acknowledgement. He remained a while longer, absorbing the enormity of their losses. When the adani within the site began to settle, he stood and returned to the clans. He would mourn the dead until the day he joined them, but his duty was to the living.

He let his eyes drift across the surviving adanists, but there was still no sign of Samora, and no one outside he might ask where she had gone. Karla, he'd learned, died protecting the clans. She and Aldrick were really the only two Samora had spent much time around. Lacking better options, he returned to the healing tent to see if Samora had said anything to Brittany.

Brittany didn't know where his sister had gone, but she possessed the clue he'd been waiting for. "She told me there was one more thing she had to do, but that it might be a while before she returned. She thanked me for everything and told me to keep a close eye on you."

"Those were her exact words?"

"Close enough."

Elian chewed on his lower lip. Those sounded more final than Elian would have liked. Brittany clearly thought Samora's "a while" would only be a day or two, but Elian wondered if it wouldn't be much longer.

"You could always ask the dragons. I know she became somewhat close with one of their elders," Brittany suggested.

Elian agreed, disgruntled he hadn't thought of it first. He had some idea of where Samora had gone, but the dragons would confirm it before he went chasing after ghosts.

He bowed his thanks, then sought out the dragons, who'd built themselves a temporary nest to the east of the clans. Elian sought out an elder and connected his adani.

The questioning didn't take long, and his adani returned soon after. "I know where she is," he told Capricia.

"Where?"

"Far from here. At the Debru circle near where the Hawks' gathering ground used to be."

"Did you want to go alone?"

Elian thought for a moment, then shook his head. "Would you join me?"

"I'd be happy to."

He and Capricia climbed on a dragon, which lifted off and carried them west, toward the setting sun.

ELIAN HAD HALFWAY EXPECTED that by the time he reached the Debru circle it would be gone and Samora vanished without a trace.

Instead, he found it whole, with Samora, Aldrick, and the elder dragon resting beside it. Aldrick and Samora were leaning against the dragon, as though it were the world's most dangerous and oversized chair.

He landed close, and Samora greeted him with a lazy wave of her hand. "Good to see you," she said. She looked like she had a lot on her mind. He didn't blame her. The flight across the deadlands had reminded him that even if the Debru had been as good as defeated, there was so much left to do. The land remained scarred, carrying the wounds of the fight that had lasted so many generations. It wasn't just the clans that needed to heal, and the task ahead seemed no less daunting than beating the Vada.

The first step was here, with his sister. He already knew her decision, could see it in the way she lounged against the dragon, the way she looked at the endless horizon. She'd never needed to tell him her thoughts, for to him, they were written in her every movement. "Good to see you, too. Thanks for saving my life."

"You're just lucky I didn't have anything better to do."

Samora patted the ground next to her, and Elian took the

offered seat. Like the others, he leaned against the dragon. She didn't seem to mind. "Using them as chairs now?"

Elian felt the dragon trying to reach out to him and he accepted the connection. The elder appeared in her human form before him. Her golden eyes glared at Elian. "We were discussing what comes next," she said.

"I assumed you two had come to close the portal. Why haven't you?"

"We were waiting for you. We're not certain what our best choice is, and I wanted to talk to you before I made the decision. We could learn much by leaving it open," Samora answered. "There are other worlds out there and other powers. Dangerous as this circle has been, a careful study might help us learn a lot more about the universe we live in."

"Or it might simply continue to serve as a gateway for more Debru." Elian figured if no one else was going to say the obvious, he would.

"Possibly, but I don't think we have to worry for a while. That was the last Vada, and I don't think the other Debru are too eager to come through unless they have guaranteed safety."

"It's not worth taking the risk. We should close it."

"You shouldn't be so hasty to dismiss the potential benefits of learning more about shadow," Samora said.

"What do we need to learn, when we can just banish it from our world?"

Samora shook her head slowly. "I'm not sure it's that simple."

"Why not?"

She didn't answer for a time, but then she said, "I'm not certain the Debru were the biggest threat we need to worry about."

Elian's nostrils flared as he thought about Father, Mother, Harald, Karla, and so many more. But as quickly as his anger flared, it cooled. Samora had suffered all the same losses. "If not the Debru, then who?"

She gave the smallest shrug of her shoulders. "The Debru were human once, too, until they changed."

Elian's thoughts leaped ahead, following the trail his sister had blazed. "Shadow."

Samora nodded.

"Do you think we're still in danger?"

His sister gave him that same small shrug. "I couldn't begin to say, but studying this circle is the only way I can think of to find out."

Elian thought he might be sick. After all they'd been through, he couldn't stomach the idea of having to keep fighting. He considered for a long time, then gazed at the circle. They couldn't know the consequences of their choices, but he knew how he felt. "No. Shadow has no place in this world."

Samora looked at the elder dragon, who looked to be deep in thought. "What do you think?"

There was another long pause, and then she said, "I agree with Elian. I don't deny the potential benefits you list, but ultimately, closing the gates to the other world seems best."

Samora nodded, as though she'd long resigned herself to that outcome. "Very well."

She closed her eyes, and in less time than it took Elian to draw breath, the circle had vanished.

His jaw dropped all the way down to his chest. "How did you do that?"

"I'd already started the process. I was just waiting for you to arrive and discuss it before I made my final decision." She looked down at her hands. "Becoming one with the heart didn't just make me stronger. It's as though I can sense everything, now. Something like this, which used to take all my focus, is easy now."

Elian grinned and shook his head. "No matter how strong I get, you always seem to be one step ahead of me."

"Only one?"

Elian chuckled, but his mirth didn't last long. He was thinking about what Samora had said about shadow. "What do we do?" he asked, and though he wasn't specific, she knew what he meant.

"The same things you would have done anyway. The land needs to heal, and humanity needs to grow so much stronger. We need more adanists, more farmers, more…everything. You'll need to guide them in that direction. Give humanity hope, the same way you've given me hope through all our darkest days."

"Without you?" he asked

She didn't seem surprised he'd guessed, and she didn't try to deny it. "I'll be in touch. The dragons have so much to teach us, and the knowledge won't do us any good if it's locked in my head. I'll teach as I travel, but no, I won't be wandering with the clan."

Elian looked over at Aldrick. "Seems to me you'll be wandering with your own little clan."

She smiled. "I like how you think."

"I'll miss your advice."

"You hardly need it. You have Capricia. I think she'll serve as a far better adviser than I."

Samora stood, and Elian scrambled to his feet after her. She seemed older, somehow. "I was saddened to hear of Tiafel's loss, but you have plenty of wisdom left. Kati, Tera, Tassan, and the healers will be particularly helpful. You won't be alone, and if there's anyone who can help rebuild humanity, it's you."

"I'm not sure I deserve that amount of praise but thank you. If there's anyone who can learn everything we've lost, it's you."

She gave a short grunt that could have been a laugh, and Elian was reminded of Karla. "I definitely don't deserve that."

They stood in silence for a time, not having anything more to say but not willing to part just yet. They watched the setting sun together, but as it dipped below the horizon, Elian became eager to return to the clans. There was so much to do, a brighter future to build. "I love you."

433

She smiled. "Love you, too. Don't get yourself too beat up while I'm gone. I'm not sure anyone else can heal that body anymore."

"I'll try, but no promises."

They hugged, and they held each other tight, and then they broke apart, each walking to their partner and their dragon. Elian gave a wave as he climbed on, and Capricia's presence behind him kept him steady when it felt as though his heart would break. Samora held on tight to Aldrick, and he was glad she'd found someone so strong and steady.

Then they took off, each in their own direction. Aldrick and Samora chased the fleeing sun west over the horizon, and Elian and Capricia rode their dragon into the darkness, eagerly awaiting the dawning of the new day.

ALSO BY RYAN KIRK

The Legend of Adani

Born of Light and Shadow

From Shadow to Flame

The Ascension of Light

A War of Light and Shadow

Waterstone

The Rise of Shadow

The Shadows Beyond

The Last Sword of the West

Last Sword in the West

Eyes of the Hidden World

A Sword Named Vengeance

Wraith's Revenge

Frontier's End

Song of the Sagani

Legend of the Sword in the West

Nightblade

Nightblade

World's Edge

The Wind and the Void

Blades of the Fallen

Nightblade's Vengeance

Nightblade's Honor

Nightblade's End

Saga of the Broken Gods

Band of Broken Gods

Fall of Forgotten Gods

Rise of the Resurrected God

Oblivion's Gate

The Gate Beyond Oblivion

The Gates of Memory

The Gate to Redemption

Relentless

Relentless Souls

Heart of Defiance

Their Spirit Unbroken

The Sentinels Saga (with Taylor Crook)

Path of the Eternal Sun

A Path Divided

A Path Reforged

Primal

Primal Dawn

Primal Darkness

Primal Destiny

Song of the Fallen Swords

These Fallen Swords

Standalone Novels

The Last Fang of God

Blades of Shadow: A Nightblade Story

ABOUT THE AUTHOR

Ryan Kirk is the award-winning and internationally bestselling author of over thirty fantasy novels spanning nearly a dozen worlds. He lives in Minnesota with his family, where he enjoys long, meandering walks outside even when the snow is high enough to cover his legs. When he isn't glued to his keyboard, he's usually in the woods, either on foot or on bike.

facebook.com/waterstonemedia
instagram.com/authorryankirk
bookbub.com/authors/ryan-kirk